Human Voices

Human Voices

Science Fiction Stories

James Gunn

Five Star • Waterville, Maine

Additional copyright information on page 6.

Five Star First Edition Science Fiction and Fantasy Series.

Published in 2002 in conjunction with
Tekno-Books and Ed Gorman.

Cover illustration © Vincent DiFate 2002

Set in 11 pt. Plantin by Rick Gundberg.

Printed in the United States on permanent paper.

Library of Congress Cataloging-in-Publication Data

Gunn, James E., 1923–
Human voices : science fiction stories / James Gunn.
p. cm.—(Five Star first edition science fiction and fantasy series)
ISBN 0-7862-4317-1 (hc : alk. paper)
1. Science fiction, American. I. Title. II. Series.
PS3513.U797 H86 2002
813′.54—dc21 2002067509

To all those from whom I have learned
and to all those whom I have tried to teach.

We have lingered in the chambers of the sea
By sea-girls wreathed with seaweed red and brown
Till human voices wake us, and we drown.
—T. S. Eliot

Contents

Introduction

Raymond Chandler introduced a volume of his short stories with an insightful essay about what he called "the gentle art of murder," in which he remarked that, "everything one learns about writing takes away from your need to write." That hasn't been my experience. People do get busier, however, as they get deeper into life, and they find less time to write stories. Time is the problem.

In my case, I got involved in directing university relations for the University of Kansas and teaching, writing novels, and writing about science fiction. So the short stories that I enjoyed so much—and feel are the ideal form of science fiction—became less frequent. Even some of the short stories were written as part of novels.

In this volume, then, I have gathered together the stories of my last quarter century. There aren't a lot of them, fewer than one every two years, but they represent the more mature vision of the years after 50. The earlier stories had been influenced by the magazines I had grown up reading and the postwar anthologies that had recapitulated the experience for me. They were written when I felt that I was primarily a writer and actually had spent several years as a full-time writer, earning my living with what I was able to sell. But the stories in this volume were written by a man who took time away from other occupations to devote to fiction, who had the experiences of an editor, a teacher, a director of university relations, and a professor, as well as the earlier experiences of student, naval officer, and husband and father.

So the stories were much more difficult to categorize, and sometimes more difficult to find a publisher for. "The Old Folks," for instance, was written for my fiction-writing class, as an example for my students of what I wanted them to produce as weekly assignments—and to trick myself into writing again. I would like to have sold the story immediately and presented the publication to my students as a validation of everything I had told them. But the science-fiction magazines said the story wasn't science fiction, and the slick magazines—there still were some of them around—said they didn't publish science fiction. Then I met Harry Harrison at the World Science Fiction Convention of 1968, in Oakland, and he said he was publishing a new anthology of original stories. Categories didn't bother him, he said, and he published "The Old Folks" in *Nova Two*, and then it appeared in a *Best SF of the Year* collection. So there was a kind of validation after all, although it came after half-a-dozen years.

"The Voices" was written as the second part of my novel *The Listeners*. I had been working as the first Administrative Assistant to the Chancellor for University Relations, and the job was so demanding that I hadn't taken any vacation for the first half-dozen years, nor had I found any time for writing anything of my own. Finally, in 1967, I decided to take my month off in the summer and devote it to writing. I started my novel *Kampus* one year, wrote the second and third sections of *The Burning* in two other years, and wrote the novelette "The Listeners," which was published in *Galaxy* and later became the first chapter of the novel and was reprinted as part of my second short-story collection, *Breaking Point*. "The

Voices," which also was published in *Galaxy*, became the second chapter.

I wrote "Fault" after I returned to full-time teaching in 1970 and after a long spell of writing such novels as *The Listeners* and such complicated historical surveys as *Alternate Worlds: The Illustrated History of Science Fiction*. The idea came from a geology professor who wanted me to write a scenario for him dealing with the psychological problem of earthquake prediction. I thought it would make a good story and so did Ben Bova, the new editor of *Analog*, who later told me that a government agency had requested copies. "Guilt" came along a couple of years later. For that I drew upon the expertise of a psychology professor who directed me to certain texts in the University's library.

"Child of the Sun" started as a proposal for a television series. CBS was looking for a series to compete with the then popular "The Six-Million-Dollar Man," and, at the suggestion of my agent, I "pitched" the idea to the west-coast office. The executives who listened seemed interested, but when it didn't get picked up, I decided to write it as a story. It was published in *Analog* and the following year in a collection of *The World's Best SF*. That attracted the attention of a Hollywood producer who took a year's option on the TV and film rights. When that didn't work out, I decided that the people who make decisions about television series believed that there weren't enough such stories to justify a series. So I wrote five more of them, published them in *Analog*, and then as a novel called *Crisis!*

"The North Wind" was a sidelight of my long-time work on a millennial novel called *Catastrophe!* (published in 2001 as *The Millennium Blues*). "Among the Beautiful Bright Children" was written for Harlan Ellison's long-postponed *The Last Dangerous Visions*. I later added two more substantial sections and some inter-chapter materials and published it as *The Dreamers*. "The Futurist" was almost another "The Old Folks." I tried it on a great many magazines in two different forms before Kim Mohan at *Amazing Stories* started working on it with me and, after some tinkering, published it—calling its publication one of his greatest pleasures as an editor.

"Man of Parts" emerged from my reading of a colleague's work on futurism. He quoted Adam Smith's anecdote in *The Theory of Moral Sentiments* that is repeated early in the story, and I began to consider what might happen if someone really was convinced that he could save people by cutting off a finger—and other pieces of himself. *The Magazine of Fantasy and Science Fiction* published that one.

Finally, "The Gingerbread Man," "The Day the Magic Came Back," and "The Lens of Time" were the products of my retirement from full-time teaching in 1993. I finished *The Millennium Blues* and decided that I'd like to write some more stories, maybe even enough to reach at least one hundred publications. "The Gingerbread Man," which was published in *Analog*, was a response to Isaac Asimov's "The Bicentennial Man," a marvelous story whose sentimental conclusion seemed to run counter to the basic rationalism displayed in Isaac's other fiction. Only a few readers recognized that the two stories were related, in spite of identical names of the protagonists and the date. "The Day the Magic Came Back," published in *Science Fiction Age*, I thought of as a response to the world's contemporary fascination with fantasy and fantastic phenomena. I had noted an increasing number of reflexive stories in SF, and I decided to write one: "The Lens of Time" was my tribute to Fitz-James O'Brien's marvelous 1858 story "The Diamond Lens." In doing my research for it I discovered that the story had made O'Brien's reputation, that he had been accused of plagiarizing the idea from a colleague who had died tragically young, and that he had defended himself by telling how he had used the expertise of an acquaintance, Dr. J. D. Whelpley. Whelpley, incidentally, also wrote SF, and his story, "The Atoms of Chladni," was published a year after "The Diamond Lens." Everything in "The Lens of Time," except the description of the meeting and the conversation, is true.

"The End-of-the-World Ball" is the final chapter of *The Millennium Blues*, although I wrote it first as a way of finding out about the characters who would wend their way through the millennial year 2000 before they ended up on December 31 at the End-of-the-World Ball. Then I went back and picked up the story on January 1, with my six characters viewpointing three chapters each as the year progressed inexorably toward the end of the second millennium. But meanwhile I answered a friend's request for a story, and George Zebrowski published it in his original anthology series, *Synergy*.

In 1999 I began a new series of novelettes, with "The Giftie," published in *Analog*. Carl Sagan sent me a copy of his novel *Contact* thanking me for the inspiration of *The Listeners*, but as I watched the film adapted from his novel, I thought: It wouldn't happen like that. So I decided to write about the way it would really happen. I hope to develop the series into a novel made up of six such episodes. I've done four of them. And I still have one more story to go before I reach one hundred.

James Gunn
Lawrence, Kansas
January 15, 2002

The Old Folks

They had been traveling in the dusty car all day, the last few miles in the heat of the Florida summer. Not far behind were the Sunshine State Parkway, Orange Grove, and Winter Hope, but according to the road map the end of the trip was near.

John almost missed the sign that said, "Sunset Acres, Next Right," but the red Volkswagen slowed and turned and slowed again. Now another sign marked the beginning of the town proper: SUNSET ACRES, Restricted Senior Citizens, Minimum Age—65, Maximum Speed—20. As the car passed the sign, the whine of the tires announced that the pavement had changed from concrete to brick.

Johnny bounced in the back seat, mingling the squeak of the springs with the music of the tires, and shouted above the engine's protest at second gear, "Mommy—Daddy, are we there yet? Are we there?"

His mother turned to look at him. The wind from the open window whipped her short hair. She smiled. "Soon now," she said. Her voice was excited, too.

They passed through a residential section where the white frame houses with their sharp roofs sat well back from the street, and the velvet lawns reached from red brick sidewalks to broad porches that spread like skirts around two or three sides of the houses.

At each intersection the streets dipped to channel the rainwater and to enforce the speed limit at 20 m.p.h. or slower. The names of the streets were chiseled into the curbs, and the incisions were painted black: Osage, Cottonwood, Antelope, Meadowlark, Prairie. . . .

The Volkswagen hummed along the brick streets, alone. The streets were empty, and so, it seemed, were the houses; the white-curtained windows stared senilely into the Florida sun, and the swings on the porches creaked in the Florida breeze, but the architecture and the town were all Kansas—and the Kansas of fifty years ago, at that.

Then they reached the square, and John pulled the car to a stop alongside the curb. Here was the center of town—a block of greensward edged with beds of pansies and petunias and geraniums. In the center of the square was a massive, two-story, red brick building. A square tower reached even taller. The tower had a big clock set into its face. The heavy, black hands pointed at 3:32.

Stone steps marched up the front of the building toward oak doors twice the height of a man. Around the edges of the buildings were iron benches painted white. On the benches the old men sat in the sun, their eyes shut, their hands folded across canes.

From somewhere behind the brick building came the sound of a brass band—the full, rich mixture of trumpet and trombone and sousaphone, of tuba and tympani and big, bass drum.

Unexpectedly, as they sat in the car looking at the scene out of another era and another land, a tall black shape rolled silently past them. John turned his head quickly to look at it. A thin cab in the middle sloped toward spoked wheels at each end, like the front ends of two cars stuck together. An old woman in a wide-brimmed hat sat upright beside the driver. From her high window she frowned at the little foreign car, and then her vehicle passed down the street.

"That was an old electric!" John said. "I didn't know they were making them again."

From the back seat Johnny said, "When are we going to get to Grammy's?"

"Soon," his mother said. "If you're going to ask the way to Buffalo Street, you'd better ask," she said to John. "It's too hot to sit here in the car."

John opened the door and extracted himself from the damp socket of the bucket seat. He stood for a moment beside the baked metal of the car and looked up each side of the street. The oomp-pah-pah of the band was louder now and the yeasty smell of baking bread dilated his nostrils, but the whole scene struck him as unreal somehow, as if this all were a stage setting and a man could walk behind the buildings and find that the backs were unpainted canvas and raw wood.

"Well?" Sally said.

John shook his head and walked around the front of the car. The first store sold hardware. In the small front window were crowbars and wooden handled claw hammers and three kegs of blue nails; one of the kegs had a metal scoop stuck into the nails at the top. In one corner of the window was a hand mower, its handle varnished wood, its metal wheels and reel blue, except where the spokes had been touched with red and yellow paint and the curved reel had been sharpened to a silver line.

The interior of the store was dark; John could not tell whether anyone was inside.

Next to it was "Tyler's General Store," and John stepped inside onto sawdust. Before his eyes adjusted from the Sunshine State's proudest asset, he smelled the pungent sawdust. The odor was mingled with others—the vinegar and spice of pickles and the ripeness of cheese and a sweet-sour smell that he could not identify.

Into his returning vision the faces swam first—the pale faces of the old people, framed in white hair, relieved from the anonymity of age only by the way in which bushy eyebrows sprouted or a mustache was trimmed or wrinkles carved the face. Then he saw the rest of the store and the old people. Some of them were sitting in scarred, oak chairs with rounded backs near a black, potbellied stove. The room was cool; after a moment John realized that the stove was producing a cold breeze.

One old man with a drooping white mustache was leaning over from the barrel he sat on to cut a slice of cheese from the big wheel on the counter. A tall man with an apron over his shirt and trousers and his shirtsleeves hitched up with rubber bands came from behind the counter, moving his bald head with practiced ease among the dangling sausages.

"Son," he said, "I reckon you lost your way. Made the wrong turn off the highway, I warrant. Heading for Winter Hope or beyond and mistook yourself. You just head back out how you come in and—"

"Is this Sunset Acres?" John said.

The old man with the yellow slice of cheese in his hand said in a thin voice, "Yep. No use thinking you can stay, though. Thirty-five or forty years too soon. That's what!" His sudden laughter came out in a cackle.

The others joined in, like a superannuated Greek chorus, "Can't stay!"

"I'm looking for Buffalo Street," John said. "We're going to visit the Plummers." He paused and then added, "They're my wife's parents."

The storekeeper tucked his thumbs into the straps of his apron. "That's different. Everybody knows the Plummers.

Three blocks north of the square. Can't miss it."

"Thank you," John said, nodding, and backed into the sunshine.

The interrupted murmur of conversation began again, broken briefly by laughter.

"Three blocks north of the square," he said as he inserted himself back in the car.

He started the motor, shifted into first, and turned the corner. As he passed the general store he thought he saw white faces peering out of the darkness, but they might have been feather pillows hanging in the window.

In front of the town hall an old man jerked in his sleep as the car passed. Another opened his eyes and frowned. A third shook his cane in their general direction. Beyond, a thin woman in a lavender shawl was holding an old man by the shoulder as if to tell him that she was done with the shopping and it was time to go home.

"John, look!" Sally said, pointing out the window beside her.

To their right was an ice-cream parlor. Metal chairs and round tables with thin, wire legs were set in front of the store under a yellow awning. At one of the tables sat an elderly couple. The man sat straight in his chair like an army officer, his hair iron-gray and neatly parted, his eyebrows thick. He was keeping time to the music of the band with the cane in his right hand. His left hand held the hand of a little old woman in a black dress, who gazed at him as she sipped from the soda in front of her.

The music was louder here. Just to the north of the town hall, they could see now, was a bandstand with a conical roof. On the bandstand sat half a dozen old men in uniforms, playing instruments. Another man in uniform stood in front of them, waving a baton. It was a moment before John realized what was wrong with the scene. The music was louder and richer than the half-dozen musicians could have produced.

But it was Johnny who pointed out the tape recorder beside the bandstand, "Just like Daddy's."

It turned out that Buffalo Street was not three blocks north of the square but three blocks south.

The aging process had been kind to Mrs. Henry Plummer. She was a small woman, and the retreating years had left their detritus of fat, but the extra weight seemed no burden on her small bones and the cushioning beneath the skin kept it plump and unwrinkled. Her youthful complexion seemed strangely at odds with her blue-white curls. Her eyes, though, were unmistakably old. They were faded like a blue gingham dress.

They looked at Sally now, John thought, as if to say, "What I have seen you through, my dear, the colic and the boys, the measles and the mumps and the chickenpox and the boys, the frozen fingers and the skinned knees and the boys, the parties and the late hours and the boys. . . . And now you come again to me, bringing this larger, distant boy that I do not like very much, who has taken you from me and treated you with crude familiarity, and you ask me to call him by his first name and consider him one of the family. It's too much."

When she spoke, her voice was surprisingly small. "Henry," she said, a little girl in an old body, "don't stand there talking all day. Take in the bags! These children must be starved to death!"

Henry Plummer had grown thinner as his wife had filled out, as if she had grown fat at his expense. Plummer had been a junior executive, long after he had passed in age most of the senior executives, in a firm that manufactured games and toys, but a small inheritance and cautious investments in municipal bonds and life insurance had made possible his comfortable retirement.

He could not shake the habits of a lifetime; his face bore the wry expression of a man who expects the worst and receives it. He said little, and when he spoke it was usually to protest. "Well, I guess I'm not the one holding them up," he said, but he stooped for the bags.

John moved quickly to reach the bags first. "I'll get them, Dad," he said. The word "Dad" came out as if it were fitted with rusty hooks. He had never known what to call Henry Plummer. His own father had died when he was a small child, and his mother had died when he was in college; but he could not find in himself any filial affection for Plummer. He disliked the coyness of "Dad," but it was better than the stiffness of "Mr. Plummer" or the false camaraderie of "Henry."

With Mrs. Plummer the problem had not been so great. John recalled a joke from the book he had edited recently for the paperback publishing firm that employed him. "For the first year I said, 'Hey, you!' and then I called her 'Grandma.' "

He straightened with the scuffed suitcases, looking helplessly at Sally for a moment and then apologetically at Plummer. "I guess you've carried your share of luggage already."

"He's perfectly fit," Mrs. Plummer said.

Sally looked only at Johnny. Sally was small and dark-haired and pretty, and John loved her and her whims—"a whim of iron," they called her firm conviction that she knew the right thing to do at any time, in any situation—but when she was around her mother John saw reflected in her behavior all the traits that he found irritating in the old woman. Sometime, perhaps, she would even be plump like her mother, but now it did not seem likely. She ran after Johnny fourteen hours a day.

She held the hand of her four-year-old, her face flushed, her eyes bright with pride. "I guess you see how he's grown, Mother. Ten pounds since you saw him last Christmas. And three inches taller. Give your grandmother a kiss, Johnny. A big kiss for Grammy. He's been talking all the way from New York about coming to visit Grammy—and Granddad, too, of course. I can't imagine what makes him act so shy now. Usually he isn't. Not even with strangers. Give Grammy a great big kiss."

"Well," Mrs. Plummer said, "you must be starved. Come on in. I've got a ham on the stove, and we'll have sandwiches and coffee. And, Johnny, I've got something for you. A box of chocolates, all your own."

"Oh, Mother!" Sally said. "Not just before lunch. He won't eat a bite."

Johnny jumped up and down. He pulled his hand free from his mother's and ran to Mrs. Plummer. "Candy! Candy!" he shouted. He gave Mrs. Plummer a big, wet kiss.

John stood at the living room window listening to the whisper of the air conditioning and looking out at the Florida evening. He could see Johnny playing in the pile of sand his thoughtful grandparents had had dumped in the back yard. It had been a relief to be alone with his wife, but now the heavy silence of disagreement hung in the air between them. He had wanted to leave, to return to New York, and she would not even consider the possibility.

He had massed all his arguments, all his uneasiness about this strange, nightmarish town, about how he felt unwanted, about how it disliked them, and Sally had found his words first amusing and then disagreeable. For her Sunset Acres was an arcadia for the aged. Her reaction was strongly influenced by that glimpse of the old couple at the ice cream parlor.

John had always found in her a kind of Walt Disney sentimentality, but it had never disturbed him before. He turned and made one last effort. "Besides, your parents don't even want us here. We've been here only a couple of hours and already they've left us to go to some meeting."

"It's their monthly town-hall meeting," Sally said. "They have an obligation to attend. It's part of their self-government or something."

"Oh, hell," John said, turning back to the window. He looked from left to right and back again. "Johnny's gone."

He ran to the back door and fumbled with it for a moment. Then it opened, and he was in the back yard. After the sterile chill of the house, the air outside seemed ripe with warm black earth and green things springing through the soil. The sand pile was empty; there was no place for the boy to hide among the colorful Florida shrubs which hid the back yard of the house behind and had colorful names he could never remember.

John ran around the corner of the house. He reached the porch just as Sally came through the front door.

"There he is," Sally cried out.

"Johnny!" John shouted.

The four-year-old had started across the street. He turned and looked back at them. "Grammy," he said.

John heard him clearly.

The car slipped into the scene like a shadow, silent, unsuspected. John saw it out of the corner of his eye. Later he thought that it must have turned the nearby corner, or perhaps it came out of a driveway. In the moment before the accident, he saw that the old woman in the wide-brimmed hat was driving the car herself. He saw her head turn toward Johnny, and he saw the upright electric swerve sharply toward the child.

The front fender hit Johnny and threw him toward the sidewalk. John looked incredulously at the old woman. She smiled at him, and then the car was gone down the street.

"Johnny!" Sally screamed. Already she was in the street, the boy's head cradled in her lap. She hugged him and then pushed him away to look blindly into his face and then hugged him again, rocking him in her arms, crying.

John found himself beside her, kneeling. He pried the boy away from her. Johnny's eyes were closed. His face was pale, but John couldn't find any blood. He lifted the boy's eyelids. The pupils seemed dilated. Johnny did not stir.

"What's the matter with him?" Sally screamed at John. "He's going to die, isn't he?"

"I don't know. Let me think! Let's get him into the house."

"You aren't supposed to move people who've been in an accident!"

"We can't leave him here to be run over by someone else."

John picked up his son gently and walked to the house. He lowered the boy onto the quilt in the front bedroom and looked down at him for a moment. The boy was breathing raggedly. He moaned. His hand twitched. "I've got to get a doctor," John said. "Where's the telephone?"

Sally stared at him as if she hadn't heard. John turned away and looked in the living room. An antique apparatus on a wooden frame was attached to one wall. He picked up the receiver and cranked the handle vigorously. "Hello!" he said. "Hello!" No answer.

He returned to the bedroom. Sally was still standing beside the bed. "What a lousy town," he said. "No telephone service!" Sally looked at him. She blinked.

"I'll have to go to town," John said. "You stay with Johnny. Keep him warm. Put cold compresses on his head." They might not help Johnny, he thought, but they would keep Sally quiet.

She nodded and headed toward the bathroom.

When he got to the car, it refused to start. After a few futile attempts, he gave up, knowing he had flooded the engine. He ran back to the house. Sally looked up at him, calmer now that her hands were busy.

"I'm going to run," he told her. "I might see that woman and be unable to resist the impulse to smash into her."

"Don't talk crazy," Sally said. "It was just an accident."

"It was no accident," John said. "I'll be back with a doctor as soon as I can find one."

John ran down the brick sidewalks until his throat burned and then walked for a few steps before breaking once more into a run. By then the square was in sight. The sun had plunged into the Gulf of Mexico, and the town was filled with silence and shadows. The storefronts were dark. There was no light anywhere in the square.

The first store was a butcher shop. Hams hung in the windows, and plucked chickens, naked and scrawny, dangled by cords around their yellow feet. John thought he smelled sawdust and blood. He remembered Johnny and felt sick.

Next was a clothing store with two wide windows under the name "Emporium." In the windows were stiff, waxen dummies in black suits and high, starched collars; in lace and parasol. Then came a narrow door; on its window were printed the words "Saunders and Jones, Attorneys at Law." The window framed dark steps.

Beside it was a print shop—piles of paper pads in the window, white, yellow, pink, blue; reams of paper in dusty wrappers; faded invitations and personal cards; and behind them the lurking shapes of printing presses and racks of type.

John passed a narrow bookstore with books stacked high in the window and ranged in ranks into the darkness. Then came a restaurant; a light in the back revealed scattered tables with checkered cloths. He pounded at the door, making a shocking racket in the silence of the square, but no one came.

Kittycorner across the street, he saw the place and recognized it by the tall, intricately shaped bottles of colored water in the window and the fancy jar hanging from chains. He ran across the brick street and beat on the door with his fist. There was no response. He kicked it, but the drug store remained silent and dark. Only the echoes answered his summons, and they soon died away.

Next to the drug store was another dark door. The words printed across the window in it said, "Joseph M. Bronson, M.D." And underneath, "Geriatrics Only."

John knocked, sure it was useless, wondering, "Why is the town locked up? Where is everybody?" And then he remembered the meeting. That's where everyone was, at the meeting the Plummers couldn't miss. No one could miss the meeting. Everyone had to be there, apparently, even the telephone operator. But where was it being held?

Of course. Where else would a town meeting be held? In the town hall.

He ran across the street once more and up the wide steps. He pulled open one of the heavy doors and stepped into a hall with tall ceilings. Stairways led up on either side, but light came through a pair of doors ahead. He heard a babble of voices. John walked towards the doors, feeling the slick oak floors under his feet, smelling the public toilet odors of old urine and disinfectant.

He stopped for a moment at the doors to peer between them, hoping to see the Plummers, hoping they were close enough to signal without disturbing the others. The old people would be startled if he burst in among them. There would be confusion and explanations, accusations perhaps. He needed a doctor, not an argument.

The room was filled with wooden folding chairs placed neatly in rows, with a wide aisle in the middle and a narrower one on either side. From the backs of the chairs hung shawls and canes. The room had for John the unreal quality of an etching, perhaps because all the backs of the heads that he saw were silver and gray, here and there accented with tints of blue or green.

At the front of the room was a walnut rostrum on a broad platform. Behind the rostrum stood the old man Sally had pointed out in the ice cream parlor. He stood as straight as he had sat.

The room buzzed as if it had a voice of its own, and the voice rose and fell, faded and returned, the way it does in a dream. One should be able to understand it, one had to understand it, but one couldn't quite make out the words.

The old man banged on the rostrum with a wooden gavel; the gavel had a small silver plate attached to its head. "Everyone will have his chance to be heard," he said. It was like an order. The buzz faded away. "Meanwhile we will speak one at a time, and in a proper manner, first being recognized by the chair."

"Just one moment, Mr. Samuelson.

"For many years the public press has allowed its columns to bleed over the voting age. 'If a boy of eighteen is old enough to die for his country, he is old enough to vote for its legislators,' the sentimentalists have written.

"Nonsense. It takes no intelligence to die. Any idiot can

do it. Surviving takes brains. Men of eighteen aren't even old enough to take orders properly, and until a man can take orders he can't give them.

"Mrs. Richards, I have the floor. When I have finished I will recognize each of you in turn."

John started to push through the doors and announce the emergency to the entire group, but something about the stillness of the audience paralyzed his decision. He stood there, his hand on the door, his eyes searching for the Plummers.

"Let me finish," the old man at the rostrum said. "Only when a man has attained true maturity—fifty is the earliest date for the start of this time of life—does he begin to identify the important things in life. At this age, the realization comes to him, if it ever comes, that the individual has the right to protect and preserve the property that he has accumulated by his own hard work, and, in the protection of this right, the state stands between the individual and mob rule in Washington. Upon these eternal values we take our stand: the individual, his property, and state's rights. Else our civilization, and everything in it of value, will perish."

The light faded from his eyes, and the gavel which had been raised in his hand like a saber sank to the rostrum. "Mr. Samuelson."

In the front of the room a man stood up. He was small and bald except for two small tufts of hair above his ears. "I have heard what you said, and I understand what you said because you said it before. It is all very well to talk of the rights of the individual to protect his property, but how can he protect his property when the government taxes and taxes and taxes—state governments as well as Washington? I say, 'Let the government give us four exemptions instead of two.' "

A cracked voice in the back of the room said, "Let them

cut out taxes altogether for senior citizens!"

"Yes!"

"No!"

A small, thin woman got up in the middle of the audience. "Four hundred dollars a month for every man and woman over sixty-five!" she said flatly. "Why shouldn't we have it? Didn't we build this country? Let the government give us back a little of what they have taken away. Besides, think of the money it would put into circulation."

"You have not been recognized, Mrs. Richards," the chairman said, "and I declare you out of order and the Townsendites as well. What you are advocating is socialism, more government not less."

"Reds!" someone shouted. "Commies!" said someone else. "That's not true!" said a woman near the door. "It's only fair," shouted an old man, nodding vigorously. Canes and crutches were waved in the air, a hundred Excaliburs and no Arthur. John glanced behind him to see if the way was clear for retreat in case real violence broke out.

"Sally!" he exclaimed, discovering her behind him. "What are you doing here? Where's Johnny?"

"He's in the car. He woke up. He seemed all right. I thought I'd better find you. Then we'd be closer to the doctor. I looked all over. What are you doing here?"

John rubbed his forehead. "I don't know. I was looking for a doctor. Something's going on here. I don't know what it is, but I don't like it."

"What's going on?"

Sally tried to push past him, but John grabbed her arm. "Don't go in there!"

The Chairman's gavel finally brought order out of confusion. "We are senior citizens, not young hoodlums!" he admonished them. "We can disagree without forgetting our dignity and our common interests, Mrs. Johnson."

A woman stood up at the right beside one of the tall windows that now framed the night. She was a stout woman with gray hair pulled back into a bun. "It seems to me, Colonel, that we are getting far from the subject of this meeting—indeed, the subject of all our meetings—and that is what we are going to do about the young people who are taking over everything and pushing us out. As many of you know, I have no prejudices about young people. Some of my best friends are young people, and, although I cannot name my children among them, for they are ingrates, I bear my son and my two daughters no ill will."

She paused for a deep breath. "We must not let the young people get the upper hand. We must find ways of insuring that we get from them the proper respect for our age and our experience. The best way to do this, I believe, is to keep them in suspense about the property—the one thing about us they still value—how much there is and what will become of it. Myself, I pretend that there is at least two or three times as much. When I am visiting one of them, I leave my checkbook lying carelessly about—the one that has the large and false balance. And I let them overhear me make an appointment to see a lawyer. What do I have to see a lawyer about, they think, except my will?

"Actually I have written my will once and for all, leaving my property to the Good Samaritan Rest Home for the Aged, and I do not intend to change it. But I worry that some clever young lawyer will find a way to break the will. They're always doing that when you disinherit someone."

"Mrs. Johnson," the Colonel said, "you have a whole town full of friends who will testify that you always have been in full possession of your faculties, if it ever should come to that,

God forbid! Mrs. Fredericks?"

"Nasty old woman," Sally muttered. "Where are Mother and Father? I don't see them. I don't think they're here at all."

"Sh-h-h!"

"I'm leaving my money to my cat," said a bent old woman with a hearing aid in her ear. "I'm just sorry I won't get to see their faces."

The Colonel smiled at her as he nodded her back to her seat at the left front. Then he recognized a man sitting in the front row. "Mr. Saunders."

The man who arose was short, straight, and precise. "I would like to remind these ladies of the services of our legal aid department. We have had good luck in constructing unbreakable legal documents. A word of caution, however—the more far-fetched the legatee, though to be sure the more satisfying, the more likely the breaking of the will. There is only one certain way to prevent property from falling into the hands of those who have neither worked for it nor merited it—and that is to spend it.

"Personally, I am determined to spend on the good life every cent that I accumulated in a long and—you will pardon my lack of humility—distinguished career at the bar."

"Your personal life is your own concern, Mr. Saunders," the Colonel said, "but I must tell you, sir, that we are aware of how you spend your money and your time away from here. I do not recommend it to others nor do I approve of your presenting it to us as worthy of emulation. Indeed, I think you do our cause damage."

Mr. Saunders had not resumed his seat. He bowed and continued, "Each to his own tastes—I cite an effective method for keeping the younger generation in check. There are other ways of disposing of property irretrievably." He sat down.

John pulled Sally back from the doors. "Go to the car," he said. "Get out of here. Go back to the house and get our bags packed. Quick!"

"Mrs. Plummer?" the Colonel said.

Sally pulled away from John.

The familiar figure stood up at the front of the room. Now John could identify beside her the gray head of Henry Plummer, turned now toward the plump face of his wife.

"We all remember," Mrs. Plummer said calmly, "what a trial children are. What we may forget is that our children have children. I do my best not to let my daughter forget the torments she inflicted upon me when she was a child. We hide these things from them. We conceal the bitterness. They seldom suspect. And we take our revenge, if we are wise, by encouraging their children to be just as great a trial to their parents. We give them candy before meals. We encourage them to talk back to their parents. We build up their infant egos so that they will stand up for their childish rights. When their parents try to punish them, we stand between the child and the punishment. Fellow senior citizens, this is our revenge: that their parents will be as miserable as we were."

"Mother! No!" Sally cried out.

The words and the youthful voice that spoke them rippled the audience like a sword tossed into a pond. Faces turned toward the back of the meeting room, faces with wrinkles and white hair and faded eyes, faces searching, near-sighted, faces disturbed, faces beginning to fear and to hate. Among them was one face John knew well, a face that had dissembled malice and masqueraded malevolence as devotion.

"Do as I told you!" John said violently. "Get out of here!"

Sally turned. She ran down the hall, pushed her way through the big front doors, and was gone. John looked for something with which to bar the doors to the meeting room, but the hall was bare. He was turning back to the doors when he saw the oak cane in the corner. He caught it up and slipped it through the handles. Then he put his shoulder against the doors.

In the meeting room the gathering emotion was beginning to whip thin blood into a simulation of youthful vigor, and treble voices began to deepen as they shouted encouragement at those nearest the doors. "A spy!"

"Was it a woman?"

"A girl."

"Let me get my hands on her!"

The first wave hit the doors. John was knocked off balance. He pushed himself forward again, and again the surge of bodies against the other side forced him back. He dug in his feet and shoved. A sound of commotion added to the shouting in the meeting room. John heard something—or someone—fall.

The next time he was forced from the doors; the cane bent. Again he pushed the doors shut; the cane straightened. At the same moment he felt a sharp pain across his back. He looked back. The Colonel was behind him, breathing hard, the glow of combat in his eyes and the cane in his hand upraised for another blow, like the hand of Abraham over Isaac.

John stepped back. In his hand he found the cane that had been thrust through the door handles. He raised it over his head as the Colonel struck again. The blow fell upon the cane. The Colonel drew back his cane and swung once more, and again his blow was parried, more by accident than skill. Then the doors burst open, and the wild old bodies were upon them.

John caught brief glimpses of flying white hair and ripped lace and spectacles worn awry. Canes and crutches were raised above him. He smelled lavender and bay rum mingled with the sweet-sour odor of sweat. He heard shrill voices, like the voices of children, cry out curses and maledictions, and he felt upon various parts of his body the blows of feeble fists, their bones scarcely padded, doing perhaps more damage to themselves than to him, though it seemed sufficient.

He went down quickly. Rather too quickly, he thought dazedly as he lay upon the floor, curled into a fetal position to avoid the stamping feet and kicks and makeshift clubs.

He kept waiting for it to be over, for consciousness to leave him, but most of the blows missed him, and in the confusion and the milling about, the object of the hatred was lost. John saw a corridor that led between bodies and legs through the doors that opened into the meeting room. He crawled by inches toward the room; eventually he found himself among the chairs. The commotion was behind him.

Cautiously he peered over the top of a fallen chair. He saw what he had overlooked before—a door behind the rostrum. It stood open to the night. That was how the Colonel, with instinctive strategy, had come up behind him, he thought, and he crept toward it and down the narrow steps behind the town hall.

For a moment he stood in the darkness assessing his injuries. He was surprised: they were few, none serious. Perhaps tomorrow he would find bruises enough and a lump here and there and perhaps even a broken rib or two, but now there was only a little pain. He started to run.

He had been running in the darkness for a long time, not certain he was running in the right direction, not sure he knew what the right direction was, when a dark shape coasted up beside him. He dodged instinctively before he recognized the sound of the motor.

"John!" It was a voice he knew. "John?"

The Volkswagen was running without lights. John caught

the door handle. The door came open. The car stopped. "Move over," he said, out of breath. Sally climbed over the gearshift, and John slid into the bucket seat. He released the hand brake and pushed hard on the accelerator. The car plunged forward.

Only when they reached the highway did John speak again. "Is Johnny all right?"

"I think so," Sally said. "But he's got to see a doctor."

"We'll find a doctor in Orange Grove."

"A young one."

John wiped his nose on the back of his hand and looked at it. His hand was smeared with blood. "Damn!"

She pressed a tissue into his hand. "Was it bad?"

"Incredible!" He laughed harshly and said it again in a different tone. "Incredible. What a day! And what a night! But it's over. And a lot of other things are over."

Johnny was crying in the back seat.

"What do you mean?" Sally asked. "Hush, Johnny, it's going to be all right."

"Grammy!" Johnny moaned.

"The letters. Presents for people who don't need anything. Worrying about what mother's going to think. . . ."

The car slowed as John looked back toward the peaceful town of Sunset Acres, sleeping now in the Florida night, and remembered the wide lawns and the broad porches, the brick streets and the slow time, and the old folks. "All over," he said again.

Johnny still was crying.

"Shut up, Johnny!" he said between his teeth and immediately felt guilty.

"John!" Sally said. "We mustn't ever be like that toward our son."

She wasn't referring just to what he had said, John knew.

He glanced back toward the small figure huddled in the back seat. It wasn't over, he thought; it was beginning. "It's over," he said again, as if he could convince himself by repetition. Sally was silent. "Why don't you say something?" John asked.

"I keep thinking about how it used to be," she said. "He's my father. She's my mother. How can anything change that? You can't expect me to hate my own father and mother?"

It wasn't over. It would never be over. Even though the children sometimes escaped, the old folks always won: the children grew up; the young people became old folks.

The car speeded up and rushed through the night, the headlights carving a corridor through the darkness, a corridor that kept closing behind them. The corridor still was there, as real in back as it was revealing in front, and it could never be closed.

The Voices

. . . a host of phantom listeners
That dwelt in the lone house then
Stood listening in the quiet of the moonlight
To that voice from the world of men . . .
—Walter de la Mare

He came past the saucer-shaped valley lined with metal plates, past the big metal dish fixed against the sky, past the parking lot surfaced with packed white sea shells.

A crater shaped to hold the silence of the stars; an empty cup waiting patiently to be filled . . .

He came out of the vertical sunlight into the dark, through the glass doors into the one-story concrete building, down its cool, brightening corridors to the office marked "Director," and past the middle-aged secretary to the office she guarded, where a man stood up behind a desk piled with papers.

They came into the corridor to watch the intruder, the pallid scientists and their own brown clerks, their faces furrowed with facts, their eyes empty of meaning like blind oscilloscopes.

"My name is George Thomas," the newcomer said.

"I'm Robert MacDonald," said the man behind the desk.

They shook hands. MacDonald had a good handshake, Thomas thought, almost gentle but not feeble, as if he didn't have to prove anything.

"I know," Thomas said. "You're director of this Project." A sensitive man could draw inferences from the way he said it; Thomas didn't care.

The room was cool and pleasant and spare, a little like the man who worked in it. The air in the corridor had smelled of machine oil and ozone, but here was a smell that Thomas knew better, a smell that made him feel comfortable, of paper and old books. Behind the simple desk were tall bookshelves built into the wall and on the shelves were books with real leather bindings in brown and dark red and dark green. From where he sat Thomas could not quite make out the titles, but from a word or two he could tell that some of them, at least, were in foreign languages.

His fingers twitched to take one in his hands, to feel the grainy, slightly slick texture of its binding, to turn the brittle pages. . . .

"*Era* magazine has commissioned me to do a profile in depth of the Project," Thomas said.

"And kill it."

Thomas was past showing surprise, almost past feeling it, he thought. "To prepare it for burial. It's already dead."

"Do you have reasons for saying so or merely prejudice?"

Thomas shifted in his chair. "The Project has continued for more than fifty years without a positive result. In fifty years even hope dies."

" 'There's life in the old girl yet.' "

Thomas recognized the quotation. "Literature survives," he conceded, "but little else." He looked at MacDonald again.

The Director of the Project is forty-nine. He looks it. But his eyes are blue and unfaded, and his long face holds within it the musculature that often accompanies strength of will and sometimes even strength of character.

"Why do you think I intend to kill the Project?"

MacDonald smiled; it illuminated his face. Thomas wondered what it would be like to smile like that.

"*Era* is the magazine of the upper classes, many of whom are mandarins, others are technocrats, and some of both are Solitarians; *Era* reinforces their prejudices, bolsters their self-esteem, and supports their interests. The Project threatens all three, in particular the effortless working of our technological society."

"You give our upper classes too much credit; they don't think that deeply."

"*Era* does that for them. And even if this all were not true, the Project still represents for *Era* a tempting target for its arrows of wit, and today's game is to see what you can kill with laughter."

"You do *Era* and me an injustice," Thomas protested casually. "The magazine's motto is 'Truth and Wit.' Note that truth comes first."

" *'Fiat justitia, et pereat mundus,'* " MacDonald murmured.

" 'Let Justice be done, though the world perish,' " Thomas translated automatically. "Who said that?"

"Emperor Ferdinand I. Do you know of him?"

"There were so many Ferdinands."

"Of course," MacDonald said. "Of course! George Thomas. You did that magnificent translation of the *Commedia*, what, ten, fifteen years ago?"

"Seventeen," Thomas said. He did not like the way the

word came out, but it was too late to call it back. He pretended to be trying to read the papers on MacDonald's desk.

"You're a poet, not a reporter. You wrote a novel a few years later, *The Inferno*. About today's damned, with a vision and sensitivity virtually equal to that of its immortal predecessor. It was meant to be the first book of a trilogy, surely. Did I miss the later books?"

"No."

MacDonald had a way of stabbing him with kindliness, Thomas thought. "What a man must be is wise enough to recognize failure and turn to something in which he has some chance of success."

"And a man must believe sufficiently in himself—or in his cause—that he persists in spite of disappointments and the inexorable metronome of the years."

They looked at each other, the older man who was not yet old and the younger man who was no longer young, and they understood each other, Thomas thought.

First a talented linguist, then an indifferent electrical engineer—as if he were deliberately preparing himself for the Project—MacDonald joined the Project twenty-one years ago. Five years later he was named Director. He is said to have a beautiful wife and a marriage in which there is some hint of scandal. He had grown old listening for voicss he had yet to hear. And what of George Thomas, poet and novelist who found success too soon and fame too young and discovered that success can be just another face of failure and fame can be a kind of death that draws the jackals of both sexes who eat up time and talent. . . .

"I'm recording this, you know," Thomas said.

"I thought you were," MacDonald said. "Is this how you

achieve the sound of reality?"

"Partly. But it's not for that. I have a good memory, and reality doesn't sound as real as you might think. Mostly I record to placate *Era*'s libel lawyers."

"You are in the right business."

"Reporter?"

"Undertaker."

"I see death all around me."

"I see life."

"Despair."

"Hope. *L'amor che muove il sole e l'altro stelle.*"

He thinks I am still in hell, Thomas thought, that I have not finished my *Inferno*, and that he is in paradise. He is a subtle man and knows me better than he lets on.

" *'Lasciate ogni speranza voi ch'entrate.'* We understand each other," Thomas said. "Hope and faith keep this Project going—"

"And scientific probability."

Thomas felt the gentle humming against his belly of the recorder clipped to his waistband. "That's another name for faith. And after more than fifty years even scientific probability becomes more than a little improbable. Perhaps that is what my profile will demonstrate."

"Fifty years is but the flicker of an eyelash on God's face."

"Fifty years is a man's working life. It has been most of your life. I don't expect you to give it up without a struggle, but it won't do you any good. Are you going to cooperate with me or fight me?"

"Is there anything we can tell you or show you that will change your mind?"

"I'll be as honest with you as I hope you will be with me: I doubt it, not because my mind is closed but because I doubt that there is anything to show. Like any good reporter, I start from a point of basic skepticism; to me this Project looks like the biggest and longest boondoggle of all time, and the only thing that can change my mind is a message."

"From the publisher or from God?"

"From another world. That's what this project is all about, isn't it?"

MacDonald sighed. "Yes, that's what it's all about. Suppose we strike a bargain."

"You know what happens to those who strike bargains with the devil."

"I'll take the chance that you are not the devil but his advocate, a man like the rest of us, lost in hell, with human fears, hopes, and desires—including the desire to seek the truth and, finding it, to communicate it to his fellow beings wherever they are."

" 'What is truth? said jesting Pilate . . .' "

" 'And would not stay for an answer.' We will stay. The bargain concerns your willingness to do as much. We will cooperate with your investigation if you will listen to what we have to say, and hear, and look at what we have to show, and see."

"Of course. That's what I'm here to do."

"I should tell you that we would have cooperated without your promise."

Thomas smiled. It may have been his first real smile since he entered the room, he thought. "I should tell you that I would have listened and looked without your cooperation."

The sparring was over, and Thomas was not sure who had gained an advantage. He was not used to feeling uncertain at this point, and it bothered him. MacDonald was a formidable opponent—all the more because he truly did not think of himself as an opponent but a colleague in the search for truth—and Thomas knew that he could never relax. He had no doubt that he could destroy MacDonald and the Project, but the game was more complex than that: it had to be played in such a way that the destruction did not include *Era* and Thomas. It was not that Thomas cared about *Era* or Thomas, but he could not lose the game.

Thomas asked MacDonald's permission to photograph him and his papers at his desk and to leaf through the papers on it. MacDonald shrugged.

Upon MacDonald's desk there are books and papers intermingled. The books are Intelligent Life in the Universe *and* The Voices of the Thirties. *The papers are of three kinds—all kinds of letters from many parts of the world, some scientific, some fan mail, some news inquiries, some crackpot notes; inter-Project memorandums, technical and formal; official reports and graphs describing the continuing work of the Project. The last are at the bottom of the neat stack on the left-hand side of the desk, like a reward for plowing through the rest, and the rest are scattered on the right-hand side with brief notes on them about the nature of the response, if any, or routing.*

When Thomas had completed his inspection, MacDonald guided his tour of the building. It was efficient but spartan: painted concrete walls, tiled floors, radiant ceiling fixtures. The offices were standard cubicles, each with its blackboard scribbled with equations or circuit diagrams, individualized only by choice of books, an occasional drape on a window or rug on a door, and a collection of personal items like clocks, radios, recorders, TVs, pipes, pictures, paintings. . . .

MacDonald introduced Thomas to the professional staff. Olsen, the computer expert, who seemed young for his peppered hair; Sonnenborn, the intense mathematician and historian of interesteller communication, verbal, curious, incisive; Saunders, the slow-talking, pipe-smoking philosopher, the lean, sandy designer of proposals and attacks; Adams, the red-faced, round-faced, sweating electronics engineer, whose responses tolled his inner doubts . . .

Thomas picked Adams to guide him through the technical aspects of the Project. The choice was natural; MacDonald could have raised no objections if he had wanted to. He smiled—it was, perhaps, a knowing smile—and said, "You will come home to dinner with me. I want you to meet Maria, and Maria will want to meet you. Bob, tell him anything he wants to know."

With MacDonald's instruction or without, Thomas thought, Adams would be the source of the inside information he needed, not just about techniques and goals but about people, and that was the most important of all. In every group there is an Adams.

The offices were places of quiet, sustained effort. In spite of its continuous history of failure, the Project maintained its morale. The personnel worked as if it were the first year, not the fifty-first.

The technical areas were different; they were lifeless. The computers and the hulking electronic consoles crouched silently, their lights extinguished, their relays stilled. Some of them had their insides spread out in front of them while men in white suits searched through them like diviners seeking oracles in the entrails of chickens. The green windows of their eyes were blank. The hum of their electronic pulse was gone. They were dead, and the sterile white walls of the rooms in which they were laid out was the operating pit in which they had died from lack of meaning.

To Adams it was different. "Here in the daytime it looks

normal enough. Everything quiet. Everything in its proper shape. But at night, when the listening begins—Do you believe in ghosts, Mr. Thomas?"

"Every civilization has its ghosts. Usually they are the gods of the last one."

"The ghosts of this civilization are in its machines," Adams said. "Year after year the machines will do your bidding, mechanically, without complaint, and then suddenly they will become possessed and do things for which they were never created, give answers for which they were never questioned, ask questions for which there are no answers. At night these machines come alive. They nod, they wink, they whisper to each other, they chuckle."

Thomas ran his hand along the front of a console. It was slick and dead. "And they tell you nothing."

Adams looked at Thomas. "They tell us a great deal. It just isn't what we asked them for. We don't know the right questions, maybe. Or we don't know how to ask them properly. The machines know. I'm sure of it. They keep telling us, over and over. We just don't understand them. Maybe we don't want to understand them."

Thomas turned toward Adams. "Why not?"

"Maybe they're trying to tell us that there's nobody out there. Think of that! That there's nobody there, nobody but us in the whole wide universe. All of it is just for us, a vast show we can look at but never touch, spread out to impress the only creature capable of understanding it—and capable of feeling lonely."

"Then this whole Project would be folly, wouldn't it?"

Adams shook his head. "Call it man's attempt to stay sane. Because we can't ever know for sure; we can't eliminate all possibilities. So we keep searching because it is too terrifying to give up and admit we are alone."

"Wouldn't it be more terrifying to learn that we are not alone?"

"Do you think so?" Adams asked politely. "Everyone has his own great fear. Mine is that there is no one there, even though my mind tells me that this is what is. I have talked to others who dreaded to hear something, and I couldn't understand them, even though I could understand how they might have feelings I feel only stirred by other terrors."

"Tell me how it works," Thomas said politely. There would be time later to exploit Adams' fears.

The listening continues as it began more than fifty years ago, largely by radio waves picked up by radio telescopes, by giant arrays of antennae built into valleys, by smaller steerable dishes, by spiderwebs of metal cast into space. The listening is mostly at the twenty-one-centimeter frequency of neutral hydrogen. Other wavelengths are sampled, but the listeners keep returning to nature's standard calibrating frequency or its whole multiples. A lifetime of engineering ingenuity has gone into multiplying the sensitivity of the receivers and canceling out the natural noise of the universe and of earth. And after it all is canceled, what is left—now as then—is nothing. Zero. And still they listen. And still they strain their ears to hear.

"Why don't you quit?" Thomas asked.

"It's been only fifty years or so. That's only a second of galactic time."

"If somebody or something were signaling, those signals surely would have been heard by now. That must be clear."

"Perhaps there's nobody there," Adams mused and then his eyes became aware of Thomas again. "Or maybe everybody's listening."

Thomas raised his eyebrows.

"It's much cheaper to listen, you know. Much cheaper. Everybody might be sitting there glued to their receivers, and nobody's sending. Only we *are* sending."

"We're sending?" Thomas asked quickly. "Who authorized that?"

"This place is pretty uncomfortable if you're not working," Adams said. "Let's get a cup of coffee, and I'll tell you about it."

The lunchroom was a converted office filled by two small tables, each with four chairs, and lined on three sides with coin-operated machines that hummed very softly as they went about their business of keeping food and drink hot or cold.

Adams sipped his coffee and went over the entire history of the Project, beginning with Project Ozma and the inspired speculations of Cocconi, Morrison, and Drake, and the subsequent contributions of Bracewell, Townes, and Schwartz, Oliver, Golay, Dyson, von Hoerner, Shklovsky, Sagan, Struve, Atchley, Calvin, Huang, and Lilly whose efforts to communicate with the dolphin gave to the infant group the name "order of the dolphin."

From the first it was clear that there *ought* to be other intelligent creatures in the universe. The process of planet formation, once thought to be the chance (and unlikely) near-collision of two stars, was recognized as a natural occurrence when stars were forming out of gaseous clouds and rock and metal fragments. One or two percent of the stars in our galaxy probably had planets which could support life. Since there were 150 billion stars in our galaxy, at least a billion, perhaps two or three, had habitable planets.

"One billion solar systems where life can develop!" Adams said. "And it seems reasonable to assume that where life can develop it will develop."

"Life, yes, but man is unique," Thomas said.

"Are you a Solitarian?" Adams asked.

"No, but that is not to say that I do not consider some of their beliefs well founded."

"Perhaps man is unique," Adams said, "although there are many galaxies. But is intelligence unique? It has high survival value. Once it has occurred, even by accident, it is likely to prevail."

"But technology is another thing," Thomas said, sipping his hot black coffee.

"Quite another thing," Adams agreed. "It happened to us only very recently, you know, about midway during the main sequence time of our sun during which life can be expected to exist. Hominids have lived on Earth only for one-tenth of one percent of Earth's existence, civilization has existed for about one-millionth of Earth's lifespan, and technical civilization, only one-billionth. Considering the late emergence of all three and the fact that there must be older planets, if there is intelligent life on other worlds some of it must be farther advanced than we, and some, much farther advanced. But—"

"But—?"

"But why don't we hear from them?" Adams cried out.

"Have you tried everything?"

"Not only the radio frequencies—we've explored gamma rays, lasers, neutrinos, even long-chain molecules in carbonaceous meteorites and absorption lines in the spectrum of stars. The only thing we haven't tried is 'Q' waves."

"What are those?"

Adams was absently sketching diagrams on the gray surface of the table. Thomas noticed that the table was covered with fainter, washed-away marks where others had sketched. "What Morrison many years ago called 'the method we haven't discovered yet but are going to discover ten years from now,' " Adams said. "Only we haven't discovered it. The only other thing we haven't tried is sending messages. That's more expensive. We could never find the funds—not now, not without some hope of success. Even then we would have to decide whether we wish to broadcast to the universe or even to one solar system the presence here of intelligent, civilized life."

"But we are sending, you said."

"We've been sending since the earliest days of radio," Adams said. "Low power, most of it, unbeamed, loaded with static and other interfering transmissions, but intelligent life has made Earth the second most powerful radio source in the solar system, and in a few more decades we may equal the sun itself. If there's anybody out there to notice, that should make Earth visible."

"But you haven't heard anything?"

"What would we hear on this little apparatus?" Adams asked, nodding toward the valley beyond the walls. "What we need is some time on the Big Ear upstairs, the five-mile-in-diameter net, or the new net being built, but the astronomers won't give us the time of day."

"Why don't you quit?"

"He won't let us!"

"He?"

"Mac. No, that's not right. Yes, it is. He keeps us together, he and Maria. There was a time, not so long ago, when it looked as if it would all come apart . . ."

Thomas took another sip of coffee. It was cool enough to drink now, and he swallowed it all.

The drive to MacDonald's house in the Puerto Rican hills was pleasant as the day closed. The shadows draped themselves across the green slopes like the legs of purple giants.

The evening breeze blew the sharp scent of salt in from the ocean. The elderly steam turbine under the hood hummed along with only an occasional vibration to betray its age.

This place must be the cleanest, quietest spot in the whole dirty, noisy world, Thomas thought, like paradise, innocent, before the knowledge of good and evil. Like a carrier I bring the dirt and noise with me. He felt a moment of irritation that this place should exist in a world of misery and boredom and a flash of satisfaction that he had the power to destroy it.

"Did you learn all you wanted from Adams?"

"What?" Thomas said. "Oh, yes. That and more."

"I thought you would. He's a good man, Bob, a man you can count on when you need a friend, a man you can call at home in the middle of the night to say that a tire has gone flat in a rainstorm, and you know he'll come. He talks a lot and complains a lot. Don't let that keep you from seeing the person underneath."

"What of the things he told me am I not to believe?" Thomas asked.

"Believe it all," MacDonald said. "Bob wouldn't tell you anything but the truth. But there is something misleading in too much truth, even more, perhaps, than too little."

"Like your wife's attempted suicide?"

"Like that."

"And the resignation you tore up?"

"That, too."

Thomas could not tell whether there was sorrow in MacDonald's voice or fear of exposure or merely recognition of the irrepressible evils of the world.

As we drive toward his home in the hills near Arecibo, hills as silent as the voices for which he listens in the concrete building we had left, he does not deny that his wife attempted suicide a year ago or that he wrote a letter of resignation and later tore it up.

The house was a Spanish-style hacienda looking friendly and warm in the gathering darkness, beams of yellow light pouring from door and window. Stepping into the house, Thomas felt it even more, the lived-in, loved-in feeling that he had known only once or twice before in the homes of friends. To those homes he had returned more than to others, to warm himself in their relationship, until he realized what was happening to him. He would stop writing. He would look for someone to ease the ache he had inside, and he would end with a casual affair that would turn to revulsion. He would flee back to his solitary life, back to his writing, to work out on his typewriter keys the agony that pulsed through his veins. And the writing would be twisted and angry like the infernal regions he described. Why hadn't he written his purgatory? He knew why: under his fingers it kept turning back into hell.

Maria MacDonald was a mature, olive-skinned woman whose beauty went deep. She was dressed in a simple peasant blouse and skirt, and she held his hand in hers and bade him welcome to her home. He felt himself warming to her gentle smile and Latin American courtesy, and fought it. He wanted to kiss her hand. He wanted to turn it over and see the scar upon her wrist. He wanted to take her in his arms and protect her against the terrors of the night.

He did none of these. He said, "I'm here, you know, to do a piece about the Project, and I'm afraid it will not be favorable."

She turned her head a little to one side to study him. "You are not an unfriendly man, I think. You are a disappointed man, perhaps. Perhaps bitter. But you are honest. You wonder how I know these things. I have a sense about people, Mr. Thomas. Robby brings them home to me before he hires them, and I tell him about them and not once have I been wrong. Have I, Robby?"

MacDonald smiled. "Only once."

"That is a joke," Maria said. "He means I was wrong about him, but that is another story that I will tell you some time if I come to know you better, as I hope. I have this sense, Mr. Thomas, and more—I have read your translation and I have read your novel, too, which Robby tells me you have not continued. You must, Mr. Thomas. It is not good to live in the inferno. One must know it, yes, so that one can comprehend the purging of the sins that one must go through to achieve paradise."

"It was easy to write about hell," Thomas said, "but I found it impossible to imagine anything else."

"You have not yet burned away your deadly sins," Maria said. "You have not yet found anything to believe in, anything to love. Some people never find that, and it is very sad. I feel so sad for them. Do not be one of them. But I am too personal—"

"No, no—"

"You are here to enjoy our hospitality, not to endure my missionary zeal for love and marriage. But I cannot help it, you see." And she put one arm through her husband's and offered the other to Thomas as they went from the entryway down the hall tiled with terra cotta to the living room. A bright Mexican rug covered part of the polished oak floor. There, in big leather chairs, they had salty margaritas and casual conversation about New York and San Francisco and friends they might have in common, the literary life, and the political scene, and where *Era* fitted into both, and how Thomas had started writing for the magazine.

Then Maria ushered them into dinner. They sat down to what she called a "traditional Mexican *comida*." The first course was soup swarming with dumpling-like tortilla balls, vegetables, noodles, and pieces of chicken. The second course was *sopa seca,* a highly seasoned dish of rice, noodles, and cut-up tortillas in an elaborate sauce; then a fish course was followed by a salad and a main course of *cabreto,* roasted young goat, and several vegetables, and this was followed by refried beans smothered with grated cheese. With it all came feathery hot tortillas in napkin-lined baskets. The dinner ended, none too soon for Thomas, with a caramelized milk pudding Maria called "natillas piuranas," with strong black coffee, and with fresh fruit.

Protesting feebly, as the meal progressed, that he could eat no more, Thomas surrendered to Maria's insistence and ate something of each dish as it appeared, until MacDonald laughed and said, "You have fed him too much, Maria. He will be good for nothing for the rest of the evening, and we still have work to do. The Latin Americans, Mr. Thomas, have this kind of meal only upon special occasions, and then in the middle of the day after which they retire for a well-deserved siesta."

MacDonald filled their glasses with a brandy he called pisco. "May I propose a toast," he said. "To beauty and good food!"

"To good listening!" said Maria.

"To truth!" Thomas said, to prove that he had not been charmed nor fed into complete subjugation, but his eyes were on the white line that cut across Maria's olive wrist.

"You have noticed my scar," Maria said. "That is a reminder of my folly that I will bear with me always."

"Not your folly," MacDonald said, "my deafness."

"It was a little more than a year ago," Maria said, "and I was feeling a little crazy. I could see that it was not going well with the Project and Robby was wearing down between the demands of keeping the Project going and his worry over me. It was madness, I know now, but I thought I could remove one of Robby's concerns by removing myself. I tried suicide with a razor blade, and I almost died. But I lived, and I found my sanity again, and Robby and I found each other again."

"We were never lost," MacDonald said. "We had just, temporarily, out of human inattention, stopped listening to each other."

"But you knew all this, didn't you, Mr. Thomas?" Maria said. "Are you married?"

"I was once," Thomas said.

"And it was wrong," Maria said. "That is sad. You must be married. You must have someone to love, someone to love you. Then you can write your *Purgatory*, your *Paradise*."

An infant cried somewhere in the house. Maria looked up happily. "And Robby and I found something else."

She moved gracefully from the room and returned in a moment with a baby in her arms. It was two or three months old, Thomas thought, and it had dark hair and bright dark eyes in an olive face, like its mother, and the eyes seemed to see Thomas where he stood by the dinner table.

"This is Bobby, our son," Maria said. If she had been alive before, she was doubly alive now, Thomas thought. This was the magnetism that turned painters toward madonnas for their subjects.

"We were lucky," MacDonald said. "We waited a long time to have a child, but Bobby came easily and he is normal, not handicapped as are some children of older parents. I think he will grow up to be an ordinary boy burdened with the love of parents old enough to be his grandparents, and I only hope we can understand him."

"I hope he can understand you," Thomas said, and then,

"Mrs. MacDonald, why don't you make your husband give up this hopeless Project?"

"I don't make Robby do anything," Maria said. "The Project is his life, just as he and Bobby are my life. You think there is something bad about it, a treachery, a deception, but you do not know my husband or the men he has gathered to work with him if you honestly think that. They believe in what they are doing."

"Then they are fools."

"No, the fools are those who do not believe, who cannot believe. It may be that there is no one out there or if there is someone out there he will never speak to us or we to him, but our listening is an act of faith akin to living itself. If we should stop listening, we would begin dying and we would soon be gone, the world and its people, our technical civilization and even the farmers and peasants, because life is faith, life is commitment. Death is giving up."

"You have not seen the world the way I have seen it," Thomas said. "It is dying."

"Not while men like these still strive," Maria said.

"You give us too much credit," MacDonald said.

"No, I do not," Maria said to Thomas. "My husband is a great man. He listens with his heart. Before you leave this island, you will know that, and you will believe. I have seen others come like you, doubting, eager to destroy, and Robby has taken them in, has given them faith and hope, and they have left, believing."

"I do not intend to be taken in," Thomas said.

"You know what I meant."

"I know that I wish I had someone who believed in me the way you believe in your husband."

"We'd better go back," MacDonald said. "I have something to show you."

Thomas said good-bye to Maria MacDonald and thanked her for her hospitality and for her personal concern for him, and he turned and left the hacienda. When he was outside in the darkness he turned once and looked back at the house with the light pouring from it and the woman standing in the doorway of the house with a baby in her arms.

The difference between day and night is of another order than the difference between light and dark. After the sun has set, the familiar assumes different proportions: distances are elongated and objects shift their places.

As MacDonald and Thomas made their way past the valley into whose arms had been built the semi-steerable radio telescope, it was not the same sterile saucer. It was a pit of mystery and shadows gathering strange echoes from the sky within its sheltered bowl, catching the stardust that drifted gently, gently through the night air.

The steerable dish that had been frozen in deathlike rigor against the sky now was alive and questing. Thomas thought he could see it quivering as it strained toward the silent dark.

The Little Ear, they called it, this giant piece of precision machinery, the largest steerable radio telescope on Earth, to distinguish it from the Big Ear, the five-mile-in-diameter network of cables in orbit. At night the visitor can sense the magic it works upon the men who think they work their will upon it. For these obsessed men, it is an ear, their ear, cocked responsively toward the silent stars, with supernal power and ingenious filters and bypasses listening to the infinite and hearing only the slow heartbeat of the eternal.

"We inherited it from the astronomers," MacDonald was saying, "when they put up the first radio telescopes on the far side of the moon and then the first of the networks in space. The earthbound equipment no longer was worth anything, rather like an old crystal set when vacuum tubes were perfected. Instead of junking these instruments, however, they gave them to us with a small budget for operation."

"Over the decades, the total must mount toward the astronomical," Thomas said, trying to shake away the effects of the evening's hospitality and the night's spells.

"It adds up," MacDonald agreed, "and we fight for our lives every year. But there are returns. One might compare the Project to a hothouse for intellects, a giant continuing, unsolvable puzzle against which the most promising minds pit themselves and grow strong. We get the young scientists and engineers and train them and send them on to solve problems that have solutions. The Project has a surprising number of alumni, many of them overachieving."

"Is that how you justify the Project, as a kind of graduate school?"

"Oh, no. That is what our predecessors used to call fallout or spin-off. Our ultimate goal and our most valuable goal is communication with other beings on other worlds. I offer you reasons that you may use to justify us if you cannot bring yourself to accept us as we are."

"Why would I want to justify you?"

"That you will have to find out for yourself."

Then they were inside the building, and it was different, too. The corridors that had seemed brisk and businesslike in the daytime now were charged with energy and purpose. The control room had been touched by the forefinger of God; where death had been there was life: lights came on and turned off, oscilloscopic eyes were alive with green linear motion, the relays of the consoles clicked gently, the computers chuckled to themselves, electricity whispered along wires.

Adams was seated at the control panel. He had earphones on his head, and his eyes studied the gauges and oscilloscopes spread before him. As they entered, he looked up and waved. MacDonald's eyebrows lifted; Adams shrugged. He pulled the earphones down around his neck. "The usual nothing."

"Here," MacDonald said, removing the earphones and handing them to Thomas. "You listen."

Thomas put one of the receivers to his ear.

First comes babble, like a multitude of voices heard afar or a stream rippling over a bed of rocks, squirting through crevices, and dashing itself over small waterfalls. Then the sounds grow louder, and they are voices talking earnestly but all together so that none can be heard individually but confused and one. The listener strains to hear, and all his effort only makes the voices more eager to be heard, and they talk louder still and even more indistinguishably. Like Dante, the listener "stood on the edge of the descent where the hollow of the gulf out of despair amasses thunder of infinite lament." And the voices change from eager pleadings to angry shouts, as if, like damned souls, they demand salvation from the flames in which they burn. They turn upon the listener as if to destroy him for temerity in thrusting himself among fallen angels, in all their arrogance and sinful pride. "Above I saw a thousand spirits in air rained down from heaven, who angry as if betrayed cried: 'Who is this who without death doth dare the kingdom of the dead folk to invade?' " And the listener thinks that he is one of those who shouts to be heard, damned like them in hell, able only to scream at the torment and the frustration of having no one to listen to him and to care what happens to him and to understand. "Even then I heard on all sides wailing sound, but of those making it saw no one nigh, wherefore I stood still, in amazement bound." And the listener thinks he is among giants "whose rebellious pride Jove's thunderings out of heaven still appall." All of them, like him, struggle to be heard in their mighty voices and cannot be understood. "Raphael may amech zabi almi, throat brutish mouth incontinently cried; and they were fitted for no sweeter note." And the listener felt as if consciousness were about to leave him.

And the voices were gone. MacDonald was lifting the earphones from his ears where, Thomas vaguely recalled, he had placed them himself. And he was shaken by the overpowering influence of those sounds, those voices, all kinds of voices struggling to be heard, blending together into an alien chorus, each participant singing a different song. . . .

Thomas had a moment of self-revelation in which he knew that he was lost, like the voices, and he would have to find his way out or be damned to live forever within his fleshy prison, as alone in his torment as if he were in hell itself.

"What was that?" he asked, and his voice was shaky.

"The sound of the infinite," MacDonald said. "We translate the radio signals into audio frequencies. It doesn't help us pick up anything. If anything is there it would show up on the tapes, the dials would flash, the computer would sound an alarm; it wouldn't come out as voice communication. But there is inspiration in hearing something when you're listening, and we need inspiration."

"I call it hypnosis," Thomas said. "It can help convince the doubtful that there really is something there, that they someday may be able to hear clearly what now they imagine, that there really are aliens out there trying to communicate—and it's only a trick to fool yourselves and perpetrate a fraud upon the world."

"Some are more susceptible than others," MacDonald said. "I'm sorry you took it as a personal attack. We aren't playing tricks. You knew there was no communication there."

"Yes," Thomas said, and it angered him that his voice still was shaky.

"But this is not what I wanted you to hear. This is background. Let's go to my office. You, too, Bob. Leave the watch to the technician. It doesn't matter."

They went to the office, the three of them, and settled into chairs. MacDonald's desk was clear now, waiting for the next day's deposit. But the scent of old books remained. Thomas rubbed his hands over the slick wooden arms of his chair and watched MacDonald.

"It isn't going to work," Thomas said. "Not all the hypnotic sounds in the world or the pleasant company or delightful meals or beautiful women or touching family scenes can ever compensate for the fact that this Project has been going on for more than fifty years and you haven't yet received a message."

"That's what I brought you here to say," MacDonald said. "We have."

"You haven't!" Adams said. "Why didn't I know?"

"We haven't been sure. We weren't sure until last night. We have had false alarms before, and they have been our most difficult moments. Saunders knew. It was his baby."

"The tapes from the Big Ear," Adams said.

"Yes. Saunders has been working with them, trying to clean them up. Now we're sure. Tomorrow morning I'm calling together the whole crew. We'll announce it." He turned to Thomas. "But I want your advice."

"You aren't going to try to trick me with something like this, are you, MacDonald?" Thomas asked. "The coincidence is too much."

"Coincidences happen," MacDonald said. "History is full of them. The projects that succeed, the concepts that prevail, somehow are rescued from destruction by the coincidence that arrives just before the moment of final success."

"And then to ask for my help," Thomas continued. "That is the oldest ploy of all."

"Don't forget, Mr. Thomas," MacDonald said, "we are scientists. We have been searching for fifty years and more without success; we have stopped thinking, if we ever did, about what we would do if we succeeded. We need help. You know people and how to move them, what they will accept and reject, how they will react to the unknown. It is all quite logical and natural."

"It's too pat. I don't believe it."

"Believe him, George," Adams said. "He never lies."

"Everyone lies," Thomas said.

"He's right, Bob," MacDonald said. "But you will believe it, Mr. Thomas, because it's true and because it's verifiable and reproducible, and when it is released, if that is what we do with it, all the scientists will say, 'Why, yes. It's right. That's the way it would be.' Why would I fabricate something that could be so easily disproved and wreck this Project more thoroughly than anything you might write?"

"I've heard that someone who wants out of service should complain of pains in the back or voices in the head, neither of which can be disproved," Thomas said.

"The physical sciences are not subjective. And anything this big will be checked and checked again by every astronomer everywhere."

"Perhaps you hope to con me into killing the whole thing in the name of public morale."

"Can I con you, Mr. Thomas?"

"No," Thomas said, and remembered the voices and said, "I don't know. Why now? Why at this moment when I came to do this profile?"

"I don't want to minimize the significance of your assignment," MacDonald said, "but you are not the first writer to come here to do a story. We have a reporter here every week or so. It would be strange if we did not have a reporter here within a day or two of the time we received our first message. It just happened to be you."

"Well," Thomas said, "what is it? How did you stumble across it?"

"We began getting tapes from the Big Ear about a year ago—tapes of their routine radio telescopy—and began to analyze them. Saunders ran them through the computer, earphones and all, and one day he thought he heard music and voices.

"His first thought was 'delusion,' but the computer said no. Saunders did what he could to clarify them, reinforce them, subtract the noise and interference. We've developed a lot of tricks in the past fifty years. The music came through recognizably and the voices, in snatches, even better. And the voices were speaking English.

"His second thought was that the Big Ear had picked up some stray transmissions from Earth or maybe something bounced off one of the other planets. But the net wasn't pointed toward Earth or another planet. It was pointed off into space. There were other tapes going back several years, and when the Big Ear was pointed in a certain direction it got the same signals."

"What were they?" Thomas asked.

"For God's sake, Mac, let's hear it!" Adams said.

MacDonald pushed one of the buttons on his desk.

"Understand," MacDonald said, "that there was much more interference, but for this purpose Saunders cut out almost all the non-intelligible parts. The ratio of noise to sound was about fifty to one, so you're hearing only about one-fiftieth of what we have."

The sound was monophonic, although it came from two speakers built into the walls to the right and left. The impact was nothing like that of the headphones in the control room, but the sounds had a fascination akin, perhaps, to that of the early days of radio when people sat around a crystal set straining at faint sounds, trying to pick up Schenectady or Pittsburgh or Fort Worth. The sounds were radiant, Thomas thought, with the possibility that they came from another world—or with the improbability that they could have come from anywhere but Earth.

The sounds are earthly. That is certain. There is music, all based on the chromatic scale, and some of it familiar, the William Tell Overture, for instance. And there are the voices, speaking English most of them but also Russian, French, Italian, German, Spanish, English. Music. From another world? It doesn't make sense. And yet we listen.

The transmission is bad. Static and other random interruptions at times obscure whatever is being transmitted, and what comes through is broken into fragments, occasionally understandable, mostly cryptic, none complete, each in a different voice. Here, indeed, is Babel, but Babel in which enough is clear that the listeners feel that all should make sense.

For a few moments the music or the voices come through clearly, fading in and fading back out as the noise level rises. The listeners waver between the impression that the voices are the dominant element occasionally interrupted by noise and the impression that the transmission of noise is occasionally interrupted by voices.

Like a Greek chorus, the voices chant their lines and imbue them with a Delphic obscurity. The listeners lean forward as if it will help them hear a little better. . . .

POPCRACKLE ice regusted CRACKLEPOP music: that

little chatterbox the one with the pretty POPCRACKLE wanna buy a duck POPCRACKLE-POP masked champion of justice CRACKLEPOPPOP POPPOPPOPCRACKLE ter eleven book one hundred and POPCRACKLEPOP here they come jack POPPOP music CRACKLE yoo hoo is anybody POPCRACKLE is raymond your POPCRACKLEPOPPOP music POPPOPCRACKLE music: wave the flag for hudson CRACKLEPOP um a bad boy POPPOPPOP lux presents holly CRACKLECRACKLE music POPPOPCRACKLE rogers in the twenty POPCRACKLEPOP music: cola hits the spot twelve CRACKLE say goodnight grace POPPOP music CRACKLEPOP could have knocked me over with a fender POPCRACKLECRACKLE knee this is rochest CRACKLEPOP music CRACKLEPOPPOPPOP matinee idol larry POPPOP music: au revoir pleasant CRACKLECRACKLE the little theater off POPPOPCRACKLE eye doodit CRACKLEPOP music POPPOPPOP who knows what evil POPCRACKLEPOP voss you dare shar CRACKLEPOP you have a friend and adviser in CRACKLECRACKLE music POPCRACKLEPOP another trip down allens POPPOPCRACKLE stay tuned for POPCRACKLE music: bar ba sol bar POP you termites flophouse CRACKLEPOPPOPOP at the chime it will be ex CRACKLECRACKLEPOP people defender of POPPOP music POPCRACKLE the only thing we have to fear CRACKLE and now vic and POPPOPOP duffy ain't here CRACKLEPOP music POPCRACKLEPOP information plea CRACKLECRACKLE music: boo boo boo boo POPPOPCRACKLE can a woman over thirty-five CRACKLEPOPPOPOP adventures of sher POPCRACKLECRACKLE music POPPOP it's a bird CRACKLE only genuine wrigley's POPCRACKLE born edits the news CRACKLECRACKLEPOP hello everybody POPCRACKLEPOP music POPPOPCRACKLE that's my boy CRACKLE check and double POP.

After the voices and the static had stopped, Thomas turned to look at MacDonald. He had more than half an hour of it on his own recorder, but he wasn't sure what he was going to do with it or even what he thought about it. "What does it mean?"

"It's from Earth," Adams said.

"We start with that," MacDonald said. He turned and selected a book from the shelf behind him. "Take a look at this," he said to Thomas, "and maybe you'll understand it better."

The book was *The Voices of the Thirties.* Thomas leafed through it. He looked up. "This is about the early days of radio, more than ninety years ago."

"What we heard," MacDonald said, "as you would discover from this book and others if you made a careful study, was broadcast during that period: music, news, comedy, drama, adventure, what they called soap operas, mysteries, fireside chats, agony shows. . . . There was a great deal of foreign language fragments, too, but we screened them out."

"You think I'm going to believe that you received this nonsense from the stars?"

"Yes," MacDonald said. "This is what the Big Ear picked up when the astronomers listened in a direction about five hours' right ascension, about fifty-six degrees declension, in the general direction of Capella."

"How could Capella be sending us this Earth garbage?"

"I didn't say it was Capella," MacDonald said, "just that it was in that general direction."

"Of course," Adams said.

"It's too ridiculous," Thomas said.

"I agree," MacDonald said. "So ridiculous that it must be true. Why would I try to deceive you with something so transparently foolish when it would be simple to plant some signals almost indistinguishable from noise. Even these could be proven false in time, but we could brazen it out and maybe pick up some real signals before our deception was discovered. But this! Easily checked—and too ridiculous not to be true."

"But it's—how could Capella—or whatever—be sending??"

"We've been listening for fifty years," MacDonald said, "but we've been transmitting for more than ninety years."

"We've been transmitting?"

"I told you, remember?" Adams said. "Ever since radio transmission began, these relatively feeble radio waves have been spreading through the universe at a speed of 186,000 miles per second."

"Capella is about forty-five light-years from Earth," MacDonald said.

"Forty-five years for the radio waves to get there," Adams said.

"Forty-five years to get back," MacDonald added.

"It's bouncing off Capella?" Thomas said.

"The signals are being sent back. They're being picked up near Capella and beamed directly back to us in a powerful, directional transmission," MacDonald said.

"Is this possible?"

"We couldn't do it," Adams said. "Not with the equipment we have now. A really big antenna in space—perhaps deep in space, far from the sun—would be able to pick up stray radio transmissions, even feeble ones like those in our early transmission history, from a hundred light-years away or more. Perhaps we would find that the galaxy is humming with radio traffic."

"Even so, it is surprising that we can discern anything at all across forty-five light-years and back. The stray signals arriving at Capella must be incredibly faint, scarcely distinguishable from noise," MacDonald said. "Of course they may be using other devices—perhaps a receiver relatively close to Earth, in the asteroid belt, for instance, which could pick up our radio broadcasts and beam them directly at Capella. This would imply, of course, that this solar system has been visited by aliens—or at least by their automated pick-up and transmission devices. It doesn't matter. The fact is that we are receiving a delayed rebroadcast, ninety years out of our past."

"But why would they do that, even if they could?" Thomas protested.

"Can you think of a better way to catch our attention?" MacDonald asked. "To tell us they know we're here and that they are there? A signal we can't miss?"

"Just a big hello?"

"That wouldn't be all," Adams said.

MacDonald nodded. "Some of the static may not be static. There seems to be some kind of order to some of it, a series of pulses, groups of on-off signals, a series of numbers, or a message in linear form or something that might make a picture if we knew how to put them together. Maybe it's nothing; maybe it's some early telegraphy. We don't know yet, but Saunders and the computers are working on it."

"It's the beginning," Thomas said. He could feel his pulse beating faster and his palms beginning to perspire. He had not felt like this since he was working on *The Inferno*.

"We are not alone," Adams said.

"What could they have said to us?" Thomas asked.

"We'll find out," MacDonald said.

"And then?" Thomas asked.

"There's that," MacDonald agreed. "Just as there is the question before us now of how we announce what we have discovered or if we announce it at all. How will people react to the demonstrated fact of other intelligent beings in the galaxy? Will they be terrified, angry, curious, pleased, excited, exultant? Will they feel proud or suddenly inferior?"

"You've got to announce it," Thomas said. He had a deep conviction that he was right. This too was something he had not felt for a long time.

"Will they understand?"

"We must make them understand. There's a race of intelligent beings out there on a world something like ours, and they must have a great deal to say to us. What great news for humanity! It demands not fear but celebration. We must get people to see that, to feel it."

"I don't know how."

"You're joking," Thomas said. He was smiling. "You've handled me like a master psychologist, steering me the way you wanted me to go each step of the way. No matter. I'll help. I can get others. We'll communicate every way we can think of: articles, television, books, fact and fiction, interviews, polls, games, toys. . . . We'll make the Project the doorway to a new world and this Earth needs one right now. It's bored with what it has, and boredom is an enduring danger to the human spirit."

"We mustn't forget," Adams said, "that there's a world of intelligent creatures near Capella who have sent us a message, who are waiting for a response. That's the main thing."

"They aren't human, you know," MacDonald said. "In fact, their environment is markedly different. Capella is a red giant—or rather twin red giants—somewhat cooler than our sun but much larger and brighter."

"And probably older, if our theories of stellar evolution are correct," Adams said.

"Capella's suns are what our sun may become in a galactic

decade or two," MacDonald said. "Think what it must have meant to have evolved with two red giant suns in the sky, with the irregularities in light and dark and in orbit itself, in the nature of the world one lives on, its growing conditions, its extremes of heat and cold! What kind of creatures will have survived such conditions—and thrived?"

"What strange viewpoints they must have!" Thomas said. "Dante descended into hell to find out how other creatures lived and what they thought. Our creatures are much more alien, and all we have to do is listen."

"We, too, have our descents into hell," MacDonald said.

"I know. Are you going to tell your staff tomorrow?"

"If you think it's wise."

"It's necessary, wise or not. Urge everyone, for now, to treat the information as confidential. I'll write my profile for *Era*, with your permission, but it will be a little different from the one they expected."

"*Era* would be ideal, but would they print it?"

"For an exclusive like this, they would come out in favor of communicating with Satan and all his fallen angels. They'll toss the Solitarians into the inferno and lead the mandarins and the technocrats into the promised land. Meanwhile I'll recruit some colleagues and we'll have a series of stories and interviews ready for all the media when *Era* hits the mail."

"It sounds good," MacDonald said.

"Meanwhile," Thomas said, "here's a thought for you: do the Capellans understand the radio transmissions they receive from Earth? And are they judging our civilization by our soap operas?"

Thomas stood up and turned off his recorder. "It's been a good day," he said. "I'll see you in the morning." And he started for the door, and, although he didn't know it until later, approached his purgatory.

Fault

The second time they made love during that long night the girl cried out. Later, as his breathing quieted and the sweat dried upon his body, he lay beside her, smoking a cigarette, not seeing the smoke but only the glow of the tip as he drew upon it, and his troubles returned. He pushed them away and asked why she cried out. He wanted her to know that he did not regard her only as a faceless female he had selected by chance from off the street with whom he coupled without affection or concern. But also, he knew, he wanted to glory another moment in his masculinity, in his ability to bring an inexperienced girl to passion and repletion.

"Didn't you feel the earth move?" she asked.

He laughed at the incongruity and his own deflation, and felt her stiffen. "You think I'm silly," she said sulkily.

"I'm sorry," he said, and put his hand on her slender thigh, once cool and mysterious under a short, pale blue, silken skirt and now as familiar as his own. "It was—it reminded me of an old book, that's all."

He swung his legs over the edge of the bed and went to the window and stood looking out over the lights of San Francisco. Union Square loomed gray and formless below, like a fortuneteller's clouded ball. He peered into it, willing it to clear, to allow him to see, if only a few days or weeks, into the future. It would be foggy today, he thought. That's what they needed most on this kind of day, he thought bitterly—fog.

"Why did you come with me?" he asked.

"The money," she said.

She was still sulking, he thought, and he remembered the chance events that had brought them together.

He had not wanted to go home with his problem, with the decision he had to make. He had been exhilarated with the feeling of power, as if he himself were in control of great natural events, and at the same time oppressed by a foreboding of disaster or, at the very least, of incredible difficulties in the days ahead.

He had walked from City Hall down Market Street, past the porno movie houses and the Palace Hotel, clear to the Embarcadero, down the Embarcadero, looking out over the bay, smelling the salt air, feeling the leather soles of his shoes abrading themselves against the sidewalk, to Broadway, past the sex shops and the little bars and the outdoor cafes and the sadomasochism movies and the girlie bars which advertised live sex acts on their stages. One barker almost dragged him into a bar by his arm before the barker recognized him and let him go, muttering an apology.

His town, Alonzo had thought, and then, more defiantly, *his town!* Sinful maybe. Degenerate maybe. But frank and free and brave and bold most certainly, and he was going to save it. If he only knew how.

He had turned and walked up Grant Street, crowded with tourists, white faces standing out among the yellow, looking at the painted buildings and the bric-a-brac and strange foods in the windows, smiling at the music of Chinese spoken by older citizens, smelling the strange foods. Alonzo had found himself studying the construction of the buildings like a termite inspector, thinking, this building or this will be the first to crumple, the first to flash into flame.

Finally he had come to Union Square. First he had noticed the crowd that was gathered around the figure of a man who stood above it, a white-haired, white-bearded old man in a long, brown robe, who had shouted, "The world is coming to an end, sinners! Repent! Repent!"

Someone in the crowd shouted, "Tell 'em, Grandpa!"

"Get thee from this town of Sodom and Gomorrah! The hand of the Lord is descending upon this sinful city!"

"Hallelujah, brother!"

"In the book of prophecy it is written that the Earth itself will tremble and fire will walk upon the land and burn upon the sea. Now even atheistic science confirms the prophets: California will be shaken from top to bottom, Los Angeles will go, San Francisco will go, Oakland and Berkeley will go, shaken into the sea."

"Gosh, Grandpa, I thought you said the whole world."

"It will seem like the whole world to thee, sinner. Get thee to the hilltops! Confess thy sins! Become one with the Lord! Repent! Be born again!"

"Where we gonna find this hilltop?"

"Go to the East! Leave this doomed city behind, leave the lechers and defilers to die with the city. Pass by the other cities of the bay! They also will die. Proceed until you reach the hills and safety where you may walk with God and together watch this place go to the perdition it deserves."

Alonzo looked around at the crowd. It was a mixed group, a polyglot group, a multi-hued, multi-garbed, many-aged slice of San Francisco. On most of the faces he could see were looks of amusement or inattention. Bottles of whiskey and wine were openly displayed or passed around. Cigarettes, cigars, and pot were being smoked. One young man was sniffing something out of what looked like a tiny, silver saxophone. Huddled on the pavement at one end of a bench was a child who could not have been more than eleven mainlining something . . .

Alonzo flipped his cigarette far out the window toward the square and turned back toward the girl. “That was a little quake,” he said. “What geologists call a premonitory effect. You’ve felt them before.”

“That’s what I meant,” she said, still pouting, hugging the sheet around her throat.

She looked very attractive and vulnerable at that moment, and Alonzo’s mood lightened. “Come on,” he said. “Let’s take a shower! Wake us up!”

The shower was small, but even in close contact the girl did not get into the playfulness of the occasion. She only huddled in a corner letting the water fall upon her. As they toweled themselves afterwards, Alonzo looked into the mirror blurred with steam, and he leaned forward and wiped it partially clear with his towel until he could see his own bemused face peering out at him as if from a great distance and he could almost hear himself saying, “You make it sound very easy, gentlemen, but it isn’t. The consequences of what you ask will be staggering.”

The scientist who seemed to be the spokesman for the others, the round-faced one named Parsons, said, “We know the consequences of refusing to act. Five hundred people were killed in San Francisco on the first day of the 1906 temblor—”

“The fire did the damage,” Alonzo said automatically.

Parsons’ eyes looked at him as if he were delinquent student, and Parsons’ voice was cold and precise. “The quake did enough, and it caused the fire. The relatively small 1971 San Fernando quake caused half a billion dollars damage to Los Angeles, killed sixty-four people, injured twenty-five hundred. Ten thousand people died in Managua in 1972, and some seventy-five percent of the city's buildings were damaged or destroyed. The Tokyo earthquake of 1923 killed more than one hundred thousand persons. Just think what another 1906 disaster would do to your city."

"I'm thinking what an evacuation would do to my city. And you say there is one chance in five . . ."

"In the next two weeks. We admit that the science of earthquake prediction is still new. Within a few years we hope to get it up to the level of accuracy of weather prediction. We're refining our equations and getting new tiltmeter and creepmeter readings, pressure wave and shear wave readings, all the—"

"What if we ride out this two-week period?" Alonzo said, looking around the long, dark table at the somber faces of the scientists. They reminded him of soothsayers urging the right course of action on a king. "What if we wait until you're more certain?"

Parsons frowned. "We've discharged our responsibilities. You're the only one who can order evacuation. It's your decision now."

When Alonzo came out of the bathroom the girl was sitting on the edge of the bed looking thin and unhappy. Alonzo sat down beside her and put his arm around her and kissed her. As he drew her down to the bed, she said, "Do we have to do it again?"

"It'll be better this time," he said. But it wasn't.

He remembered how he had seen her—he had almost knocked her down as he turned abruptly away—at the edge of the crowd in Union Square. She was slender and pale and young—perhaps twelve, he thought first, and then revised his estimate to fourteen or fifteen. He had caught her by her thin shoulders to keep her from falling, and laughed and apologized for his clumsiness while he thought how pretty she was—like a pretty child—with her long dark hair and her blue eyes and her smooth, unformed face.

She laughed, too, and said, "That's all right," in a childish soprano but with a quick, precocious sophistication.

"You're beautiful," he said, and heard the words as if a stranger had said them. He clamped his lips tightly on other words such as "I love you," although, indeed, he did: he loved her for being young and for being beautiful. So much in this world was old and sordid and ugly and difficult.

"You're kidding me," she said. But she turned her head and looked up at him as if she liked it.

She seemed to be alone. He knew she was not a tourist because she wore no sweater or jacket. Only natives found temperatures in the low sixties comfortable without wraps.

He heard himself saying, "I'm going to get a hotel room over there. Would you like to share it with me?" And he tried to look unconcerned, as if he did this every day, while he wondered why he had said it and what she would say. What were the chances that she would call a cop? Ten to one? It seemed to be a day for decisions.

"How much?" she said.

That wasn't one of the responses he had anticipated. "A hundred?"

She looked at him fully for the first time, from his shoes to his face, almost insolently, and said, "Why not?"

Afterwards, in the room, as the girl lay on her side of the bed and he lay on his, he said, "Why did you come with me?"

"The money," she said.

He knew it wasn't the real reason, but he let it go. More important was why he had asked her, why a married man with a loving wife and two children, a man of position and respectability who had never done anything like this before, had scarcely even thought of it, had taken a young girl to a hotel room and engaged all night in a kind of sexual gymnastics he would have thought impossible. He had not even had a drink.

Perhaps it was the weight of a decision he had yet to make. Maybe it was the psychology of disaster; people who live on the side of an active volcano or on top of a major fault don't give a damn about consequences: they're ready for anything. What was he going to do? Was it better to do nothing, to let come what will come? Or should he act and take the responsibility for the upheaval of nearly a million lives, the death of some, the certain injury of many, the privations of all, on a—on a witch doctor's hunch, on the word of augurers stirring the entrails of a dead chicken . . . Scientists had no pipeline to the future; at best they had an imperfect forecasting device called the scientific method.

He probed gently at his conscience and felt no guilt. Perhaps that was the way the peasants felt on the slopes of Vesuvius. When you may die tomorrow, today's small sins are inconsequential unless you believe strongly in damnation. He had never sinned greatly; he had never dared to sin magnificently even in his dreams.

Who had he hurt? Not his wife, for he felt no less love for her than he had felt before. Perhaps the girl, or her family, whoever they were. But how was this different from some frantic coupling in a musty barn or a dusty attic with a fumbling youth her own age? Girls did not remain virgins long these days.

Perhaps it was all true, but he also knew it was all sophistry. He had seduced this girl, though gently and not without concern for her, but in love, if at all, not with her but with the things she was: young, beautiful, inexperienced . . . He had used her as an object. He did not know her name. He did not want to know her name.

Perhaps the prophet was right, and they were all sinners and this was their Sodom and their Gomorrah, and they would all be destroyed tomorrow by fire from heaven—or from below.

He thought of all the unspeakable sins going on throughout this lovely, lovable, libertine city of his, and it did not comfort him. He was like the Puritans, he thought, with their stern sense of right and wrong which didn't keep them from sinning, only from enjoying it.

He had not thought himself capable of what he had done tonight. Clearly there was a buried fault within himself which had chosen this moment to shake the foundations of his self-knowledge. Now he was here on the slopes of Vesuvius with his decision still unmade, but he had made himself feel real for a moment by returning to the primitive.

"There sure wasn't anything else," the girl said.

For a moment Alonzo didn't know what she was talking about and then he realized that she hadn't come with him for the money, that she had expected something else, some secret excitement, some ultimate fulfillment.

"You've got a right to be disappointed," he said. "Listen. I'm going to leave now, but you can stay here as long as you like. You have a family in San Francisco, right?"

"Yes."

"When you go home tell them—tell them you met a city official on the street and he told you—he told you to get out of San Francisco before noon. That there's going to be an announcement at noon. San Francisco is being evacuated. Some people won't want to leave. Some will want to get out first. There's going to be the biggest traffic jam, the most trouble, the most danger, that anybody has seen since 1906. Those who get out before noon are going to be the lucky ones."

He had come to a decision. He didn't know whether history would prove it to be the right one, but it was the only one.

"Yeah," she said skeptically.

"Believe me," Alonzo said earnestly. "It's the best thing I can do for you."

In the dark, by the light of the window beginning to gray with dawn, he got back into his clothes. He peered into his billfold and pulled out five bills. "Much more valuable than this hundred dollars," he said, putting the money on the bureau. But she was asleep.

After he had paid the bill to a sleepy night clerk at the desk, he stopped at a pay telephone in the lobby. "Hello, Joan?" he said.

"Where have you been?" a woman's voice complained. "I kept calling City Hall, and they kept saying you weren't there."

"I had to get out and walk."

"All night?"

"So I got drunk. Satisfied? That's all unimportant. Listen! I want you to pack the station wagon for a trip—you and the kids. You're going to go visit your parents. I want you on your way to Utah by nine."

"Why?"

"For once don't ask any questions. San Francisco is being evacuated beginning at noon, and I want you out of here." He hung up the telephone and then immediately called again. "Look. I'm sorry. Don't tell anybody, but scientists have predicted a major earthquake will hit us within the next two weeks."

"Oh," she said.

"I love you," he said. He was glad he said it and glad he meant it.

"Me, too," she said.

The telephone clicked as she hung up. He stood in the telephone booth for a moment and felt absently in the coin return slot. It was empty.

He walked out into the chill gray of morning. It was foggy, all right.

The announcement came at noon. Alonzo stared without expression at the television set in his office as a news announcer said, "Before the news, Mayor John Alonzo has a message of major importance for citizens of San Francisco and surrounding areas. The message was taped just an hour ago in his office . . ."

Alonzo wondered briefly if the girl were watching, if she would identify him, if she would accuse him to her friends, to the authorities, what he would have to pay for a moment's impulse . . . and what was left of his religious training reveled in the reflection that he would be punished. But if she had done as he had urged her to do she would not have seen him . . . The wages of virtue, he thought.

". . . that the science of earthquake prediction is in its infancy," his image on the screen was saying to him, "but we cannot ignore the advice of experienced, qualified scientists who warn us that the chances—I repeat, the chances—of a major, 1906-type earthquake are significant. Therefore, in consultation with the county and city governments which have jurisdiction over other communities which lie along the San Andreas Fault or which will be directly affected by what we do in San Francisco, and in consultation with state and federal authorities, I have ordered martial law in this city and the beginning of an evacuation which should leave San Francisco empty within forty-eight hours, with the exception of essential government services—key city and county officials, police, firemen, and the National Guard . . ."

His announcement was followed by some additional justification and then detailed instructions for an orderly evacuation, with the city divided area by area and then street by street; routes to bridges, interstate highways, and public transportation—buses and trains had been massed at terminals, and citizens were urged to use public transportation whenever possible. Lists followed: essentials to be carried along, things to be done before the homeowner left his premises, locations considered safely beyond the area of devastation, public accommodations, available camp grounds, medical stations, gasoline suppliers on evacuation routes, ambulance and ambulance substitutes and ambulance trains for the hospitalized, recommendations from the US Geological Survey and the Office of Emergency Preparedness . . .

And for those who might refuse to leave, the curious, the fatalists, the revelers, the looters: electricity and gas would be cut off at noon the following day, water to everything except the fire mains twenty-four hours later. The National Guard had orders to shoot looters. The hoarding of essential supplies was declared a crime . . .

Two weeks later John Alonzo sat in his office studying the papers which measured out his days.

Three hundred and forty-nine persons lost their lives in automobile accidents during the evacuation.

Sixteen died of carbon monoxide poisoning in the traffic jams.

Twenty-eight critical patients died while being moved to other hospitals or because of inadequate facilities at their destinations.

Twenty-two persons were crushed to death in a theater when a manager made a rash announcement.

Forty-three looters and two National Guardsmen were shot to death.

Fifteen persons died in fires.

Injured and wounded were many times the dead.

The evacuation had cost an estimated one billion dollars, directly or indirectly through lost business and damage to property. Already one billion dollars in lawsuits had been filed against the city. And the pressure of the population to return to the city was becoming unbearable. The National Guard no longer could keep them back . . .

The male voice of his assistant came over the intercom. "A young lady on line one, sir," he said.

Alonzo's face tightened and then he reached for the telephone.

"Hello, Daddy," a little girl's voice said.

"Ginny!" Alonzo said. "Where are you calling from?"

"We're home, Daddy. We didn't want to stay away any longer. We wanted to come home."

And then it was his wife saying that it was so, that they couldn't stand it in Utah any more: her parents couldn't stand it, she couldn't stand it, the kids couldn't stand it, and so they had come home like everybody else.

"Why didn't you call me first?"

"I knew you would tell us not to come. Is it all right, John?"

"I hope so," he said, and hope was all he had as San Francisco began to fill up again as rapidly as it had been emptied, as the business of life began again, as normality crept like fog across the city.

The next day his secretary told him that Dr. Parsons and the other geologists were back, and they insisted on seeing him.

The carousel had come around again—the meeting with

the scientists, the prophet in the park, the unheeding city, the girl and his own shocking behavior—and he reached out for the brass ring of reality: the ground was shaky under his feet but at last he knew himself, his weakness, his impotence in the face of impending events.

"Tell them," Alonzo said, "tell them to go kill their chickens somewhere else. We've had our disaster. Tell them it doesn't matter what they predict now. We can't move these people again. Not even if we wanted to."

Two days later, at 5:32 A.M., the earthquake began. It hit 8.5 on the Richter scale.

Guilt

I.

All of us feel guilty. All of us have something to feel guilty about. The problem is that some of us don't feel guilty enough.

—The 2020 Hearings on the Hardister Plan for Justice Reform.

Judge Meredith Nelson scanned the verdict on his bench one last time. He always tried to give the citizen the benefit of every doubt. "It is better," Sir William Blackstone wrote, "that ten guilty persons escape than one innocent suffer."

But there was no scrap of uncertainty in front of him. Intent read too high; restraint, too low. Regretfully, though with a faint thrill of power that he always felt and always tried to repress, he pushed the button on his bench marked "Execute."

II.

Guilt is the special form of anxiety experienced by humans-in-society, the warning tension of life principles violated, of conditions of human social existence transgressed, of socio-spiritual reality ignored or affronted, of God alienated, of self being destroyed.

—*Edward V. Stein.*

Patricia Williams stopped with the spoonful of mock-turtle soup almost to her lips, like Galatea turned back to stone by an angry god. Then her hand began to shake. The soup trembled from her spoon, splashing on her white blouse in ugly dark blotches like old blood, marring the spotless tablecloth. Her face was flushed. Shudders jarred her body.

Gary Crowder stared at the woman he loved. "Pat! What's the matter?"

The spoon dropped to the bowl. She let it go as if glad to be rid of the responsibility for holding it steady. "Nothing," she said.

In the elegant room at the top of the Harlem Hotel, with its understated color panels and its broad windows revealing the lights of the city slowly turning around them, the other diners stared at Patricia. Gary wanted to take her tender body in his arms, wanted to calm the panic of her heart, wanted to shelter her from the knowing looks of those who were her inferiors in every way. But that would only call more attention to her condition.

"Are you having an attack?" he asked.

But he knew what the matter was. The others in the room knew what it was, too, and he could feel them draw back, as if Patricia had been stricken by the Plague and that by distancing themselves from her they could avoid contagion. But it was a blacker plague, a moral plague. In the great judicial buildings that towered near the foot of the island, Patricia had been found not guilty enough.

Resentment surged through Gary, despite a lifetime of suppression—resentment at a system that would inflict such agony on an innocent like Patricia. What criminal urges could she have? What acts of hers need be restrained?

Somehow the system had failed.

III.

A fundamental inequity in our system of justice is that the law abiding must pay for the entire cost of the police and judicial system, as well as the punishment of the convicted. The ideal arrangement would be an automatic monitoring system and self-punishment.

—*The 2020 Hearings on the Hardister Plan for Justice Reform.*

Times had changed since Blackstone's day, Judge Nelson thought. Then the criminal was punishable only after he had committed a crime; even then his guilt had to be proved by the testimony of uncertain and unreliable witnesses, and in most cases some residue of doubt remained. No wonder Sir William had been concerned about the miscarriage of justice. In his day—why, even as recently as the twentieth century—only one criminal in ten was ever caught and only one-tenth of those were ever brought to trial.

Today the city was free of crime. The potential criminal was detected before he had committed his criminal act, and his guilt was increased to the point where he could not do it.

His father should have lived to see this day, his big, hearty, successful father, who had been a policeman back in the days when there still had been a need for men to stop crime or arrest criminals, his father who had died in the street facing a mob who had been throwing bottles and stones.

Nelson could not imagine living in a city where footpads

lurked in every dark corner, where harlots brazenly walked the streets, where rapists waited for decent women, where thieves looted homes at will, where swindlers misused positions of trust, where bands of juvenile muggers tormented the old and the weak.

His wife and daughter could walk anywhere in the city, even at night. It was a city without bars, and he would return to a home without locks.

Nelson pushed himself back from his bench and stood up. He felt pleased with himself, satisfied with his role in a world that handled antisocial problems so well.

IV.

If we are going to aim at the ideal system, we should try to detect the criminal before he commits his crime and stop him. We don't attempt anything like that now because we have no reliable means of detecting the intent to commit a crime and no effective means of stopping its commission. But it's our lack of ability rather than our ethics that holds us back.

—The 2020 Hearings on the Hardister Plan for Justice Reform.

Patricia was like a spastic, scarcely able to move without stumbling, but Gary helped her out of the sky-high restaurant, down the glass-enclosed elevator that Patricia had found so exciting on the way up, and into a taxi. All the way she had told him not to be angry, that what had happened was all right.

"I'm guilty," she kept saying. "I'm guilty."

But Gary knew it was only the guilt-syndrome speaking. Every school child knew how it worked. The pituitary was ordering her adrenals to pour adrenaline into her blood stream. The adrenaline was increasing her heart action. It was taking blood from the skin and rerouting it to the brain and the muscles. It was increasing the blood-sugar level. If she had been in the jungle, her body would be ready for fight or flight.

It was the guilt syndrome, a warning that every time she thought about committing a crime she would feel like this again.

Gary told the taxi Patricia's address, enunciating clearly so that there would be no mistake. He didn't dare get into the taxi himself because his anger was running too high.

What had happened to Patricia was all wrong. She was not the kind of person who would even consider committing a crime, she was too good, too innocent for that. Gary knew it. He also knew that if he entered the taxi his anger might be reported to the Department of Justice.

No one was sure where the readings were taken. Everything else was revealed about the system but that. Inevitably, then, suspicion fell on every enclosed space that might conceal an encephalograph, a sphygmomanometer, a polygraph, or any of the more advanced devices that singly or in combination detected and analyzed emotional and mental states.

Detection might lie anywhere, in subways, elevators (had it been a mistake to use the elevator down from the restaurant?), telephone booths, even hair dryers, circumsenses, or door knobs. All of them, or none. Perhaps it was all done by light or air; maybe it came out of the sky like the finger of God.

Whatever it was, he couldn't take the chance that he might be stopped before he could correct the injustice that had been done to the girl he wanted to marry, whom he wanted to make happy, whom he wanted to protect from fear and uncertainty.

The evening had started so hopefully. After dinner in the most expensive place he could afford he was going to tell her about his promotion to first supervisor. Then would come the proposal. And after that, he had daydreamed, in his apartment or hers, the night-long ecstasy of excitation and fulfillment. She could no longer put him off—he did not resent it; it was by this he knew her innocence, her desirability—she would no longer have a reason.

He knew her well enough to be sure she was thinking about the same thing, though her dreams were spiced with the thrill of the forbidden.

V.

Guilt is the most important problem in the evolution of culture.
—Sigmund Freud.

Judge Nelson was only an average-sized man, just about six feet tall. He was much smaller than his big, blue-clad father had been, but there was scarcely room for him to stretch in the cubicle he occupied six hours a day, every other day. It was pleasant enough, with its soothing, color-varied walls, but not big. It was sufficient for the work he had to do; justice needed no larger sphere than this.

The little room held all he needed: a comfortable chair, the bench that gave him the readings from the computer when he pressed the button marked CASE, and the three buttons clustered beneath his right hand—EXECUTE, PROBATION, and DISMISS—that symbolized the discretionary part of his work.

For this he bore the title of "Judge." It was an honorable title, with a long and noble tradition, and he would do nothing to diminish it.

Actually, the only button on his bench that looked at all

used—part of the white, incised lettering had been worn away—was the one marked "execute." That bothered him sometimes, but then he told himself that the computer put a case on a judge's docket only when it was ready for action. The system provided for human judgment; no case could be decided merely by machine response. Every few days a case would appear—almost as if to test the alertness of the judge—in which the readings seemed ambiguous or marginal. The probation button sent such cases back into memory for further investigation. Seldom was there the kind of clear error that called for dismissal.

But it had happened, and Nelson was determined to mete out justice. He remembered Reinhold Neibuhr's wisdom: "Man's capacity for justice makes democracy possible, but man's inclination to injustice makes democracy necessary."

Who knew what decisions were reached by the judges on the other shifts; some, even, who occupied this room, whose fingers rested upon these buttons? Certainly Nelson didn't know. He didn't want to know. From casual conversations in the judges' lounge, however, he had the feeling that he was more lenient—more careful was how he thought of it—than some others. Some, he thought, a bit scornfully and perhaps unkindly, were mere button-pushers.

VI.

How can we punish a person for what he has not done, some of you ask? The answer is simple: the prevention of crime is no more a punishment than the discipline of a child to prevent harm to himself or others is cruelty.

—The 2020 Hearings on the
Hardister Plan for Justice Reform.

Gary looked toward the Tower of Justice, distant at the foot of the island but clearly visible against the night sky. It stabbed upward, tall, slender, bathed in white light from base to spire. Once he had thought it the symbol of justice untouched by human passions, above the petty concerns of mortals; clean, unsullied, humanity's finger straining like Adam's toward God. Now it seemed more like a straightened question mark, struggling to regain its crouch.

The Tower was a good ten kilometers away, and he had to traverse that distance all on foot. It would have been more sensible, he knew, to have gone home, to have slept his anger away, and to have set about correcting the injustice to Patricia tomorrow when he was calmer. But he didn't care. Perhaps tomorrow his courage would leak away. Tomorrow the Department of Justice might monitor his emotional condition and lay on him an inhibiting load of guilt. If he waited he might never act.

His sister Wylene, had she lived, would have been Patricia's age. He squared his shoulders, fanned the flames of his indignation, and set out down the island across territory he had seldom traveled by foot.

VII.

If we could know with absolute certainty that a person intends to commit a crime and will do it, given the opportunity, and if we could stop it who among us would say, "First let him break the law, first let him steal or rape or murder, then we will punish him"? The person who would let the crime occur would be a monster.

—*The 2020 Hearings on the Hardister Plan for Justice Reform.*

Judge Nelson turned toward the door of his courtroom as his fourth-shift replacement entered. The man was dark, undersized, surly, and, as usual, ten minutes late. His name was Kassel, and Nelson knew no more about him. Nelson chose his friends as carefully as he performed his duties, and he had few friends in the Department of Justice. The work he did every other day was difficult enough; he wanted to leave it all in the courtroom.

His position carried significant prestige. Judges were supposed to be anonymous servants of justice, but family knew what he did, and friends. Nelson knew he was admired by some, respected by others, perhaps feared by a few. It was the work he had chosen, that he had been selected for, and he accepted it and everything that went along with it.

The biggest part of his job was the responsibility. Every working day he affected people's lives; he considered the evidence, reached a decision, adjusted someone's guilt to the proper level. It was a weight he bore reluctantly but well; someone had to do it, and Nelson did it better than anyone.

Now he allowed himself a rare comment on someone else's performance. "You're late," he said to Kassel as he passed the man in the doorway.

"No matter," Kassel said, glancing back under heavy eyebrows. "I'll catch up quick and then do all the cases you had left over from your shift."

Nelson feared that Kassel was one of the button-pushers. "Not if you're thorough," he said mildly.

"Don't tell me how to do my job, Nelson!" Kassel said. "If you badmouth me I'll see that you get taken care of." He threw himself into the padded chair behind the bench.

"I've had less antisocial cases than yours among those that appear on my bench," Nelson said. It was as much a departure from his judicial reserve as he could allow himself.

As he started down the hall toward the judges' lounge, Kassel shouted after him, "That's it, Nelson! I'll show you who's antisocial."

VIII.

The troubles from which the world suffers at present can, in my opinion, very largely be traced to the manifold attempts to deal with the inner sense of guiltiness, and therefore any contribution that will illuminate this particular problem will be of the greatest value.

—*Ernest Jones.*

At 110th Street, Gary decided to take a shortcut through Central Park. Once the decision would have been reckless, a bit later, foolhardy, and a few decades after that, suicidal. Now as he skirted Harlem Meer and The Loch he passed couples strolling hand-in-hand or arms about each other, old people on park benches talking about the past, joggers improving their physical condition, sportsmen tossing frisbees in the moonlight, wild animals ambling across the meadows between air-curtain walls.

He began to hear sounds of music as he neared the Reservoir. As he rounded the curve on its western side he came upon the musicians. They were dressed in makeshift uniforms, and they were playing a mournful, syncopated kind of music that made Gary think of death and grieving, of matters left undone that should have been done, of Wylene and, strangely, of Patricia.

As he tried to move past the group, a hand caught his shoulder and pulled him into the midst of the marchers. He found a clarinet in his hands and tried to give it back. "I can't play," he said.

"Play, brother!" a black face said.

"I'm in a hurry," Gary said.

"Nobody's in that much of a hurry," the other replied, as if they were the lyrics to the music the group was playing. "Play, brother!"

Reluctantly Gary put the mouthpiece to his lips and blew into it. To his surprise music came out, and not just any music but music that fit what everybody else was playing. It was a magic instrument he held that not only made magic music but magically made him feel as if he were making it.

For the moment he lost himself in the experience. He blew and blew, and the sad, guilty music came out, and the music the others made reinforced it, lifted it, made it part of something wonderful. He marched along to the slow beat, blowing music into the air, music that talked about death and sorrow and somehow, by making them into music, eased the pain of loss, made suffering into art.

IX.

Guilt is the process by which we socialize ourselves. Guilt is the unpleasant feeling we experience when we fail to live up to our ideals. Guilt is the internalized parent who says, "Thou should have, or thou should not have!" Without guilt we would still be savages.

—*The 2020 Hearings on the Hardister Plan for Justice Reform.*

Judge Nelson sat in the judges' lounge, sipped his after-duty drink of espresso and brandy, and quoted Blackstone to

Judge Thornhill. Thornhill was an older man of sufficient distinction and maturity that Nelson felt respect for him, perhaps even a bit of the awe that others felt for Nelson. After all, Thornhill had been a judge when Nelson was only a clerk—not much more than a computer jockey. He might have known Nelson's father.

Thornhill sipped his scotch on the rocks. "Of course Blackstone had it all wrong. Today the innocent suffer. The guilty do escape. Though, indeed, he meant it differently."

Nelson looked around the pleasantly darkened lounge, seeing shadowy figures here and there but not caring who they were, as if in his courtroom he saw too much and here he could turn off his vigilance. The quiet and anonymity gave reassurance that the city and its system of justice were running smoothly. "Perhaps we shouldn't stretch our comparisons too far," he ventured. "The innocent do not really suffer. Their guilt is enhanced. A bit of guilt never did anyone any harm."

"Or, to quote Hardister, 'All of us feel guilty. All of us have something to feel guilty about. The problem is that some of us don't feel guilty enough.' Have you ever seen one of them when it hits them?"

"When the button is pushed?"

"Yes."

"I suppose. It's hard to miss seeing that sort of thing once in while if one is out in public at all."

"Not a happy sight, is it?"

"A little shock," Nelson said. "It must have some effect to serve as an effective notice. It soon wears off. And the citizen is better for it."

"Than without? I wish I could believe that."

"Than if he had been allowed to commit the crime that was welling up?"

"Oh, that," Thornhill said. "Of course. It just seems to me that there's a lot of it these days."

"More than there used to be?"

"By comparison with the amount of crime."

"But there isn't any crime," Nelson said.

"Exactly. Then why all the casework? Why all the citizens we observe getting notice?"

"Even if criminal impulses have been eliminated, we still find antisocial tendencies—"

"That isn't our job. Our job is to prevent crime, not to repress legitimate emotions, not to fine-tune society. How much honest dissent are we suppressing? How much variation in human response are we leveling?"

"I've always said," Nelson agreed, "that there are too many button-pushers."

"It's not that either." Thornhill drained his glass. "The cases come to us with little room for discretion. We're all button-pushers, when it comes to that. Sometimes I think our role is ornamental."

Nelson bristled a bit in spite of his respect for Thornhill. "It isn't as if guilt were bad. Actually we're in remarkably good shape as human history goes. No crime. No poverty. No human misery. Art is flourishing. . . ."

"Art is one of the few areas where emotions can be expressed safely, without fear of repression," Thornhill said gloomily. "Besides, art feeds on neurosis. We push things down in one place, and they spring up in another."

He put down his glass, got up slowly, and, nodding at Nelson, left the lounge. Nelson stared after the old man. He must be due for retirement soon, never having served as an appellate judge, much less a member of the Review Board. No wonder he sounded a little querulous.

X.

Out of guilt comes hope. Guilt holds up for us an ideal state that has not yet been realized; because of that ideal we are able to endure present inadequacies and the pain they cause. Excessive guilt is an overwhelming pain that makes even future bliss inadequate; insufficient guilt stems from an inability to imagine a better future.

—*The 2020 Hearings on the Hardister Plan for Justice Reform.*

Columbus Circle was filled with an outdoor sculpture exhibition. Strange shapes fashioned out of rubber or plastic had been inflated to float in the air or bob along the ground; others changed their shapes or colors, and some emitted serpentine hisses, beastly groans, or half-human sighs. Even stranger-looking creations were fashioned out of plastic, extruded or shaped by flame or knife. A gigantic piece of ice was being carved by a woman wielding a blowtorch no bigger than a cigarette lighter into something grotesque but compelling.

Almost every piece of art moved Gary in ways that he could not explain. They crouched. They loomed. They moved ponderously or swayed ominously. They were the figures out of nightmares or the demons one pushes into the back of one's mind, out of sight, where no one will suspect their existence, where the omnipresent instruments of the Department of Justice can never find them.

Gary ducked and weaved his way through the exhibition trying not to think about the objects he was moving among or the feelings they inspired in him. He was almost to the other side when he felt a strong hand on his arm. He looked in annoyance into a stranger's cheerful, sweating face. "Come along," the stranger said, "you're drafted."

"I'm busy," Gary said, and tried to pull away.

"Come along," the other said, undeterred. "This is living sculpture. Be part of it!"

Protesting, Gary was dragged to a spot where living men and women stood in unusual poses among white foam people. All of them—meat creatures and foam things—were pointing in seeming horror at an empty platform; it was like a game of statue played in a wax museum. Then, as the sculptor drew Gary through the group, the platform was empty no longer. Gary was standing on it.

The sculptor pressed a white, foam figure into his arm and placed a knife in Gary's other hand. Then Gary felt the hands of the sculptor on his body shaping him into position as if he were just some other kind of plastic material.

Gary looked around him, unable to understand what was happening. The crowd that surrounded the platform was pointing at him. The crowd was pointing at him! He felt uneasy, disturbed, guilty. It was like a nightmare. He had nothing to feel guilty about. He wanted to shout at them, "I haven't done anything!" But he choked it back and looked away, turned his eyes down.

The foam figure in his arms had been shaped into the form of a woman. Her head was thrown back, her body was arched away from him, or perhaps from the threat of the knife in his hand. He could see only her chin and the long sweep of her throat and the upthrust cones of her plastic breasts.

"Go on," someone said. "Do it!"

Gary looked toward the voice. There was a man where the voice had spoken; he was motioning with his hands. Gary recognized him almost immediately. The sculptor.

"It's all right," the sculptor said. "It's art."

The real people and the plastic people were pointing. He looked back and forth between them and the sculptor, and then down at the figure in his arms, dreading the knife, yet asking for it, begging for it.

"Do it!" the voice urged. "It's art. Not real. No one can call you to account! It's all right to feel things! You can do it and no one can demand justice!"

To be accused and to commit no crime. It was like what had happened to Patricia, or Wylene. Rage rose in Gary's throat. Desire made his arm tremble. A sense of power surged through his body. The world turned glittery. He drove in the blade. Again and again he struck, feeling the blade plunge through brief surface resistance and then slickly up to the hilt.

And the figure in his arms moved. He felt it move, and horror swept through his body, occupying all the places the feeling of power had existed. He held up his hand. It was shaking. The movement flipped red drops from the blade. The white bosom he held in his arm was red with something spurting through a multitude of cuts, and the body was moving, coming apart in his arms, crumbling, falling in bits of plastic onto the platform, and Gary turned and ran, dropping the knife, pushing his way through the pointing figures. . . .

XI.

Injustice is relatively easy to bear; what stings is justice.
—Henry Mencken.

Judge Nelson was already halfway from the elevator to the great doors of the Tower of Justice, past the massive central figure of Justice covering her eyes with one hand while the other pressed a button on the bench in front of her, when a clerk clattered across the floor behind him. "Judge Nelson!"

Nelson turned and waited until the young man caught up with him.

"Judge Nelson!" the clerk repeated breathlessly. "I'm glad I caught you. The Review Board wants to see you."

"Now?" Nelson asked.

"Yes, sir. Before you leave."

Nelson thought about the pleasant walk home he had been anticipating, the welcome from his wife, who always waited up for him no matter how late his shift, the moment he allowed himself to look down upon the face of his sleeping daughter, secure in her bed because of the work he did. And he shrugged and returned to the elevator with the blond-haired young man. The clerk seemed relieved and talkative now that his mission had been accomplished, and Nelson responded to his remarks absently, thinking it had not been so many years ago since he had been young and breathless like this clerk, wondering what challenges and fulfillments the future would bring.

It had brought satisfaction, though never moments as exciting as the promise when he had been named to the bench. Well, it was part of growing up to seek maturer gratifications and not to surrender to vain regrets or idle speculations, such as why the Review Board wanted to see him.

XII.

Guilt gives us ourselves, a sense of what we are as individuals measured against some social ideal; it gives us not only freedom but the possibility of transcending the self.

—*The 2020 Hearings on the Hardister Plan for Justice Reform.*

Times Square was clean and uncluttered. All the tawdry,

little shops had been replaced by handicraft and art stores, with imaginative displays and bright little signs. The garishness was gone. There was advertising, of course—but tastefully and cleverly done, even though all the men looked a bit too worldly and the women looked wholesomely attractive but as if given the chance they would be naughty, a bit like Patricia when she was most appealing.

The theater had returned to Times Square: billboards were everywhere and marquees announced new productions and revivals of old favorites. Even the streets—now cleared of tramps, pimps, and prostitutes—had been taken over by the players.

Gary found himself in the midst of a street production of "Oedipus Rex," and, to his dismay, cast in the title role.

The actors moved around him like electronic wraiths, yet they were as solid and real to Gary as his own flesh. He felt the emotions and the words as if they had been imprinted on his brain, as indeed they were. To an external observer, the action of the play would have seemed a blur, but it seemed to Gary as measured as a dream; each scene, each speech, seemed precisely paced, even though the key scenes stood out from the background like van Gogh objects outlined in black.

"There is a horrid thing hid in this land," Creon said, "eating us alive. Cast out this thing, and all will be right again."

Gary-Oedipus replied, "For my own sake, I'll see this sin cast out. Whoever killed Laius, let the same murderous hand find me too. Caring who killed Laius is like caring who killed my own kin."

Tiresias, the blind seer, said to him, "You sought the killer of Laius. I tell you he stands here. Blind, who once had eyes, beggared, who once had riches, he shall make his way across the alien earth, staff groping before him, voices around him calling, 'Behold the brother-father of his own children, the seed, the sower, and the sown, shame to his mother's blood, and to his father, son, murderer, incest-worker.' "

Later he heard himself confess, "At Pytho I asked God if I were indeed the son of Polybus, king of Corinth, and was denied an answer; instead His voice gave other answers, things of terror and desolation, that I should know my mother's body and beget shameful creatures, and spill my father's blood."

When his wife, Jocasta, was introduced to the stranger from Corinth, he heard the leader of the Chorus say, "She is his wife and mother—of his children."

And at last, with guilt and grief raging through his body, he shouted, "Enough! Everything will come true. I have seen too much misery to see more. I am revealed in all my sinfulness—born in sin, married in sin, killed in sin."

He stabbed out his eyes and felt the pain as if it were his own and knew it as less than the pain he felt inside.

Leaving the scene it seemed to Gary as if he were blind, feeling his way with a staff, and he heard the Chorus say, "Look, citizens. Here comes Gary Crowder, who answered the Sphinx's riddle and became the most powerful of men; good fortune loved him, and when he passed people turned to watch him. Now he is miserable and low. Citizens, beware, and do not count anyone happy or fortunate until the full story is told and death finds him without pain."

Suddenly Gary was free of the street theater, free of the electronic impulses that enslaved him to actions he had never taken, emotions he had not felt, and pain he had not earned. In actual time only a few minutes had passed. The Tower of Justice was not much farther now, and he moved on toward it, unpurged.

XIII.

Guilt creates God. Out of the family unit—mother, father, child—comes guilt; and out of guilt comes God, the ultimate parent, who sets for us the highest model, the impossible goals.

—*The 2020 Hearings on the Hardister Plan for Justice Reform.*

The Board Room was at the top of the Tower, commanding a view of the city on all sides, like the eye of God. With compulsory smoke and fume suppression, the air was as clear as the moral climate, and the visitor could see from the Battery to the Bronx, from Queens to the Palisades. Nelson had been in the room twice before, when it was open for employee tours, but then it had been day and he had not been summoned.

The judges who made up the Review Board were all elderly. They had been elevated from the ranks of the appellate judges at the time other appellate judges were retiring. When one member of the Review Board died, or became too infirm to serve, the other two members elected a third. They were, after all, in the best position to judge. They had information on all judges and cases at their fingertips.

Literally it was true. They sat behind a long bench opposite the elevator door, their backs to the windows as if disdaining another reality than the one in front of them. Each section of the bench angled to follow the curve of the outer wall so that Nelson had to stand almost clasped within the arms of the bench looking from one judge to another.

To Nelson they all looked alike. They were alike in dignity and power, even though one was a woman, small, white-haired, and wrinkled, another was tall, thin, and black, with little silver curlicues in the black wool of his hair and beard, like turnings from a metal lathe, and the third was big and tanned and dark-haired. Nelson thought that the dark hair was a wig. They were named Barington, Stokes, and Fullenwider. Nelson knew them by their pictures. But there was something particularly familiar about Fullenwider.

Judge Stokes sat in the middle. "Judge Nelson?" he asked.

"Yes, sir."

"We have received complaints about your work."

"From the appellate division?" Nelson asked. He could not keep surprise from his voice.

"Not from the appellate division," Judge Barington said. Her voice was surprisingly big and strong. "Your judgments are seldom appealed."

"That in itself raises questions," Judge Stokes said. "Too few appeals suggests excessive leniency, just as too many suggests excessive severity."

"But what we are chiefly concerned about is the amount of your work, not the quality," Judge Barington said. "There have been complaints."

"By whom?" Nelson asked, though he thought he knew.

"That is irrelevant," Judge Stokes said.

Nelson wondered why Judge Fullenwider didn't say anything, and why he looked familiar.

"The evidence is available from the computer," Judge Stokes was saying. Nelson had missed something but perhaps it didn't matter; he couldn't believe he was standing here listening to his life being reduced to numbers. "You have the lowest case load of anyone in this jurisdiction. You are thirty percent below the average."

Nelson struggled to remain calm, to behave the way a judge should behave. "Perhaps I'm more careful than the others," he said. In spite of his efforts, alarm was fluttering in his throat.

"If you don't handle your share of the cases, the work load increases for everyone else," Judge Barington said.

"A judge must make judgments," Nelson responded automatically; glad that he could pull these phrases out of past conversations, that he did not have to think. "That takes time."

"Nonsense!" Judge Stokes said. "The work isn't that difficult. 'All of us are guilty.' "

"Indecision can disqualify you from the exercise of your authority," Judge Barington said. "You can be removed by a vote of this Board if it finds you incapable of performing your duties."

"I know," Nelson said. It had come to this. "But surely there are more serious faults. I know some judges who no longer even have faith in what they're doing."

Judge Fullenwider spoke for the first time. "Who?"

Nelson hesitated, the puzzling familiarity still bothering him. "I don't know any names. One hears things. One puts things together."

Judge Fullenwider shrugged. "If there is disloyalty, if there is lack of faith, it will reveal itself. For now you are warned. Get your caseload up to the average. You will not receive a second warning."

Now Nelson knew why Judge Fullenwider looked familiar. He looked the way he remembered his father. If he had been dressed in blue, with a cap on his head, the resemblance would have sent Nelson to his knees. Instead, he only nodded numbly and turned to the elevator.

On the way down to the lobby he thought, I'll have to be faster. I'll have to turn into a button-pusher like the others.

That made him feel worse. At least, he told himself, I didn't name anybody when they asked. But he knew he would have named Thornhill if his father—if Fullenwider had pressed him, and that was just as bad.

XIV.

Of all manifestations of power, restraint impresses men most.
—Thucydides.

Gary Crowder was coming out of the appeal booth when Judge Nelson emerged from the elevator. Both looked shaken.

Gary stopped Nelson with a hand upraised in his path. "Are you a judge?"

Nelson frowned. The lobby was public territory but he cherished his anonymity, now more than ever, when his judgment, his professional conduct, had been questioned and his future was in the hands of others. "Yes," he said reluctantly.

Gary brought his hand forward to grasp Nelson's arm. "I've been trying to appeal a judgment," he said, "but they say I can't."

"They?" Nelson repeated. He was still thinking about the Review Board.

"The appeal booth there." Gary motioned with his free hand.

Nelson freed his arm with an impatient jerk of his shoulder and looked where Gary pointed. The glass-sided appeal booth, open and honest, was connected directly to the computer. It should accept an appeal automatically and refer it to the appellate court. "What did you say?" he asked, as something in the young man's babbling suddenly made sense.

"They said I couldn't appeal someone else's case," Gary repeated. "That's—"

"That's right," Nelson said, relieved of the need to act. He walked toward the door that opened into the night. Gary trotted along beside him, half-turned to look at Nelson's face. "It has to be your own case. Obviously we can't have people going around appealing anybody's case."

Gary looked ridiculous as he took a little hop to keep up. "But it's a girl!"

"Young women come under our jurisdiction, too," Nelson said with an irony that was wasted on the young man. The door opened for him, and he went out into the friendly night. Out there, where he had hoped to regain his composure and his confidence in himself, he was annoyed to discover that the young man was still with him.

"The way Patricia feels," Gary said, his voice high and tight—Nelson spotted it immediately as a symptom of adrenaline flow—"she can't appeal. Don't you see—she feels guilty? And she doesn't know what she's done."

"I assure you," Nelson said impatiently, "her case was considered carefully. The decision was justified. She had something to feel guilty about. 'All of us,' " he quoted, and felt compromised for having resorted to it, " 'have something to feel guilty about.' "

"But it's not fair," Gary said. "You don't know Wylene the way I do. You don't know how innocent she is, how pure and good. And now—"

"Wylene?" Nelson echoed.

"Did I say 'Wylene'?"

Nelson shrugged. "Wylene, Patricia. . . . I don't want to know her. The Department of Justice, in its wisdom, knows her far better than you do. You can believe that! Or not. It's immaterial to me and to the Department."

He turned away from the young man. As he turned he saw in front of him on the sidewalk the shadow of an upraised arm cast by the light from the doorway behind. It was an image out of every nightmare he ever had, and he waited for his father to strike. When the blow did not come, he turned and found the young man standing behind him, rigid, like a statue dedicated to anger.

Then the statue came to life like stone cracking. The upraised arm dropped to the young man's side, its crime unperformed.

"Young man," Nelson said, "are you all right?" But he knew what had happened. He summoned a taxi and helped the sick young man into the back seat. "Can you take care of yourself now?"

Gary nodded weakly. "I'm sorry," he said. "I shouldn't have—I'm sorry."

XV.

Guilt creates society. Without guilt society would have no ultimate power to persuade. Without society we would be barbarians.

—*The 2020 Hearings on the Hardister Plan for Justice Reform.*

In the morning Judge Nelson awoke with his heart pounding as if he had been running for many minutes. He was breathing rapidly. His muscles trembled. His hands were wet; his face was hot. He had the fading memory of a nightmare—no, not the memory but the feeling of inescapable terror, the need to flee and the inability to move.

He knew what it was. He'd had enough experience with it second-hand. Guilt. He never knew what it was for.

Child of the Sun

Ten thousand suns burned in the valley as Ellen McCleary climbed from the desert past the staff village to the cottage on the hills above the project.

Ten thousand giants bestrode the mountains holding lightning in either hand as she opened the cottage door and moved into the cool darkness calling, "Shelly? Shelly? I'm home. Where are you? Michelle? Mrs. Ross?"

Ten thousand trumpets shouted in her ears as she read the message scribbled in red across his bathroom mirror—and moments later found the housekeeper, tied and gagged with her with her own stockings, behind her bed.

He never knew whether he was troubled by memory or nightmare.

Every few weeks he dreamed about a pendulum. It swung back and forth like the regulator on a clock. He sensed the movement and he heard a sound, not a tick but a swoosh, as if something were moving rapidly through the air. At first he had only a vague impression of things, but gradually details forced themselves into his awareness. The pendulum arm, for instance, was more like a silvery chain with wires running through it down to the weight at the end.

Then scale became apparent. The entire apparatus was big. It swung in a cavern whose sides were so distant they could not be seen, and the wires were thick, like busbars. The weight was a kind of cage, and it was large enough to hold a person standing upright. Somewhere, far beyond the cavern, unpleasantness waited. Here there was only hushed expectancy.

In his dream he could see only the glittering chain and the cage: it swung back and forth, and at the end of each swing, where the pendulum should have slowed before it started to return, the cage blurred as if it were swinging too fast to be seen.

At this point he always realized that the cage was occupied. He was in the cage. And he understood that the pendulum marked not the passage of time but a passage through time.

The dream always ended the same way: the cage arrived with a barely perceptible jar, with a cessation of motion, and he awoke. Even awake he had the sense that somewhere the pendulum still was swinging, he still was in the cage, and eyes were watching him—or perhaps a single eye, like a camera, that occasionally revealed to him a scene of what might be. . . .

He opened his eyes. He was lying on a bed. The sheets and blankets were tangled as if he had been thrashing around in his sleep.

He looked up at the ceiling. Cracks ran across the old plaster like a map of a country he did not recognize. On his left a window let a thin, wintry light through layers of dust. On the right was the rest of the room: shabby, dingy, ordinary. In the center of the room was a black-and-white breakfast table made of metal and plastic; pulled up to it were two matching metal chairs. Beyond the table, toward what appeared to be the door to the room, was a black plastic sofa; a rickety wooden coffee table stood in front of it, and a floor lamp, at one end. Against the left wall was a wooden dresser whose walnut veneer was peeling and, beside it, an imitation-walnut wardrobe. Against the right wall was another door which led, no doubt, to a bathroom. Next to the door four-foot partitions separated from the rest of the room a stove, a sink, a refrigerator, and cabinets.

Newspapers advertised it as a studio apartment; once it was called a kitchenette.

The man swung his legs out of bed and sat up, rubbing the sleep out of his face with open hands. He appeared to be a young man, a good-looking man with brown, curly hair and dark eyes and a complexion that looked as if he had been out in the sun. He had a youthful innocence about him, a kind of newly born awareness and childlike interest in everything that made people want to talk to him, to tell him personal problems, secrets they might have shared with no one else.

But after meeting him what people remembered most were his eyes. They seemed older than the rest of him. They looked at people and at things steadily, as if they were trying to understand, as if they were trying to make sense out of what they saw, as if they saw things other people could not see, as if they had seen too much. Or perhaps they were only the eyes of a man who often forgot and was trying to remember. They looked like that now as they surveyed the room and finally returned to the table and the hand-sized tape recorder that rested on it.

He stood up and walked to the table and looked down at the recorder. A cassette was in place. He pushed the lever marked "Play." The cassette hissed for a moment and then a man spoke in a clear, musical voice but with a slight accent, like someone who learned English after adolescence and speaks it better than the natives.

"Your name is Bill Johnson," the voice said. "You have just saved the world from World War III, and you don't remember. You will find stories in the newspapers about the crisis through which the world has passed. But you will find no mention of the part you played.

"For this there are several possible explanations, including the likelihood that I may be lying or deceived or insane. But the explanation on which you must act is that I have told you the truth: you are a man who was born in a future that has almost used up all hope; you were sent to this time and place to alter the events that created the future.

"Am I telling the truth? The only evidence you have is your apparently unique ability to foresee consequences—it comes like a vision, not of the future because the future can be changed, but of what will happen if events take their natural course, if someone does not act, if you do not intervene.

"But each time you intervene, no matter how subtly, you change the future from which you came. You exist in this time and outside of time and in the future, and so each change makes you forget.

"I recorded this message last night to tell you what I know, just as I learned about myself a few weeks ago by listening to a recording like this one, for I am you and we are one, and we have done this many times before. . . ."

After the voice stopped, the man called Bill Johnson picked up a billfold lying beside the recorder; near it were a few coins, a couple of keys on a ring, and a black pocket comb. In the billfold he found thirty-six dollars, a Visa charge card and a plastic-encased social security card both made out to Bill Johnson, and a receipt for an insured package dated three weeks before.

He tossed the billfold back to the table, walked to the stove, ran a little water from the hot water tap into a teakettle, and put it on the stove. He turned on the gas under it and tried to light it several times before he gave up and turned the knob off. He went into the bathroom, came out a few minutes later, and opened the front door. A newspaper lay on the dusty carpet outside. He picked it up, shut the door, and turned on the overhead light. The bulb burned dimly, as if the current was weak. He made himself a cup of instant coffee with tap water and took it to the table.

The newspaper was thin, only eight pages. The man leafed through it quickly before he stopped at one item, stared at it for a long moment as if he were not so much reading it as looking through it, tore it out, folded it, and put it into the billfold. He stood up, went to the dresser, put on his clothes, removed a scratched plastic suitcase from the top of the wardrobe, and put into it two extra pairs of pants, three shirts and a jacket, and a handful of socks and underwear; he put his dirty clothes into a paper sack and packed it, remembered the tape recorder, closed the suitcase, picked up the assorted objects on the table and slipped them into his pockets, and walked to the door.

He looked back. The room had been ordinary before. Now it was anonymous. A series of nonentities had lived here, leaving no impression of themselves upon their surroundings. Time itself in its passage had left a cigarette burn on the table, torn a hole in the cushion of a chair, ripped the sofa, scratched the coffee tables and the walls and the doors a thousand times, deposited loesses of dirt and lint in the corners and under the bed.

Johnson smiled briefly and shut the door behind him.

Downstairs he stooped to drop the keys on the ring into the mail slot in the door marked with a plaque on which was spelled out the word "Manager." Just after the keys hit the floor, the door opened. Johnson found himself looking into the face of a middle-aged woman. Her gray hair was braided and wound around her head; her face was creased into a frown of concern.

"Mr. Johnson," she said. "You're leaving? So sudden?"

"I told you I might." His voice was the voice he had heard from the tape recorder.

"I know. But . . ." She hesitated. "I thought—maybe—you were so good to my daughter when she had . . . her trouble. . . ."

"Anyone would have wanted to help," he said.

"I know but—she thought—we thought . . ."

Johnson spread his hands helplessly, as if he saw time passing and was unable to stop it. "I'm sorry. I have to leave."

"You've been a good tenant," the woman said. "No complaining about the brownouts, which nobody can help God knows, or the gas shortages. You're quiet. You don't take girls to your room. And you're easy to talk to. Mr. Johnson, I hate to see you go. Who will I talk to?"

"There are always people to talk to if you give them a chance. Good-bye," he said. "May the future be kind."

Only when Bill Johnson was alone did he feel like a person. When he was with people he felt that he was being watched. Those occasions had a peculiar quality of unreality, as if he were an actor mouthing lines that someone else had written for him and he was forced to stand off and watch himself perform.

Seeing himself at the corner of the block, windswept paper and dust swirling around his legs, waiting without impatience for a city bus to come steaming around the corner. Sitting uneasily over torn plastic protecting the seat of the pants from the sneaky probe of a broken spring, arriving at last at the interstate bus terminal surrounded by buildings with plywood-boarded windows scribbled with obscene comments and directions. Purchasing, with the aid of his credit card, a ticket automatically imprinted with a Las Vegas destination; waiting in a television-equipped chair—the viewer long broken and useless—until a faulty public-address system announced the departure of his bus in words blurred almost beyond understanding.

Hearing the unending whine of tires on interstate concrete, broken only by chuckhole thumps and the stepdown of gears as the bus pulled off the highway for one of its frequent stops to expel or ingest passengers, to refuel with liquefied coal and resupply with boiler water, to allow passengers to consume lukewarm food at dirty bus stations or anonymous diners. Enduring the procession of drowsy days and sleepless nights. Watching people enter and depart, getting on, getting off, individual worlds of perceptions and relationships curiously intersecting in this other world on wheels careening down the naked edges of the world.

Feeling bodies deposited in the seat beside him, bodies that sometimes remained silent, unanimated lumps of flesh, but sometimes, by a miracle as marvelous as the changing of Pinocchio into a real boy or the mermaid into a woman, transforming themselves into feeling, suffering, rejoicing, talking people.

Listening to the talk, this imperfect mechanism of communication, supplemented in the light by gesture and expression and body position, anonymous in the night but perhaps thereby as honest as the confessional.

Listening to an old man, hair bleached and thinned by the years, face carved by life into uniqueness, recalling the past as the present rolled past the window carrying him to the future, a retirement home where he never again would trouble his children or his grandchildren.

Listening to a girl, with blonde hair and blue eyes and a smooth, unformed face ready for the hand of time to write upon, anticipating rosily her first job, her first apartment, her first big city, her life to come with its romances, pleasures, possessions, and faceless lovers.

Listening to a man of middle years, dark-haired, dark-eyed, already shaped by a knowledge of what life was about and how a man went about facing up to it, touched now by failure and uncertainty, heading toward a new position, determined to make good but disturbed by the possibility of failing again.

Listening to a woman of thirty, her life solidified by marriage and family but somehow incomplete and unsatisfying, achieving neither the heights of bliss nor the bedrock of fulfillment, unconsciously missing the excitements of youth, the uncertainty of what the day would bring, the possibilities of flight and pursuit, looking, although she did not know it, for adventure.

The young man inspected the unrolling fabric of their lives and past it to that part yet concealed from them, and he was kind, as everyone must be kind who knows that the future holds bereavement, disappointment, disillusion, and death.

Besides, the times were hard: like the curse of the witch who had not been invited to the christening, the Depression had lain like death across the land for five years, the unemployment rate was nearly eighteen percent, and the energy shortage was pressing continually harder on the arteries of civilization. A little kindness came cheap enough, but it was scarce all the same.

Between conversations on his rolling world, the man named Bill Johnson occasionally removed a newspaper clipping from his billfold and read it again.

CALIFORNIA GIRL ABDUCTED

Death Valley, CA (AP)—The four-year-old daughter of Ellen McCleary, managing engineer of the Death Valley Solar Power Project, was reported missing today.

McCleary returned from her afternoon duties at the

Project to discover her housekeeper, Mrs. Fred Ross, bound and gagged behind her own bed and the McCleary girl, Shelly, gone from the home.

Authorities at the Project and the local sheriff's office have refused to release any information about the possible abductor, but sources close to the Project suggest that oil interests have reason to desire the failure of the Project.

McCleary was recently divorced from her husband of ten years, Stephen Webster. Webster's location is unknown.

Authorities will neither confirm nor deny that the abductor left a message behind.

Below the hill the valley was a lake of flame as Bill Johnson climbed toward the cottage some two hundred yards from the little group of preformed buildings he had left behind. Then, as the path rose, the angle of vision changed and the flame vanished, as if snuffed by a giant finger. Now the valley was lined with thousands of mirrors reflecting the orange-red rays of the dying sun toward a black cylinder towering in their center.

The air coming up the hill off the desert was hot, like a dragon's breath, and brought with it the scent of alkali dust and the feeling of fluids being sucked through the skin until, if the process continued long enough, only the desiccated husk would be left behind for the study of future archaeologists. Johnson knocked on the door of the cottage. When there was no answer he knocked again, and turned to look at the valley, arid and lifeless below him like a vision of the future.

A small noise and an outpouring of cool air made him turn. In front of him, in the doorway, stood a middle-aged woman with a face as dry as an alkali flat.

"Mrs. Ross?" Johnson said. "I'm Bill Johnson. I talked on

the telephone to Ms. McCleary from Las Vegas, but the connection was bad."

"Ms. McCleary gets lotsa calls," the woman said in a voice like dust. "She don't see nobody."

"I know that," Johnson said. He smiled understandingly. "But she will want to see me. I've come to help in the disappearance of her daughter."

Mrs. Ross was unmoved. "Lotsa nuts bother Ms. McCleary about stuff like that. She don't see nobody."

"I'm sorry to be persistent," Johnson said, and his smile illustrated his regret, "but it is important." His body position was relaxed and reassuring.

The housekeeper looked at him for the first time and hesitated about closing the door. As she hesitated, a woman's voice came from within the darkened house, "Who is it, Mrs. Ross?"

"Just another crank, Ms. McCleary," the housekeeper said, looking behind her, but grasping the door firmly as if in fear that Johnson would burst past her into the sanctity of the cool interior.

Another woman appeared in the doorway. She was tall, slender, dark, good-looking but a bit haggard with concern and sleeplessness. She stared at Johnson angrily as if she blamed him for the events of the past few days. "What do you want?"

"My name is Bill Johnson," he said patiently. "I called you from Las Vegas."

"And I said I didn't want to see you," McCleary said and started to turn away. "Shut the door, Mrs. Ross—" she began.

"I may be the only person who can get your daughter back for you," Johnson said. It was as if he had leaned a hand against the door to keep it from closing.

The tall woman turned toward him again, her body rigid with the effort to control the anxiety within. Johnson smiled confidently but without arrogance, looking not at all like a nut or a crank or a criminal.

"What do you know about my daughter?" McCleary demanded. Then she took a deep breath and turned to Mrs. Ross. "Oh, let him in. He seems harmless enough."

"The sheriff said not to talk to anybody," the housekeeper said. "The sheriff said you was to—"

"I know what the sheriff said, Mrs. Ross," McCleary interrupted. "But I guess it won't matter if I talk to this person. Sometimes," she continued, her voice detached and distant, "I have to talk to somebody." She brought herself back to this place and time. "Let him in and go stand by the telephone in case I find it necessary to call the sheriff." She looked at Johnson as if warning him against making that step necessary.

"I wouldn't want you to do that," he said submissively, and moved forward into darkness. More by sound than sight he followed her footsteps down a hallway into a living room where returning vision and the light filtering through closed drapes over a picture window let him make his way to an upholstered chair. McCleary sat stiffly on the edge of a matching sofa; it was covered in velvet with variable-width stripes of orange and brown and cream. She lit a cigarette. The lingering odors of stale smoke and a littered ashtray on the glass-covered coffee table in front of her suggested that she had been smoking one cigarette after another.

"What do you know about my daughter?" she asked. She was under control now.

"First of all," he said, "she is an important person." He held up a hand to forestall her questions. "Not just to you, overriding as that may be at the moment. Not just because she is a person in a society that values every individual. But because of her potential."

"What do you know about that?" she demanded. A note of doubt had crept into her voice.

"It's hard to explain without making me seem like a crackpot or a fool," Johnson said, leaning toward her to emphasize his sincerity. "I have—special knowledge—which comes to me in the form of—visions."

"I see." Doubt had crystallized into certainty. "You're a psychic."

"No," Johnson said. "I told you it was difficult. But if that's the way you want to think of it—"

"I've had dozens of letters and telephone calls from psychics since my daughter was abducted, Mr. Johnson, and they've all been phonies," she said coldly. "All psychics are phonies. I think you'd better go." She stood up.

He stood up along with her, not submitting to but resisting his dismissal. He looked into her eyes as if his eyes had the power to compel her belief. "I think I can find your daughter. I think I know how to get her back. If I thought you could do it without my help, I wouldn't be here. I want you to know that I could find myself in great difficulties and my mission in jeopardy."

"Where is my daughter?" It was not the tone of belief but of a final examination.

"With your husband."

"You guessed."

"No."

"You know about the message."

"Was there a message?"

"You're from Steve. He sent you."

"No. But I sense danger to your daughter and perhaps to your husband as well."

She slumped back to the sofa. "What are you then?" she asked. "Are you just a confidence man?" Her tone was pleading, as if it would comfort her if he admitted her guess was right. "What do you want from me? Why don't you leave me alone?" If she had been a more dependent person she might have turned her face from his and cried.

"All I want is to help you," he said, sitting down again, reaching toward her with one hand but not touching her, "and to help you find your daughter."

"I don't have any money," she said. "I can't pay you. If you're preying on my helplessness, it won't gain you anything. If you're seeking notoriety, you will be exposed eventually."

"None of these things matter beside your daughter's safety and her future. Moreover, you may not be able to control the events of your life as you have been accustomed to doing, but you are not helpless. I don't want any money. I don't want any word of my part in this to get out to anyone, and certainly not to the press. It would be dangerous to me."

"Then what do you want?"

"I want to get to know you," he said, and as she stiffened he hastened on, "so that I can find your daughter." His glance moved around the room as if he were looking at it for the first and the last time. At the picture window that looked out over the desert valley and the solar power project when the drapes were drawn. Michelle had stood there and watched for her mother's return. At the electronic organ in the corner that neither McCleary nor her daughter could play. At the doors that led to bedrooms where a woman and a man had slept and made love and lain awake in the night. At other doors that led to baths, to the hall, to the kitchen and dining room on the other side of the hall. "I want information about your work, your daughter, your husband, the circumstances of your daughter's abduction. . . ."

She sighed. "Where do you want to start?"

"The message. What did it say?"

"The sheriff told me not to describe it to anyone. He said that knowledge of it would either be guilty knowledge or proof of the abductor's identity."

"You've got to trust somebody some time," Johnson said.

"And the police are not to be trusted, Mr. Johnson?" Through her concern flashed the perceptiveness that had made her director of a major research project.

"From the police you get police-type answers," he said. "Investigation, surveillance, evidence, apprehension. I think you want something else—your daughter back safely and preferably without your husband—"

"My former husband," she corrected.

"Your former husband's injury or punishment."

"Ms. McCleary," said the voice of Mrs. Ross from the hall doorway, "the sheriff is here to see you."

"Thank you, Mrs. Ross," McCleary said.

"Come in, sir," Johnson said. "I've been expecting you."

The room was not much of a jail cell. It was a small room without windows. The walls were paneled in plywood faced with mahogany and decorated with framed prints of famous racehorses. In the center of the room was a long table lined with chairs on either side.

It had never been intended for a cell. It was a small dining room off the main cafeteria, where groups could get together for luncheon conversations. Now a young man sat across the table from Johnson, silent and nervous, uncertain about his duties and privileges as a jailer.

He was a junior engineer on the Solar Power Project, and

he had been asked to guard the prisoner while the sheriff made arrangements to transport the prisoner to the county jail some forty miles away. The young man fidgeted in his chair, clasped and unclasped his hands, and smiled uncertainly at Johnson.

Johnson smiled back reassuringly. "How is the project going?" he asked.

"What do you mean?" The engineer was a pleasant looking young man with sandy hair bleached almost white by the sun, a face peeling perpetually from sunburn, and large hairy hands that he didn't know what to do with.

"The Solar Power Project," Johnson said. "How's it going?"

"What do you know about the project?" the engineer demanded, as if he suspected that Johnson, after all, was the hireling of the oil interests.

"Everybody knows about the Solar Power Project," Johnson said. "It's no secret."

"I guess not," the engineer admitted. He looked at the metal table with its printed wood grain as if he wished it were a drawing board. "This is an experimental project, and we've demonstrated that we can get significant amounts of power out of solar energy."

"How much is that?"

"Enough for our own needs and enough more to justify the overhead towers that cross the hills toward Los Angeles," the engineer said with a mixture of pride and defensiveness.

"That is a significant amount."

"During daylight hours, of course."

"Then why is the project still experimental?" Johnson asked.

The young man at last found something to do with one hand. "Well," he said, rubbing his chin and making the day's stubble rasp under his fingers, "there's one problem we haven't solved."

"The daylight problem?"

"No. Energy can always be stored by pumping water, electrolyzing it into hydrogen and oxygen, with batteries or flywheels. The problem is economics: it's cheaper to burn coal, even if you toss in the cost of environmental controls and damage. Almost one-fourth as cheap. And nuclear power costs less than that. Other forms of solar power, including power cells for direct conversion of sunlight into electricity, are either less efficient or more expensive."

"If the project has accomplished its purpose," Johnson asked, "why is it still going on?"

Both the engineer's hands were in motion now as he defended his project and his profession. "We still hope for a breakthrough. Producing cheaper solar cells through integrated factories. Maybe cheaper computer-driven mirrors. Maybe putting solar power plants in space where the sun shines twenty-four hours a day, if we could solve the problem of getting the energy back. Maybe some new method of converting sunlight into useful energy like chlorophyll or the purple dyes found in some primitive sea creatures."

"Nature's method of converting sunlight into energy may still be the most efficient," Johnson said. He looked up at one of the racehorses. It was a shiny red, and it was happily cropping blue grass inside a white rail fence.

"We're trying that, too," the engineer said. "Energy farms for growing trees or grasses. But put it all together and it doesn't add up to a third of the energy needs of the world that once were satisfied by cheap oil."

"What about nuclear energy?" Johnson asked.

"Inherently dangerous—particularly the breeder reactor. Not basically any more dangerous in its total impact than coal or oil, but the risks are concentrated and more visible. So the moratorium on the building of new nuclear power plants has effectively ended the effort to make nuclear energy safe."

"Well," Johnson said, "there's a lot of coal."

The engineer nodded. By now he was treating Johnson like an equal instead of a prisoner. "That's true," he said, "but unlike oil, coal is dirty. It has to be dug, and that damages the miners—or the land if it's strip-mined. Sulfur has to be removed, in one way or another, to avoid sulfur-dioxide pollution. And the coal will run out, too, in a century or so."

Johnson looked sad. "Then the energy depression is going to get worse until the coal runs out, and after that civilization goes back to the dark ages."

The engineer clasped his hands in front of him, almost in an attitude of prayer. "Unless we can come up with a workable technology for nuclear fusion."

"Fusing atoms of hydrogen together?"

"Making helium atoms and turning into energy the little bit of matter that's left over." The engineer's index fingers had formed a steeple. "The true sunpower—the solar process itself, clean, no radioactivity, inexhaustible, unlimited power without byproducts except heat, and maybe that could be harnessed to perform useful work if we're clever enough. Why, with hydrogen fusion man would have enough power to do anything he ever wanted to do—clean up the environment, raise enough food for everybody, improve living standards all around the world until everybody lives as well as we used to, return to space travel in a big way, reshape the other planets or move them into better orbits, go to the stars—" His voice stopped on a rising note like a preacher describing the pleasures of the life to come.

"But we haven't got it yet," Johnson said.

The engineer's eyes lowered to look at Johnson, and his

hands folded themselves across each other. "We just haven't got the hang of it," he said. "There's a trick to it we haven't discovered, and we haven't got much time as civilizations go. For the past decade we've been through an energy depression that shows no signs of letting up. How much longer can we go on? Maybe thirty or forty years, if we're lucky and don't have a revolution or a major war; and if we don't discover the secret to thermonuclear fusion by then the level of civilization will be too low to apply the technology necessary to bring it into general use, and after that there'll be no one capable of thinking about anything except personal survival."

"Pretty grim," Johnson said.

"Ain't it?" the engineer said, and then he smiled. "That's why we keep working. Maybe we can buy a little time, ease the pressures a bit. Maybe somewhere a breakthrough will occur. If we don't find it, maybe our children will."

The engineer was a dreamer. Bill Johnson was a visionary. He knew what was coming, but the engineer jumped when the knock came at the door like the future announcing itself.

"George?" said the voice of Ellen McCleary. "Open up. I want to talk to the prisoner."

Outside the day had turned to night. The stars were out, bright and many-colored, and the Milky Way streamed across the sky like a jeweled veil. The reflected heat from the desert below seemed friendly now against the cool evening breeze pouring down from the hills.

Ellen McCleary stopped a few yards from the cafeteria building and turned to face Johnson. "I guess you think I'm a silly woman, not able to know her own mind, first having you arrested and then setting you free."

"I may think many things about you, but not that you're a silly woman," Johnson said. "That battle has been won; you don't have to keep fighting it. Your presence here as director of this project is proof of that."

"I thought about it," she said, shrugging off his interruption but not looking at him, "and I decided that I couldn't throw away the chance that you might be able to help. If I can get Shelly back—" She didn't finish the sentence. Instead she held out an oblong of stiff white paper. It was a Polaroid snapshot.

He took a few steps back into the light that streamed through the front window of the cafeteria building. The picture showed writing—red, broad, smeared—against a shiny black background.

"He wrote it on the bathroom mirror with my lipstick," she said.

Johnson read the message:

> *Ellen—The Court gave Shelly to you, but I'm going to give her what you never could—the full time love of a full-time parent.*

"Is that your former husband's handwriting?" Johnson asked. He seemed to be looking through the picture rather than at it.

"Yes. His language, too. He's a madman, Mr. Johnson."

"In what way?"

"He—" She paused as if to gather together all the fugitive impressions of a life with another person. She took a deep breath and began again. "He thinks that the way he feels at the moment is the only thing that matters. That he may feel differently tomorrow or even the next moment doesn't count. He'd be willing to kill himself—or Shelly—if he felt like it at the moment." She let her breath sigh out. "That's what I'm afraid of, I guess."

"Are you sure he's homicidal?"

"I'm making him sound crazier than he is, I know, but what I'm trying to say is that he's an impulsive person who believes that people should only do what feels right to them. He doesn't believe in the past or the future. Now is the only thing that exists for him. He thinks I'm cold and unfeeling, and I see him as childish, and—but I'm talking as if you're a marriage counselor. We tried that, too."

They talked together now in the darkness, two voices without faces, sound without body. "That's all right," Johnson said. "It helps me get the feel of things. Did he have a profession, a talent, a job?"

Her voice held the hint of a shrug. "He was a bit of a lot of things—a bit of a painter, a bit of a writer, a bit of an actor, but a romantic all the time. What really broke things up, though, was when this project got started and I was selected as director. I was in charge, and he was just—around. He had nothing to do, and conditions were pretty primitive for a while. That's when Shelly was conceived—as sort of a sop to his manhood. But it didn't last. He left for a few months when Shelly was about a year old, came back, we quarreled, he left again, and finally I divorced him, got custody of Shelly, and that's about it."

"Not much for what—ten years of marriage?"

"Yes." She sighed. "Shelly is all, and he's taken her."

"Where did you meet?"

"In Los Angeles. At a party at a friend's house. I was a graduate student at Cal Tech; he was an actor. He seemed romantic and strong. I was—flattered, I guess—that he was interested in me. We got married in a whirlwind of emotion, and it was great for a few months. Then things began going bad. I irritated him by worrying about my career, by wanting to talk about where we were going to be next year, ten years from now. He annoyed me by his lack of concern for those things, by his unrelenting demands upon my time, my attention, my emotions. Part of my emotions were invested in other things—in my work, for one—and he could never understand that, or forgive it."

"I understand," Johnson said. "The times your husband left—did he return to Los Angeles?"

"I think he did the first time, although we weren't communicating too well then. But that's where he said he'd been when he came back."

"The second time?"

"I don't know. We didn't communicate at all until the divorce, and then it was through lawyers. Until that." She indicated the photograph in Johnson's hand, a shadowy finger almost touching the white rectangle.

He held it in his fingertips, almost as if he were weighing it. "I suppose the police checked all his friends in Los Angeles."

"And his relatives. That's where he was born and grew up. But they didn't find anything. Nobody has seen him recently. Nobody knows where he might have gone with Shelly."

"Did he have any hobbies?"

"Tennis. He liked tennis. And parties. And girls." The last word had an edge of bitterness.

"Hunting? Mountain climbing?" Johnson's words were tentative, as if he were testing a hypothesis.

She seemed to be shaking her head. "He didn't like the outdoors. Not raw. If he'd liked to hike or hunt, he still might be here," she said ruefully. The blur of a hand gestured at the mountains that rose to the east and the north and the west of them.

"He sounds restless," Johnson said. "Could he stay in one place for long at a time? If he starts moving around, the police will find him."

"He never has been able to stay still before, but if he thought that was the only way to hurt me he might be able to do it."

"Is Mrs. Ross sure he's the one who tied her up?"

"She never knew Steve. I hired her after he left. But she identified his picture."

"There was nobody else with him? Nobody who might be making him do what he did?"

"Not that she could tell. She said he seemed cheerful. Whistled while he tied her up. Said not to worry, I would be back at six o'clock—that I was like a quartz watch, always right on the second. He hated that." She paused and waited in the darkness. When he didn't say anything, she asked, "Is there anything else?"

"Do you have any of his personal belongings?"

"I threw them out. I didn't want anything to remind me of him. Or to remind Shelly either, I guess. Except this." She handed Johnson another white oblong.

He took it into the light. It was the picture of a blond young man in tennis clothing, looking up into the sun with the net and court behind him, squinting a little, laughing, strikingly handsome and vital and alive, as if time had been captured and made to stand still for him and he would never grow old.

"Can I keep the pictures?" Johnson asked.

"Yes," she said. Her disembodied voice held a nod. "Can you find Shelly for me?"

"Yes," he said. It was not boastful nor a promise but a statement of fact. "Don't worry. I'll see that she gets back to you." That was a promise. "May the future be kind," he said. Then he walked out of the light into the darkness. His footsteps sounded more distant on the path until the night was still.

★ ★ ★ ★ ★

Los Angeles was a carnival of life, a sprawling, vivid city of contrasts between the rich and the poor, between the extravagant and the impecunious, between mansions and slums.

The smog was gone, removed not so much by the elimination of automobile exhaust fumes but by the elimination of the automobile. Except for the occasional antique gasoline-powered machines that rolled imperiously along the nearly deserted freeways, the principal method of transportation was the coal-fueled steam-powered bus. The smokestacks, too, had been stopped, either by smoke and fume scrubbers or by the Depression.

Johnson was sullen. Unlike an earlier period when minorities had felt that they were being cheated of an affluence available to everyone else, the citizens shared what was clearly a widespread and apparently growing distress and general decline in civilization. The riots of discrimination were clearly past, and the riots of desperation had not yet begun.

Through this strange city went a man who did not know his name, troubled by a past he could not remember and visions of a future he could not forget, trying to put together a portrait of a man who had as many images as there were people who knew him, seeking the vision that would reveal a place where a man and a child might be unnoticed, asking questions and getting always the same replies.

At a Spanish bungalow with peeling pink stucco, "No, we don't know him."

At a walled studio with sagging gates, echoing sound stages, and decaying location sets that looked like a premonition of the society outside its walls, "No, we haven't used him in years."

At a comfortable ranch house in the valley, surrounded by orange trees, "The police have been here twice already.

We've answered all their questions."

At a tennis club still maintaining standards and the muted *sprong-sprong* of court activity, "He hasn't been around for months."

At a high school where hopeless teachers tried to impart knowledge whose value they no longer found credible to listless students who were there only because society had no other place for them, "We can show you only the yearbooks," and in them pictures of a face without character and listings of activities without meaning.

And then, unexpectedly, at a bar along the Strip, half-facade and half-corrupt, like a painted whore, "Yeah, I seen him a couple of months ago, him and a fellow with a cap on—you know one of those things with a whatchmacallit on the front . . . yeah, a visor—like a sea captain, you know—yeah, Gregory Peck as Captain Ahab. Reason I remember—it wasn't his style, you know. It was always girls with him. You could see him turn up the charm like one of those things that dim and brighten lights . . . a rheostat?—yeah, I guess. With guys he was cool, you know?—like he didn't care what they thought of him. But with this guy it was different. Like he wanted something from the guy. . . . No. I didn't hear what they was talking about. I had sixty-seventy customers in here that night. The noise you wouldn't believe sometimes. You're lucky I remembered seeing him."

A search of the dock area, all up and down the coast, until finally at the small boat marina near Alamitos Beach State Park, a marina with many empty docks, "Steve? Sure, he borrowed my cruiser for a couple of hours about two weeks ago. . . . No, he didn't tell me where he was going, but I trusted him and he brought it back. Of course I didn't think he was running dope past the border. There's no point in that now, is there? What with the new laws and everything'? Anyway, he was gone only a couple of hours. . . . Well, I gave him the keys about one o'clock in the afternoon, and he was back with them before four. . . . Sure I'm certain about the time. I remember—I told him I was having a party on board that evening, and I had to get her cleaned up and provisioned. Matter of fact, I asked if he wanted to join the party—a guy like Steve gives a party real class, and the girls come back—but he couldn't. . . . You can push her up to thirty knots, but she's a real fuel eater at that speed. . . . No, I didn't see anybody with him. May have been, but I didn't see anybody. Want to look at the boat? Why not? I bought it from a fellow in Long Beach five years ago when fuel got so expensive. Now I hardly ever go out in it. Use it sort of like a floating bar and bedroom. . . ."

Brass rails, gleaming teak decks, white paint shining in the sun, the spoked wheel, touch it, feel its response, sense the directions it has gone, the hands that have held it and steered the boat. The cabin below, all compact and efficient, bunks and tables, kitchen and head, immaculate, haunted by ghosts, crowded together here laughing, crying, drunken, reckless, desperate. . . .

And back to the dock, certain now, seeing a vision of a place available by water within an hour's range of the cruiser, at most thirty nautical miles from the small boat marina. . . .

And at the head of the dock, waiting for him, a tall, slender woman, dark-haired, dark-eyed, good looking but a bit more haggard now. "So," she said, "he took her away by water. I would never have suspected him of having that much imagination."

Johnson looked at her and saw the past. "You didn't give him credit for much."

"You don't seem surprised at seeing me," she said.

"No."

She hesitated, looking down at her feet in their red canvas

shoes that matched her red slacks. "I guess I owe you an apology," she said finally.

"No."

"I suspected you," she went on, looking up at him, letting him see her guilt. "The police suspected you too of having had some contact with Steve, of being his emissary, at least of knowing him, perhaps where he was living, perhaps being willing to sell him out."

"You have reason to suspect people," Johnson said. The odor of fish and oily salt water surrounded them.

"So we had you followed. And you did the police work to find him. You don't know how difficult this is for me, do you?"

"Yes," he said.

"You did it better than the police. You found him. Maybe you really are what you say you are."

"That's a reasonable assumption."

"The world isn't reasonable," she complained. "People aren't reasonable. You did find him, didn't you? Tell me that you found him."

"I found him," Johnson said simply, "but I haven't gone to him yet. I haven't got Shelly back for you yet."

"I'm not asking you to tell me where he is," Ellen McCleary said, a bit unsteadily, looking at Johnson's face hopefully, "but I'm asking you to take me with you."

"I can get Shelly back without damage to her or your former husband if I go alone," Johnson said. "With you along the chances get much slimmer."

She got angry at that. "Who are you to say? What do you know about him or me or Shelly? What right have you to meddle in our lives?"

"Only the outcome can justify any of us," he said. "Good intentions, emotional involvements, rights—all these are only the absolution we give ourselves for lack of foresight. Look out there." He motioned toward the smooth blue swells of the Pacific gleaming with highlights in the sunshine. "Quite a difference from your wasteland. That's fertility. That's promise. We came from the sea, and in the sea lies our future."

"My desert is not as lifeless as it looks," she said. "We get energy from it, energy we need, energy we must have."

"The lowest kind of energy—heat. You waste a lot when you have to pump it up into electricity."

"Like all energy it comes from the sun."

"Not all," he said. The wind was coming in off the ocean and blowing away the old smells of rot and waste. "I won't take you with me. You can have me followed, of course, but I ask you not to do that. What will it be? Your desert of old memories or my sea of hope?"

She shook her head slowly, helplessly. "I can't promise."

"Then neither can I," he said, and left her standing at the edge of the water as he walked quickly to the street and the nearest public transportation.

The ferry ride was a pleasant interlude, a break in the feeling of urgency that drove Johnson. He could not hurry the ship, and he existed for the moment, like the smiling young man in the tennis clothes, outside of time. From San Pedro Bay to Santa Catalina, he watched the blue water curl under the bow, white and playful, and the smooth blue surface of the Pacific extending undisturbed to the end of the world.

Johnson studied it as if he had never before seen the protean sea or the creatures that lived in it—small darting fish, dark shapes changing instantly into silver when pursued by large solitary predators, and distantly, across the horizon, the gray unbelievable backs of whales. The breeze, laden with salt, blew across his face and tugged at his hair and clothing, and he smiled.

He left the ferry at Avalon as soon as the ship had tied up in its slip.

Few people got off the ferry—the pleasure business was an early casualty of the Depression—and Johnson paid no attention to them. He rented a bicycle from a stand at the end of the pier and pedaled up the main road among the wooded hills, got off and walked the bicycle where the hills were too steep to ride, stopped for a moment when he had reached the high point, with Black Jack Peak to his right and the Pacific spread out in front of him again like hope regained, then coasted rapidly down the hills, past Middle Ranch and along the west coast where the ocean flashed blue between the trees.

Just short of Catalina Harbor, he stopped, pulled the bicycle off the road and behind some trees, and walked up through the woods along a barely discernible path until the trees began to thin and he found himself close to a small clearing with a small cabin in the middle. As Johnson stood without moving, the sound of a child's happy voice came to him and then a man's deeper voice followed, surprisingly, by a third voice and a fourth, the child's squeal of laughter, and a man's chuckle.

Johnson moved through the last of the trees into the dust of the clearing. Now he could see the front porch of the cabin. On the edge of the porch sat a child with short dark hair and lively blue eyes. She was dressed in a red, knitted shirt and dirty jeans. Her feet were bare, her hands were squeezed ecstatically between her knees, and she stared enraptured at finger puppets on the hands of a light-haired young man.

In a hoarse voice the young man chanted:

"Today I'll brew, tomorrow bake;
Merrily I'll dance and sing.

Tomorrow will a baby bring:
The lady cannot stop my game . . ."

The little girl shouted with delight, "Rumpelstiltskin is my name!"

The young man was laughing with her until he saw Johnson. He stopped laughing. The puppets fell off his fingers as he reached behind him. The little girl stopped laughing, too, and looked at Johnson. In repose her face looked a great deal like the face of Ellen McCleary with the young man's blue eyes and spontaneity.

"Hello," Johnson said. He moved forward slowly, like a man moving among wild animals, so as not to frighten them into flight or attack.

"Don't tell me you've come to read the meter," said the young man sitting on the porch, "or that you just wandered here by mistake."

Johnson eased himself down in the center of the clearing with his back to the ocean that gleamed through the trees a deeper blue than the sky. He sat cross-legged and helpless in the dust and said, "No, I came here to talk to you, Steve Webster."

Webster brought his right hand out from behind him. It had a revolver in it. He supported the butt on his knee and pointed it in Johnson's general direction. "If you're from my wife, tell her to leave me alone—me and Shelly—or she'll regret it." Webster's voice was harsh, and the little girl stirred nervously beside him, looking at her father's face, down at the gun, and then at Johnson.

"I've talked to your former wife," Johnson said, "but I'm not here in her behalf alone. I'm here as much for your sake as hers, but mostly for Shelly's sake."

"That's a lot of crap," Webster said, straightening the gun a little.

"You're frightening your daughter," Johnson said to him.

"She wasn't frightened before you came," Webster said.

"I realize that you and your daughter have been happy together," Johnson said. He spread his hands as if he were weighing sunbeams on his palms. "But how long can it last? How long before the authorities locate you?"

Webster waved the ugly gun in the air as if he had forgotten he held it. "That doesn't matter. Maybe they'll find us tomorrow, maybe never. Now we're happy. We're together. Whatever happens can never change that."

"Suppose," Johnson said, "it could last forever. You can't always be a little girl and her father playing games in a cabin in the woods. Shelly will grow up without schooling, without friends. Is that the thing to do for your daughter?"

"A man has got to do what he thinks is right," Webster said stubbornly. "Now is all any of us have got. Next month, next year, maybe something else will happen. Something good, something bad—you can't live for that. Nobody knows what's going to happen."

Johnson's lips tightened but Webster didn't seem to notice.

"Nobody's found me yet," Webster said, and then his eyes focused on Johnson again. "Except you." He noticed the gun in his hand and pointed it more purposefully at Johnson. "Except you," he repeated.

The little girl began to cry.

"Wouldn't that spoil it?" Johnson said. "Having Shelly see me shot by her father?"

"Yeah," Webster said. "Run inside the cabin, Shelly," he said, looking only at Johnson. The little girl didn't move. "Go on, now. Get in the cabin." The little girl cried harder. "See what you're making me do," he complained to Johnson.

Johnson put his hands out in the dust in a gesture of helplessness. "I'm not a threat to you, and you can't save anything by getting rid of me. If I can find you, others can. In any case, you couldn't stay here long. You'll need food, clothing, books. Word about a man and a little girl living here is bound to get out. You'll have to move. The moment you move the police will spot you. It's hopeless, Steve."

Webster waved the gun in the air. "I can always choose another ending."

"For yourself? Ellen said you might do that."

"Yeah?" Webster looked interested. "Maybe for once Ellen was right."

"But that's not the way it ought to be," Johnson said. "You're old enough to make your own decisions, but you ought to leave Shelly out of this. She's got a right to live, a right to decide what she wants to do with her life."

"That's true," Webster admitted. He started to lower the gun to his knee again, and then lifted it to point at Johnson again. "But what does a little girl know about life?"

"She'll get bigger and able to make her own decisions if you give her a chance," Johnson said.

"A chance," Webster repeated. He raised the gun until it pointed directly at Johnson, aiming it, tightening his finger on the trigger. "That's what the world never gave me. That's what Ellen never gave me."

Johnson sat in the dust, not moving, looking at the deadly black hole in the muzzle of the gun.

Gradually Webster's finger relaxed. He lowered the revolver to the porch beside him as if he had forgotten it. "But you're not to blame," he said.

"I suppose I'm to blame," a woman's voice said from the edge of the clearing. Ellen McCleary stepped out from among the trees.

Webster seemed surprised and delighted to see her. "Ellen," he said, "it was good of you to come to see me."

"Mommy," Shelly said. She tried to get up and run to her mother, but Webster held her wrist firmly in his hand and would not let her go.

"That's all right, Shelly," Ellen said, moving easily toward the porch where her former husband and her daughter sat. She no longer seemed tired, now that she had reached the end of her search. "Let Shelly go," she said to Webster.

"Not bloody likely," he said.

"Not to me," Ellen said. "Let her go with this man."

Webster glanced at Johnson. Neither of them said anything.

"Let's leave Shelly out of this," Ellen said. "It's between us, isn't it?"

"Maybe it is," Webster said. His fingers loosened on Shelly's wrist.

The little girl had stopped crying when her mother appeared. Now she looked back and forth between her parents, on the edge of tears but holding them back.

"We did it to each other," Ellen said. "Let's not do it to Shelly. She's not guilty of anything."

"That's true," Webster said. "You and I—we're guilty, all right."

"Go to Mr. Johnson, Shelly," Ellen said. Her voice was quiet but it held a quality of command.

Webster's hand fell away, and he pushed the little girl affectionately toward Johnson. "Go on, Shelly," he said with rough tenderness. "That man's going to take you for a walk."

Johnson held out his arms to the little girl. She looked at her father and then at her mother, and turned to run to Johnson.

"That's a kind thing to do," Ellen said.

"Oh, I can be kind," Webster said. He grinned, and his face was warm and likeable.

Johnson got slowly to his knees in the dust of the clearing and then to his feet.

"It's a matter of knowing what kindness is," Webster said.

"If you're fixed in the present," Ellen said, "I suppose that would be a problem."

Johnson took Shelly's hand and began moving out of the clearing.

"Now, now," Webster cautioned, "let's not be unkind. We are put here on this earth to be kind to one another. And we have come together now to be kind to one another as we were not kind before."

Johnson and Shelly had reached the protection of the trees and moved among them. The odor of green, growing things rose around them.

"The problem," Ellen said, "is that we don't know what the other one means by kindness. What is kindness to you may be unkindness to me, and the other way around."

As Johnson and Shelly moved down the path, they could hear the voices behind them.

"Don't start with me again," Webster said.

"I'm not," she said. "Believe me, I'm not. But it's all over, Steve. I didn't come here alone, you know."

"You mean you brought police," he said. His voice was rising.

"I couldn't find you by myself," she said. "But I didn't bring them. You brought them. By what you did. Don't make it worse, Steve. Give yourself up." The rest was indistinguishable. But the sound of voices, louder, shouting, came to them until hands reached out of bushes beside the path to grab them both.

A man's voice said, "You're not Webster."

Another man's voice, on the other side of the path, said, "That's all right, little girl, we're police officers."

A shot came from the clearing some two hundred yards away. For a moment the world seemed frozen—the leaves were still, the birds stopped singing, even the distant sea ceased its restless motion. And then everything burst into sound and activity again, bodies pounded past Johnson toward the clearing, dust hung in the air, and Shelly was crying.

"Where's my mommy?" she said. "Where's my daddy?"

Johnson held her tightly in his arms and tried to comfort her, but there was nothing he could say that would not leave her poorer than she had been a few moments ago.

Then he heard footsteps approaching on the path.

"Hello, Shelly," Ellen said heavily.

"Mommy!" the little girl said, and Johnson let her go to her mother.

After a moment, Ellen said over the child's head, "You knew what was going to happen, didn't you?"

"Only if certain things happened."

"If I had not come here Steve might still be alive," she said, "and if you hadn't been here both Shelly and I might be dead."

"People do what they must—like active chemicals, participating in every reaction. Some persons serve their life purposes by striding purposefully toward their destinations; others, by flailing out wildly in all directions."

"What about you?"

"Others slide through life without being noticed and affect events through their presence rather than their actions," Johnson said. "I am—a catalyst. A substance that assists a reaction without participating in it."

"I don't know what you are," Ellen said. "But I've got a lot to thank you for."

"What are you going to do now?"

"I'm going to sit down and think for a long time. Maybe Steve was right. Maybe I was neglecting Shelly."

"Children can be smothered as well as neglected," Johnson said. "They must be loved enough to be let go by people who love themselves enough to do what they must do to be people."

"You think I should go back to my project."

"For Shelly's sake."

"And yours?"

"And everyone's. But that's just a guess."

"You're a strange man, Bill Johnson, and I should ask you questions, but I have the feeling that whatever answers you gave or didn't give, it wouldn't matter. So—let me ask you just one." She hesitated. "Will you come to see me again when all this is over? I—I'd like you to see me as something other than a suspicious, harried mother."

An expression like pain passed across Johnson's face and was gone. "I can't," he said.

"I understand."

"No, you don't," he said. "Just understand—I would like to know you better. But I can't."

And he stood on the hillside, dappled by the light that came through the leaves and was reflected up from the ocean, and he watched them walk down the path toward the road that would take them back to the boat, back to the mainland.

In the distance a frigate bird sailed alone in the sky, circling a spot in the ocean, turning and circling and finding nothing.

The rented room was lit only by the flickering of an old neon sign outside the window. Johnson sat at a wooden table, pressed down a key on the cassette recorder in front of him, and after a moment began to speak.

"Your name is Bill Johnson," he said. "You have just returned to her mother the little girl who will grow up to perfect the thermonuclear power generator, and you don't remember. You may find a small item in the newspaper about it, but you will find no mention of the part you played in recovering the girl.

"For this there are several possible explanations. . . ."

After he had finished, he sat silently for several minutes while the cassette continued to hiss, until he remembered to reach forward and press the lever marked "Stop."

The North Wind

The North wind doth blow,
And we shall have snow,
And what will the robin do then,
Poor thing?
He'll sit in a barn
To keep himself warm,
And hide his head under his wing,
Poor thing!

—*Nursery Rhyme*

The ice sheets on the North American continent advanced as much as fifty kilometers that winter, but almost nobody was around to notice. Virtually everybody had gone south. They were huddled in battered Florida or troubled southern California, or had pushed farther toward the equator through shattered Mexico or island-hopping through Cuba, Jamaica, Haiti, and Puerto Rico in a bloody reverse migration.

About forty miles from the Kansas border with Missouri, John Reed still farmed the sheltered valley that had been farmed by his family for nine generations. For him it was the winter when the first arm of ice thrust over the flint ridge at the northern end of the valley.

For twenty years, half Reed's lifetime, the glaciers had been driven south by the relentless pressure of the ice behind.

At first they came down the easy descent of the Missouri River valley, starting at the Garrison Reservoir in North Dakota and, after grinding its massive dam into powder, pushed down through South Dakota, split Nebraska and Iowa more effectively than any flow of water, and then hesitated where the Missouri River valley turned east toward the greater ice flow that had replaced the Mississippi River. Now the rivers of ice had turned into sheets, engulfing the land from horizon to horizon and steadily surging south.

That was the winter, too, that Reed discovered the girl in the ice.

For several years after the riots in the cities were over but predatory bands were looting their way across the countryside, Reed had lived in a cave located in what once had been called "Hidden Valley," abandoning his home to the brigands who had made Kansas bleed as it had bled two centuries before. That was after his wife and children had been killed while he was transferring food to the cave. He had returned to find the men drunk in his living room. Quietly and efficiently, as he had done everything in his life, he killed them. He buried his wife and children in the old family cemetery on the hill, which had not been used since they opened the cemetery in town a century and a half before. He dug a common pit for the looters and shoveled dirt over their bodies for sanitary reasons.

For a while he had no contact with anybody; he had been numb, and by the time the numbness was gone the others were gone, too, from the town and from the other farms. Some of them had gone to where a little warmth still came from a spotless sun; others had been driven away by the looters, or killed. In the aftermath of his personal tragedy he had removed the rest of the food and the tools and the weapons and anything else that might be of use to anyone.

And the books. He still liked to read in the evening by the sheltered light of his antique Coleman lantern. He read the old words mostly: Browning and Tennyson and Frost. "These are the times for Frost," he would say to his wife, before her death, looking up and chuckling. And she would frown at him in mock reproval while they listened to the north wind whistling around the corners of the house and the snow piling up on the roof, making the rafters creak.

Eventually wounds stop bleeding. The looters stopped coming. The Great Plains, where there was nothing to stop the wind or the glaciers, got too cold for them, and there was nothing left to loot. They, too, went south, and died or survived in the melee there. After waiting two years—he, like the ice, had patience—Reed repaired the damage the looters had done and the weather had done after them; he rebuilt what they had burned and moved back into the house his great-great-grandfather had built, where generations of Reeds had lived while they farmed the land, and died and were buried.

He, too, farmed the land. It was difficult and it got steadily more difficult, but he planted spring wheat at the beginning of the short summer, when the glaciers did not so much retreat as paused for a few months as if to gain new strength, and he harvested, if he was lucky, before the snow started to fall again. He found and penned a few chickens in the barn. And he hunted—northern animals had been pushed south: caribou and moose, and also the wolves that preyed upon them and made short work of the domestic dogs that had turned wild.

When he wasn't farming or hunting or doing chores around the house, he sometimes went to the north ridge and looked toward the approaching ice. At first there was nothing, then a white haze in the distance that he could see only when the day was clear. Then as it got closer the haze turned bluer, in some instances almost indistinguishable from the sky, and he began to estimate how soon it would enter his valley.

It had come sooner than he expected, but he knew he would not be driven out. The looters had not done it and the ice would find him just as stubborn. He would stay there until the end, keeping what was his by right of inheritance, by right of the blood in his veins and the blood of Reeds spilled upon the ground, and by right of the sweat that had turned a wilderness into a human place. The wilderness might reclaim it, but not without a struggle.

There, looking at the ice looming where he had been accustomed to stand upon the flint ridge, he saw the girl for the first time. She was only a glimmer of color within the face of the ice. He thought it was an illusion, but he stepped closer to the blue mass, feeling it suck the warmth from his face and his hands, and brushed at the snow adhering to the surface of the ice. He saw more color and tried to peer deeper. Then it was too dark to see anything. Next morning he returned with an axe and a shovel and shaved away enough ice to see clearly.

Inside the ice, lying as if asleep, was a young woman, a girl. She had dark hair and a fair complexion, and she was dressed in a fur coat—muskrat, perhaps—and she had fur-lined boots on her feet. She was lying almost horizontal with her eyes closed and her face peaceful.

She was not beautiful, at least not at first, but Reed could not get over the wonder of her there in the ice.

The snow came down in the night in large, wet flakes. That was the first time he dreamed about Catherine. When he awoke he couldn't remember what she had said to him, only the urgency in her voice and the feeling that she wanted him to do something.

The snow fell all the next day and the next night—a meter or so in all—but the following day was bright and clear. The sunlight glinted off the mounds of snow like a knife to the eyes. Reed discovered in himself an unusual impatience, but he forced himself to rebuild the fires, restock the supply of firewood inside the house, and feed the chickens before he set off again for the face of the glacier.

This time he wore snowshoes that he had made himself and carried a broom. The glacier was twenty kilometers from the house, and he was out of breath by the time he got there. The last hundred meters he almost ran.

The glacier seemed closer. It had moved into the valley, well beyond the flint lip. He did not care about that, but it spoke of dynamic processes within the ice that threatened the vision he had seen there. For a few moments he leaned on the broom, reluctant to begin the work of unveiling that might reveal his vision as nothing but a dream inspired by loneliness, or worse, that the girl in the ice had been destroyed by the inexorable movement of the glacier.

He should measure the rate of progress, he told himself. If the glacier moved as fast as the ice had been advancing generally, it would approach his house by the end of winter, and the next winter its first advance would engulf it. But such considerations were only a means of delaying the moment of reality and were swept away as easily as the snow that covered the glacier face.

Once more he peered into the ice. She was there—just as before—and he felt a vast sense of relief. The uneven strains and pressures within the ice that made it crack and groan as he stood there, that made it surge forward at irregular intervals, had left the girl untouched.

He had not realized until now how much he had come to depend upon her existence, and how much, during the two nights and a day he had been imprisoned by the snow, he and his imagination, he had come to question the magic of her appearance. By what processes, natural or supernatural, had she got here? Standing in front of her on his snowshoes, with the north wind cold around his face and plucking at the folds of his coat, he looked at her lying peacefully within the ice, like someone who had just lain down for a moment's rest, and he wondered again.

Had she been caught in a blizzard far to the north? Had she wandered helplessly through its blinding fury until, at last, she had given up the hopeless struggle and lain down to wait for the end, huddled to retain her body's heat? And toward the end, had she felt the chill fade into a deceptive warmth so that her body relaxed and stretched out as it was now? Had the snow around her body compressed itself into ice, and had the ice carried her all the way to this spot, untouched by the terrible forces that pushed it forward, indifferent to all obstacles?

It was too astonishing to think about, but he kept returning to it again and again, constructing fancier and more fantastic scenarios to explain her presence almost at his doorstep. Finally he believed in it because it was real, and he came to accept it, as sinners accept God's grace. He even constructed philosophic justification for miracles. All unique events, he told himself, appear miraculous to those to whom, by chance, they happen. Mammoths and other creatures of an earlier ice age had been found in glaciers. Why not a person today? Once in a million years—if that was the frequency—was not so incredible.

For a while, then, chin on the handle of the broom, he was content just to look at her, to enjoy her company almost as if she were a living person come to relieve his solitude. Finally a grinding noise from the glacier and the loud crack of ice splitting stirred him from his contemplation.

"What shall I do with you?" he asked the frozen figure. "Shall I leave you here to the mercy of the glacier that brought you this far? Shall I carve you out and take you down with me into the valley? It's a long trip, but I could make a sledge—I'm handy with tools, you know—and I would tie you down securely so that you did not fall off. I could bury you up on the hill with Catherine and Billy and Josie, and all the other Reeds. They wouldn't mind."

But the ice was inexorable. It would grind its way across the hill as well as through the valley. It would grind the hill flat and with it all the bodies, corrupted and uncorrupted, lying there. Oddly, he did not mind that his family and his ancestors should be pulverized by this great, impersonal, natural phenomenon; everything would be turned to dust and returned to the soil eventually, and someday, if the ice ever retreated, a part of the land would be more fruitful because of it. But that this miraculous apparition should have come so far without damage only to be destroyed by his intervention seemed sacrilegious.

He could keep her near him to wait, like him, for the end, but that, too, seemed unfit, as if he were to capture the rainbow and keep it in a jar for his convenience. And, since he was a man who considered consequences, he thought of the brief summer when the ice would melt and his frozen miracle would thaw into clay like the mud in which she would lie.

No, he decided, it would be better to leave her where she was, to the forces that had brought her this far. He would return when he could to see if she was all right. At the moment of that decision he heard the ice shift and saw it plunge toward him by almost a meter. He staggered back, clumsy on his snowshoes, and then looked with sudden alarm toward the face of the ice. The girl was still there; she was still all right.

The incident stirred him to action, however, and he climbed the snowy hill beside the ice until he could see the blinding horizon where the unblemished sun had climbed two hands' breadths into the sky. Cool as it had turned, he could not look at it, nor in that direction. He would have to make some snow glasses, he thought. To the west, in places where the snow had been blown free of the ice beneath, he could see that the glaciers had advanced generally. He looked upon a scene of desolation, like the north pole, ice and snow as far as he could see; they had consumed everything in their path, leveling and then concealing what they had destroyed.

He should find a way to keep track, he thought: It would not do to be engulfed without warning. He wanted to meet the end, when it came, awake and aware of what was going on, and he wanted to know how long it would be. Landmarks still stood at the edge of the desolation—a hill in the distance with a tower on it, a tree still struggling to survive a few hundred meters from the frozen wasteland—but he would need a theodolite to measure angles and a way to mark the spot on which he stood. Until he could make something that would serve, he descended the hill, slipping only once, and paced off three snowshoe lengths and then three more from the glacier's face toward the valley and scratched a deep mark at each place on the brown flint rock that had been protected from the drifts.

He turned and looked once more at the girl in the ice, and turned toward the valley and home.

Reed returned the next morning. The sky was overcast and the clouds were heavy with snow, but he could not keep away. Nothing else demanded his attention; there was not much to do in the long winter except repairs, and he had done all of those. Even if he could have been out in the fields, he didn't think it was any use. Last summer nothing had grown; next summer the snow might never melt.

He walked up to the face of the glacier in his snowshoes, carrying a bundle of laths on his shoulder. He was surprised to discover that the advancing ice had obliterated his marks on the flint ridge; in fact, the ridge itself had disappeared under the glacier and the hill on which he had stood yesterday was distant and capped with the ice that filled the entrance to the valley at a level some meters above the hill.

The ice was like a living creature advancing upon him faster than he had imagined. But when he thought about it he realized that forty kilometers a year was an average of nearly one hundred fifty meters a day over the ten months the glaciers advanced. This arm of the glacier had moved at least that far in the past twenty-four hours.

He had given up the idea of the theodolite. After toying for a while with an old telescopic gun sight, he had realized that he soon would have difficulty climbing to that point of land, and he wasn't really interested in the general progress of the ice sheet, only the part that had begun to occupy his valley.

He was not surprised to find the girl in the ice untouched. At its base the glacier carried along rock debris that chewed up the soil and stone beneath, and the ice that held the rock flowed like slow water, but neither affected the girl. Reed was beginning to think of the girl as indestructible, as a gift carried into his life as compensation for the destruction of the past years and that yet to come. She was lying in the same position, as if she had been waiting for him.

"Ice is plastic under pressure, you know," he said to her. "It flows like a liquid, only very slowly." He thought about its progress in the past few days. "Maybe not so slowly." He stopped, a bit embarrassed by the sound of his voice in the wasteland, by the way it bounced back at him off the ice. Then he shrugged and leaned his bundle of sticks against the face of the glacier. He removed his snowshoes and put them down in the snow where he could sit on them, close to the girl but not so close that he would be struck by a sudden lurch of the ice.

"No one thought," he said, "that an ice age could develop so quickly. The scientists said that even if the conditions were right the ice sheets would take centuries to become a factor. 'The continental glaciers were not formed in a day,' they said. Of course they had no experience with glaciers except those left from an ice age that ended twelve thousand to thirty-eight thousand years ago. During an ice age, glaciers behave differently. It may have had something to do with what they celled 'catastrophe theory.' The glaciers over Greenland and the Antarctic moved a few inches a week, and even the valley glaciers of the Arctic, only several feet a day."

He leaned back and put his hands behind his head, making himself comfortable. He hadn't had anybody to talk to for several years. He had been alone too long, in silence too long. That did bad things to a man.

"Then came what the scientists called a 'snow blitz,' when the snow didn't melt in the northern latitudes all summer. Then came another. Each of them brought a hundred feet of snow or more. The glaciers spread down from the Arctic, and up from the Antarctic. They covered Canada within a decade. Scandinavia, too, we heard on television, and the northern half of Russia. Siberia went under even quicker. The Baltic Sea froze over and the North Sea. Scotland was covered with ice and parts of Germany and Poland. In the later stages we were getting reports only by radio, and then that stopped, too."

He glanced at the girl from time to time as if checking to see if she were listening. "What the scientists called 'the albedo effect' took over. Ice and snow reflected more sunlight; the more sunlight they reflected the less heat was retained by the earth. That made the summers even colder." He shifted his position so that he could look at the girl while he was talking. "Looking back upon it," he said, "I wonder if the new ice age didn't begin about the time I was born. Temperatures got steadily cooler for a couple of decades, and then the sunspots disappeared almost entirely. Radiation from the sun dropped by ten percent. Or so they said."

A snowflake hit Reed's face and melted, and then another. He looked up to see if it was blowing off the glacier, but it was coming from the sky. He could see the flakes, large, laden with moisture, slowly drifting down. Another storm was developing, but it would be several hours before the drifting flakes became a blizzard. He had become expert at predicting snowfall.

"I was ten, I guess, before the Arctic ice began surging down over Canada. No one believed in an ice age. Everyone thought the cold summers and colder winters were simply statistical aberrations, that temperatures would average out. 'All we need is one good hot summer,' the optimists said. Of course a few alarmists said that it was the beginning of an ice age. Boy! Were they surprised when they turned out to be right." He laughed.

"There were anomalies. Scandinavia had a warm spell that held back the ice for several years, but then it came with a rush. Finally scientific data began to accumulate: the absence of sunspots, the average decrease in temperature worldwide, the accumulations of snow and ice, the lowering of ocean levels. Theories were proposed and checked. Finally everybody agreed, cheerfully enough at the time: we were in for an ice age. It wouldn't be like the last one; we had civilization, we had science. We would dig more coal, create more heat, add more carbon dioxide to the atmosphere, start a greenhouse effect that would counteract the sun's betrayal. Science would find an answer."

The snow was getting heavier. Reed looked once more into the sky and knew he would have to get started home soon. "Some northern cities thought they could protect themselves with heat barriers; they would build more nuclear generators and let the waste heat keep the ice away. Others thought they could divert the ice with huge vertical knife-edged barriers made from old automobile bodies backed with rock and earth and cement. But the forces that could wear down mountains pushed them aside as if they were built of sand.

"Eventually the northern populations began trickling south, slowly at first. The Canadians were accepted in this country without question; the Swedes and the Norwegians met more opposition because the population was denser, but they finally were allowed into Denmark and then, as the ice pushed on, they and the DaNes were admitted into Belgium and the Netherlands, Germany, and even France and England. The Finns, though, were turned back at the Russian border; they, too, moved into western Europe. In most places everything was friendly; it was like temporarily out-of-work relatives moving in for a brief stay."

Reed got up and put on his snowshoes. "Science had no good answers, it turned out—not against the kind of forces gathering against humanity. Before the radio went off, I heard a few partial answers. Maybe a few individuals had answers like mine. I thought I could hide until things quieted down, but I waited too long. Now the ice that I thought might never reach here has come for me. You've come for me."

He looked at the girl again. "Did you say something?" Then he laughed. "Of course you didn't say anything." He picked up his bundle of sticks and paced off one hundred meters from the face of the glacier, pushed a stick into the snow, and then, as the world began to be obliterated by the universal whiteness, he headed back toward the farmhouse, inserting a stick into the snow every five meters until they ran out.

Next morning the snow still fell from the sky so thickly that Reed could not see the barn. By mid-day, however, it let up long enough for him to reach the face of the glacier to check his markers. Only the top thirty centimeters or so stuck above the snow, and only a few of them remained. He estimated that the glacier had advanced another one hundred sixty meters. If that rate continued, the ice would reach his house before it slowed and stopped during the brief summer. He couldn't clear away enough of the snow before the blizzard enclosed him again to see if the girl was still there in the ice, still all right, but he was sure she was. He had come to count on her.

The snowstorm lasted for almost a week. He had to climb out a second-story window to shovel snow off the roof before it caved in from the accumulating weight, and he had to tunnel through the snow, now five meters deep, to reach the barn. He had rigged a wood stove there to keep the chickens from freezing, and it, like the chickens, had to be fed. Fortunately, the temperature was relatively warm; the gulf air bringing the moisture up from the coast always kept the temperature from falling more than a dozen degrees below freezing.

He was profligate with firewood now. This would be his last winter, he knew, and what he did not use up the ice would take. If necessary he could move the remaining chickens into the farmhouse cellar and use the barn for firewood. For him there would be no more farming, no more hunting, no more caring for animals and fowl; all that was left was dying.

Sometimes during the long nights he dreamed of Catherine again. She asked him why he stayed in the land of death, why he did not go south where there was life and hope, no matter how difficult. He answered, "Why, Catherine, I can't leave you and the children," for in his dream they still were alive but for some reason could not go with him. She chided him then for the sin of self-destruction; she always had had an unshakable faith in God, even when the winters grew long and bitter, perhaps even when she was being abused by the brigands after they had killed her children. He did not share her faith, but he never mocked it either. "I'm only staying where I belong," he replied. "If God wants to save me, he can spare this valley or stop the ice from covering the world."

Sometimes little Billy would be with Catherine, clinging to her hand. "But, Daddy," he said, "if you're waiting for God to take you or spare you, why do you keep up the house and the barn and the tools and everything?" And he said, because children needed to know these things, "That's what a man does, Billy."

Josie never appeared in his dream. He thought that was his punishment for loving her best.

On the sixth day the sun finally came up. It was a wintry sun, pale and chilly, and the temperature had dropped during the night. His thermometer read only to minus thirty degrees Celsius, and he knew it was colder than that. He was not surprised: he was living in the Arctic; it had come down to engulf him.

As soon as he had stoked the fires and fed the chickens, he

set off for the glacier. It was difficult travel, even on snowshoes. The last layer of snow had turned to powder as the temperature dropped, and when he fell his arms and shoulders, sometimes his head as well, would go deep into the drifts, and he had difficulty regaining his feet. Sometimes he had to dig himself out with the shovel he had brought with him to dig his way down to the girl. The snow had covered everything; the hills were impossible to distinguish from the drifts. If he had not known the valley and had the sun to guide him, he might have become lost in this silent, glittering wasteland, where nothing moved, nothing lived.

The wind was almost still, but even his slow passage through it brought the cold biting through his skin until he pulled a cloth mask over his face and the snow glasses he had made over that. He wished he had learned to ski, but it was too late for that.

By the time he reached the spot where he thought the glacier should have been, it was almost mid-day. He looked around at the mounded snow, trying to distinguish a casual drift from an indication of a feature beneath. But there was no clue to the location of the glacier. For a moment his heart felt as cold as the wasteland around him, and then he realized that all it took to find the face of the glacier was work.

He dug down through the snow—some five or six meters in places—until he reached ice. The lowest, compacted levels of snow were almost ice already; that was the way the glaciers grew. He dug down half a dozen times, each time five meters farther south, and he was getting tired, a little desperate, and a bit faint with the cold and the effort when he found the excavation going deeper than five meters, deeper than six meters, and he moved a little north and found the face of the ice.

The glacier was at least a kilometer from the place where he judged the entrance of the valley to be. He shoveled his way down the face, leaving plenty of room for the ice to move if it chose to do so, and cutting steps in the snow as he went. It was hard work on top of everything that had gone before, and his ears were ringing from the effort by the time he reached the bottom. There, however, like the Holy Grail, the figure of the girl waited for him.

He sat down to rest and leaned back against the snow, feeling the sweat freezing in his clothes even though he was protected here; he knew he should not stay here long if he wanted to get back to the farmhouse. He was very tired; it was not certain he could get back; he was not sure he wanted to. He was comfortable here, almost as if he and the girl were alone in a darkened room lit only by the reflection of the sun from the snow at the top of the excavation. In the relative darkness, the face of the girl was not as clear, almost as if she were receding from him. But he remembered what she looked like. He was comfortable with her now, and he thought she was the most beautiful woman he had ever seen.

He knew that this might be the last time he would see her, one way or another; even if he gathered the strength and the will to return to the farmhouse, the next snow might obliterate the glacier beyond the reach of anyone's efforts. For now, though, it was just the two of them, together, in the icy room. He had someone he could talk to about the events that had happened to him and to the world.

"It's been a while," he said after his breathing had slowed. But he was still light-headed. "I told you about the neighborliness of people at first. It didn't last." The snows and the glaciers kept descending. Food became scarce as growing seasons got short and undependable. The panic began. The steady trickle of movement south became a river and then a flood. "When conditions got bad, nobody wanted the refugees." Fences were thrown up. Armed guards turned back those fleeing the cold. If they tried to sneak through, or rushed the barricades, they were shot down. Some got through—there were troops and arms north of the fences—and fanned out across the countryside.

"Walled cities returned," he said. "Citizens guarded them by day and night, frantic to keep what was theirs, never thinking that they, too, might have to head south in their turn. Some governments fell apart. Soldiers and police formed their own protection businesses. Others began to band together for their own protection and to preserve their stocks of food and weapons."

—Why didn't you go south?

"I couldn't see killing my fellow humans to make a place for myself and my family," he said. It would have come to that. On a larger scale it came to that: the Russians took over the Middle East, but when it tried to move into Africa, U.S., British, French, and German troops fought the Russian armies, not so much to protect the African countries as their own warm-weather rights. The Russians withdrew when the Chinese attacked along their common border. Eventually Russia collapsed, and what was left of the Chinese soldiers battled back through China and into Indo-China followed by hundreds of millions of Chinese, most of whom soon starved.

"Here in this country, most attention was on the invasion of Mexico. By the time organization and communication broke down, parts of some groups had battled their way as far south as Brazil." The Japanese took over the Philippines and fought the British for Indonesia. Australia moved into New Guinea and Micronesia. The population of India slowly drifted south, dropping along the way from starvation and disease. The remainder huddled in the southern provinces while their leaders conquered Sri Lanka.

"Here and there pockets of sanity remained. Scientists

and engineers kept a few northern cities free of ice for a few years by sprinkling powdered coal on the snow to encourage melting, sometimes buying enough time for the population to move underground." Pennsylvania and West Virginia coal mines provided natural spaces for underground living; all they needed was tools, food, furnaces, hydroponic gardens, and air-handling equipment. In Montana and Wyoming they could dig caves in the rock near supplies of coal, or take nuclear reactors underground. "But who knows what they will be like when they come out—if they ever come out, if the ice ever retreats."

—Humanity must survive!

"Sometimes I wonder why," he said. The same things must have been happening in the southern hemisphere, but except for Australia and South Africa, the news had been almost non-existent. It was reported that the Antarctic icecap floated out over the ocean and occasionally broke off in big icebergs that littered the sea. They must finally have frozen together. "North and south, civilization collapsed in the space of thirty years."

—There's still time to leave.

By now he had lost track of what was thought and what was spoken. Here in this cold, white room, reality was shattering around him like frozen light. "I've lost whatever reason I had to live," he said. "I won't join the savages scrambling to survive on any terms. Most of them are doomed to death by starvation, disease, or violence."

—It doesn't have to be that way. Conditions are better now. Order is beginning to emerge. They need your skills. They need your courage and determination. You can stay alive; you can help others stay alive.

Death, he thought, was not black, but white. It came glittering and shining and cold. "I'd rather stay here with you," he said. He held up his shovel. "I could carve out a place for myself beside you, and we could share eternity together, frozen side by side, going south in style."

He imagined how it would be as the snow filtered in around him and he reached out for her through the ice, the warmth of his hand melting its way to her until he held her frozen hand in his. Then he would be satisfied.

—No! I am dead, but you are alive.

Just for a little while, he thought.

—It is the business of the living to stay alive. Humanity has been in difficulties before. People haven't given up. If they had given up as easily as you, humanity never would have got out of the jungles.

No! he tried to say. My roots are here. My ancestors bought this place for me with their labor and their dying. This is where I belong.

—You've got feet. Use them! Go south! Survive! Wait until the glaciers retreat, whether it's a hundred years or ten thousand! Don't forget! Come back to a world scoured clean, ready to be built on again! Come back then and make it a better world! You can if you don't forget! If you struggle! If you survive!

He had closed his eyes against the brightness, but now he opened them. Afterward he knew she hadn't spoken. The voice had come from inside him. It was the same voice he had heard when Catherine spoke to him in his dreams. It was the voice of his ancestors going back through the eons of struggle to stay alive against fire and ice, drought and flood, plague and hunger and all the other animals that were stronger and swifter and more deadly. It was the ancient voice of humanity demanding struggle, demanding survival.

He said goodbye to the girl in the ice and climbed from the pit he had dug and began his long journey home.

* * * * *

The next day he began work on the sledge. When it was finished he loaded it with tools and weapons and provisions, and finally his books. He made one last trip, not to the glacier but to the hill where his family was buried. By some kind chance it had been swept clear of snow. When he returned he started south. He did not look back.

Among the Beautiful Bright Children

The beautiful bright children spilled into the room like a handful of golden coins.

How long had it been since anyone had held a golden coin? Laurence wondered. How long had it been since anyone had thought of a golden coin? Perhaps only a historian would remember what it was.

He sat in his study, interrupted at his work, not caring, smiling benignly at the young men and women as they streamed out of the lift shaft and filled the sterile room with life and laughter.

Golden coins spilling from the hand, turning as they fall, glinting in the light. . . .

They seemed like actors, an Elizabethan company capering through Stratford shouting "Players!" or a commedia dell'arte troupe appropriating an Italian square.

The forgotten console clicked, and a new display appeared upon its screen.

Oh, happy people of the future who have not known these horrors and will, perhaps, class our testimonies with fables. We have, perhaps, deserved these punishments—but so did our forefathers. May posterity not merit the same.

One of the young men began to sing. The song was one of

those contemporary melodies haunted by echoes of the past, but it was not the song or the words that brought tears to Laurence's eyes but the clear tenor itself. Beautiful, beautiful—like one of the legendary castrati.

Others took up the song, here and there, toying with it as if it were a colorful balloon—a red one, perhaps; yes, red would look right in the all-white room—tossing it here and there and then holding it up, steady, with their mingled voices and the intensity of their desires. And all the while they went about their games: in groups of twos or threes they danced or courted or walked about admiring the room as if it were a work of art, and it was all one whether they danced or walked. They moved with the grace of ballet dancers and the innocence of children.

Ching-a-ching go the golden coins. *Ching-a-ching* rings the music clear. . . .

Not really children, Laurence thought, more like courtiers playing an elaborate game of manners without a thought of tomorrow, without a thought of the rest of the world, as if here and now were all the world. The boys were muscular and masculine, and the girls were rounded and feminine, but they all had an air of unstudied directness, like children, without lurking reservations or sullen needs. . . .

One by one they wandered past his study to run their marveling fingers over the console's plastic top, to lean past the console and touch his hand or his shoulder, to murmur a word to him.

"Honor."

"Pleasure."

"Sweet."

"Adorable."

"Keep working."

"We love you."

One of the blooming girls touched his cheek with her lips. She was slim and blue-eyed and beautiful. He had not been this close to anyone since his wife died, and he felt their human warmth as they passed and smelled the spice of their bodies, driving away the old stale odors that he never smelled anymore, the odors that the room could never quite exhaust.

Click.

When has any such thing ever been heard of or seen? In what histories has it been read that houses were left vacant, cities deserted, the country neglected, and a fearful and universal solitude over the whole earth? Will posterity ever believe these things when we, who have seen them, can hardly credit them?

Some of them made love like children, innocent and free, with no one to tell them shame, wherever they happened to be, or on the round bed that rose, at the touch of a button, like a white altar from the center of the floor.

"They wanted to meet you," one of them said. She was standing beside the console in her brief suit, shining in his eyes until he had to blink. "Father," she had added. "Father." But he couldn't be her father. It was only yesterday, wasn't it, that he had taken a little girl to a crèche when her mother died? A few months? A few years? He had seen her, of course, looking in upon her through the console's screen, visiting her remotely in her happiness, soft and gentle, and she had been pleased that she could see him in return and speak to him, and each time she was larger. But now—had it been so long?

He rose and embraced her. She wound her golden arms around his neck and held him against her yielding body and kissed him, and Laurence felt old.

Hold the coins tight in a sweaty hand, the knuckles white over the bone, the coins biting into the fingers.

"Particularly Virginia," his daughter said as she released

him at last, laughing, pleased. Geraldine? No, of course not. Genevieve. Jenny. "I bring you Virginia."

Behind Jenny was another golden girl, slighter, quieter, but just as beautiful. Perhaps—if it was not unfatherly to think so—even lovelier, with short dark hair and eyes as big as sunflowers that looked at him as if they two were all alone in the room. The pupils of her eyes were black mirrors in which he could see himself reflected, doubled, enhanced.

"Women have served all these centuries," Laurence said softly, "as looking glasses, possessing the magic and delicious power of reflecting the figure of man at twice its natural size."

"You are witty," Virginia said. Laurence was pleased with her voice. It was soft and low, like the breath of a lover upon the ear.

His knees felt weak. He sat down again and ran his hands over the white plastic of the chair in which he spent most of his waking hours, feeling it moist and slick under his palms. "That wasn't original with me," he said. "A woman wrote that long ago. An author. Another Virginia."

"You know so much," Virginia said.

"You are famous, Father," Jenny said happily. "You do not know how famous. Everybody knows your name. The author of this, the author of that. Your work is read by the dreamers, and we live their dreams. Your reality, Father."

"I don't understand," Laurence said. He could not stop looking at Virginia, and at the eyes that looked at him.

"Not many historians are left," Jenny said. "Without historians where would we be? And you're the greatest of them."

"I seem to recall a phrase like 'history is irrelevant.' "

"That was cycles ago, Father. Now we know better. Without historians the past would be forgotten, and our way of life would be limited. Also, a recent cap of a historian was popular a few cycles ago. Anyway, everybody wanted to meet you."

"An old man like me?" They made him feel old, Jenny, Virginia, and the rest, full of eager health and blossoming energy, their skins packed to bursting with self.

Click.

Imperfect as ancient history is, in regard to the accounts of diseases, and the extraordinary phenomena of nature, we find that between the years B.C. 480 and the Christian era, a number of violent plagues occurred, most of which coincided in time with the following phenomena, comets, eruptions of volcanoes, earthquakes, drouth, severe winters, diseases among cattle. . . .

"You're not old," Virginia said. "Just older."

"Virginia has this thing about older men," Jenny said wickedly, but her wickedness was like the face of a child determined to be stern but unable to keep the natural good humor from breaking through in smiles.

"About real people," Virginia corrected. "It only happens that most of them are older." The way she said "older" made it seem like an uncommon virtue. And all the while she spoke, she did not take her eyes from his face, as if she wished to memorize it and keep it with her always.

And then—moments later or hours?—Jenny was gone and the others were gone and the room was empty of all but Laurence and Virginia. She had talked—no, he had talked and she had listened, leading him on with a shy question when he paused, a discreet exclamation when he said something that pleased her.

It was he who had unfolded—or been unfolded with delicate golden hands—like a Chinese puzzle box, each box smaller and better hidden than the one before, until he lay all exposed before her sunflower eyes that seemed all black pupil, and she clapped her hands in delight and laughed.

"You're wonderful," she said.

Stack the coins, one upon another, carefully, so that the tower does not topple. . . .

He told her about his childhood. "Children were different then," he said, but he didn't really know that. He thought they were different, but he hadn't known many other children when he was a child, and he didn't know any now. "We had books."

"Books!" she said as if they were the most marvelous objects.

"Histories, biographies, novels. . . ."

"Imagine!" she said. "Reading!" Reading, too, was a miracle.

He told her how the people in the books had become real to him, more real than people.

"I know," she said, as if she really knew.

He told her how their world—the world of the self-sufficient urban centers—had developed naturally out of early experiments with chemical memory. How chemical memory had been perfected until people no longer needed to learn things from books or how to do things from other people: They simply injected themselves with knowledge. Computers, too, were improved, and the computers created better machines; society became more productive, more efficient; the urban centers were built; and people were liberated from toil, freed to do whatever they wanted. Some pursued the pleasure of sensation, and some, like himself, sought out knowledge that had not yet been reduced to proteins. For him it was knowledge of the past.

He told her how he had thought about the past until it seemed like a living tapestry interwoven with the color of people's lives, breathing the incense of their desires. He told her how he had come of age more curious about the past than the present until he met the woman who was to become his wife and the mother of Genevieve.

"How beautiful," she said.

His wife had been older and more worldly.

Virginia approved of that.

They had met at the home of her parents when they first moved to the building in which his parents lived. She had made the decisions—that they would be married, where they would live in the building, that he would be a scholar and write, that they would have one child. She had taken care of all the practical concerns of life.

"She must have been a wonderful woman," Virginia said.

"She was," he agreed. "Lovely, too, with pale blue eyes and fair skin and long brown hair. Her name was Susan, and I loved her. And yet—"

"Yes?" Virginia said.

"Nothing."

"Tell me," she pleaded.

"Oh, sometimes I wonder if my life would have turned out the same. I've missed so much, you see."

"Oh, no!" she said quickly. "You're real, and you have made things real for other people. But Susan died."

"Yes. It was a silly thing. She didn't have to go out at all. We were happy here. We could have lived here forever and never gone anywhere. But she got bored and went out."

"Outside the building?"

"Yes. It was a strange thing to do, and she was not that kind of person at all. I never understood it."

Click.

Mezeray relates that in China, the disease originated from a vapor, which burst from the earth, was horribly offensive and consumed the face of the country through an extent of 200 leagues. This account may be inaccurate, but is not to be wholly rejected.

That some action of subterranean heat was instrumental in generating the disease is very probable; or at least that some phenomena of fire accompanied it, because this supposition is consonant to the whole series of modern observations.

After that, he told her, he had taken Jenny to the crèche.

"The best place," she said. "Most of us were raised there."

And he had blinked, and he was middle-aged. Jenny was grown and the world had passed him by, and he did not know where life had gone.

"Our world is not so wonderful," she said.

What is not wonderful about bright gold and its music? Add one more to the stack. One more.

"Without the caps we'd be nothing," she said.

Nothing? This child, this girl, this creature of joy?

"And it is you who make the men who make the caps."

He felt tears welling in his eyes and blinked them back. When he could see again, she was standing beside him, leaning toward him until he felt the radiant warmth of her body caressing his face and the sweet smell of her filled his head with fantasies. Her lips touched his cheek like a bubble bursting. And before he could think or move, she was gone.

The tower toppled *ching-a-ching,* the coins rolling in different directions, ending in corners and other hidden places. Impossible to catch, impossible to find, impossible to put back together.

The beautiful bright children spilled into the room like quicksilver. The shimmering stream broke into glistening beads, coruscating in the light like prisms, eternally moving, changing. . . .

A week had passed since the children had first come to him. Laurence knew it was a week because he had marked off the days, like a prisoner scratching with a nail upon his prison wall.

What would they think of that, the children who knew nothing of prisoners and nails? There was so much, he realized, he did not know about them and the world they lived in, but there was as much or more that they did not know about him and the world they all had come from.

It was ironic, he thought, that a lifetime had passed while he was not looking and a week had struggled by so painfully. But now it was over, and he searched the glitter for a face he knew, a face with eyes as big as sunflowers.

Then he saw her, and he felt suddenly young and giddy. It was a ridiculous feeling, and he did not understand it, but he knew that he was happy, even though Virginia did not come to him, even though she dallied with a young man dressed in black, moving quickly around him, coming close to him and retreating in one fluid movement, speaking quickly, breathlessly, her eyes not black mirrors (did she save that for Laurence?) but surging pools flashing with light. . . .

She looked so different, Laurence thought. No wonder he could not pick her out at once.

Click.

The symptoms of this fatal malady were violent affection in the head and stomach, buboes and other glandular swellings; small swellings like pimples or blisters; usually a fever, and a vomiting or spitting of blood. The swellings in the glands were infallible signs of the disease; but the most fatal symptom was, the pimples or blisters spread over the whole body. Hemorrhages from the mouth, nose, and other parts, indicated a universal and sudden disorganisation of the blood. The patient usually died in three days or less—which denotes the virulence of the poison, or rather the activity of the disease, which destroyed the powers of life in half the time, which the bilious plague usually employs.

Laurence watched the flow of life through the room and was content. No one came to him as they had come before. It was as if a pageant was being continued before his eyes, a pageant that had started somewhere else and would go on in still another place when it had left his room. Momentarily it paused here to gleam in this white room, silver on white.

The beads flowed together into larger beads and split apart, clinging until the final separation, into smaller beads again, whole and complete in themselves.

Everything happened so swiftly that he could not understand it, but clearly the flow of the young people had a pattern. He tried to understand what was going on, tried to make sense of it, but it was too complex for him. He sighed. He was content that the room was full of life again, as if the world had opened a casual hand and let its protean stuff surge in around him. He filled his eyes with movement and his ears with the sound of their mercurial voices and his nostrils with the perfume of their bodies.

"Father," someone said. Laurence looked up hopefully, but it was, of course, his daughter Jenny. "Someone else wanted to meet you," she said in a silvery voice. "I bring you Samuel. Samuel is a dreamer, and he dreams the most exquisite adventures."

Beside Jenny was the young man dressed in black, the young man around whom Virginia had danced her courtship. Now that he was near, Laurence could see that he was not so young but more an old-young man. He was thin, and he had a pale, drawn face and eyes that were weary and dark, and looked, sometimes, as if they were turned inward toward some interior vision of hell or heaven.

"I thought you would never return," Laurence said to Jenny.

"You know, Father," Jenny said, fidgeting on one foot as if

staying in one place were painful. "Historians went out. Since then we have had musicians and painters and scientists and sculptors and composers and—oh, I forget them all. But now it is dreamers, and Samuel, Father, is the most precious dreamer." Then she was gone.

Click.

The peripneumony which was epidemic about the same time, appeared in a burning fever, insatiable thirst, a black tongue, anxiety and pains about the heart, short breath, a cough, with expectoration of a mixed matter, open mouth, raging delirium, fury, red, turbid or black urine, restlessness, and watchings, black eruptions, anthraces, buboes, and in some, corroding ulcers over the whole body. The disease usually terminated the 4th day, sometimes not till the 7th. The blood was black and thick; but sometimes greenish and watery or yellowish. Venesection was certain death. The disease baffled medical skill—the only remedies that appeared to relieve, were laxatives early administered, cupping and scarification, leeches applied to the hemorrhoids, and inwardly, infusions of mild, diaphoretic, attenuating, pectoral vegetables.

"I did want to meet you," Samuel said in a slow, soft voice that contrasted with Jenny's volatility. "You have given me some of my most effective dreams—your Nero was magnificent, with all the intrigues and orgies and murders and persecutions and torture, and your Masada was almost as evocative, though of a different sort, of course."

Laurence looked at him. "I do not understand."

"You are my favorite historian," Samuel said simply, turning out his hands as if to reveal their stigmata. "You must be very deep, full of exquisite passions, to make it all so real."

"I don't understand what you do," Laurence said.

"I dream. That is all. I let your words—or someone else's words—I must move with the fashions in dreams, after all—

flow over me like lava, engulfing me, consuming me—music plays—incense drifts through the air—my bed embraces me—sometimes I pop a little—not much, you understand, or what I dream would be someone else's dream, and what I produce would be secondhand, so to speak—just enough to get the juices flowing. But the most important part of the whole process is the material, and that you provide. We are sort of partners, you and I; you perform your research; you create a world and people it; and I produce the dream."

"You dream," Laurence repeated.

A dark eyebrow lifted on Samuel's pale forehead. "You are an innocent, aren't you? Jenny said you were out-of-it, and I didn't believe her. You don't pop and you don't dream."

"I dream," Laurence said. Dreams slithered through his nights like serpents or crept like snails, leaving their slimy trails across his waking memory.

"They dream," Samuel said, waving a casual hand at the quicksilver children shining behind him, never stopping long enough to assume a fixed shape. "You live. You're real."

"That's what Virginia said."

Try to hold quicksilver and it slips away, slides into other forms, breaks into tiny fragments, forms itself into heavy little balloons flattened on one side, unable to fly; try to close your fingers around it and it is not there.

Laurence tried to identify Virginia again and found her at last. She was involved in a kind of flickering, intricate pattern of movement with a young man, like a kind of feathered courtship performed to an unheard arabesque.

"I have a talent," Samuel said. "I dream. I dream so vividly that my dreams are like memory, my memory like knowledge. And while I am dreaming, the little needles come and drink my blood, and then the laboratories analyze the proteins—the peptides, to be precise—and synthesize them, just as the brain does, and put them into little capsules, and the poppets pop it, you see? And then they live my dreams."

Click.

This plague was so deadly that at least half or two-thirds of the human race perished in about 8 years. It was most fatal in cities, but in no place died less than a third of the inhabitants. In many cities perished nine out of ten of the people, and many places were wholly depopulated. In London 50,000 dead bodies were buried in one graveyard. In Norwich died about the same number. In Venice died 100,000—in Lubec, 90,000—in Florence the same number. In the east perished twenty millions in one year. In Spain, the disease raged three years and carried off two-thirds of the people. Alfonso 2d. died with it while besieging Gibraltar.

"They feel my emotions, my fears, my anxieties, my hopes. Or someone else's—whoever happens to be popular that cycle."

"What are they dreaming now?" Laurence asked huskily, feeling his mouth and throat all dry. He put his hand on the slick console top. That, at least, was solid and real.

"The latest thing is some composer. They're in the allegro phase right now. See how briskly they move? They hear music—heavenly music, I understand. I wouldn't know. I don't pop—well, hardly at all, you know. Honestly, it's because I prefer my own dreams to someone else's, and I do enjoy the status. We're alike, we two. Real people. We keep the world spinning for the poppets."

"Are they always like this?"

"Oh, no," Samuel said. "The largo really drags. And sometimes there are darker caps, grimmer dreams. . . . Oh, I must go. They're leaving. It must be time for another cycle to begin, and I don't want to miss it. This is my hour, you see. Dreamers are in, and I should enjoy it while I can. I may add to my psychic energy, my dream stuff, so to speak."

And then they disappeared, as if a time sequence had been reversed, and all the scattered silver beads drew back together into a liquid silver stream that poured back down the drop shaft and was gone. . . .

The beautiful bright children poured into the room like honey, honey-slow and honey-sweet.

They were all languid grace and weary courtesy. They moved like dreamers, enraptured by events beyond their control.

Virginia came directly to Laurence, walking as if all the delicate bones in her delightful body were cushioned in oil.

Click.

Along the trade routes between China and Europe the Plague traveled. In 1346 it was passed on to a warrior horde, a band of Kipchaks who were besieging a Genoese trading post in the Crimea. Their own death was certain, but the Kipchak leader ordered that the plague-infected corpses be catapulted into the town, where the Plague immediately broke out.

Ten days had passed. Laurence had tried to work. He had studied the original documents, trying to get a feeling for the era, trying to get inside the doomed people, and he had even dictated a few paragraphs, but they were worthless. The past no longer seemed as important. The present pressed in upon him, and the possibilities that awaited him in the uncertain future tormented his waking moments and disturbed his sleep. Perhaps he was innocent, but he was not a fool. He recalled all the old men in history and their infatuations with young girls, and he told himself how foolish they had been—and how foolish he was—and how it always ended badly.

He was not worldly-wise, but he knew something about people from his studies and he knew something about himself from the experience of projecting himself into the historical characters about whom he wrote. In his way, he told himself, he had lived a thousand lives already, more than any of these children, with their capsule fictions, whatever they were, could imagine.

He knew, then, that his fantasies were foolish, but he could not put them away.

Sugar in the gourd and honey in the horn, I never was so happy since the hour I was born.

And Virginia said to him in her slow, sweet voice, "I have come back."

"Yes," Laurence said.

"I want you to talk to me again," she said.

"I will do anything you say," he said.

She sat at his feet while the rest of the children moved around them as if in an underwater ballet, and he spoke to her, at first hesitantly about generalities, and then as she listened attentively, her sunflower eyes focused on his face, he talked more swiftly, more confidently, almost as if he were dictating to the console. Only this console was a living creature, lovely and receptive.

He spoke to her about savages and civilizations, about wheels and wanderings, about monuments and minarets, about warriors and weapons, about serfs and soldiers, about farmers and farthings, about priests and prisoners, about philosophers and philanthropists, about forests and fortresses, about barristers and barbarians, about commerce and continents, about tigers and tarantulas, about alchemists and alloys, about scientists and sacrifices, about empires and emperors, about intrigue and incest . . . about the vast movements of peoples, about changes in the earth, about the operation of chance or fate that put here a great idea, there a great discovery, and there a man or woman of iron will or whim, and things happened for good or ill and usually both.

But most of all he spoke about love and lovers, about kings and queens, about princes and princesses. . . .

Click.

At the beginning of October, in the year of the Incarnation of the Son of God 1347, twelve Genoese galleys were fleeing from the vengeance which the Lord was taking on account of their nefarious deeds and entered the harbor of Messina in Sicily. In their bones they bore so virulent a disease that anyone who even spoke to them was seized by a mortal illness and in no manner could avoid death. When the citizens of Messina discovered that this sudden death came from the Genoese ships they hurriedly expelled them from the town and the harbor. But the evil remained in the town and caused a fearful outbreak of death.

While he was speaking, Virginia took his foot into her soft lap and stroked it. His voice shook then, and something in his chest trembled.

When his words slowed and he looked up, the others were gone. They were alone, he and Virginia, and she came slowly, liquidly, to her feet and said, "Come."

She took his hand and led him to the altar-bed and unbelted his robe and pushed it from his shoulders. He let it slide down his body to the floor, feeling his senses come alive to her. Slowly, languorously, she drew him down to her, and she was sweet, honey-sweet, until he thought that he would drown.

He awoke, his body still languid and slow with its memories, the taste of honey sweet upon his tongue, and she was gone.

Panic paralyzed him. The honey turned sour in his mouth. His throat tightened. A chilly hand squeezed his stomach.

He sat up and searched the room with his eyes. There was no place for her to hide. The only pieces of furniture in the room were the console and the bed. The lavatory door was open, and he could see from here that it was empty. The kitchenette, with its autochef, its little round table and chairs, was empty too.

And he was empty.

What he had known the past twelve hours had been a dream, as fleeting and as impermanent.

He was alone. Now it was different. Now he knew he was alone.

Slowly he gathered himself together. Slowly he moved toward the lavatory. Slowly he showered. Slowly he took a new robe from the dispenser in the lavatory wall. Slowly he put it on. And felt someone watching him. He swung quickly toward the door.

Virginia was standing in the doorway, her eyes like polished volcanic glass.

He knew happiness again.

Joy was a lump of tears in his throat.

He could not speak. He held out his arms, and she came into them like a child.

Click.

I say, then, that the years of the fruitful Incarnation of the Son of God had attained to the number of one thousand three hundred and forty-eight, when into the notable city of Florence, fair over every other of Italy, there came the death-dealing pestilence, which, through the operation of the heavenly bodies or of our own iniquitous dealings, being sent down upon mankind for our correction by the just wrath of God, had some years before appeared in parts of the East and after having bereft these latter of an innumerable number of inhabitants, extending without cease from one place to another, had now unhappily spread towards the West.

A bit later he noticed the small case she held.

"With all my worldly goods—" she said. "You're wonderful in your way, Laurence, but you're a bit out-of-it, you know. You have no cap catalog, no dispenser, no injector niche. We'll have to fix that if I stay."

"If you stay . . ." he repeated.

She smiled at him, and he remembered sweetness. "Not to worry, Laurence. I'll stay. For now. But I had to get my hand injector and my favorite caps. It took some thinking, too, I can tell you, to weed them down to those I could carry. If I need the latest, I'll just have to go out."

He was filled with unreasoning fear. "I never want you to go out."

"Not out of the building, silly," she said, putting both hands flat upon his chest. "You do fret! But I like that."

"When will we be married?" he asked.

"You mustn't get notions," she said quickly. "That's not our way. Things change too fast. Enjoy. Enjoy. Happiness is now. Don't make it a prisoner."

Laurence shook his head, trying not to be concerned, realizing that he was irritating her with his importuning, conscious that he might lose her. He held a butterfly in his hands and he could not hold it too tightly: it might break its wings or, when he relaxed for a moment, it would fly away. But he could not help himself. "And I don't want you to take any more capsules."

She patted his cheek and then reached up to kiss him. "But that's what you like, Laurence," she said as she leaned back. "And you'll like it even more. When I'm Helen, Cleopatra, or Poppaea, Isolde or Héloïse, Madame Pompadour or Mata Hari, and a dozen other women who have no names in history but are just as entrancing. . . ."

"What do you know of those women?" he asked.

"I know what they did and how they felt. . . ."

"You know what some dreamer thought they did and how they felt."

"But they're very good, the dreamers," Virginia said. "Besides, what do you know of those women?" She smiled.

Click.

In men and women alike there appeared at the beginning of the malady, certain swellings, either on the groin or under the armpits, whereof some waxed of the bigness of a common apple, others like unto an egg, some more and some less, and these the vulgar named plague-boils. From these two parts the aforesaid death-bearing plague-boils proceeded, in brief space, to appear and come indifferently in every part of the body; wherefrom, after awhile, the fashion of the contagion began to change into black or livid blotches, which showed themselves in many first on the arms and about the thighs and after spread to every other part of the person, in some large and sparse and in others small and thick-sown; and like as the plague-boils had been first (and yet were) a very certain token of coming death, even so were these for every one to whom they came. . . .

She came to him as Helen and silenced his apprehensions with her consciousness of beauty that shone through her face and body like sunlight through alabaster.

She came to him as Cleopatra and the millennia-old incestuous royal blood heated her tutored body to an intensity that burned his flesh.

She came to him as Poppaea, and her corruption coiled around him like a leperous white snake.

She came to him as Isolde, and her guilt made their lovemaking a frantic coupling upon the slopes of smoking Mount Vesuvius.

She came to him as Héloïse, and her sin turned her to unresponsive ice that melted suddenly into boiling urgency and tears.

She came to him as Madame Pompadour, and her consciousness of courtly intrigue gave every word a dozen meanings, every act a myriad of purposes.

She came to him as Mata Hari, and her duplicity drove her to lay siege to his senses.

She came to him as a ballet dancer . . .

A pubescent girl . . .

A whore . . .

A desperate virgin . . .

A reluctant bride . . .

An Amazon . . .

A slave . . .

She came to him as all women. Each one enraptured him, whipped him into new intensities of passion, and sickened him, for what he wanted beyond desire was the honey-sweet girl he had known first, the girl he thought of as the real Virginia. But the honey was gone, and what she gave him in its place was biting and sometimes bitter.

One morning he awoke with the consciousness that he was alone. He lay dully on the bed wondering where Virginia had gone. Finally he roused himself and looked around the room. She was gone, and he felt a moment of relief. Perhaps, he thought, she had gone to renew her supply of capsules. But he knew that he was telling himself fantasies. He sensed that she was gone for good, and relief turned into an old sickness that climbed from his loins into his chest.

Slowly he moved to the console and discovered that a week had passed. Virginia had stayed with him for a week.

A week. He had learned more in a week than he had learned from a lifetime of studying books and old manuscripts.

Click.

Some were of a more barbarous way of thinking, avouching

that there was no remedy against pestilence better than to flee before them; wherefore, moved by his reasoning and recking of nought but themselves, very many, both men and women, abandoned their own city, their own houses and homes, their kinsfolk and possessions, and sought the country seats of others, or, at least, their own, as if the wrath of God, being moved to punish the iniquity of mankind, would not proceed to do so wheresoever they might be, but would content itself with afflicting those only who were found within the walls of their city, or as if they were persuaded that no person was to remain therein and that its last hour was come. . . . This tribulation had stricken such terror to the hearts of all, men and women alike, that brother forsook brother, uncle nephew, and sister brother and oftentimes wife husband; nay (what is yet more extraordinary and well nigh incredible) fathers and mothers refused to visit or tend their very children, as they had not been theirs.

Where was she, he wondered. Where was his honey-sweet girl?

He thought he could work again. He tried to work, but the manuscripts, the documents, the pages, kept flipping past his eyes on the screen, and he had not read them.

Click.

Of this abandonment of the sick by neighbors, kinsfolk and friends and of the scarcity of servants arose an usage before well nigh unheard, to wit, that no woman, how fair or love-some or well-born soever she might be, once fallen sick, recked aught of having a man to tend her, whatever he might be, or young or old, and without any shame discovered to him every part of her body, no otherwise than she would have done to a woman, so but the necessity of her sickness required it; the which belike, in those who recovered, was the occasion of lesser modesty in time to come . . .

He found himself telling the console about Virginia, recalling for this unloved, unmoving, plastic machine all the intimate moments and surprises of their relationship. When he awoke to what he was doing and asked for the information to be recalled for him so that it could be wiped from memory, he was surprised to discover that what he had talked about was not obscene.

He was, he realized, not sensual but romantic. It was a remarkable discovery, because until a few weeks ago he had been neither and then for the past week he had thought he was all sensualist. Even the sick desires that plagued his waking moments and twisted his sleepless limbs at night faded beside the idealization of Virginia that grew in his imagination to something impossible to realize. He knew it. This was a worse sickness than the sickness of the flesh, he knew, but there was no cure.

The days passed like plague victims crawling to hiding places to avoid the pest house. Laurence was a patient man and a healthy, slender, agile man, but he found himself becoming more distracted and nervous; he lost interest in food and grew thinner; he developed a cough and he thought he ran a fever at times. At last he tried to call Virginia, but the room reported itself empty and without information as to the whereabouts of the inhabitant.

She's living with someone else, he thought, or reveling with the children through some euphoric masque.

He tried to contact his daughter, but Jenny, too, was not at home.

Until that moment he had not realized how free the society was in which he found himself. It was so free that people could cut themselves away from it without restraint, could drop out of it without concern, fade out, be unavailable, do whatever they wished whenever they wished.

He tried to think of someone else he could reach who

might know where he could locate Virginia, but even the central computer was helpless.

Click.

Few, again, were they whose bodies were accompanied to the church by more than half a score or a dozen of their neighbors, and of these no more worshipful and illustrious citizens, but a sort of blood-suckers, sprung from the dregs of the people, who styled themselves pickmen and did such offices for hire, shouldered the bier and bore it with hurried steps, not to that church which the dead man had chosen before his death, but most times to the nearest, behind five or six priests, with little light and whiles none at all, which latter, with the aid of the said pickmen, thrust him into what grave soever they first found unoccupied, without troubling themselves with too long or too formal a service. . . . The consecrated ground sufficing not to the burial of the vast multitude of corpses aforesaid, which daily and well nigh hourly came carried in crowds to every church—especially if it were sought to give each his own place, according to ancient usance—there were made throughout the churchyards, after every other part was full, vast trenches, wherein those who came after were laid by the hundred and being heaped up therein by layers, as good as stored aboard ship, were covered with a little earth, till such time as they reached the top of the trench.

Laurence left a standing call for Virginia and Jenny, and turned to research—this time on the nature of the society in which he lived, about which, it seemed, he had known so little.

It had started with chemical memory. Memory, it was discovered, was first encoded in complex protein molecules, later engraved in synaptic pathways. Chemical memory had changed society more than the Industrial Revolution. Schools disappeared. Only the perverse individual learned to read.

Whatever anyone needed to know how to do was available in a capsule. If a computer broke down and some person had to fix it—nobody needed to do that anymore; the computers fixed themselves and everything else as well—why, all he needed to do was inject the right capsule and he not only knew the technical information but how the technician felt when he was applying it. If brain surgery was necessary—few surgeons were left—all a person had to do, if he wanted to, was inject the right capsule and he knew what had to be done, how to do it, and how it felt to do it right.

But chemical memory had more exciting possibilities than supplying information or skills. A person could get out of a capsule the feeling itself without the burdensome information; he could feel like a surgeon or a technician. Or he could feel like more exciting people, people who lived vividly, felt intensely. Nothing remained for most of humanity to do but pursue sensation. Enjoy! Enjoy!

Hence the dreamers. Hence the beautiful bright children who had nothing to do with their time but pursue pleasure and, when pleasure palled, sensation beyond pleasure: guilt, humiliation, sin, degradation, decadence, sorrow, grief, pain. . . .

He knew them by name; he had felt them all. And so long as people wanted them, dreamers would provide them.

Laurence knew all this, and yet he could not stop himself from wanting Virginia back.

Click.

Moreover I say that, whilst so sinister a time prevailed in the city, on no wise therefore was the surrounding country spared, wherein, throughout the scattered villages and in the fields, the poor and miserable husbandmen and their families, without succor of physician or aid of servitor, cried, not like men, but well nigh like beasts, by the ways or in their tillages, or about the houses, indifferently by day and night. . . . To leave the country and return to the city, what more can be said save that such and so great was the cruelty of heaven (and in part, peradventure, that of men) that, between March and the following July, what with the virulence of the pestiferous sickness and the number of sick folk ill tended or forsaken in their need, through the fearfulness of those who were whole, it is believed for certain that upward of a hundred thousand human beings perished within the walls of the city of Florence, which, peradventure, before the advent of that death-dealing calamity had not been accounted to hold so many?

The dreamers . . .

He remembered a dreamer named Samuel. Perhaps. Perhaps? He asked the computer to call Samuel's residence. No one answered, but the glass in Laurence's console lit up and revealed a scene.

For a moment Laurence could not interpret what his eyes saw. The room was darkly red; the walls and floors were red and the room was dimly lit so that it was difficult to see at all. Slowly, however, Laurence began to make out shapes and then figures. The figures seemed naked. They were men and women; they lay in tangled heaps about the floor. At first Laurence thought they all were dead, and then he saw, here and there, a figure moving slowly.

In the center of the room was a chair. Samuel was seated in it. He, too, seemed naked, although Laurence could not be sure. He was leaning back in the chair as if exhausted; his eyes were closed. One arm dangled over the arm of the chair. From Samuel's hand something was dripping, a dark fluid was dripping into the mouth of a girl lying on the floor.

The girl lying there with dark stains on her lips was Virginia.

★ ★ ★ ★ ★

The beautiful bright children crawled around the floor like dark-red slugs.

Somehow Laurence had found Samuel's residence. The computer had given him a map, but he had not left his room for so long that he soon became confused. He blundered into several other rooms by lift shaft or drop shaft before he came upon the red room he had seen upon his console screen.

The room was hot. Laurence could feel himself sweating as soon as he stepped into it. It smelled of incense and sweat and blood. It throbbed with a primitive beat like the still-living heart of a dead reptile.

Laurence threaded his way across the floor, not wanting to touch any of the bodies that undulated across his path. He arrived at the chair in which Samuel sat bleeding from his palms.

Laurence picked up Virginia and held her in his arms, trying not to look at the smears around her mouth or the way her tongue licked out across her lips. She seemed almost insensible and scarcely stirred.

Samuel opened dark, shadowed eyes in his pale face and smiled. "The ultimate dream," he said weakly. "We have eliminated the middle man. Straight from producer to consumer." And he closed his eyes again.

Click.

The Brotherhood of the Cross they called themselves. The Flagellants arose in Hungary and created an order, complete with regulations and uniform, out of the formless and spontaneous wanderings of homeless people. They were robed in sombre garments with red crosses on the breast, back and on the cap and bore triple scourges tied in three knots in which points of iron were fixed. On arrival at a town, they handed the citizens a copy of a remarkable letter from Jesus Christ which they claimed had fallen from heaven. It set forth a horrifying plan which they claimed God had devised for the punishment of man. The punishment could be avoided if the example of the Flagellants was followed. Each procession was to last for thirty-three and a half days—one day for each year of Christ's life. At every place they visited, they entered the church and closed the door and each one divested himself of his upper clothing. Then marching in procession around the church, each scourged himself until the blood ran down over his ankles.

Laurence could not remember later how he had maneuvered Virginia down drop shafts and up lift shafts, nor how he had found his way, thus burdened, back to his room. But she did not stir until he had placed her on the bed, had sealed and locked the room so that no one could enter and no one could leave without his voiced instructions, and had begun to clean her face and hands with a cloth from the lavatory. She moved then and tried to sit up, but he held her down by a shoulder. She blinked and tried to make out his features and squinted at the white walls and slowly relaxed.

"Laurence," she said. "It's all over, Laurence. You can't keep me here. The past is past. Enjoy! Enjoy!"

"I think you're mad," he said, "but I love you."

"I'm not mad just because our ways are different," she said. "Society determines what is normal, and everybody does what I have been doing, what we have been doing. Everybody pops but a few real people like you."

This time when she said "real people" it sounded like profanity.

"Let me go," she said, her body undulating a bit in spite of the position in which he held her. "This was a good cap."

"I'm not going to let you go until you're free of this need to be somebody else," he said. "I'm not going to let you go until you—the real you, not someone else—can decide what you want to do."

"That's ridiculous," she said. "You can't keep me. You can't keep me from popping."

"I can," Laurence said grimly, foreseeing darkly what lay ahead, "and I will. I am going to speak to the real Virginia."

She screamed. It was the scream of a wounded cat, filled with pain and anger and incredulity. But it was nothing to the way she screamed later.

With a robe pulled tight around her and her face contorted with anger, she screamed at him and reviled him with language Laurence had encountered only occasionally in his research. She was not beautiful now, he thought; indeed, she was not nice to look at, and yet he thought he loved her more. He felt a strange sense of pleasure that it was not her beauty that enslaved him.

He sat at his console and ignored her anger. He was not afraid, even when she pounded at him with her fists. Knowing she was there, he was not even distracted. His work went well.

Click.

NOTICE TO BE GIVEN OF THE SICKNESS.

The Master of every House, as soon as any one in his House complains either of Botch, or Purple, or Swelling in any part of his body, or falleth otherwise dangerously sick, without apparent cause of some other Disease, shall give knowledge thereof to the Examiner of Health within two hours after the said sign shall appear.

SEQUESTRATION OF THE SICK.

As soon as any man shall be found by this Examiner, Chirurgion or Searcher to be sick of the Plague, he shall the same night be sequestred in the same house. And in case he be so sequestred, then though he afterwards die not, the House wherein he sickened shall be shut up for a Moneth, after the use of due Preservatives taken by the rest.

A day later Virginia pleaded with him to let her go. "I will never be anything but a burden to you. I will never be anything but hateful. You will get no joy of me. Please let me go. Don't do this to me."

"You have enjoyed similar caps of imprisonment and suffering," Laurence said. "Why can't you enjoy this one?"

The next day she was sullen and would not speak. She sat on the edge of the bed, her back to him, her body bent over her hands.

She was not even attractive, Laurence thought. The golden girl with the quicksilver moods and the honey-sweet taste was gone. She had been replaced by this drab creature. But Laurence did not relent. Someday soon, he told himself, she would cast off the remnants of her capsule personas like a snake shedding its winter skin and she would be herself. That self, he knew, had to be beautiful and loving and kind.

The fourth day she crawled to him and kissed his feet and begged him for one little cap. "I'll do anything," she said. "Just one little cap. You can pick it out. And then we'll be like we were before. I'll be anything you want me to be. I'll stay with you. I'll—"

"All I want," he said gently, "is the real you."

An hour later she was back. She let her paper robe drop to the floor and tried to shape her shaking body into an enticing pose. "You want me?" she said. "Take me. Do anything you want with me. Just let me have one cap."

He did not find her desirable. Her face was haggard and twisted; her body was dull and flaccid. She did not value it anymore, and he could not want it.

He shook his head.

"Damn you!" she screamed. "Damn you! What are you? What kind of fiend? What kind of pervert? You're getting even with me for what I did to you, aren't you! Admit it!"

"You didn't do anything to me," he said.

She laughed harshly. "I found you innocent and alone and contented, and I seduced you. I did it deliberately. I took you away from your studies and your writing and taught you what it is to feel things. Now you're no longer innocent. You're no longer contented. You feel dirty and betrayed, and you want to hurt me."

He shook his head again. "I love you," he said. "I don't want to hurt you. I want to find you. And if you must hurt for a little, it is only to let the real you come out from behind all the masks you've been putting between yourself and the world."

"The real me!" she said. "The real me! Don't you understand? There is no real me! I am what I pop. Strip that away and there's nothing left. I'm nothing. Nothing."

"I don't believe that," he said. But he was shaken.

"Believe this, then," she said. "I left you because you bored me. You're the most boring person I ever knew. You have only two emotions: tolerance and a pallid sort of pleasure. I thought perhaps I could find something else beneath that wishy-washy exterior, but there isn't anything else. Nothing I could do could induce you to let loose and enjoy. All the time holding back, preaching and disapproving! You're dull and boring, Laurence, that's all. And I couldn't stand it anymore. I had to go find something alive."

He *was* shaken now; what she accused him of confirmed all the fears he had ever known, all the self-doubts and inadequacies that had kept him from participating in life.

"What's more," she said, "I know why your wife left you. Jenny told me. She is too kind to tell you, but I'm not. Your wife left you because she was bored. She didn't die. She went to another building, a strange building. Can you imagine that? Rather than continue to live with dull, boring Laurence, she went to a strange building and found herself another life among strangers. Because she couldn't stand you anymore. She couldn't stand—"

Laurence slapped her. The blow was unpremeditated, and as soon as his hand touched her face, he was sorry. She sprawled on the floor and looked up at him, holding one hand to her cheek.

He did not speak. He sat down at the console and tried to read the manuscript page the computer had put before him.

Click.

EVERY VISITED HOUSE TO BE MARKED.

That every House visited, be marked with a Red Cross of a foot long, in the middle of the door, evident to be seen, and with these usual Printed words, that is to say, Lord have mercy upon us, *to be set close over the same Cross, there to continue until lawful opening of the same House.*

When he awoke, the beautiful bright child was back, golden in his bed, quicksilver in his arms, honey-sweet to his lips, and for a moment he rejoiced. But then suspicion swept joy aside.

He unwound her from him and went to the lavatory. The capsule was gone—no doubt she had cast it into the waste disposal—but the injector was too big for the lavatory, and the waste disposal had rejected it because it was metal.

She could have obtained them only one way: in the night she had discovered how to instruct the console to provide her with what she craved.

When he turned, sickness trembling along every nerve, she was standing beside the bed, holding out her golden arms. "Love," she said tenderly, "we've been cruel to each other when we should have been kind. People should make each other happy. Enjoy! Enjoy!"

He let her lead him back to bed and into paradise.

Later, when she was asleep, he sat at the console one last time. In one hand was the injector, in the other a capsule marked "Abélard."

On the screen of the console was a new page of manuscript.

Click.

This day, much against my will, I did in Drury Lane see two or three houses marked with a red cross upon the doors, and "Lord have mercy upon us" writ there; which was a sad sight to me, being the first of the kind that, to my remembrance, I ever saw.

He inserted the capsule in the injector, pushed back his sleeve, and pressed the nozzle of the injector to his arm. For one brief moment, before the synthetic peptides began to reconstruct his memories, his eyes filled with tears and he could not read.

The Futurist

The sphinx materialized on the United Nations plaza at 3 A.M. on October 9, 2009. At that time of night no one was injured, but several metal sculptures were crushed under its apparently substantial mass. At least the sculptures were never seen again, and their remains were presumed to rest beneath the dull, black figure.

A United Nations guard happened to be looking at the spot when the object appeared. It didn't shimmer or look insubstantial at any time. "One instant it wasn't there," he said later—not once but many times; "the next instant it was. I couldn't believe my eyes, I can tell you. I blinked a couple times, thinking I was seeing things or maybe dreaming. But there it was."

There it was indeed. One hundred meters exactly from human head to lion's tail, and twenty meters tall at the shoulders, forty meters at the head. And it was heavy. Although it had arrived without apparent impact or sound, it had sunk almost a meter into the pavement and the soil and rock beneath. Nothing and no one could move it. Construction firms tried to elevate one end or the other without any result other than to break their equipment, and a floating crane succeeded only in tilting the wide barge on which it rested.

Acids did not react with the surface of the object, drills simply slid off, diamonds made no mark on it, and torches did not even heat up the surrounding area. Even a thermite wand did no damage. The object apparently had infinite capacity for absorbing heat, or diverting it, although instruments mounted nearby could detect no radiation from it, in any part of the spectrum. It attracted compass needles, however, and airplanes flying overhead had to compensate for its presence. Gravitometers registered the presence of an object several hundred times the mass that the size of the object would justify under any reasonable assumption of density.

It responded to no attempts at communication. Messages in all languages, living and dead, were directed at it in every form known to humanity. At first the messages were cautiously friendly; at the end they turned impatient, even truculent. Nothing moved it. The sphinx sat there, stolid and unresponsive, staring blindly at the north entrance to the United Nations, asking its eternal riddle of those who came and went. Not "what walks on four legs in the morning, two legs at noon, and three legs in the evening?" But "What am I, what am I doing here, and what does it mean?"

Many people thought they had the answer. Some said that since its measurements were so precisely metrical it had to be of human origin, but others said that the meter was an easy measure to deduce, much easier than the foot or the yard, for instance, and that this fact in itself meant nothing. Nevertheless, an industry developed to speculate about the ways in which the measurements of this enigmatic object were intended to predict the future, and as a consequence great things were in store for humanity; others insisted, on the basis of equally valid extrapolations, great misfortunes.

Some said that the sphinx was a human concept, emerging from human mythology, and therefore the object had to be humanly constructed. Others, citing its weight, mysterious appearance, and the unknown material from which it was constructed, said, even more vehemently, that it clearly was alien.

Some mystics suggested that the object proved that the Earth had been visited thousands of years ago by aliens, and that this was the Second Coming, or at least the second coming. They insisted that the Egyptian sphinxes were proof of such visitations and speculated that they might not be mythological but carved, so to speak, from life.

The aliens, they said, could reasonably be supposed to be sphinxes. And since sphinxes came in all sizes, though many were quite large, the present example might be life-sized. And a few, though they were a schismatic group, maintained that the object on the United Nations plaza was a living alien. It had an incredibly slow metabolism, they said, and therefore lived an incredibly long time, perhaps comparable to the life spans of stars or galaxies. In time, they said, it would open its eyes, and perhaps its terrible mouth, and see the world and judge it.

"What rough beast?" they quoted, and fell to their knees in reverence or in fear.

The scientists, however, though clearly puzzled, maintained that the object was not only inanimate but always had been and always would be. When asked how it had got to its present location without moving, they insisted that it hadn't moved under its own power. And when asked to explain its appearance suddenly out of nowhere, they replied that they had only the guard's word for that.

It was there, indisputably there, and its presence did the name of science no good. Science had no explanation for it, not one, and the mystics had many. Too many.

The object sat there for a solid year, guarded day and night. Sensible people might have expected the speculation and the psychological uproar to fade away, the enigmatic presence of the sphinx to be accepted at last as no more marvelous than the Great Sphinx at Giza. But it didn't and wasn't, and finally, precisely a year later, on October 9, 2010, the sphinx opened its jaw.

The jaw dropped, or gaped, as one of the guards put it. Fortunately no sphinx-worshipers were present at that hour or they might have fainted in anticipation or dread, or expired on the spot. But the object emitted no sound. Instead, a tongue emerged as if in preparation for a giant raspberry and turned into a stairway complete with railings that ran out silently until it reached the ground.

Nothing more occurred for long seconds—long enough for guards to draw their weapons, sound the alarm, summon help, and run around madly shouting, turning on additional lights, and approaching the stairway with caution befitting their individual supplies of courage.

Before the Secretary General arrived, or any of the undersecretaries, or even the mayor or the chief of police, the boldest of the guards, who had forced his reluctant body within ten meters of the stairway, observed a pair of bare feet appear at the top of the stairs, one after the other, the calves of smooth, tan colored legs topped by loose white trousers or culottes, and then a face.

The guard almost fainted at the vision, and, indeed, as he later confided to a friend, although not the media or even his immediate superior, came within a hair of shooting the creature there and then, seeing in that terrible moment the face of an alien growing directly out of the creature's thighs. Only as he was leveling his pistol did he realize that the creature was bending over, peering out.

Seeing the gun, the creature shouted, in understandable English, "Don't shoot!" and quickly came down the stairs, its hands held high, to stand trembling in front of the guard. "I come in peace!" it said hastily, although one of the guards reported that he thought the creature said, "Hack 'em in pieces!"

If confusion had been a proper description for the state of affairs when the sphinx opened its mouth, panic was the condition that followed. A creature stood on the plaza surrounded by milling guards; it was soon joined by throngs of curious passersby even at that hour of the morning. Lights came on in nearby office buildings and condominiums. Sirens raped the air. Someone finally thought of forming a line of guards and ushering the stranger through it to the north doors of the General Assembly building. Unfortunately, no one had a key.

In the midst of the turmoil, the stairway retracted itself into the mouth of the sphinx and the jaw closed. No one noticed, but when one of the guards looked, and raised a shout, the sphinx was as impenetrable and as enigmatic as ever. It had emitted, however, an oracle.

Fortunately, at this time the Secretary General arrived. He was a man of great international distinction and even some wisdom. Once he had been informed about recent events, he looked at the human-like creature in white tunic and culottes and bare feet standing close to the broad front doors with an air of uncertainty, or perhaps even of timidity, he ordered that the doors be opened and the creature taken to his office. After some delay a key was located, and the creature was escorted—no one wanted to touch it—to an elevator and up to the proper office.

Following these events witnessed by many, much of the rest of the events that followed is supported by tape recordings, video tapes, and interviews. The Secretary General recalled that he motioned toward a chair and when the creature sank into it, its knees working as if accustomed to such equipment for sitting, the Secretary General took a first full look at the creature's lack of weapons, apparent defenselessness, and absence of threat, and told the guards to leave, warning them to say nothing about the events of the evening until they were given the opportunity to do so in official circumstances. As soon as they emerged from the building, they began telling everything they knew to the reporters who by now had gathered.

In the office, the Secretary General said when they were alone, "I understand you speak English. Where do you come from?"

"I think," the creature said, its eyes moving uneasily between the Secretary General and the door, "you should call an emergency meeting of the permanent members of the Security Council."

The Secretary General's eyes had been opened from a sound sleep by the events of the past hour, hut now they opened a little wider. "Well, you do speak English, and very well. And you know our organization. I will do as you suggest. Do not concern yourself about that. But you can talk to me first."

The creature shook its head. "From this moment anyone who spends any time alone with me is under suspicion of knowing more than anyone else. No one will believe that you do not know more than you are willing to reveal. I do not think you want your authority undermined in that way. It is better if you know nothing."

The Secretary General stroked his chin, a little stubbly at this hour in the morning. "There's that, of course. But I can't get all the members of the Security Council to a meeting in the middle of the night, and not even the permanent members without some idea of what the subject of the meeting will be."

"That's obvious," the creature said, turning its alien brown eyes toward the Secretary General. "Me."

"Well, yes. I'm sure the permanent members of the Security Council would think that enough reason to gather. But couldn't you give me some hint as to what you want to communicate?"

"I will tell you when I tell the others. There are reasons, including the one I gave. My time is limited. I hope you are recording this."

"Of course," the Secretary General said, having already pushed the button on his desk that turned on the video cameras behind pictures and mirrors in his office when he sat on the edge of his desk. "Are you going to give us a revelation? An ultimatum? Will it create panic? Will it cause war?"

The creature shook its head. "I will tell you when I tell the others."

So it was that at 4:30 A.M. on October 9, 2010, sleepy and tousled ambassadors gathered in the Security Council chamber, glaring about them and conferring grumpily with their entourage of assistants. Shortly after the last group had entered, the Secretary General emerged, followed by the barefoot creature from the sphinx. It looked around the room with unconcealed curiosity, somewhat like a tourist observing Westminster Abbey or the House of Parliament, the British ambassador reflected. He remembered thinking that it might take out a camera at any moment and begin snapping photographs.

"This crea—person," the Secretary General said, "has emerged from that object that has been sitting in front of this building for the past year. I have tried to interview it without success. It has told me nothing except to call a meeting of this body."

The Russian ambassador rose like a sullen bear. "Russia finds this difficult to believe. We refuse to accept this information, since it is so ridiculous that it cannot be true."

"Is it harder to believe than the object in front of this building? But that exists, and there are witnesses to the fact that the object opened, let down a staircase, and this person came out."

The Russian waved a heavy hand. "Witnesses!" he said, expressing his scorn of such easily suborned evidence. "Where do you come from?" he demanded of the creature.

"I come from the future," the creature said.

The ambassadors sat back in their padded chairs, silenced, for once in their professional lives, by the creature's revelation. And then as the implications of the last statement began to occur to them, questions burst forth.

"Did we—?"

"Will we—?"

"Then has socialism—?"

"How do we—?"

"What do you—?"

The Secretary General held up his hand. "Ambassadors! Perhaps I might put to this—person—some of the questions that have occurred to us all. After that, you may present individually the questions that I do not cover."

The ambassadors nodded or grumbled assent.

The Secretary General turned to the stranger. He was unusually good looking, the American ambassador recalled, and films confirm her impression; she also remembered thinking what a great, even tan he had on his legs and face and arms. "Now," the Secretary General said, "perhaps you will tell us why we should believe you. It is easy to claim time travel, but difficult to imagine. Or to prove."

"Is it any more difficult to imagine than the time machine I arrived in?"

"That is a time machine?"

"Doesn't it look like one? Actually, it's the only kind there is."

"But how do we know?" asked the American ambassador, a handsome dark-haired woman, and then glanced apologetically at the Secretary General.

"You'll have to take my word for it," the creature said.

"But you could verify your statement, if you wished," the Secretary General said, "by telling us about important events that will happen."

"Since they haven't happened, that would be no proof. I could make up anything and you wouldn't know the difference. Unless it were something that is to happen in the next hour or day, and I don't have that information. And my time here is too short to wait for the occurrence of events months or years away."

"You must tell me," the Russian ambassador broke in. He had accepted the new free enterprise system but he had grown to maturity in the heady days of Soviet power, and old ideologies reasserted themselves. "Communism ultimately prevailed, da?"

The person from the future looked down at its hands. "Yes and no."

"What kind of answer is that?" the Russian shouted.

"The only kind that is accurate," the stranger said hesitantly. "Look: If someone had asked one hundred years ago whether the United States would be a socialist country by the year 2000, what kind of answer would you give?"

The Secretary General held up his hand again. "Perhaps we could approach this subject in another way: How far in the future do you come from?"

"Exactly one hundred years."

"And how many does your—time machine—hold?"

"I'm the only one."

"How were you chosen?"

"It was sort of a—lottery," the stranger said. "Among qualified persons."

"Are you male or female?" the American ambassador asked.

The stranger looked down at its hands, hesitating. "We don't ask that question where I come from. But I realize that your culture does not feel comfortable without that knowledge. You can consider me male."

"And this time machine," the distinguished French ambassador said in his distinguished Gallic accent, "of what different substance is it made?"

"I don't know much science," the visitor from the future admitted. "I am a kind of specialist in Twentieth Century history and culture. All I know is that the machine is built from a substance obtained from distant astronomical bodies and that this substance has something to do with its ability to reverse time's flow."

"That means," the British ambassador said, with Holmesian deduction, "that you have interstellar flight."

"So it would seem," the visitor said. "In any case, the machine is more permanent than stone and virtually indestructible. It has to be, you see, because it must endure until 2110 in spite of your attempts to penetrate it and, that failing, to destroy it."

"We wouldn't do that," the Secretary General protested.

"And why must it endure until 2110?" said the ambassador from the People's Republic of China.

"Travel into the past is possible by reversing time's arrow," the visitor said, "but you can travel into the future only moment by moment. By their permanence you can identify time machines."

"I see," said the Chinese ambassador, and then his eyes

clouded. "No, I do not see. How do you reverse—as you call it—time's arrow?"

"I don't have the slightest idea," the visitor said, "and if I did I would not have been chosen for this mission. As I said, I am not a scientist. And even if I knew I couldn't tell you, because, you see, the reversal of time's arrow was not possible until 2090. Even if I told you, you couldn't do it—because you didn't. Do you understand?"

"I see," the American ambassador said. "You mean that the future is fixed. If it didn't happen, it won't happen."

"Yes," the visitor said, "and no. There are anomalies, real and unreal, created by my presence here."

"How can it be both yes and no?" the Russian ambassador asked disgustedly.

The visitor from the future looked unhappy. "If I have come from the future, it means that there is only one future and therefore it is unchangeable. That is right. And wrong, too. It is both right and wrong in the same way that your physicists consider light to be both a particle and a wave."

"I don't understand that either," the French ambassador said.

"Actually, our scientists have said that it is neither," the visitor said. "The problem is that you don't have the mathematics to express the time anomalies or the intellectual history to understand them."

"Don't underestimate us," the Secretary General said. "We have scientists who understand these things."

"How would you explain indeterminacy to an intelligent Roman?" the visitor asked.

"But we're only one hundred years behind you," the British ambassador observed, "not two thousand."

"In absolute time that is true," the visitor said. "In scientific time, one hundred years of future development is equivalent to two thousand years of history. Knowledge increases exponentially, and the difference is greater between me and you than between you and that Roman. In our time . . . well, I'll get to that in a moment, but let me say this—even we think that our children are strange, and their children we can't understand at all."

"But if you can't change the future," the Secretary General said, "why are you here?" His eyes widened as a thought occurred to him. "Are you a refugee?"

"No. I realize this would make you more comfortable, because it is a term you understand, but I am an emissary."

"Then why?" the Secretary General demanded. Even his inexhaustible patience seemed to be reaching bottom.

"Because the future would be different, in a way that I will explain to you in a moment, if I had not come in my machine to speak to you about the future. How could it be otherwise? I am what is known in my time as a causality loop. I am here because I was here. Understand?"

"I don't understand," said the Russian ambassador, "and I think we should subject this man to expert interrogation until he speaks truth."

No one in the room had any doubt what he meant by interrogation. Even the visitor from the future shivered.

"That would be unwise," the Secretary General said. "Even if it were not inhumane, we do not know what powers our visitor has—or his machine—or the future that sent him."

"The United States would veto that course immediately," the American ambassador said.

The visitor tried to look powerful, without success. More than anything else, he looked like a beggar asked to deliver a revelation to the Pope.

The American ambassador turned to the visitor. "But you should tell us *something* about the future."

The visitor from the future looked beleaguered. "I know that you don't understand, and that is one reason I have come here to speak with you. But all the things I want to tell you, you don't want to hear. All you want to know is what the future holds."

"That's the only subject about which you're an authority," the British ambassador said, "and the only reason we're gathered together at this ungodly hour."

The visitor looked around the table at the mixture of faces and expressions. "All right, I'll tell you," he said. "You wouldn't like it."

Horror jumped from face to face as one after another, according to their quickness of wit, each ambassador and aide understood the implications of what the visitor had said.

"You see?" said the visitor unhappily. "The first thing I have told you, and you're upset. What you must understand about the future is that you wouldn't understand it."

"Now just a minute," the American ambassador said. She was the quickest of the group, as everyone later agreed. "You're here. That's something."

"Yes," the visitor said. "That's something you can understand and appreciate: The future exists. All the problems you consider life threatening have failed to wipe out the human race. Surely that is cause for self-congratulation. You have reason to celebrate."

The visitor waited. No one celebrated, although a few of those present looked relieved and some even smiled.

"But there are so many problems," said the French ambassador. "Overpopulation, pollution, war—"

"Economic disorders, racism, imperialism," the Russian ambassador added.

"Energy shortages, revolution, religious intolerance, terrorism," the American ambassador continued.

"These and others that your wisest people and gloomiest prophets have not yet foreseen," the visitor agreed. "They caused great misery of body, mind, and spirit. But something your era has not yet learned: Misery isn't terminal. Put that with your other epigrams that sum up the wisdom of your time, such as 'There ain't no such thing as a free lunch,' 'The map is not the territory,' 'This too shall pass,' 'Whatever can go wrong will go wrong,' and 'Winning is something but surviving is everything.' "

"That isn't one of our sayings," the American ambassador objected.

"Of course it isn't," the visitor said, rubbing his forehead. "Sometimes I get confused. It's not easy trying to remember what is appropriate to this era and what isn't."

"Do you realize," the Russian ambassador said, "that we are accepting the truth of what this [here he used a Russian word for a person who is not only a liar but a traitor to the state] has said: that he comes from the future?"

"Do we have a choice?" asked the Secretary General.

"We only assume," said the Chinese ambassador, who had been silent for some time.

"What is the point?" the British ambassador asked.

"For the human race," the visitor said faintly, "the point is that problems are meant to be solved. It got where it is by solving problems. When humanity stops solving problems it will stop being humanity and become another domesticated animal, suited for a single set of conditions and no other."

"This is wisdom," the Chinese ambassador agreed.

"Wisdom?" said the French ambassador.

"There is something to be said for domesticated animals," the Russian said.

"I am afraid," the American ambassador said, "there are

some among us who already are domesticated, preferring to retreat to conditions they know rather than solving problems."

"On the other hand," the Secretary General broke in conciliatorily, as his office demanded, "our visitor tells us that the problems will be solved. That is something."

"But how will they be solved?" the Russian broke in. "That is all-important."

"I can't tell you," the visitor said. "There isn't time, and even if I had the time and you the patience, some wouldn't believe me and others would believe me too readily and wouldn't exert themselves to do what must be done."

"Why does our visitor keep referring to time?" the Chinese ambassador asked. He smiled inscrutably. "Surely a time-traveler has all the time in the world."

"I wish it were so," the visitor said weakly. "But time travel is more exhausting than anyone thought, and I have only a few moments with you before I must return to my time machine and the artificial hibernation that will allow me to survive until 2110, if everything goes according to plan."

"Nonsense!" the Russian said.

"I'm not sure, old man, that leaving would be quite cricket," the British ambassador said.

"This man is free to come or go as he wishes," the American said. "What of this future awakening?"

"There will be a great celebration," the visitor said dreamily. "All my dear ones will be present: my nest mothers, my nestlings, my youth-wife, my mid-wife, my sex partners . . ."

The American ambassador looked shocked.

"We're discussing matters of great importance with a pervert," the Russian said.

"These matters are best kept in the home," said the British ambassador.

The French ambassador smiled inscrutably.

"I apologize for offending your sense of morality," the visitor said. "It is such a delicate thing, this sense of morality. I do not mean to suggest that we are not a moral people. We, too, are offended by immorality."

"That's hard to believe," said the American.

"Our morality is not your morality. Of all the things I had to learn about you and your times, your morality was the most difficult."

"How did you learn about us?" the Secretary General asked.

"We have records of your time: films, tapes, documentaries, fiction. . . . But you should understand that your period is not particularly interesting."

The ambassadors sat back, offended more by this remark than by those earlier.

"I spent years studying it at great personal sacrifice," the visitor hastened on. "After my time machine arrived, you must have wondered why it stood without opening or even announcing its purpose for a year."

"That question did come up," the Secretary General remarked.

"I was sampling your society in *situ,* so to speak, absorbing your television and radio shows, your news, your music, your advertisements, your art, your disagreements—which no one in my time can understand. They seem to us like debates about how many angels can dance on the head of a pin."

"We have weapons that can destroy the world," the Russian growled.

"But no comparable-sized issues," the visitor said.

"Well, freedom—" began the American ambassador.

"Brotherhood," said the Frenchman.

"Equality," said the Russian.

"Your belief, if I interpret it correctly," the visitor said hesitantly, "is that there are differences between people usually ascertainable by visual observation. Or if not that, by a comparison of values."

"Come now," said the British ambassador.

"That is how it appears. Some are shorter or taller; some are closer to some arbitrary standard of esthetics; some are pigmented differently; some speak other than the prevailing language or dialect; some are better favored by birth or inheritance—"

"It was otherwise in the late Soviet Union," the Russian said gloomily.

"Or education or fortune or talent. You make judgments, as well, about attributes you can't see, such as personality or temperament, but a person's most basic nature—goodness, kindness, wisdom, honesty—is beyond you."

"Surely these things are beyond all men," said the Chinese ambassador.

"Of course you do not have the psychometricon," the visitor said, "which allows us to ascertain such matters early in life and to make appropriate adjustments."

Everyone but the Russian looked shocked, and he looked interested.

"What kind of devil's work is this?" asked the Briton.

"How can you interfere?" the American said. "Who are you to decide what people should be like?"

"You prefer children to grow up unhappy and maladjusted until they must be turned over to the art of a psychologist or the punishments of a penal system," the visitor said. "Better, you say, to leave human personality to chance, or to God."

"Amen to that," said the American.

"And yet we leave to personal choice many intimate aspects of life that you wish to control. You believe that people should have only one mate at a time, although in some circumstances, to some of you, casual sexual partners are permissible."

"Not in the right circles, old man," said the Briton.

"Not since AIDS," the American added.

"This makes no sense to us. People, we know as you do, relate to each other in many ways, from the most casual to the most intimate. How can one person relate to one other person, and the other way around, in every satisfying way, all the time for many years? We encourage a variety of relationships to serve as many socially meaningful and personally pleasing functions as is desirable for the individual or society."

"Well, I call it immorality," the American said.

"If that is what the future holds, we shall have no part of it," the Briton said.

"Now, there may be something in what the visitor says," the Frenchman observed.

"Yet you or your children or your children's children will have a part of it; in fact, you will create it, and you will call it moral. A society gives approving names to what it approves. We have youth-wife, mid-wife, mature-wife, companion-wife, sex-wife, and, of course, females have just as many male relationships, and each has same-sex relationships as well. . . ."

"That is disgusting," the American ambassador said.

"Western perversions," said the Russian.

"We should not be judgmental," the Frenchman said.

"This society of yours," said the visitor, "has many more words for disapproval than for approval. It is a symptom of a repressive society."

"Now who speaks words of disapproval?" the Chinese ambassador asked.

"Who are you to judge us?" asked the Secretary General.

"I am, of course, the perfect judge," the visitor said. "I am the only judge you will ever have—the future. From my vantage point it seems clear that your society is sick. It is easy to judge the past; it is impossible to judge the future."

The Russian pushed himself back from the table and lumbered to his feet. "I move that we execute this creature as a danger to world peace and get back to our regular business."

Outside the United Nations building a crowd had gathered, summoned by the mysterious force that draws ill-assorted humans into silent spectators of fires and accidents or into mobs inciting each other to violence. All nationalities were represented, as befitted the location, and all ages, and the entire spectrum of political, social, and religious convictions. There were those in the group who would have killed their neighbors without compunction if they had known what they were thinking, and others who would blow up an entire cluster of strangers, including children, if they thought it would further their cause. Still others would have clapped into prison people in the crowd who looked dangerous or dressed or talked differently or held opinions contrary to theirs. But now they were protected from each other by their proximity and their ignorance and their mutual focus on great, if enigmatic, events. People kept adding themselves to the throng and the north plaza, already crowded by the sphinx, was getting filled. At first silent, the crowd had begun to shout questions at the doors of the slab-shaped building, and the group itself was gaining its own identity with a slowly building roar. The guards, now reinforced, had nervously summoned help from the New York City police.

Inside the Security Council chamber, the uproar was comparable to that in the plaza when the sphinx had uttered its oracle. People shouted and shook their fists at one another. In the midst of the turmoil, the visitor sat cringing in his chair, holding his hands to his ears. As if in response to a situation that they could neither hear nor witness, the crowd outside shouted a protest at nothing in particular.

Finally the Secretary General's quiet voice brought order once more. "The motion of the Russian ambassador has been ruled out of order. This meeting will continue. The ambassador may leave the meeting, but it will continue without him, and what this visitor from the future has to say will be heard. He will tell us what he has to say in his own way, and perhaps soon he will get to what he has come about."

"Our visitor claims perfection," said the Chinese ambassador, who had remained seated and silent throughout the disturbance.

The Russian looked at the door and slowly returned to his seat.

The visitor shook his head. "We know that society will continue to change, that what we consider moral and reasonable will give way to something considered more moral and more reasonable that we will consider as sinful as you consider us. But we have something you do not. . . ."

"And what is that?" asked the American.

"We have a sense of the future; we know we must accept it," the visitor said. "We have made a beginning where it counts—with children. We have established the right of children to be wanted, to be loved, and to be brought up in an environment capable of developing, without warp or frustration, the potentials of a genetic heritage as free from flaws as we can make it. . . ."

"You not only tamper with their minds," the American

ambassador said, "you tamper with their genes as well."

"In the right hands," the Russian said, "not a bad idea."

"For once I agree with my Russian colleague," said the Chinese ambassador.

"The administration I represent does not approve of abortions," the American said.

"Of course no abortion is involved," said the visitor. "No one would want to become pregnant or to impregnate someone else if the child's right to those conditions was not assured. No one would wish to bring a new life into this world if its essentially happy nature might be frustrated by its circumstances, if it might experience more pain than joy."

"Certainly no one would disagree with that," said the Secretary General, trying to bring the group back together.

"Of course this is all theoretical," the visitor said. "All children are conceived and brought to term extra utero—"

"He means in test tubes," said the American. "Like *Brave New World.*"

"We know what he means," said the Frenchman.

"Once born," the visitor said, "children are given to a child-rearing system whose personnel are suited by temperament and prepared by training to provide a healthy environment for the growing child."

"That sounds pretty unhealthy to me," the American woman said, sounding more and more like the Russian. "Like a bunch of test-tube orphans."

"They are not orphans," the visitor said firmly, "but nestlings. You allow every untrained, ill-tempered, overburdened parent to raise a future citizen. We call that barbaric, stupid, and potentially disastrous."

"More words of disapproval?" the Chinese ambassador asked.

"You speak of poverty cycles and criminal patterns and do

nothing about them. On the other hand, a solution to these problems you imagine as children ripped from loving parents and incarcerated in unfeeling institutions."

"Some matters are better left to chance," said the Frenchman.

"You'll never find anyone more concerned about raising children than the parents themselves," the Briton added.

"Chance seldom provides the love and care a child needs. Primitive instincts have a darker side," the visitor said.

"We must commend our visitor for honesty," the Secretary General said. "He told us we wouldn't like it."

"Maybe so; maybe not. This world that he describes sounds more and more like the old communes," the Russian said.

"If you were transported to my world," the visitor said, "you would feel like your great-grandparents if they were moved from their gaslight and horse-and-buggy world to your world of electricity and electronics, of airplanes and space travel, of television and terrorism and hydrogen bombs."

"We are not our great-grandparents," the American said.

"At first you would be astonished by all the marvels," the visitor said. "Then you would be disturbed by the changes. Sprats and chundleys and go-forths and willy-nillies and—but these are only words, and I no more have time to tell you what they describe than to tell you how you are going to solve your problems."

"What are you going to tell us, then?" the Secretary General asked.

"You want me to tell you about the future," the visitor said, "and I must tell you that you would experience astonishment, discomfort, then psychological disorientation. In my world, events move faster, life scurries by, and yet there are few jobs and a great deal more leisure. Less is said and more is understood. You would find that unsettling. But to all of this you could become accustomed; you never would feel quite at home, but like your great-grandparents you could learn to live with it and maybe even to appreciate it."

Outside the United Nations building, the crowd was growing even larger—and more unruly. The time was 6 A.M., and the gathering of night people and news gatherers had been augmented by early risers and early workers. The entire north plaza was covered with upright bodies from the sphinx to the doors of the Assembly building, and those doors were being threatened by occasional surges.

The Secretary General lifted his head as if he could hear the gathering crowd, but that was impossible. "I understand," he said, indicating the receiver in his ear that some might have mistaken for a hearing aid, "that we must release some information soon or face the possibility of mob violence."

"That mustn't happen," the visitor said, agitated by more than the prospect would suggest. "I have come to bring you a gift from the future. Announce that to the crowd and the news media."

The Secretary General nodded to an aide who walked swiftly from the chamber. "Now, what gift can the future bring the present?"

"A cure for cancer or for AIDS?" the American said.

"Inexhaustible energy?" the Briton ventured.

The visitor shook his head impatiently.

"A foolproof system of birth control," said the Chinese ambassador.

"A way to make food out of rock," the Frenchman said.

"An end to war," the Russian said. "You will destroy our hydrogen bombs."

"You must do that yourself," the visitor said. "No, none of those—"

"He was speaking about life in the future," the Secretary General said, "and he was saying there was something we could not become accustomed to."

"Yes," the visitor said with relief. "The social system."

"Nonsense," said the Russian. Later he explained that a nation that had been through two revolutions had nothing to fear from evolution.

The British ambassador looked puzzled. "Is this what you have come back one hundred years to tell us? That we would not like the future? That we could not accept your social system?"

The visitor from the future spread his hands wide in a gesture of helplessness that had not changed. "It may not seem like much, but the experts of our era believe it is vitally important."

"I think we are wasting our time," said the Frenchman.

"All things eventually become clear," the Chinese ambassador said.

"Your time," the visitor said, "was the first to think seriously about the future. You gave birth to the futurists—those half-blind social scientists who began poking about in the leavings of the science-fiction writers."

"Futurists?" the American ambassador said.

"They talked about shaping the future through a developing system by which thoughtful people could explore possible futures, then choose among them by making the right decisions."

"That seems sensible enough," the American said.

"It is," the visitor continued, "if you are dealing with technology."

"What does technology have to do with it, old man?" the Briton asked.

The visitor looked at him as if he had asked a stupid question in class. "Technology determines what members of a society can do and can't do, what they can think and even how they can think."

"That is the function of government," the Russian said.

"Of some governments," the American responded.

"These decisions you can make," the visitor said. "You can decide how you are going to transport yourself and your goods, what you will use for energy, what goods to produce, and how you are going to communicate. You can decide how to allocate to these activities common resources, including the environment. You can decide whether to live on the moon or in the ocean depths. You can decide what weapons to use in the next war."

"Thank you very much," said the Briton.

"You can do this," the visitor said, "because though these are vitally important decisions, their consequences are elusive: No one knows what effect they will have on people's lives. Not the futurists. Not you. Not me. No one could know enough to project the chain of causality from the automobile, say, to the decay of the inner cities and the lives of the people who live in them."

"Our Marxists did," the Russian said.

"You have the problem without the cars," the American said.

"All this may be very interesting," the Secretary General said, "but is it relevant?"

"This is the gift I bring you from the future," the visitor said. "You must avoid the decisions you most desire: the ones that control people's behavior, the legal determination of what is lawful and the ethical determination of what is moral."

"But that is what governments and religions are instituted to do," the Frenchman said stiffly. The visitor from the future finally had touched him, too, and even the ambassador from China seemed repulsed.

"You can try to control morality," the visitor said. "Every society does. But every society has the morality appropriate to its circumstances, or else it is bound in chains forged by the past. Every generation, if it could, would set down for all time what is good and true, what is right and wrong, but each new generation redefines them, either through freedom to explore and innovate, or through rebellion."

"I can't agree with that," said the American.

"Focus your decision-making on technology," the visitor said. "That doesn't matter, because its ultimate significance is beyond us. Leave morality alone. You would like to set down the rules by which we, a century from now, will live, but I urge you to think. Those great-grandparents of yours—what if you had to live by their rules?"

All the ambassadors looked skeptical, if not rebellious.

"I cannot tell you all the problems people in my time have had because of disputes about morality, and I have been sent back to your time to say to you—"

"Now we're getting to it," the Secretary General muttered.

"That the future is waiting for you and that you will hate it and that it doesn't matter."

"Stupid!" the Russian ambassador shouted.

"Ridiculous!" said the Briton.

"Absurd!" said the Frenchman.

"Well!" said the American.

"Have we been gathered together at this hour," said the Chinese ambassador, "to listen to such ramblings of small meaning?"

"You have begun to denounce me," the visitor said. "Before the events of this morning are completely analyzed, you will have joined against me. For the first time in the history of the planet, everyone will be united—united against the future."

"We have seen the future," the Secretary General murmured, "and it doesn't work."

"Somehow, each of you is thinking, we must prevent it. But gradually what I have said will seep into the minds of some of you and then a few more and a few more. You will remember that I said, 'You will solve your problems. The world will continue.' Then you will say, 'Even if it isn't a future I would care to live in, I don't want this world to end too soon; I want to see that future.' And then you will say, 'Let us make a better one.' "

The ambassadors were arguing among themselves. Virtually unnoticed by all but the Secretary General, who had his own reasons for not speaking up, the visitor from the future had gotten to his feet during his last speech and was at the door. When the others looked for him, they saw only an empty doorway.

No one ever saw the man from the future again. No one admits to having seen him make his way from the Security Council meeting room to the front doors and through the crowd that had gathered on the plaza to his time machine. Perhaps he left through a side door. Perhaps he spent a day or several days in a safe place until he could once more regain the sanctuary of his gigantic artifact. If that were true, someone had to help. When asked directly about this possibility, the Secretary General denied participating in any such maneuver.

There are, of course, diplomatic denials that are not the same as lies.

What is undeniable is that the last words of the man from the future created as much of an uproar in the world outside as they had in the Security Council chamber. What had been announced as a gift was universally denounced as interference in the personal lives and beliefs of every person on the planet. The man from the future was attacked in every political forum, from every pulpit and lectern, in every bar, on every street corner, in every living room. Mobs gathered; rage rose; violence boiled just below eruption.

What is undeniable, as well, is the presence on the United Nations plaza of the massive black sphinx. Whether or not the visitor from the future is within its protective walls, sleeping his way into the future, the sphinx remains a constant reminder that the future is inexorably approaching, second by second. Scientists and fanatics have attacked its smooth surface without damage to anything except themselves.

There it will remain, apparently, until 2110, or perhaps forever, as humans understand such terms.

What is not clear is why the society that has come to be in the year 2110 sent the Futurist back, knowing that his appearance might keep the future from arriving. The Futurist would say that he came back because he had come back, the kind of statement that was not intended for 21st-century minds. Somewhere the causality loop had to begin—or did it? A moebius strip has no beginning.

On the other hand, some philosophers have speculated that what has happened as a consequence of the Futurist's visit was a necessary condition to the world of 2110. That future, they have said, may have needed to avert the kind of concern about morality that has led to most of the organized violence in the world. By attacking the attempts to legislate morality, the future may have instigated a defense of it that may lead, in time, to a wiser future—or at least to a future.

Perhaps, some have continued, the last, great moral crusade loomed ahead like the end of the world and the Futurist's mission was to cut it off before it cut off the future.

But the only way the world will find out is to achieve the future in the only way possible. A day at a time.

The violence never surfaced, of course; the mobs dispersed; the sermons and the political diatribes died away. There was nothing to attack. A new air of reasonableness has begun to replace the old atmosphere of suspicion and accusation in international and personal relationships. People finally began to listen to what the visitor from the future had said to the Secretary General and then to the permanent members of the Security Council.

People have started to think more seriously about the riddle of the sphinx.

And they have begun to forget about ancient injuries and old hatreds and to think about the future.

Man of Parts

This story begins and ends in a hospital. It is about death and suffering and self-mutilation in a number of unpleasant ways. Christ, you say, who wants to read a story about hospitals and death and suffering and self-mutilation? Well, it is about life and miracles and self-sacrifice, too, and maybe about the salvation of the world, and if you read it in the right spirit, it will make you feel good about the human race.

It begins, in a way, in 1759 with a book by Adam Smith, *The Theory of Moral Sentiments*. Smith wondered how a man with normal human feelings might respond to the news that a fearful earthquake had swallowed up millions of Chinese. Smith believed that the man would go on with his business or his pleasure as if nothing had happened. But if he were told that he would lose his little finger the next day, he wouldn't be able to work or sleep for worrying about it.

Benny Geroux knew nothing about Adam Smith. In fact, all he knew at the moment about himself was that he was thirty-five years old and his mother was sick. That upset him. His mother was almost never sick, and it was her refusal to be sick that led to Benny's surprising discovery. After months of watching his mother get thinner and paler, Benny finally persuaded her to enter the hospital for tests. They revealed that she had cancer of the liver.

There was no doubt about it. Benny was as certain as if the

doctor had held out the traitorous organ to him in the operating room and said, "See? Cancer. There's no hope." Not that he had faith in doctors, but in cause and effect. Benny was allowed to look at the specimen under the technician's microscope. It was an unusual courtesy to allow a man with no more stature or powers of persuasion than Benny, but he was a stubborn man and he loved his mother better than life itself.

Many people say that, but Benny meant it. He loved his mother better than life itself. As he sat by her hospital bed while she was sleeping away the postoperative trauma, he looked at her pale cheeks and her gray hair spread upon the white pillow and whispered, "Please, God, take me, not her."

But her breathing continued raggedly in the quiet room. It would stop for long periods when he thought he had lost her, and then it would suddenly start up again. Maybe he was being too passive, he thought, leaving the decision to someone else.

"O.K.," he said to the empty air, and stood up and walked quietly down the redolent corridor. He rode in the elevator to the first floor, walked out to the parking lot, opened the door to his mother's Chevrolet, stuck his finger in the doorjamb, and slammed the door on it.

The doctor who trimmed and sewed the stump said, "You must have been thinking about your mother."

"That's true," Benny said. The moment after he had slammed the door had been filled with pain worse than anything he had imagined. Surely it hurt worse than death. At the same time, his whole being had been swept by a thrill of satisfaction.

When he went back to look at his mother, her breathing was regular and her eyes were open. She recognized his face and smiled. "Benny, I feel better."

He felt a surge of happiness such as he had not experienced in any of his previous thirty-five years. His sacrifice had been accepted. "I'm going to be all right," his mother said. And she was.

Benny would not have thought any more about that matter, other than a periodic thankfulness for his mother's recovery, had not his mother brought up the matter of the astronauts in their faulty capsule. The capsule was *Apollo 13*, the date was April 11, 1970, and the three "juniors"—Lowell, Haise, and Swigert—were hurtling toward the moon in a capsule with a defective power supply. "There they are," his mother said. "They can't do nothing. It's a real pity nobody down here can help them."

Benny nodded and said nothing, but he thought about it. What was a finger to him compared to life for the astronauts and the honor of his country. This time he lopped off the little finger of his right hand in a paper cutter. It was neater and less painful. His mother turned on the car radio as she was taking him to the emergency room at the hospital. They both heard the announcement that the moon landing had been canceled but that the crew was safe and the capsule was returning to Earth.

The stinging in Benny's right hand was replaced by a feeling of power. Perhaps the rest of the world was helpless, but he was not. He thought about the other three astronauts who had been killed in a flash fire while their capsule had been sitting on the ground. There had been no warning of that, or he might have saved them, too.

The next opportunity came a few months later. A child was dying of leukemia. Benny didn't know the little girl personally, but she lived in his town and the newspaper ran an article about her disease and her courage. Benny thought she was remarkably pretty. He cut off his left little toe with a chisel while he was working on a model boat in the basement. The little girl made a recovery that had her doctors shaking their heads in disbelief, and people began commenting about Benny's clumsiness.

Even his mother, who seldom noticed Benny's mistakes or odd ways, thought something was strange about it. "Can't understand why you was working down there in your bare feet," she said, shaking her head. "Don't see either how you could get your foot up there."

Benny shrugged. He didn't talk much, and he particularly didn't want to talk about this.

Benny was a dishwasher. He had been a poor student, though he tried hard. His teachers said he had a reading problem, but he read murder mysteries all right. He liked the kind that didn't have violence or blood in them. He thought it was because his mind was logical, and he liked to figure them out.

His father had died before Benny could remember him. His father had been an alcoholic who beat his wife when he was drunk and would have beaten his infant son if his wife had not always interposed her body between them. One evening his father had fallen down drunk on a cold, wet night, caught pneumonia, and died within three days. Occasionally Benny felt a moment of regret when he thought that he could have saved him if it had happened when Benny had become aware of his power.

His mother, Ellen, was a strong woman. She had raised Benny all by herself, without help from anyone. When she was young and not bad looking, she had worked as a waitress. Later she tended a machine that made envelopes in a greeting-card factory. When the others stopped at a bar after work for a few beers or went bowling, Ellen went home to Benny.

Her devotion and his father's death may have made Benny excessively dependent upon her—and made other women seem vain and self-centered by comparison. He had never married. He had never even had a date with a woman.

Benny was a master dishwasher. He had a precise blend of speed and thoroughness. He had got his first job in a diner when he was still in high school. When he had dropped out of school at the age of eighteen without a diploma, continuing to wash dishes was the easiest thing to do. Since he lived at home, the pay was okay; he contributed most of it to household expenses. Most important, he liked washing dishes. He could stand with his hands in hot, soapy water and let his mind wander; his hands worked better when he didn't think about them. He graduated from the diner to a restaurant and then to the best restaurant in town. The money wasn't much better, but in Benny's field it was success.

Benny wasn't religious. He didn't go to church; he didn't think what the Sunday school teachers tried to tell him was logical. But he had faith. His mind wandered around to that while he was washing dishes. There had to be a reason for things, he thought. That's why there had to be a God. But there were reasons for other things as well. Good and bad luck, for instance. He had considered all the standard superstitions about bad luck and found them inadequate: black cats, ladders, Friday the 13th, broken mirrors, stepping on cracks, knocking on wood—all the possible ways one could incur or avoid bad luck didn't work. He had tried them all. There was a reason somewhere, but he hadn't found it.

The same with good luck. Some people were lucky; some were not. This he had observed over his thirty-five or so years, but he didn't know the reason. It wasn't God, he felt pretty sure. God wasn't arbitrary, giving good luck to people who didn't deserve it and bad luck to those who deserved it even less. And he didn't buy the bit about "working in mysterious ways." There was no reason God should want to be mysterious; in fact, Benny could think of lots of reasons God shouldn't want to be. It was something else, a connection Benny hadn't discovered, something people did or didn't do that made them winners or losers. That is why Benny didn't find strange his ability to buy life for someone else at the price of a part of himself. He had simply stumbled onto the right cause and effect.

Sometimes he wondered whether other people could do it, too. He thought of asking them, but one by one he considered all the people he might ask, and one by one he discarded them. Even his mother might think he was talking crazy, and he knew there was a cause-and-effect relationship between talking crazy and ending up in a mental institution, and people had mentioned that before. What he was doing and thinking now, he felt certain, fell into an area that most people thought was crazy.

Once he hinted at it to his mother. "Mama, do you think people can heal other people?" he asked.

"Doctors do it all the time," she said.

"I mean healers. Like faith healers."

"I don't know," she said. "I ain't never seen it."

"What if you saw it?"

"Then maybe I'd believe it."

But Benny decided in the end not to test his mother's tolerance. In any case, he liked having a secret, and he believed his situation was special. No one else did what he could do because no one else could do it. Otherwise, there would be a lot more miracle cures and rescues. Of course it was possible that other people could do it but didn't know about it, or that they knew about it and didn't want to do it. But that seemed so unlikely that Benny discarded the idea immediately. Perhaps because he was so unimportant in other ways, he had been made important in this way. There was a reason for everything.

He couldn't wash dishes for a while after he lost his little fingers, but his boss was understanding and Benny and his mother had some money saved. That plus his mother's social security and small pension paid the bills until his stumps could heal. Four fingers on each hand was not an intolerable handicap. And the bit of pain he endured was more than compensated by a feeling of accomplishment, of doing something for the world that nobody else could do—not even the wealthiest philanthropist—and yes, he had to admit it, a feeling of power.

After the third amputation, life became more difficult. The staff at the emergency room had begun to make remarks, and even his mother accused him of being clumsy when he dropped the old refrigerator onto the little toe of his right foot as they were making room for the new one. That was after news had come of a man and his wife lost in the Rocky Mountains for two weeks; she was discovered in good health in a cabin, but the husband had died of a heart attack before the news about them was released.

Other occasions arose, and Benny had to think of increasingly ingenious methods of self-sacrifice in order to avoid the worst aspects of suspicion. Several cases of too little or too much rain came in a row over the next few years. The Mississippi threatened to flood almost the entire Delta area, but the rains stopped and the river crested lower than expected. An entire population of natives was starving in a drought-stricken area of Africa that Benny had never heard of; it didn't matter to Benny: the rain began to fall. The monsoons failed two years in a row in the subcontinent—wherever that was—but the second year they came unexpectedly late, bringing welcome floods to withering crops. On the other hand, a hurricane bore down on Florida before swerving suddenly and harmlessly out to sea.

The local medical community had begun to talk about Benny not simply as accident-prone but as a classic case because of the way his fingers and toes dropped in so regular a fashion. Benny would have varied the order, but each time he had to consider the question of how much the next sacrifice would incapacitate him for simple survival. And then his mother was killed in an automobile accident.

Death was instantaneous. Benny had no fingers or toes left, but he cut off his left hand with a saw. It didn't help. Ellen was dead, and Benny couldn't bring her back. As he bandaged Benny's stump, however, the doctor told him that his mother's liver had been fine right up until the end.

"But, Benny," the doctor said gently, "you're going to have to go into the hospital."

"I don't want to," Benny said.

"But, Benny—you can hardly walk and you can't hold anything."

"I can get by," Benny said stubbornly.

The doctor looked at him suspiciously. "If you lose anything else, you'll have no choice. I'll have no choice."

Getting the United States out of Vietnam took Benny's left foot and put him into the hospital—the psychiatric wing he had always dreaded. But they allowed him a television set, and on it, one day, he saw the assassination attempt on President Reagan. He pulled himself into a wheelchair, and when everybody else was watching the television set in the lounge, he took the freight elevator to the basement, where a repair project was under way and a table saw had been left unattended.

Now Benny was virtually without mobility, and the entire staff was instructed to watch him closely. Though he seemed reasonable enough to talk with, he was, everyone said, definitely and completely round the bend. When the news came of the attempt on the pope's life, Benny had to pull himself out of bed and fall to the floor, then drag himself down the hall to the elevator by one arm to offer his remaining hand to the elevator's descending floor.

The psychiatrist in charge of Benny's case sometimes forgot his professional cool when he couldn't get any answers out of the lump of flesh that was left of Benny. "Can't you give me some idea why you've undergone this crazy program of self-mutilation?" Dr. Frederick asked. He wasn't supposed to use words like crazy, but he was past discretion.

Benny shook his head.

"Was it your mother?" Dr. Frederick asked. "Your father's brutality?"

Benny's eyes flickered, but he didn't speak.

"There had to be a terrible amount of self-hatred to make you cut yourself up this way," Dr. Frederick said.

Benny looked scornful.

"With the world going to hell the way it is," the psychiatrist said despairingly, "surely it doesn't need any help from you."

Benny's eyes moved from the psychiatrist's face to the television set above the doctor's head, where tanks were rumbling in parades and missiles were being raised into firing position.

"It's gonna happen, isn't it?" Benny asked.

It was going to happen, finally, the Armageddon everyone had feared for almost half a century, which Mutually Assured Destruction had finally stopped deterring. Benny knew it as certainly as he had known about his mother's cancer.

"What's going to happen? What?" the psychiatrist asked impatiently.

"That." Benny nodded at the television screen.

"Television?"

"The war. The bombs. The end."

"Maybe."

"I can stop it," Benny said.

"You?"

Benny nodded and began to tell the psychiatrist, calmly, the story of how he had learned about his power and what he had done with it. When he finished, the doctor looked at him for some time in silence.

Finally, he said, "You believe this?"

"It's true." Benny said simply.

"Why haven't you told me this before?"

"I haven't told anybody."

"Why not?"

"I figured they'd put me in a mental institution."

"You are in a mental institution."

"I know. Now it doesn't matter." The talking head stuck on the appendageless torso would have unnerved the keeper of an eighteenth-century snakepit.

"And now you think you can stop World War III by means of a similar bodily sacrifice?" Dr. Frederick asked.

"The last one," Benny said steadily. "It's gonna take a big one this time. But I need help."

"What kind of help?"

"I can't get out of bed. You got to hold the knife."

"You must be out of your mind," Dr. Frederick said. He had done it again.

"But, Doctor—!" Benny began.

"Of course I can't do that," the psychiatrist said. "But I can help in another way."

"Yes?" Benny prompted.

"I can have the nurse give you a tranquilizer."

"Not that! Don't you understand? We're all going to die. Better just me than everybody."

"Nurse!" the doctor called.

"Doctor!"

"Nurse!"

Benny struggled on the bed, but it was no use. He could not evade the pacifying needle. His past sacrifices had left him helpless. Next morning, however, they found his limbless trunk half off the bed. His head was discovered behind the bed, where it had been removed with surgical precision by the adjustable frame. The head was smiling.

Adam Smith was wrong. Benny Geroux was right. Oh, there was no connection between Benny's sacrifice and the events that followed, you understand, but Benny thought there was, and was willing to sacrifice himself for others. The night he made his final sacrifice, the missiles did not arrive.

Now it's up to us.

The Gingerbread Man

Andrew Martin began his transformation on July 4, 2076. It might not have happened at all had he not been interrogating himself about the purpose of life. "The purpose of life," he muttered, looking deep within, "is to avoid pain."

But he was thinking of the pain inflicted upon the psyche by other people and how it would be better not to care what they said or did, or, indeed, to have anything to do with them. In any case, it started, as most things do in life, by accident. In fact, it was the rarest of rarities, an automobile accident. With automated roads and computerized controls, a car could collide with another, or with a stationary object, only by total malfunction, and even malfunctions were programmed to fail-safe. In Andrew's case, however, a computer chip failed at a critical junction, short-circuiting the steering mechanism and the fail-safe devices, and allowed his vehicle to propel itself into and under the back of a computer-driven semi.

Although the airbag seized him in a lover's embrace, it could not totally protect his legs, and his left foot was mangled beyond repair. Having failed at its most important task, the automobile's computer sensed Andrew's physical condition with instant accuracy and tightened a cuff around his lower leg, injected him with a painkiller and a tranquilizer, and summoned an ambulance, which arrived with whumping blades even before the tourniquet needed loosening.

Andrew opened his eyes to the sterile blankness of a hospital ceiling. On the left wall was a window opening on a sunny meadow strewn with red, yellow, and blue wildflowers. A brook babbled through it. Behind the meadow was a green forest rising in the distance to blue mountain peaks capped with snow.

"What's going on?" Andrew asked.

"You're in regional hospital five seven two," the computer responded in a pleasant, concerned female voice. "You have been involved in an automobile accident—"

"An automobile accident!" Andrew interjected.

"An automobile accident," the computer repeated. "Your left foot was crushed. We have replaced it with prosthetic model eff two one eight three. Can you move the toes on your left foot?"

It certainly felt as if he could move the toes on his left foot. Andrew pulled his left leg from under the light thermal covering and held it up for inspection. The leg above the ankle revealed a bit of bruising, but otherwise the leg, including the foot, didn't look any different, and he certainly could move his toes, and without pain. "Are you sure it's the left foot?"

"We do not make mistakes," the computer said pleasantly. "Can you stand on the replacement?"

Andrew swung his legs over the side of the bed and stood on the warm resilient floor beside it. He felt a bit of residual soreness in the calf of his left leg and a bit of stiffness in his back and neck, but his left foot felt fine. In fact, it felt better than fine. He not only had a sharper sense of the temperature of the floor with his left foot than his right, he could feel the small depressions his heel and the ball of his foot and his toes made in the floor covering. In addition he had a feeling of well being in his foot to which he was not accustomed, like power waiting to be unleashed. He rose on his toes and felt a moment of shame that his right foot did not do as well.

"I see that the foot is working," the computer said.

"Indeed," Andrew said.

"Then we have an inquiry about your condition if you are prepared to receive it."

"Who has made the inquiry?" Andrew asked, wondering if it was Jennifer and hoping, perhaps, that it was. But Jennifer had said she never wanted to see him again, and it was from that dismissal he had been fleeing when the accident had occurred, almost as if the computer chip had shared the disorder in his brain.

"A Mrs. Martin," the computer replied.

"But I'm not married," Andrew said.

"She has been identified as your biological mother."

"I will accept the inquiry, of course," Andrew said, although he wondered why his mother had gotten in touch with him now, after twenty years. It wasn't as if they had argued, as he had with Jennifer; they had simply grown apart gradually until they had nothing left to share.

The square on the left wall that had been functioning as a window turned into the face of a woman who looked as young as Jennifer. He compared it with the memory of his mother that still was stored there, but he would never have recognized her.

"Mother," Andrew said, "you have had your face redone."

"Do you like it?" she said, brightening. "Well, it's you I've called about. I was notified of your accident. Imagine having an accident on the highway! Imagine traveling on the highway! Andrew, I can't imagine what got into you! Well, I can't tell you how surprised I was after all these years to be notified that my son, my only son, had been injured. Well, I see you've quite recovered." Her image began to fade into the sunny landscape.

"They replaced my foot, Mother," Andrew said quickly.

His mother's image steadied. "How efficient of them," she said. "Well, if you need anything—"

"And, Mother," Andrew said before she could fade again, "it works so well that I have decided to have the other one replaced as well." He hadn't known he was going to do it until he spoke, but now that the words were out he knew it was what he wanted to do. He could not go through life limping on a less-than-perfect real foot.

A day later Andrew walked out of regional hospital 572. It was located at the intersection of two major highways surrounded by growing crops clear to the horizon. No one else was in sight. It was a virtually silent and efficient scene in which vehicles of various sizes and purposes, but only a single, silvery color, traveled on either side, moving rapidly in several directions and effortlessly maintaining the same distance from the others. None of them was occupied; none of them, indeed, had any windows. He could understand his mother's surprise. He shared it.

He stepped into the waiting taxi and allowed it to whisk him to his home, and when it lowered him onto the landing pad of his apartment building twenty minutes later, he made his way quickly to the elevator and then to his rooms. There were four of them: a bedroom, a living room, a bathroom, and a dining room. With computer service, who needed more? They were decorated according to his own taste for comfort and muted colors, but with easy-to-clean surfaces. He would have liked to have commented to someone about his new vitality, but he had met no one. As soon as he had settled himself into his favorite chair, he called Jennifer.

"I will accept your call this time," Jennifer's image said frostily, "since I have been notified that you have been involved in an accident. But my earlier statement still holds."

"You don't understand," Andrew said. "I feel as if I have wings on my feet, and I'd like to dance. You have criticized my remoteness, my lack of involvement, and I wanted you to know that I feel like getting involved. I want to dance."

"Well—" she said.

They met at a neutral site, at a studio where dancers performed for a television audience. But it was little used any more. Computers could construct new performances from previously recorded routines, Fred Astaire and Margot Fonteyn, say, or Rudolf Nureyev with Isadora Duncan. So Andrew and Jennifer had the studio all to themselves. "Play something fast," Andrew said to the computer while he removed his shoes to allow his new feet more freedom. They began to dance.

The joint exercise lasted only a few minutes, with Andrew and Jennifer scarcely coming closer than a meter or two. Jennifer looked at Andrew and his magic feet, as if waiting for him to make the first move toward companionship, and abandoned the attempt to keep up. Synchronized with the music, Andrew's feet seemed to dance on their own. Jennifer stood against one wall and watched them caper while above them Andrew's body seemed to follow rather than to lead and his face seemed frozen in a look of amazement. After a few more minutes his body began to sag while the feet pounded on untiringly.

Finally Andrew stopped, breathless, his legs trembling but his feet still wiggling beneath him as if eager to continue.

"You dance divinely," Jennifer said, "but you're still the same remote jerk you always have been. I'm going home."

"Wait," Andrew said. "It's my legs. They just can't keep up." But she was gone already, and Andrew dismissed his taxi. He walked his aching body back to his apartment. Scurrying streetsweepers kept the pavement neat, but Andrew met nobody except two police robots who asked politely if he were lost or in need of assistance.

It was then he decided to have his legs replaced.

Afterwards, however, Jennifer refused his calls, and his legs were so filled with energy he allowed them to take him out to run. A green, groomed park was nearby, bisected with paths paved with yielding synthetics, dotted with beds of colorful flowers, redolent with the scent of the outdoors. He seemed to have it all to himself, but as he went by an underpass a group of well-dressed teenagers, who had been hiding themselves from the watchful gaze of the park's monitors, burst out upon him, and he took off with a burst of speed that startled the gang members and surprised Martin himself.

His skill and speed gave him a feeling of invulnerability, and he began to play games with his pursuers, slowing as if he were tiring to allow them to gain on him and then outrunning them once more. He felt exhilarated with a sense of well being and high purpose even though his heart was pounding and his lungs were burning. Moving so swiftly made the air rush past his face; he could see bushes and trees and buildings zoom past and, when he turned his head, his pursuers dwindling.

He remembered a story his computer-generated nanny had told him when he was a child. "I'm the ginger-bread boy, I am, I am, and I can run away from you, I can, I can."

It was his own speed, and his hubris, that doomed him as he caught up with another group of hooligans. They grabbed him and began beating his head and body with sticks and fists. The world went dark as he thought he heard an approaching helicopter and the peremptory voice of a police robot.

He awoke to disorientation. The ceiling looked the same as the one he had stared at so intently when his foot was injured, and the room seemed identical down to the scene in the picture window. "What's going on?" he asked.

The same woman's voice said, "You are in regional hospital five one six. You received irreparable injuries to your chest and internal organs, and we have had to replace them all including your heart, which had gone into arrest. Do you feel all right?"

Andrew thought about it. Except for his head, which ached abominably, he felt good, as if his entire body had the strength and vitality that he had felt before only in his feet and legs. "Yes," he said. "I feel fine. Except for my head."

"Just a moment," the voice said, and he felt a slight pressure against the back of his neck. "Is that better?"

The pain in his head ebbed. "Yes. But my arms feel different."

"They, too, have had to be replaced. It was too difficult to reattach your old ones to your new body."

Andrew flexed them. They seemed as good as new—in fact, new seemed better. "What happened to me?" he asked.

"You were attacked in the park near your home by a group of lawless humans, all under the age of twenty, and the majority of them sixteen or younger."

"And what has happened to them?"

"They have all been sentenced to therapy from six months to two years, according to age. After a second offense, each will be administered daily injections of anti-testosterone."

"Then the process is not effective."

"Recidivism is likely."

Andrew thought about it, although it hurt his head. People apparently had different concepts of the meaning of life: some thought that life meant excitement and were willing to risk punishment and pain, to themselves and to others, to experience it.

"Perhaps you could suggest some other method of treatment," the computer said.

"I can't even make sense of my own life," Andrew said. When he was released he returned to his apartment and tried to get in touch with Jennifer. His call was still blocked. He thought of going back to the park and, with his new body, wreaking vengeance on the gangs that hid there—or on their counterparts if the ones who had attacked him had been disrupted. But he discarded that as unworthy of his new vitality. Still, he needed to do something with this restlessness he felt inside.

He turned to the educational channel. It sprang to life immediately like a genie long imprisoned in a bottle.

Andrew went through the index and finally selected the origins of his society, beginning with the perfection of the computer and its ability to take over the work of the world, the endless services it was able to provide, and the retreat of humanity, with all its needs provided, into self-contained living units from which it seldom ventured. He had been happy enough with that life himself until he had become involved with Jennifer on a network bulletin board. They had corresponded incessantly and then talked image to image before, in what he had considered an incomprehensible fit of pique, she had broken off with him. He went back over their correspondence and conversations to discover what had happened, and the only thing he could find was a conversation in which she had suggested that they meet. He had hesitated. As nearly as he could remember, he had been considering how he might feel in her actual presence. And then he had taken that ill-advised trip to see her, and they had stood at opposite sides of the room while Jennifer yelled at him.

He turned to psychology, hoping to find there the answers to the questions of human behavior, particularly Jennifer's, that had disrupted the comfort and efficiency of his existence. The computerized professors were responsive and well informed, but nothing they said explained why Jennifer had called him remote and unresponsive. The professors said he was normal—that is, he was like everybody else. And they gave many explanations for the behavior of the youth gangs and why they rejected the freedom from social friction that was everybody's birthright and turned to violence, but none of them suggested an answer.

Finally he turned to areas for which there were answers, to physics and astronomy and chemistry and biology and particularly to mathematics. He was told why manned spaceflight had given way to unmanned flights, that the state of knowledge about physics and chemistry had not progressed beyond what was needed to serve known human needs, and about the development of biology to provide repairs to the human body and lengthen the lifespan. Andrew could understand the general outline of what the professors said, but a request for explanation of the details got him nowhere. He didn't have the background necessary to understand. And mathematics left him baffled. What was the good of solid geometry, for instance, and of algebra, much less of calculus?

Eventually he decided to begin at the elementary level. He kept himself and his professors working day and night, scarcely pausing for rest or food. His body felt little need for either but his head began to ache and his eyes, to burn. He felt feverish. His thoughts were jumbled in his head until he could not distinguish what was outside and what was inside.

Finally the light reddened in front of his eyes and he began to lose consciousness.

When he awoke his head was crystal clear for the first time in his life. He understood solid geometry, and as for algebra, he could solve quadratic equations by mental manipulation alone. He could even comprehend human behavior, including his own and he was filled with a longing to be of service. He knew what it was. He needed no computer to tell him: His overworked brain had suffered a disabling breakdown and had been replaced with a positronic model, just like the robots that did the world's work, and his personality, with all its memories, had been impressed upon it. All the makeshift fluids of his body had been replaced, and the replacements were working together as the originals never had. The hormones that had so delighted and confused him had been replaced by electrical impulses. He was now as efficient a human being as a human being could possibly become, and he had abilities that no human being could ever aspire to.

He was linked electronically with the computer network of the world. He knew what it knew, and where others had to communicate their needs by the imperfect mechanism of speech, he could obtain information and command action instantaneously. In fact, he was a part of the computer network at the same time that his personality impress maintained a sense of individual identity. But it was his relationship to the network, he knew, that gave him his need to serve, to put himself and his humanity to use.

What would he do with his new abilities? He considered the possibility of self-sacrifice, of cutting himself free from his new-found abilities, one by one, until at last he relinquished the immortality he had gained through his transformation, or of allowing himself to be destroyed by other humans in some dramatic fashion that would inspire and reform the human species. But it was only for an instant: Salvation was not to be found through sentimentality or by encouraging humanity's tendencies toward belief in the unknown and the unknowable.

He could create art: paintings and sculpture and fiction and drama and music and dance. He knew he could do those things and the act of knowing was simultaneous with the creation itself—the creations were there, stored in the network for production when the occasion was right. All the suffering and exaltation of being human was expressed in those works, ready for contribution to human understanding and redemption. "Let there be art," he thought, and there was art.

He could create an outlet for the misdirected aggressions of the juveniles that had beaten him. What humanity needed was a new frontier, he thought, and he instructed the network to reinvigorate the space program and to create a system of inducements and rewards that would encourage ambitious young people to challenge the unknown and spread humanity as far as human energy and creativity were capable of carrying it.

He could reverse the conditions that had encouraged humanity to retreat to the isolation of the individual cave. Social change had come too swiftly, he understood, and the perfection of the computer network had allowed people to isolate themselves in perfect comfort. He understood them well; he had been one of them. People must be given incentives to interact. He rejected the idea of cutting off computer services and forcing the cave dwellers back into the marketplace; that would create too much suffering and chaos. Instead he instructed the network to develop a system of attractive meeting places and to release the art and the ideas that would support a culture of sharing. That would take longer but the result would be more lasting.

Finally he called his mother. "Mother," he said to her bewildered image, "I appreciate the sacrifices you made to bring me into the world and to nurture me to maturity, and I want you to know that I love you. I know that you have your life and that frequent contact would disrupt that life, but I want you to know that I am fine and you will receive confirmations of that from time to time."

Then he called Jennifer. Call blocking was still in effect, but with his new powers that was easy to override. "Jennifer," he said, "I know that I have given you much to complain about, but I want you to know that I love you and I want to share a life with you, to touch and be touched, to love and be loved."

"Why, Andrew," she said, "I never thought I'd ever hear those words."

He understood now; he had to replace the fallible human parts of himself to be truly human. And he understood that the purpose of life was to discover what a person was good for and then find a way to put it to use.

The Day the Magic Came Back

Dr. Knowland looked around the isolation room at the masked faces of the nurse and of Susan Grinnell, his resident physician in internal medicine, and then back to the face of the child on the hospital bed. Her name was Linda Constant. She was seven years old. With her red cheeks and her long, golden hair spread out upon the pillow, she looked like an angel, but the color in her cheeks came from fever, not good health. Her eyes were closed. Knowland thought they might never reopen. If she were awake to see the three of them standing over her he wondered if she might think they were apparitions from the past, witch doctors come to drive the demons from the body they had possessed.

But the powers of medicine were more limited. Knowland's gaze went to the two bottles of antibiotics hanging inverted from their stands, one on each side of the bed, each with a tube leading to a pump on the IV pole and from there to a needle inserted into a vein at the inner elbow of each small arm. All their medical knowledge, all their armamentarium, were failing before the onslaught of this child's illness, and he was dreading the moment when he would face her parents and tell them that science had been defeated by a simple bacterium, *mycobacterium tuberculosis*.

Knowland turned and walked from the room. He was a man of medium height and graying hair and a slight paunch.

He walked on his heels with his feet turned out, like a duck, as he made his way down the hall. But no one smiled. He was a man of great dignity, and his patients, and many of his co-workers, thought he was the next thing to God.

He went to the nearest lavatory, washed his hands, and removed his mask. When he emerged Susan was waiting for him.

"Isn't there something else we can try?" she asked. Ordinarily she was a plain woman, but when concern transformed her face Knowland thought she was beautiful and that even though her husband was frequently neglected for her nursing duties, he was luckier than he knew.

Knowland shook his head. "The strain is antibiotic-resistant. We've tried the whole spectrum."

She looked at him as if willing him to work a miracle. Knowland shook his head again, this time as if trying to rid himself of a heavy burden. "I'm going to have to tell them."

"The Constants? Do you want me to do it?"

"You'd be better at it," Knowland said, "but they need to hear it from me."

"They've asked if they could bring in someone to see Linda."

"What kind of someone?"

"Someone to pray for her."

Knowland folded his arms across his chest. "They've lost faith in me—I can understand that—but they might have asked me."

"They belong to a sect that believes in healers. They feel that they sinned by bringing Linda to a hospital. They were too afraid to go with their own beliefs. Now they're afraid again. Afraid to ask you."

"If they can bring in a healer?"

She nodded.

"Why not?" Knowland said.

"You're going to let them?"

"We've failed. Why shouldn't they try what they believe in? I've never understood why medicine should deny people the comfort of alternatives."

"You think there's a chance—?"

Knowland looked at her like a teacher disappointed in a promising student. "Faith healers and snake oils don't work. Medicine doesn't oppose them because of that but because they keep the ill from seeking effective treatment. Well, the Constants have tried that and it's failed. Now they can make peace with their daughter's dying in their own way."

Over the next few days Knowland got accustomed to seeing the tall, thin man sitting next to the bed of the tubercular child. He was of that indeterminate age reached by some men between the middle years and the old. He had dark eyes and a beak of a nose like an owl. His hair, though thin, was still black and his skin was unlined, but his face reflected the serenity obtained through long years of experience with the world's tragedies. He said nothing. When he was offered a mask, he shook his head. He held the child's hand and stared at her as if the power of his will was enough to force open her eyes, to turn on her smile, to make her well again.

Linda's parents, one at a time or together, often were present as well, but they stood on the other side of the bed, smoothing their daughter's hair or cooling her fever with a wet cloth. They asked Susan and then Knowland to stop the antibiotics. They pointed at the places on the child's arms and hands where the needles had left ugly hematomas on their daughter's delicate skin and agonized over the nurses' struggles to find new places to insert heparin locks.

"I can't," Knowland said. "If you want the treatment to stop, you'll have to remove her from my care."

"You said you can't help her," the mother said. She was a sturdy woman with freckles and a sunburned nose. Her hair had once been yellow, like her daughter's, but now was an indeterminate brown.

"I know," Knowland conceded, "but I can't stop trying. Just as you can't." They were standing outside the isolation room. He nodded toward the door where their healer sat with the sick child.

The Constants gave up their efforts to stop the medical treatment. They feared removing her from the antisepsis and the round-the-clock attentions of the hospital, and their healer seemed not to care. He did not care, either, about the activities of the hospital staff around him. He kept his vigil and ignored everything else, leaving only, Knowland presumed, to take care of his physical needs. It was a presumption on Knowland's part: The healer was always there when the doctor opened the door on his rounds.

On the fourth day, the healer was gone and Linda looked better. Her temperature had dropped, and the false flush of fever in her cheeks had faded. She had not opened her eyes, but she had summoned the strength to cough again.

On the fifth day she was awake and recognizing her parents. On the sixth day she was sitting up and talking to everyone, her parents, the nurses, Susan, even Knowland. She had been everyone's favorite patient in the hospital and they all celebrated the normality of her temperature and pulse. Her cough had disappeared, and her chest sounded better. A few rales and cracks, but even they seemed to be diminishing. The sputum samples came back negative.

"When are you going to release her?" Susan asked.

"Tomorrow."

"Shouldn't we continue the antibiotics for a few more days?"

Knowland did not like questions about his judgment, and sometimes he snapped at students. But this time he seemed distracted. "Look at the record," he said mildly. He had admitted to himself, although he had not yet come to the point of admitting it to his resident, that the antibiotics had done nothing.

"If it wasn't the antibiotics," Susan said, "then what was it?"

Knowland shook his head. Next day, as the Constants checked their daughter out of the hospital, Knowland asked them the name of their healer.

"Mr. Alma," Constant said. He was a robust man, a farmer, with weathered hands, a pale forehead, and a brown face from the cheeks down.

"That's his real name?"

"That's his name," Constant said.

"Why didn't you call him in sooner?"

"He was on another mission," Mrs. Constant said. And then she added, as if admitting a lapse of faith, "We were afraid."

"And where can I find Mr. Alma?"

"Why do you want to?" Constant asked.

Knowland shrugged. "I don't know. We might have something talk about." He didn't know what it might be, yet.

A week later he had figured it out. The address the Constants had given him turned out to be a storefront in a part of the city that had completed a good part of the cycle from decent housing to slum to restoration. The storefront, however, was still in the slum stage. It had once been a hardware store, but the glass had been broken out of the front windows and replaced by plywood. The plywood had been painted green at one time, scrawled with graffiti, and then painted pink, graffitied, painted blue and later other colors so that now words, drawings, and colors came through indistinctly like palimpsests from the beginning of the world. Where a sign had once said "Hardware" other words had been neatly lettered: "All Souls Chapel."

The first time Knowland knocked at the battered wooden door he got no answer. The second time, a service of some kind was in progress—he could hear someone speaking and the mumble of an audience—and Knowland couldn't wait. The third time, late in the afternoon, he heard a voice asking him to enter. The interior of the room was gloomy after the sunshine outside, and a few moments elapsed while his vision was adjusting. The room was neat and clean but shabby. Folding chairs were arranged carefully across the floor, eight across and eight deep. Beyond them was an old wooden desk. Behind the desk was the dark-haired man the Constants had called Alma.

"I'm Dr. Knowland," he said.

"I know you." The man's voice was thin and reedy, and Knowland realized it was the first time he had heard it.

"I wanted to ask you about Linda Constant."

Alma nodded.

Knowland approached the desk that perhaps also served as a rostrum or pulpit or maybe even an altar. "How is she?"

"She's well," Alma said, "but you don't need me to tell you that."

"No," Knowland said. He sat down in one of the folding chairs, suddenly feeling as if his knees were unable to support him. He looked down at his soft, white hands and then up at Alma waiting patiently behind the desk. "How did you do it?"

"It weren't you and your medicines?"

"You know it wasn't."

"Most doctors take credit for what happens in their hospitals," Alma said.

"I'd failed. I know that. I want to know why you succeeded. Was it faith? Some kind of supernatural intervention? God?"

The tall, thin man stood up, towering now above the seated physician. "None of them. You may use it agin me, but I'll give you the truth—"

Knowland waved his hand impatiently. "I just want to know one thing. All my life have I been wrong about the world and the way it works?"

"Once upon a time people would have called me shaman and honored me," Alma said. "Later folks'd call me a witch and burn me at the stake. Today I'm called a faith healer and scorned." His soft voice was without passion. "All I do is put sick people right with the way things is, underneath, where the real stuff is."

Knowland's hands tightened and he was sorry he had come, but he could think of no easy way to leave, and as he listened to Alma's soft voice he began to realize that what the man was talking about in his inadequate vocabulary was physics and biology.

Later, he was seated in his office when Susan arrived for their daily conference. His desk was broad and polished, and he had an oriental rug on the floor, a broad window behind him opening on trees and a carefully tended green lawn dotted with flower beds, and bookcases filled with medical texts on either side. For several minutes he stared without speaking at a medical file in front of him. Finally Susan asked if something was bothering him.

"The healer's name is Alma," Knowland said without looking up. "That isn't his real name, of course, but he wouldn't tell me that. He told me other things. It is easier to be considered a preacher than a healer, he said. Preachers are unregulated; anybody else can be prosecuted for practicing medicine without a license."

Susan looked at him with concern. "Why did you go to see him?"

"Something happened in that hospital room with Linda Constant, and I wanted to know what it was. No, that's wrong—I had to know what it was."

"The antibiotics finally took effect," Susan said.

"You know that isn't true," he said. "It was something else, something frightening."

People have always understood, Knowland said, that the mind could influence the body. Even medical science conceded the reality of psychosomatic illnesses and sometimes the fact that recovery was aided by a positive attitude. It could be called psychosomatic healing. But medical science had no mechanism for the operation of psyche on the soma, and it denied the ability of someone else's mind to heal another person's sickness.

Alma had come up with a mechanism, and as Knowland had listened to Alma's thin voice only able to hint at the abstractions the healer was attempting to describe, Knowland had come to understand it, too. The underlying reality of the universe, Alma had said, lies far beneath the perceptions of the creatures that live within it. "In the beginning was the word," said an astronomer named Harlow Shapley, Knowland thought, "and the word was hydrogen."

Humanity cannot see or hear or touch or smell or taste the basic reality, because it is atomic and molecular and cellular. The only thing humanity has that can compare with that intangible micro-stuff from which all the macro-stuff is built is the mind. Thought, like atoms and molecules and cells, exists without being tangible, and thought not only can encompass the basic reality it can influence it. Alma could persuade the body's cells and the bacteria and the viruses to work together rather than like selfish individuals.

That is what Alma had told the physician. In spite of the evidence provided by Linda's recovery, Knowland could not accept such farfetched claims, but he also could not deny the bare possibility that Alma might not be a charlatan.

Once Alma said, magic had worked because people believed in it. It wasn't a case of ignorant people trying to explain a world filled with uncontrollable forces and inexplicable events by peopling it with spirits and demons and gods. A few of them, the shamans, perceived a deeper truth than the deceptive world of everyday reality. And the perceptions enabled some of them to shape that deeper truth to the needs of the people around them. Of course, it was easy to make mistakes or, as such positions brought honor and privilege, to pretend to a power that one didn't possess. Sometimes the truths also became confused and turned into visions that were interpreted differently by prophets and messiahs, becoming religions and superstitions, but were reflections of the underlying reality that is and always has been unified and available. It was nature, not the supernatural. And then science came along, with its objective reality and demonstrated power over nature, and faith weakened and shamans forgot and were forgotten. The magic was lost.

"And you believed this?" Susan asked.

Knowland could see she was concerned about his mental stability. Had the experience with Linda unhinged his mind? "What's remarkable about it is that this man of almost no education has come up with a theory about the nature of the universe that is not much different from that of our most learned physicists."

Susan frowned. "That sort of thing is out there in the popular press and on science programs. If it worked, that would be remarkable."

"Yes," Knowland said. "It seemed to work in the case of Linda Constant."

"Medical literature is filled with spontaneous cures."

"Do you know how weak that sounds? What we cannot explain we call spontaneous, as if that explains anything."

"What are you going to do?"

"I've asked Alma to let me go along on a few of his healing sessions. You may have to cover for me."

"Of course. But aren't you concerned about being too—?"

"Gullible?" He knew his expression reflected an inner turmoil, and he knew Susan was watching him for signs of a mental breakdown. But he could not conceal the doubts that were eating away at a lifetime of belief. "Of course I am. My reputation would be ruined if anyone found out I was taking Alma seriously. But I'm also concerned, as a man of science, about denying the existence of phenomena that I can see in front of me."

They formed an odd team, the tall, thin healer and the shorter, plumper physician. Their visits never took them to hospitals. Instead they met in bedrooms of decaying houses and apartments. Sometimes the bedroom was the only room or the only one presentable enough for visitors, and the ailing person had been moved into it. Many were neat, but whether the rooms were clean or filthy, Alma went about his business without a glance or a word.

He allowed Knowland to check the ailing person's pulse, temperature, and blood pressure, and to make a routine physical examination, listening to the heart and the lungs and feeling the lymph glands. Knowland would take a blood sample and come to a tentative diagnosis that he later checked, as best he could, in the laboratory. Then the vigil began. Knowland could not take time away from his normal practice and teaching to monitor the entire process of healing, but checked on each person at the beginning of the vigil, in the middle and at the end. Over a period of four weeks, Alma had recorded a remarkable string of successes.

As nearly as Knowland could tell without full clinical examinations, one elderly woman had a blood infection, an old man had kidney failure, a middle-aged woman had pancreatic cancer, a middle-aged man had pneumonia, and a ten-year-old boy had leukemia. All were poor and some were virtually without means. Two lived in the country on small plots; one was a squatter, and the other lived on land that had been left from what had once been a more extensive farm. Three lived in the inner city. The rural residents, at least, had gardens and neighbors. Those in the inner city subsisted on welfare and food stamps and junk food.

Knowland resisted the urge to get them into a hospital where their conditions could be treated. He tried to tell himself that this was a scientific experiment, but he could not shake the feeling that he had violated his Hippocratic Oath and, more important, his personal principles. He thought about the studies in syphilis allowed to continue in Alabama and the experiments conducted in Nazi Germany under the guise of science. He felt that way, that is, until the ailing individual began to show improvement. All but the old man with the renal condition were out of their beds and back to normal activities after a week. They seemed, as far as Knowland could discern, to be cured, although if his original diagnoses had been correct, the pancreatic cancer at least had been terminal. The leukemia might have gone into remission, but the rapidity and the extent of recovery were uncharacteristic. Without proper diagnoses and data, the cases were without scientific standing and would be worthless as anything but anecdote, but Knowland knew that with the best of luck he might have been successful with only two of the illnesses.

At the end of the month, Knowland congratulated Alma on his healings. They were standing outside one of the tenements surrounded by litter and uncollected garbage. The odor was strong, but Knowland ignored it. "If anybody had told me about these cases, I wouldn't have believed him."

"They'll not believe you, either," Alma said.

"What about the man with the renal condition?"

"The what?"

"The old man with the kidney problem. The one who died."

"He'd much to overcome," Alma said. "And I couldn't reach his—I know not what to call it."

"How many do you lose?"

"A few. Here and there. Sometimes I can't touch their will to live. Sometimes my power fails. Sometimes they fight me."

"Skepticism?"

"I give it no name," Alma said. "Some cling too strong to the world of the senses; some won't hold with the unseen."

"Have you ever tried to teach someone else to do what you do?" Knowland asked.

"People can be shown how to heal if they can see the hidden truth and if they has the power. I was taught as a boy and have taught some others the same; many cannot learn. But those that can, they spread far and wide. Beyond the seas, there may be many, I sense. Maybe some places never lost the truth."

Knowland thought for a moment and then asked, "If I

could set up some controlled experiments, would you participate? While you worked could we check your pulse, your blood pressure, your brain waves?"

"No," Alma said.

"No?" Knowland said. "And yet you allowed me—"

"You cared about Linda. You let me help her. But this other would not work. Even with evidence, people would doubt, and I would be shamed. My people would wonder. Maybe question my power." Alma looked at Knowland. "This troubles you."

When Knowland spoke, his voice was uneven. "How can we control this power, turn it into a science, if we cannot study it?"

"Some things science warn't meant to control," Alma said.

Susan found Knowland in the doctor's lounge, a clean, sterile room with shiny chromium furniture, a coffee maker, a small refrigerator with soft drinks, and no humanizing touches, not even curtains at the windows. "Look who I've got," Susan said, too brightly. She was holding Linda Constant's hand, and the seven-year-old was hanging back, the other hand to her mouth, looking overwhelmed by the building and its official-looking occupants. "Her mother brought her to say hello."

"Hello, Linda," Knowland said gently, holding out his hand.

The child hesitated for a moment and then reached for his hand with the hand that had been at her mouth and put it trustingly in his. It felt wet, but Knowland shook it and said, "How are you feeling, Linda?"

"I'm fine," Linda said. "You don't have a mask."

"No, it isn't necessary now, is it?"

The little girl shook her head. "I feel all well," she said.

"That's good," Knowland said. "Stay that way."

"I will," she said with conviction, and turned toward the door. She looked back. "My mother said to tell you 'thanks,' " she said.

"You're welcome," Knowland said.

When Susan returned, Knowland was looking at his stethoscope, turning it over and over in his hands as if he had never seen one before and was trying to figure out what it was good for. He looked up. "Por nada," he said.

"She's well again," Susan said. "That's what counts."

"Is it?" Knowland looked toward the window where the afternoon sunshine was struggling through the leaves of the giant pin oak that shielded this side of the hospital.

"You can't blame yourself for someone else's success. If that is what it was."

"That would be mean-spirited, wouldn't it," Knowland said. "Alma's method works. He heals people."

"Even if that's true," Susan said, "there has always been room in the world for the people of faith and the people of science. You'll have plenty of work to do."

Knowland turned on the bench seat of the couch. "You think I'm concerned because Alma and his kind will put me and you out of business?"

Susan looked surprised at Knowland's question.

Knowland looked back toward the window. "I suppose there's some of that. Some jealousy is hard to avoid. But more than that is at stake here."

"What is at stake?" she asked.

"It's not just the healing. It's science itself. The ability to manipulate the basic reality of the universe may start with restoring people to health, but what is to stop it from working miracles of other kinds?"

"Like what?" Susan asked.

Knowland shrugged. "Creating food. Loaves and fishes, say. Or gold. Or death for our enemies and good fortune for our friends. Energy for free if our supplications are proper; atomic explosions if they are not. Once magic is let loose upon the world again, there is no place it cannot touch."

"I didn't have your experience with Alma. But even if magic worked," Susan said, catching her breath in the middle, "surely there would be rules and controls."

"The very essence of magic is that there are no controls," Knowland said. "Only other magic."

Susan raised her chin stubbornly. "Then you'll just have to learn how to do it yourself."

"That's just it," Knowland said. "I can't. I'm too tied to the sensory world I perceive around me, that I have lived with all my life. I'm too committed to science, to ways of understanding that have nothing in common with faith. I'm bound by the physical laws I learned long ago."

"Is that why you're upset?"

"No," Knowland said. "That isn't it. The important thing is not who does it but that it can be done only by those chosen by some unseen power to possess this unique ability. Like the princess and the pea or King Arthur and the sword in the stone. Not earned but given. The image of the future is the Middle Ages. That's Camelot under another name. The divine right of kings and the magical rites of the Elect."

"Even so," Susan said, "isn't it worth a great deal to have something to fall back on? Something that can help when medical science can't?"

"To everybody seeking mercy, the appeal of magic is irresistible," Knowland said. "But it means that medicine and science are finished. All science can offer is justice. Science has much to answer for, including its neglect of mercy, but it transformed the world into something egalitarian instead of hierarchical. Science created democracy and affluence and individual choice. Now the magic has come back and the world is going to be changed beyond recognition, and it is not going to be in the hands of those who work hard and study and understand but of the Elect. They may do good, they may do evil, but science is ended, and with it any possibility of getting ahead, and of pulling the rest of humanity along, by anything but good fortune or the blessings of the Chosen."

"I don't think I ever told you," Susan said, "that my brother is HIV positive."

Something snapped. As Susan watched, Knowland walked to the wastebasket beside the coffee machine and dropped into it his broken stethoscope.

The Lens of Time

Broadway swarmed with life like water in a stagnant pond. Scarlet and yellow omnibuses raced through the open parts of the street and locked wheels where it was narrower. At irregular intervals they stopped to discharge passengers. When the passengers stretched their hands through a hole in the roof to pay the conductor his ransom for release, he pulled a cord that opened the door and deposited them in a sea of slippery mud, to run a gauntlet of cart wheels and horses' hooves, before they could reach the relative safety of the pavement next to the buildings. Loaded stages stopped in front of hotels such as the Astor House or the St. Nicholas. Railway cars holding as many as thirty persons and drawn by two or even four horses came down the side streets. All these among the carriages, the commercial wagons, and the foot traffic contributed to the clutter and the crush. Next to the buildings or leaning over into the gutters were boxes, buckets, lidless flour barrels, baskets, decayed tea chests, rusty iron pans, and earthenware jars full of ashes and vegetable refuse. All contributed their share of foul odors to that of the horse dung steaming in the ankle-deep mire of the street.

The man in the black cloak stood at the corner of 8th street and Broadway looking at the turmoil around him with the observant gaze of a scientist, absorbing the scene as a panorama before isolating the individual parts and analyzing them. What passed him was a polyglot mix of workmen and gentry, settled citizens and confused immigrants with their bundles of clothing hung over their backs. Some spoke American English, but many conversed in German and others in English transformed in Ireland into music.

In all that confusion of traffic and appearance and dress, no one paid any attention to the man in the black cloak. He picked his way down Broadway, staying close to the buildings to avoid being splashed by the on-rushing vehicles and horses, and worked his way around heaps of refuse, until he reached Jones street. His eyes focused on a sign attached to a building on the west side. The sign read "Pfaff's" and stairs led down to a cellar entrance.

As the man in the black cloak opened the door his ears were assailed by the confused clamor of laughter and multilingual conversation, clattering dishes and clinking glasses, and voices shouting, and he breathed in the heady odor of lager beer and rich German food. The room was filled with wooden tables and chairs that extended to a modest bar against the wall, flanked by a swinging door leading to a kitchen. As the man in the black cloak stepped into the room, he could see that the room extended into an alcove under the sidewalk. There, at a huge table set with dishes and glasses, some twenty young men and a couple of women were talking with great animation. All but one were fashionably dressed.

The man in the black cloak seated himself at an unoccupied table nearby and ordered a glass of wine before he turned to watching the table of revelers in the alcove. Occasionally he could overhear a scrap of conversation or song, but mostly the competition for attention created only a hubbub of noise. From time to time someone left, lingeringly, as if tearing himself from loved ones, and sometimes one or more persons arrived to a chorus of welcomes and clasps of fellowship.

Finally a man arose unsteadily from near the head of the table, and with many long farewells, made his way toward the door. He had a young face, although at the moment it was flushed and the eyes were a bit glazed. He had a broad forehead from which his long brown hair had already started to recede, a substantial nose that had been broken at least once, and a receding chin that he partially concealed by a bushy, swooping mustache. As he passed, the man in the black cloak arose from his chair and said, "Mr. O'Brien?"

"You have my name, sir," the other said, a touch of Ireland in his voice. "But you have the advantage of me."

"You are Fitz-James O'Brien, the noted poet, playwright, and author?" the man in the cloak continued.

"The same," O'Brien replied with a hint of impatience.

"Let me apologize for accosting you thus," the man in the cloak said, "but my name is T. J. Whelpley. I am a physician, and a writer, though not by any means of your stature and renown, and I have been waiting to speak to you on a matter of some urgency."

"And what would that be, Dr. Whelpley?"

"Will you come to my rooms, Mr. O'Brien, so that I can show you something interesting and we can talk at leisure?"

"Do you have any beer?" O'Brien asked.

"I have some reasonably good claret."

"Claret will do," O'Brien said. "I was going to my room to work on a new poem, but, to tell the truth, it was only duty that called me and not Calliope or Erato. Lead on, my dear Dr. Whelpley."

In the common spots of mould, which my mother, good housekeeper that she was, fiercely scooped away from her jam pots, there abode for me, under the name of mildew, enchanted gardens, filled with dells and avenues of the densest foliage and most astonishing verdure, while from the fantastic boughs of these microscopic forests hung strange fruits glittering with green, and silver, and gold.

They emerged into the night of Broadway, lit now by gas jets and scarcely less busy than by day. Indeed, it was crowded even more by the parade of a uniformed company of the New York Seventh Regiment.

"The latest census counts more than 600,000 residents of this small island," O'Brien said, "and it has almost doubled in the past decade. Where will we put the people and the horses and the vehicles when there are a million?"

"They will come sooner than you think," Whelpley said. "But there is much room for growth north of Forty-second Street. Steam soon will replace horses, and who knows, the new Central Park may one day be aptly named."

A clanging sound down the street was followed by the appearance of a fire engine dragged along by a crew of more than twenty men followed by a mob of shouting and cheering boys. The volunteers wore large boots, dark pantaloons held up by leather belts, thick red shirts, and firemen's helmets.

"Many famous people of the literary and theater world were gathered at your table," Whelpley said.

O'Brien laughed. "The Bohemians. A hearty, hard-drinking lot. But redeemed by genius. Or so we tell ourselves."

"Was that Mr. Whitman, the poet, sitting on the other side of the table? The one with the open-necked shirt and the flowing hair?"

"You mean the editor of the *Brooklyn Daily Eagle*?"

"His *Leaves of Grass* came out two years ago."

"And a queer, unrhymed thing it was, too. Hardly any meter either. Yet it has a strange power," O'Brien mused. "Perhaps I will try this free verse myself one day."

"Have you ever considered," Whelpley asked, "the power you wield over the soul of this developing city and nation?"

O'Brien laughed again, boisterously. "We Bohemians? You give us too much credit. We are poor scrabbling fools trying to scratch out a living by our wits and our influence is as ephemeral as the paper on which our words are printed."

The two men were silent as they made their way along the paved pedestrian walk, a few inches above Broadway's mire. Whelpley moved purposively, O'Brien, a bit unsteadily. Ragged women, some not twelve years old, tugged at their clothing and tried to look desirable.

"Get along with you, girls," O'Brien said gruffly. He turned to Whelpley. "Is it far? I'm getting thirsty."

"We're almost there," Whelpley said. They had been passing business buildings with ornate stone or cast-iron fronts, but now a row of decaying mansions was on their left, massive staircases leading to small porches. "Here," Whelpley said.

O'Brien looked up at the building. "Like me, you live in a boarding house. Where will we put those million people, do you think?"

"Housing will be built, some kinds of apartments, I would guess."

Whelpley led the way, unlocking the front door, and entering a once stately hall, now stained and marred by time. To the left was what had once been a sitting room, with a cheerful fireplace and a scattering of chairs and tables. To the right was a dining room with a big table surrounded by chairs. This part of the house, at least, had been kept up, although the hall smelled of boiled potatoes and onions and fried meat. Ahead was a broad staircase leading to an upper floor. Up that staircase Whelpley led O'Brien and then, ignoring the smaller staircase leading to the upper floors, he turned right and unlocked a door.

Inside was not simply the single room of most boarding houses but several rooms. Whelpley lit a gas jet to reveal the first of them, a physician's office with desk and chairs and bookcases, examining table and glass cases filled with instruments and bottles filled with pharmaceuticals, and charts of the human anatomy upon the walls. Beyond, to the right, O'Brien glimpsed what seemed a bedroom; to the left, as Whelpley lit the gas there as well, O'Brien could see a third room fitted out as a kind of laboratory. Racks of chemicals filled the walls and experimental tables, equipped with retorts and tubes and bottles of fluid, were arranged neatly about the bare floor.

"You are a scientist as well as a physician," O'Brien observed. "Now about that claret. . . ."

Whelpley motioned O'Brien into the laboratory. Indicating a stool in front of a bench on which stood some kind of instrument draped with an off-white canvas cover, Whelpley left the room and a few moments later returned, absent his cloak, with a decanter half full of reddish liquid and a couple of tumblers. "Forgive the absence of amenities," he said. "I don't entertain in my rooms." He poured both tumblers half full.

"Nor do any of us unlanded gentry." O'Brien picked up the glass and sipped it as if judging its age and character. "That is good stuff," he said, "as good as ever I had in London or Paris." He drained it in a couple of swallows and held out his glass for a refill.

"First let me show you what I brought you here to see," Whelpley said. He lifted the cover from the instrument on the table in front of O'Brien. It was a microscope, almost a work of art with a slender brass barrel extending above brass feet, an exquisitely machined knob on the side, and a silvered mirror below. Whelpley lit a small gas jet on the table, took up an eyedropper full of water from a nearby jar, squeezed a drop onto a glass slide, and slipped it into arms just above the mirror. Looking through the eyepiece, he adjusted the mirror and the knob to bring the slide into focus. "Now," he said, lifting his head and gesturing for O'Brien to take his place.

O'Brien hesitated and then, shrugging, peered into the eyepiece. He raised his head. "I don't see a thing."

"Take a moment for your eye to adjust," Whelpley said. "Just relax. Don't try to make something happen."

O'Brien sighed and looked again through the eyepiece. After a moment he twitched and said, "Fascinating!"

"What do you see?"

"Lots of little creatures moving around as if in another world. What is it?"

"That's a drop of water I got from a nearby well. And those little creatures, or animalcules, are part of the process of life. We drink them. They live within us or they die. They may even make us ill. They share our world, but they—and we—know nothing of the other. Until now."

Like all active microscopists, I gave my imagination full play. Indeed, it is a common complaint against many such, that they supply the defects of their instruments with the creations of their brains. I imagined depths in Nature which the limited power of my lenses prohibited me from exploring. I lay awake at night constructing imaginary microscopes of immeasurable power, with which I seemed to pierce through all the envelopes of matter down to its original atom.

O'Brien looked at the microscope with greater respect. It was not only an artificer's work of art, it had the unsuspected power of revealing the unknown, perhaps the unknowable. "I've heard of the microscope, of course, but I had no idea—What kind of microscope is it?"

"It's called a Spencer Trunion," Whelpley said. "But that's not important."

"To a writer everything is important." O'Brien was excited now. He had forgotten about the claret. Once more he peered into the eyepiece and studied the slide. "Incredible!" he muttered.

"What is incredible is what it means."

"Of course. What a fine story it would make."

"Perhaps you can use it for one of your 'Man About Town' columns for *Harper's*."

"It's too good an idea to waste on a column. No, it should be a story in its own right. Someone looks through a microscope, maybe a really big one, and sees—what? Something wonderful!"

Whelpley half-filled O'Brien's glass but O'Brien ignored it. "Perhaps we should talk in the other room where there are chairs."

The physician picked up both glasses and moved into the examination room. He put the glasses on the desk, took his seat behind it, and motioned O'Brien into the chair in front.

"You want me to write about the unsuspected creatures that lurk around us, that we breathe in and we drink, that may make us ill," O'Brien said.

Whelpley shook his head. "They may indeed injure us. A German physiologist has already speculated about the microscopic basis of life itself, and biology is destined to become the queen of the sciences. But what I am concerned about is even more basic than that, and that is the growing conflict between reason and emotion."

"What if a microscopist should actually see another

world?" O'Brien said. "It would have to be a different kind of microscope, of course, or someone would have seen it before."

"People will make better microscopes," Whelpley said, "just as they improve on everything. McCormick's reaper has been around a quarter of a century, the telegraph for two decades, nitroglycerin for a dozen years. Invention is changing our lives. Why, I hear that someone has invented an elevator, which means that the height of buildings in Manhattan no longer will be limited by the distance people can climb stairs."

"How could a better microscope be built?" O'Brien said. "More lenses? Different materials? Is there something exotic one could make a lens out of? A diamond, perhaps?"

"Actually a diamond was used for a lens sometime in the 1820s with no improvement in resolution," Whelpley said. "What I want to talk to you about, however, is the way science is changing our lives. A couple of European political philosophers commented on the process a decade ago." He removed a book from the shelves behind his desk, flipped it open, and began to read from it. " 'The bourgeoisie during the rule of scarce 100 years has created more massive and more colossal productive forces than have all preceding generations together. Subjection of nature's forces to man, machinery, application of chemistry to industry and agriculture, steam navigation, railways, electric telegraphs, clearing of whole continents for cultivation, canalization of rivers, whole populations conjured out of the ground—what earlier century had even a presentiment that such productive forces slumbered in the lap of social labor.' "

"Maybe one could use this new all-purpose stuff, this electricity, in combination with a lens made out of diamond," O'Brien went on.

"Look at what the railroad has done to this country, already, linking distant places," Whelpley said. "Why, there's a state in the southwest as big as five New Yorks, and one clear on the other coast less than a decade old, with fields of gold sufficient to satisfy everyone's greed. And in another decade we may be able to travel to both of those states by railroad. Distance will be annihilated. And one day we'll fill up all that empty space with people."

"But how would some innocent experimenter find out about such a process?" O'Brien mused.

"Look at what has happened in electricity," Whelpley said. "Every decade, beginning in 1800, has come a new development: the storage battery, the electric motor, the electric generator. . . . What will come next? Electric lights? The harnessing of sound, voice communication over long distances?"

"Perhaps a medium might put him in touch with some long-dead microscopist," O'Brien said.

"And basic science. Like the nature of matter or chemical combination, or the origin of life. There's a French scientist trying to figure out why wine turns sour. Who knows what may come of that?"

"I could write a story about someone building a fantastic microscope using a lens made of diamond," O'Brien said.

"What the world needs," Whelpley said, "is a better understanding of science and how it is changing the world for the better. Or the worse. Of course invention has been applied to warfare as well—rifle bullets for instance, and the firearm magazine, and the revolver. Ways to kill more people faster."

"But where would he get a diamond big enough to use as a lens?" O'Brien said.

She swept out from between the rainbow-curtains of the cloud-

trees into the broad sea of light that lay beyond. Her motions were those of some graceful Naiad, cleaving, by a mere effort of her will, the clear, unruffled waters that fill the chambers of the sea. She floated forth with the serene grace of a frail bubble ascending through the still atmosphere of a June day. The perfect roundness of her limbs formed suave and enchanting curves. It was like listening to the most spiritual symphony of Beethoven the divine, to watch the harmonious flow of lines.

"Look at that," Whelpley said, gesturing at a drawing hanging on the far wall. O'Brien turned to look at it. The drawing displayed the human body, with the skin removed to reveal the muscles and the internal organs. "The part that distinguishes us from the animals, the brain, is so small compared to our oversized genitals. Our lusts, our emotions, are more important to us than our rational processes."

"My microscopist would have to fall in love with something," O'Brien said. "Maybe a beautiful female creature living in a world far beyond his reach, beyond even the ability to hear or understand his hopeless passion."

"People fear thought when they ought to fear uncontrolled emotion," Whelpley said. "You and your friends, these men of genius, could help explain and dramatize the issues, the prospects for the future, could give readers a sense of what the future will bring and how their own humanity may be enhanced by it."

"Of course it would be futile," O'Brien said.

"Because if we don't do something, the passions accumulating in the world will find expression that may shatter every hope. Revolution is epidemic in Europe, and in this country events move us toward civil war."

"War? Here?" O'Brien said. At last Whelpley had claimed his attention.

Whelpley reached into the shelf behind him and removed a book that he pushed across the desk toward O'Brien. "Have you read this?"

O'Brien picked up the book and looked at its title. "Dear Sentimental Mistress Stowe," he said ironically. "One doesn't read a book like this, one browses through it."

"Thousands of people have read it, and it has inflamed their imaginations. I believe in the abolition of slavery and the freeing of the slaves, but rationally—not through bloodshed and anger."

"Surely it will not come to that," O'Brien said.

"Perhaps not for slavery alone, but for political reasons dividing the northern and southern states. The fighting in Kansas is only the prelude to a larger battle. Already a senatorial candidate in Illinois has told his state convention that 'a house divided against itself cannot stand.' If someone like that gets elected president, what do you think the southern states will do?"

"Why, they will work like hell at the next election, of course," O'Brien said.

"If they behaved rationally," Whelpley said. "But fear and hatred are powerful emotions, and I foresee great tragedies ahead unless thinking men and women work together to quench the flames of passion with the cool waters of reason."

"A sort of volunteer fire-fighting company of the mind, eh, Dr. Whelpley?" O'Brien said.

"You joke," Whelpley said. "Yet I am perfectly serious. A war between the states would shatter this nation for generations and create hatreds that would last for a century. If war should start after the next presidential election, you yourself would be one of the first to volunteer, and being the romantic Irish gentleman that you are, you would seek the heat of the battle and be killed within the first year along with hundreds of thousands of young men north and south."

"You may be right," O'Brien said. He did not seem disturbed at the prospect. "To die in the service of one's adopted country would not be so terrible a fate." He reflected upon the matter for a moment. "It would, at least, settle my debts once and for all. My microscopist would have to die, of course. Or perhaps go mad."

"If you insist on writing a story about a microscopist," Whelpley said, "then make him a scientist, discovering the causes of disease, perhaps ministering to dying soldiers and discovering the causes and treatments of putrefaction."

O'Brien smiled knowingly. "You may understand microscopes, but you don't understand human nature. To make a perfect microscope is an act of hubris, and it must be punished by Nemesis."

"It's you, my dear O'Brien, who do not understand science. To explore more deeply is not an act of hubris but a use of those faculties that distinguish mankind from the brutes, and to discover the ways in which the Universe works is to free oneself from Nature's tyranny rather than to invoke the wrath of the Gods. And that is the vision I would hope you would help make available broadly before it is too late."

"It wouldn't work," O'Brien said, lifting his glass and draining its contents. He looked longingly at the decanter and then rose to his feet, no longer unsteady. "I don't have the power. None of us has the power. And not a person is changed by poetry or literature except those who don't need changing. The people you want to reach don't read *Harper's* or *The Atlantic*. But I want to thank you for a good claret, a stimulating conversation, and a wonderful idea for a story which, if I deal with it properly, may make my reputation—or at least a hundred dollars.

"And so good night to you, Dr. Whelpley. If I may, I

would like to call upon your expertise again to assist me with the details of my story which I think I shall call 'The Diamond Lens.' "

O'Brien bowed and made his way to the door and down the broad stairs into the night while Whelpley stared, his glass forgotten in his hand, at the drawing of the flayed human body on the far wall.

The End-of-the-World Ball

December 31, 2000

9 P.M. William Landis stepped out of the express elevator that had transported him, like a redeemed sinner, from the lobby of the World Trade Center to the bar and restaurant at the peak of this manmade mountain, this towering skyscraper, this one-hundred-and-ten-story monument to international networking and the power of commerce. As the year 1000 had reached its end, believers had gathered on mountain tops to await the Second Coming; one thousand years later, skeptics had built their own mountain and assembled at its summit to celebrate a moment consecrated in their forgotten faith.

For this occasion the entire top floor of the World Trade Center had been taken over by the Twenty-First Corporation for its end-of-the-millennium celebration. The tables had been removed to form a ballroom and the main bar was supplemented with smaller tables around the periphery. Between the bars were buffet tables laden with food that featured a wide variety of cuisines prepared by Manhattan's most famous chefs. On the periphery of the room wide windows during the day had offered views of a winter storm over New Jersey, clouds over Coney Island, smog over midtown, ships in the harbor, and helicopters flying below. Tonight the sky was clear, and the stars shone down in all their awesome splendor.

This evening everything was free. The occasion must be costing the Twenty-First Corporation a fortune, Landis thought, not only for the food and drink but for the rent of this prime location on the restaurant's most profitable evening of the year. The public relations benefits could not possibly be worth the costs. Landis made a mental note to add to his final chapter, when he got back to his hotel room and his laptop computer, a paragraph or two about potlatch and the earning of status by ostentatious gifts and entertainment. Or maybe the richest corporation in the world knew something he didn't know and was spending its resources in a final "you can't take it with you" gesture.

Just outside the elevator doors stood a Gothic arch carved from ice. It dripped, but the drips were caught by clear plastic and led to reservoirs at either side. On the arch had been engraved, as if in marble, and the letters outlined in black to make them readable, "Lasciate ogni speranza, voi ch'entrate."

Landis looked at the inscription, and wondered how many other guests would read, and recognize, Dante's Latin. On the other side of the arch, a naked young woman wearing a black mask ran squealing from a fat and sweaty satyr. Landis felt a brief chill as he stepped through the archway. Hell had frozen over.

On the other side of the arch a young man in the quietly elegant blue-and-white corporation uniform accepted the engraved invitation Landis extended to him. A woman who was passing the entry stopped and stared at Landis. She was in her early forties, perhaps, and behind her gauzy mask and pale make-up, and a simple crimson, calf-length cocktail gown, was a face and figure that promised remarkable beauty.

"You're William Landis," she said. "The writer. I heard your talk this afternoon."

He was of medium height and slender, with blue eyes and brown hair, and he was dressed in formal black. "Guilty," he said.

"I'm Elois Hays," she said.

"The actress? I saw your play night before last."

"Guilty," she said. "You're not in costume."

"This was a costume ball?"

"You know it was. The end-of-the-world ball." She put a hand on his black-silk sleeve.

"Then I am," he said. He looked down at her hand and covered it with his.

"You were supposed to dress up as your favorite catastrophe," she said accusingly. "What catastrophe do you represent?"

"Ladies first," he said.

"I'm radiation sickness," she said.

"No sores?" he asked. "Leave it to the good-looking women to choose a catastrophe that does not diminish their beauty."

"Leave it to the men to be grotesque," she replied. "Or refuse to participate."

"Well, as for that," he said, "I am in costume. I decided to come as Satan."

"Where are your horns," she said, "and forked tail?"

"I'm a modern Satan. No external stigmata."

"No mask either."

"The devil doesn't need a mask. But then, I'm more of a devil's advocate."

"For what?"

"For hope. I'm not sure this is the end of the world."

"What makes you think that's hopeful?"

A masked and costumed couple brushed past them, entering the ballroom. The man was dressed like a Visigoth, the woman like a captive Roman, her robes artfully ripped to display tempting expanses of rosy flesh.

"Is the thought of the world's survival that wearisome?" Landis asked.

"Not to me," she said. Her pale hands were an art form. "Though I wouldn't care very much, I think. But what better time to end the world than the conclusion of the second millennium?"

"Is there a good time for catastrophe?"

"If you've spent as many years as I have on the stage, you would know that timing is everything. No one should linger after her exit line."

The naked young woman raced past them again. She was giggling. The satyr was farther behind and panting heavily.

"They're at it already," Hays said.

Landis looked at his watch. "If the world is going to end in three hours, even the minutes are precious."

She tucked her hand under his arm. "Is that your philosophy? Eat, drink, and be merry?"

"It's one of them," he said. "I think we all have a bit of that feeling. Particularly on an evening like this. Besides, who are we to criticize these others? I don't know about you, but I'm not without sin—or at least a hope for sin."

She made a ruefully attractive face. "For one thing, that fat satyr is my former husband. For another—well, I've always been fascinated by intellectual men."

He patted her hand. "And I by actresses. But you're a real actress, and I'm only a popularizer of other people's ideas."

"Perhaps we should both have faith," she said.

"In this place where Dante said we should abandon all hope? But if you will be my companion for the rest of the evening, perhaps we will find faith or hope before it is over."

* * * * *

9:15 P.M. Persistent reports of Russian troops assembling on the border of Georgia have just been confirmed by United Nations surveillance satellites. Earlier announcements by the United States met with skepticism by a number of nations and denials by the new Russian right-wing leaders. An emergency meeting of the Security Council has been called, although any action voted by the Council is certain to be vetoed by the Russians. This comes at a time of continuing revolution or guerrilla warfare in half a dozen Latin American nations, the never-ending religious wars of the Middle East, undeclared wars in Southeast Asia, and the reports of Chinese Army maneuvers near the Russian border. Out of any one of these could come a provocation that might lead to an exchange of nuclear missiles.

9:30 P.M. The open floor was almost as big as a football field. It might have dwarfed some groups, but there were many dancers, most in costume. Strangely, no orchestra played, and each couple was doing a different step to a different rhythm. It was like a medieval drawing of the dance of St. Vitus.

Paul Gentry studied them from his position with his back to one of the broad windows framing the night. He was a tall, dark-complexioned man with gloomy features and eyebrows like black caterpillars. He wore a dark business suit and a rope shaped into a noose dangling like a tie from his neck. "I beg your pardon," he said to a slender, blonde woman standing nearby, "but could you tell me why those people are behaving like idiots?"

She turned and held out a small, sealed, plastic bag. Gentry took the bag and looked at it. Inside were a pair of earplugs with dials. His eyebrows moved up.

"You put in the earplugs and dial whatever channel you want," the woman said. "There are fifty channels, half for music, half for voice. You can listen to your favorite music or news or discussion, or the commentary to what you see on the screens."

She waved a hand at the glowing theater-sized screens spaced around the room above the temporary bars and in the spaces between windows. One showed places and streets that seemed Parisian; they were filled with people and revelry. A second presented motionless groups gathered on high places; many of the people were staring at the sky. A third displayed throngs in oriental apparel and appearance, while others framed mob violence or church services or quick cuts of missiles and tanks and people dying in battle. One seemed to be portraying various kinds of threats to the continuation of human existence, from the icy majesty of advancing glaciers to the waterless sands of deserts, from the abandoned children of crowded slums to the slime of polluted rivers and seas. Here and there, scattered among the others, lines of letters scrolled up screens with news about impending catastrophes like the words written on the wall at Belshazzar's feast.

It must have seemed to the dancers on the ballroom floor as if they were located at the center of the world, as if from the top of this artificial mountain they could see around the entire globe. But none of them seemed to be paying any attention.

"Of course," the woman said, "the views from other parts of the world are tapes sent back earlier. What with the record number of sunspots and solar flares, electronic communication with the rest of the world has been cut off."

Gentry handed the unopened bag back to the young woman. "No, thanks," he said. "I'll spend my last hours in this millennium doing my own talking and seeing." He looked back toward the dancers. "But isn't it typical of our times that they are all individuals, together but separate, each dancing to his or her own music?"

"You're Paul Gentry, aren't you?" the young woman asked. "The—"

He shrugged his heavy shoulders. "Ecologist. Environmentalist. Give me whatever name you think fits."

She smiled. It was an expression that transformed an otherwise businesslike face. "How about propheteer? That's what *Time* called you."

"If you like," he said. "And what is your name and occupation?"

"I'm Sally Krebs, and I'm in charge of a camera crew for CNN." She was wearing a yellow jumpsuit that could have been either evening wear or a uniform.

"Where's your crew?" he asked in his sardonic baritone.

"They're around. You just don't see them. What's wrong with individualism? Aren't people better off?"

"Materially, perhaps, but actually not in any meaningful sense. In most periods of the past, people have had enough to eat, and they have enjoyed a much greater sense of security."

"We can destroy ourselves," Krebs said, "but we can choose not to do so. Surely our ancestors faced perils like flood, plague, and barbarians over which they had no control at all. That must have given them the terrible fear that they existed at the whim of supernatural forces."

"They accepted these calamities as part of the natural order," Gentry said. "The security I am talking about is being part of a sturdy social matrix that is capable of surviving the blows of nature or of fate."

"But not," Krebs added, with a sly smile, "of technology."

"True. Science and technology could be created only by individuals, and once created could not be stopped until they brought us to this point. To this." He waved a hand at the ballroom. "The idle rich consuming their idle riches. Is this the finest accomplishment of Western civilization?"

"Maybe it isn't very serious," Krebs said. "But it's not contemptible, either. Today people have what no one ever had before: choice."

"When people can do anything, they find that nothing is worth doing. People are social animals. Like wolves and monkeys, we belong in groups, and when the groups are gone, and the reason for the groups is gone, we find that the reason for humanity is gone."

"What you see here is just a small part of life," Krebs said. "The ceremonial part."

"Ceremony is a group function we have lost. We get together as individuals making gestures at group feeling but discover that we cannot really surrender our individualism."

"The group should determine what we think and feel?"

"The group thinks. The group feels. The group survives."

"Why exalt the group above the individual?"

"What leads to the destruction of the species—indeed, if our best scientists are right, to the destruction of all life on earth—is automatically wrong and evil."

"So that is your favorite catastrophe!"

"Self-destruction every time," Gentry said. "That's why I wear this noose." He fingered the rope around his neck.

"I thought that was to make it handy for the lynching party."

"Me?" he said in mock surprise.

"No one is going to be happy when your jeremiads come true."

"We stand on different sides of most fences, my dear," Gentry said, "but on this one we stand together. You know what they do to bearers of ill tidings."

"That's my profession."

"And pointing out the consequences of human folly is mine."

"You've done very well out of preaching catastrophe."

"And you've clearly done well out of reporting it."

She laughed. "It's no wonder people find you fascinating. Your ideas are so unrelievedly pessimistic that anything that happens comes as a relief."

A slow smile broke the dour lines of his face. "My dear, I'm glad you find me fascinating, but why are we standing here talking when we could be making love?"

Krebs laughed. "I said 'people,' not me. Besides, I'm working."

"You won't always be working."

"We've been filming and recording this conversation," Krebs said. "May we have your authorization to telecast it?"

Gentry smiled. "Everything I say is on the record. Including my final suggestion."

"End of interview," she said into the air.

"But not, I hope, the end of our relationship."

She offered him the possibilities of an enigmatic smile.

"The only time we have a certain grasp on reality," Gentry said, "is when we hold each other, pressed together flesh to naked flesh."

9:45 P.M. The reputation of environmentalists is not what it used to be. Like the boy who cried "wolf," they have shouted "catastrophe" once too often. From *Silent Spring* to *The Population Bomb* and *The Poverty of Power*, their texts have raised specters that, though frightening, turned out to be only skeletons in the closet. Undeterred, Paul Gentry, the most prominent of the breed today, recently called attention to a substantial die-off of plankton in the Gulf of Mexico, a sharp decline in krill production off Antarctica, an increase in radiation to which the average citizen is exposed in his lifetime, and an increase in acid rain after the small reduction that followed governmental restrictions on coal-fired generating plants in the early years of this decade. He has lots of other data, but it all adds up, he says, to death by pollution in the next century. In the next decade, he says, we should expect such problems as decreasing agricultural yields in a period when water has become scarce and fertilizer has become almost prohibitively expensive, a decrease in an already limited harvest of seafood, and an increase in the wholesale destruction of wild life. That is, he says, if we don't destroy ourselves first.

10 P.M. Murray Smith-Ng stood at the seafood buffet loading his plate with shrimp and salmon. He was short and round, and his gray eyes glittered. He was dressed in the dark cloak and conical hat of a medieval astronomer, but his face had been darkened as if by a severe burn. Nearby but at a respectful distance, like a well-trained dog awaiting his master's signal to be fed, was a young man dressed in the scorched rags of a nuclear survivor. They displayed to good advantage his slender legs and muscular chest. His name was Lyle, and he had been a student in Smith-Ng's seminar on catastrophism.

"Dr. Smith-Ng, may I help you to some of this lobster?" Lyle asked.

Another young man, dressed in imitation furs to look like an ice-age savage, paused in the process of picking up a plate. "The Dr. Smith-Ng?" he asked.

"I'm sure there aren't any others," Smith-Ng said.

"The catastrophist?"

"The only one of those, too."

"Maybe you could answer a question that's always bothered me," the young man said.

"If I can," Smith-Ng said.

"I thought catastrophe theory was a mathematical discipline."

"Oh, it is," Smith-Ng said, setting down his plate to wipe mayonnaise from his chin. He picked up the plate again. "At least, that's how it started. Gradually people began to see practical applications for the mathematics, and that's where I did my work."

"What kind of applications?" the young man asked.

Smith-Ng popped a shrimp into his mouth. "Read my book, young man."

"Like volcanoes and meteor strikes," Lyle said impatiently. "Plagues and wars. Tornadoes and earthquakes."

"Some processes are continuous," Smith-Ng said around a mouthful of poached salmon. "They can be charted as familiar curves: straight lines, sines, hyperbolas. . . . Some are discontinuous. They start suddenly and break off just as abruptly."

"Like chain reactions and critical mass," Lyle said. "And the dinosaurs."

Smith-Ng gave Lyle the look of respect reserved for the good student. "And other life forms," he said. "The dinosaurs are simply the most dramatic. For a century after Darwin published his theory of evolution, scientists believed that evolution proceeded at the same even pace: as conditions changed, certain secondary genetic characteristics were selected to cope with them. Scientists of that kind were called 'uniformitarians' or 'gradualists.' Then, with the discovery that certain species, and at some periods most species, disappeared simultaneously and, in evolutionary terms, almost overnight, evolutionists all became catastrophists."

"If you had read *Catastrophe: Theory and Practice*, you'd know that," Lyle said.

"The discontinuous process is more prevalent than we ever suspected," Smith-Ng said, "although there was evidence enough around. Learning, for instance. Everyone had noticed that no matter how much you learned, you were still in a state of ignorance until something magical happened and all you had learned suddenly fell into place. Everyone had observed the plateau theory of learning but pretended that learning proceeded smoothly."

"It was the same way with catastrophe theory," Lyle said. "Suddenly everybody was a catastrophist."

"Some earlier than others," Smith-Ng said.

"But don't the times have something to do with it?" the other young man said.

Smith-Ng lifted his face from his plate.

"I think I read that somewhere," the young man said.

"Some ideas seem to have a better chance in certain periods than in others," Smith-Ng admitted cautiously.

"Now I remember," the second young man said. "In a series of articles William S. Landis has been writing about catastrophe, he quotes a theory about 'steam-engine time' that he attributes to a fellow named Charles Fort."

" 'In steam-engine time people invent steam engines,' " Smith-Ng said. "And he applies that to catastrophism. 'In catastrophic times, people invent theories to explain catastrophes.' But what you've got to understand is that Landis's book is catastrophism masquerading as uniformitarianism. It merely pushes the origin of the catastrophe back to the mystical. The questions remain: What changes the times? What brings about the sudden acceptance of this theory or that? I prefer to put my faith in something I can measure."

Landis and Hays had stopped nearby, unnoticed, to listen to the conversation when they heard his name. "The question is, Smith-Ng," he asked now, "what catastrophes do your theories predict for the end of this evening?"

"You must be William Landis. I recognize you from your photographs," Smith-Ng said genially. "Of course you would be here. This will make a great concluding chapter for your book."

"If it all doesn't conclude here," Landis said. "But what's your prediction? Surely you have run everything through your equations."

"As for catastrophes," Smith-Ng said, "I predict all of them. But not for quotation."

"You certainly won't be quoted if you are no more precise than that," Landis said and smiled.

"You heard my talk this morning," Smith-Ng said, "I saw you in the audience. And that was for the record."

"You were talking in terms of centuries," Landis said. "Can't your theory do better than that?"

"And you want to pin me down to hours? Ah, Landis!" He waggled a pudgy finger at him. "But if you insist, I would hazard a guess that the world will end promptly at midnight."

Lyle chuckled appreciatively.

"But how?" Landis persisted. "That's too quick for a new ice age or the hothouse effect. Meteor? Nova? Nuclear war? Can't you pinpoint it a little better than that?"

"By the Second Coming, of course," Smith-Ng said and laughed. But he sounded as if he would be pleased if his theories were proved correct, no matter what happened to him or the rest of the world.

Lyle eyed him as if he were the end of Lyle's world.

10:15 P.M. The mathematician who titles himself a "catastrophist," in a speech today to the fancifully named "Twenty-First Century Conference" at the Twenty-First building in New York City, called attention to what he termed "a sharp rise" of one-half degree in the world's average temperature over the past decade. The speaker, Dr. Murray Smith-Ng, noted that the rise in temperature is paralleled by a similar rise in the amount of carbon dioxide in the atmosphere over the same period. He called these increases "catastrophic changes" and an indication of what he called the beginning of the "greenhouse effect" that will turn Earth into an embalmed twin of Venus. Disagreement was registered from the floor, however, in particular from one expert in atmospheric phenomena who said that his measurements and calculations indicated the beginning of a new ice age instead.

10:30 P.M. Barbara Shepherd presided over a gathering of true believers on the rooftop of the skyscraper. The weather was comparatively warm for December, but the stars, slightly distorted by the air currents rising past the sides of the building, glittered coldly overhead.

The terrace was protected from the gulfs of space by a waist-high wall. Tracks for the tower's movable window-washing machine ran along the edge of the wall. A turntable occupied each corner. Steam issued from chimney pots scattered here and there about the roof, as if there were a direct connection with the nether regions. In the middle of the roof was a turnip-shaped metal tower and a sixty-foot metal pole for microwave transmissions. The metal pole was studded with ten red beacons to warn aircraft.

Shepherd stood on a platform draped in white linen facing the forty-odd chairs almost filled by her audience. She wore a flowing white gown with wide and diaphanous sleeves. When she raised her arms, they looked like gauzy wings. The platform had been placed close to the south wall of the terrace. Sometimes she looked as if she were about to soar above the audience like Gabriel.

Landis and Hays stood in the distant doorway by which they had reached the tower's top. "Has she really lost touch with reality?" Landis asked softly.

"She says that she's finally found it," Hays replied.

"This is the time foretold," Shepherd said, needing no amplification, her voice ringing as if it were the instrument of Gabriel itself. "This is the day of judgment. Scarcely more than an hour remains for the people of this world to repent their sinful ways and accept salvation. Ninety minutes from now the world will end, and everybody will be sent to their eternal homes. To heaven, to hell. It is our choice, each one of us."

She paused, as if gathering her thoughts, and then continued more quietly. "When I was a girl," she said, "I thought that the purpose of life was to shape my body into a perfect instrument, so that it would do whatever I told it to do. And I worked hard, and I came as close as anyone."

"You can't get much closer than Olympic gymnastics," Landis whispered to Hays.

"And then I thought that the purpose of life was to understand the way the universe had been created and the laws by which it worked, and I went to school and learned everything I could."

"Can you imagine going from the Olympics to a Ph.D. in philosophy from Berkeley?"

"And then I thought that the purpose of life was to express my creativity, and I became an actress and lived other people's lives for the sake of audiences."

"She was a pretty good actress, too," Hays said, "but she

ran out of parts and maybe out of her range."

"Each of those things in turn proved to be folly, and I decided that the only purpose of life was to seek pleasure, and I lost myself in that."

"That was what she was really good at," Hays murmured.

"And I nearly lost myself for all eternity," Shepherd said, "but now I know that the only purpose of existence is to prepare us for the life to come." Her voice lifted a fraction. "And that time is almost at hand. All we need is belief and faith."

"Where do you think all this is leading?" Hays asked.

"I don't know," Landis said, looking at his watch, "but it's getting on toward eleven. Do you want to go join the revels—or perhaps find a quiet spot for some conversation?"

Hays shivered and he put his arm around her shoulders. "It's like a good play," she said. "I've got to see the curtain go down. Anyway, what better place to greet the new millennium than the top of this mountain?"

10:45 P.M. The approaching end to the second millennium of the Christian era has produced a resurgence of religion, including increased attendance in formal church services and unscheduled outbreaks of what has been compared to the mania of the Middle Ages, such as speaking in tongues, fits, snake handling, and preaching on street corners. A kind of public resignation to the end of the world, however visualized, has been accompanied by an outbreak of militant fundamentalism in some Christian countries as well as Islamic nations in the Middle East, involving an increase in terrorism, a quest for martyrdom, and the threat (or promise, as some see it) of Armageddon. One of the most unusual public conversions has been that of Olympic athlete, actress, playgirl Barbara Shepherd, who plans a prayer meeting for the top of the World Trade Center during an exclusive, invitation-only End-of-the-World Ball.

11 P.M. The pace of the evening accelerated as the hands of the invisible clock passed eleven in their inexorable progression toward midnight. Food and drink of all kinds was constantly replenished in all the bars and buffets. Drugs were almost as openly available as alcohol, and only slightly less in evidence than the food and drink; in some of the bars, they were laid out to be smoked, inhaled, or ingested, or, even, with the aid of neatly clad nurses and sterile syringes, injected.

But this was not a junky's paradise. These were the world's leading citizens, and the drugs were available, like the food, only to enhance their enjoyment of this moment that would not come around again for another thousand years. To be sure, a few, out of boredom or terror, or loss of self-control, over-indulged themselves in drugs as some did in food or drink, and rendered themselves insensible to the approach of the millennium's end, collapsed in a corner or nodding in a chair or over a table like any common drunk. One died of an overdose, and another of a cocaine seizure. If the world survived this millennium, the Twenty-First Corporation would be tied up in courts throughout the century from which it took its name.

Some sought their surcease in other ways. Sexual couplings that earlier in the evening had been consummated discreetly in staircases and rooms made available in the floors immediately below, began to overflow into more public areas and to be joined by third and fourth participants as the evening proceeded. In some places the floor became a sea of writhing bodies, as if the protoplasm that had evolved into the shape of humanity was returning, in the space of a few hours, to the amoeba-like stuff from which it had come.

"There is more to this of panic than of passion," Gentry said, looking on from the periphery.

Krebs took a deep breath. "I'm beginning to feel a bit of that myself."

Gentry smiled, lifting his eyebrows at the same time. "The panic or the passion? Are you ready to take me up on my offer?"

"And join the anonymous heaps of flesh?"

"I was thinking of something a little more private."

"I thought you were in favor of groups," she said.

"Even primitive societies approved the privacy of some functions."

Suddenly she pointed to the ballroom then. "Isn't that—?"

"I believe it is," Gentry said, tracing her finger to the shape of a tall, lean person in the sepulchral costume of Death itself. "It's the President, all right. It would be difficult to hide that figure and that way of moving."

"But why is he here?" Krebs asked.

"Isn't everybody?" Gentry responded.

"Even you and me, yes," she said distractedly. She spoke into the microphone pinned inconspicuously to her lapel. "Bob," she said, "get a camera on that figure of Death dancing with the willowy lady in green. That's got to be the President, and that's not the first lady. Lloyd can do what he wants with it, but we're going to feed it to him."

11:10 P.M. The New Genes Laboratory in California has announced the development of a hybrid wheat that resists drought and heat and most, if not all, diseases, including mosaic, but most important fixes its own nitrogen fertilizer with the aid of symbiotic bacteria. The National Disease Control Center in Atlanta has issued a general warning to physicians about a new viral infection, popularly called the Moscow flu, that is affecting large centers of population and particularly schoolchildren. Its victims display many of the symptoms of influenza but the disease has produced early mortality rates higher than pneumonia, AIDS, and what was once called Legionnaires Disease. A consumer watchdog group blames the new disease on genetic experimentation, and a spokesman for the Preservation of Democracy, on bacteriological warfare, possibly originating in the Middle East.

11:20 P.M. Smith-Ng had progressed to the meat buffet and loaded his plate with rare roast beef. He still was followed by the two young men. "Isn't that the President?" Lyle asked suddenly.

"Of course," Smith-Ng said, swallowing. "You can tell by the men in dark suits around the edges of the crowds."

"What do you make of that?" the other young man asked.

"Either he thinks he won't be recognized, or he doesn't care," Smith-Ng said.

"Why wouldn't he care?" the other asked. "When the activities at this place get reported, nobody present will be able to get elected garbage collector."

"Maybe the news that he wasn't here would be worse politically," Lyle said. "As if he wasn't invited."

"Now you're beginning to think like a catastrophist," Smith-Ng said. "But not enough like one."

"What do you mean?" Lyle asked.

"What if a catastrophe occurs?" the other young man said. "Then it wouldn't matter, and he might as well enjoy himself." He gestured at the displays of flesh and folly. "Like everybody else."

"And?" Smith-Ng prompted in his best Socratic manner.

"And what, sir?" Lyle asked.

"And what if he knows it?" Smith-Ng concluded with gluttonous satisfaction.

Lyle looked at the figures on the ballroom floor as if he had just begun to consider the possibility that catastrophe theory might turn into reality.

11:30 P.M. The Orbital Observatory adds some new concerns as the western world approaches the end of the second millennium of the so-called Christian era: sunspot activity has picked up after the relative quiet of the past decade, an indication, say some authorities, of possible solar instability that might result in a solar flare or even an explosion that could wipe out all life on earth. Nonsense, say other experts; that hot ball of gases in the sky is good for another eight billion years yet. An increase or decrease in its output of a few per cent could be fatal to life on earth, however. The Observatory also is watching a possible explosion at the heart of our Milky Way galaxy that might reach us any day now; or a massive black hole ejected from galactic center could be upon us before we know it. Meanwhile, work is pressing toward completion of the world's pioneer space habitat, which some proponents say is the first step toward insuring humanity's survival, perhaps even its immortality. The good news, at least for some, is that the Observatory now has discovered a second star, other than earth, with planets, and confidence is growing among some cosmologists that the formation of planets, around some kinds of suns, at least, is a normal process.

11:35 P.M. On the highest terrace, Barbara Shepherd's voice had grown more intense as midnight grew closer, as if, indeed, some truth was struggling for expression, some message was demanding to be heard. Members of the informal congregation had shifted uneasily from smiles to frowns, from chuckles and comments to uncomfortable glances at their neighbors, and some had left for more enjoyable pastimes. Others, as if hearing about what was occurring on the terrace, had arrived to take the empty places, and almost every chair was filled.

"This is the millennium described in Revelations. For a thousand years Satan has been bound and cast in the bottomless pit. Now that millennium has expired and Satan has been loosed to deceive the nations of the earth and to gather them together to battle. Is this not the world we see about us? Deceived by Satan? Gathered to do battle?"

Hays studied the people seated in the chairs. "Are all these people believers, do you suppose?"

"I think they're here for the same reason we are," Landis said.

"And why is that?" Hays asked.

"To see how far she's going to go."

Shepherd raised her wings. "Can we doubt the predictions in Revelations? That fire will come down from God out of heaven and devour us all? Some of you think that when the fire comes down from the sky that it will be missiles and hydrogen bombs raining down upon us, that we will be destroying ourselves, but it will be God's fire and His triumph—and our triumph, too. Because the devil who deceived us will be cast into the lake of fire and brimstone, and we will all be judged.

"If you think that I am afraid to be judged, you are right. I have sinned."

"That's certainly true," Landis whispered.

"I have fornicated, and I have committed adultery," Shepherd said. "I have profaned the temple of my body with drugs. I have born false witness and denied my God. I have broken all of the commandments and discovered others to break that would have been commandments if the ancient Hebrews had known about them. But fearful or not, I welcome judgment as the beginning of the eternal glory to come."

She had been a beautiful woman and she was beautiful now, filled with a passion as real as any she had experienced in the arms of a man. It shook her body as she spoke and made her voice tremble. "In that day of all days, we will stand before the throne of God, we the dead, small and great, and we will be judged by the works written in the book of life.

"The sea will give up its dead, and death and hell will deliver up their dead, and every person will be judged according to their works. And whosoever is not found written in the book of life will be cast into the lake of fire. And so it is up to you. Will you repent before it is too late? Will you write your name in the book of life? Will you join me in life everlasting? Or spend eternity with Satan in the fires of hell?

"Because if you do not believe me, if you do not believe that Satan walks the earth, if you do not believe that the fire of God will rain down on the earth this very night, if you do not believe that this is the day of judgment and that this begins our eternal lives in heaven or in hell, look yonder!" She stretched out one gauzy arm toward the space near the door.

"There stands Satan with his paramour!"

In spite of themselves, the audience turned to look at the figures of Landis and Hays watching the scene with detached fascination. "She recognized you," Hays muttered.

"And you," Landis said.

11:40 P.M. The World Energy Council announced today that the price of oil, which began its present climb in 1997, has reached $150 a barrel. For all except special or emergency needs, oil no longer is classified as a fuel. After the panicky hiatus of the 1980s and 1990s, the United States has resumed building nuclear generating plants. The rest of the world, which now boasts 90 per cent of nuclear-generating capacity, never stopped. Generating plants that once burned oil have been abandoned or converted to coal, sometimes in a liquefied form, in spite of the cost in human life and acid rain. Synthetic fuels once more are being pursued. Meanwhile research presses forward into the elusive thermonuclear process for fusing hydrogen. Laboratory operations have demonstrated that the theory works by getting back more energy than is consumed, but so far efforts to scale up the methods to commercial size have proven too expensive. The search goes on, however, since success would solve the energy problems, now pressing hard on the arteries of the world, for the next thousand years.

11:43 P.M. The ballroom floor was crowded now that the magic hour had almost arrived, as if the assembled guests were seeking the protection of numbers or the sacrament of ceremony. The filmed scenes flickered from screen to screen around the walls in dizzying procession until they blurred into a continuous panorama of motion uniting all the places of the world into one frantic montage of anticipation.

Here and there fights broke out between men and between women, and even between men and women, over drunken insults or sexual privileges. Women were raped, sometimes by groups of men, and occasionally a man was attacked by a group of women. Weapons carried for show were put to ancient uses; men and women, injured, staggered away for aid, or, dead, lay where they had fallen. Blood seeped into sticky puddles, and vomit and excretions dried upon the floors. Uniformed attendants who had worked diligently at keeping the tables filled and the complex clear of refuse had stripped away their emblems and joined the melee struggling desperately to forget the desperate hour. Here two thousand years of civilization disintegrated into barbarism.

And others went on with their own lives, pursuing their own visions of catastrophe.

11:45 P.M. Vulcanologists have had a great deal to watch recently. Old volcanoes in Hawaii, Mexico, Italy, Iceland, Indonesia, Nicaragua, Costa Rica, Chile, and Japan have erupted or shown signs of imminent activity, and new volcanoes have opened smoking fissures. So far none has demonstrated the destructiveness of Mt. St. Helens and El Chichon in 1983, but vulcanologists do not rule out that possibility. One or more eruptions the equal of Krakatau in 1883 or Tambora in 1815 might inject enough ash and smoke into the atmosphere to rival the nuclear winter predicted by many scientists in the 1980s to follow a nuclear war.

11:47 P.M. On the balcony Krebs listened to her earphone and then looked quickly at the ballroom floor. "He's leaving," she said.

"Who's leaving?" Gentry asked.

"The President. As if he's in a hurry. One of the Secret Service men ran over to him and spoke a word or two—nobody could pick up what was said—and he's almost running out of here."

Gentry shrugged. "It probably doesn't mean anything. Maybe he doesn't want to get caught in the midnight crush."

She made a face at him. "You're supposed to be the realist."

"Are you ready then for my realism?"

She looked at him for a moment without speaking, and

then she said, "If you were anybody else, I might say 'Yes,' and to hell with the job. But if the world survives I'm going back to the Midwest and find a more meaningful way of life, and you, for all your above-it-all earnest cynicism, you use people—you use life itself—for your own selfish satisfactions."

He seemed speechless for the first time that night, and then he said, without his customary condescension, "Do you think I don't know that? My cynicism doesn't come out of superiority, but out of fear. I'm afraid. I've always been afraid."

"Maybe so," she said, "but you'll have to live with it like everybody else. I've got to go. I've been told there's something happening on the roof top."

11:50 P.M. Astronomers today announced the discovery of a new comet that promises to be larger and brighter than Halley's comet. The comet, as yet unnamed, may be making its first pass through the solar system, possibly disturbed in its billions of years' orbit in what is known as the Oorts Cloud by a distant companion sun to Sol called by some scientists "Nemesis." Preliminary calculations indicate that the new comet may pass close to earth, but alarmist reports of a possible collision have been dismissed by scientists as "next to impossible."

11:52 P.M. Smith-Ng looked up from the dessert table in the restaurant on the second balcony. "What did you say?" he asked Lyle, who still tagged along behind him.

"The President. He's gone. What does that mean?"

"Maybe nothing," Smith-Ng said, wiping a glob of whipped cream from his upper lip. "Maybe catastrophe."

"Shouldn't we—couldn't we—find some place quieter?

More alone?" Lyle's teeth made an uncontrollable chattering sound, and he put his hand on Smith-Ng's shoulder as if he were steadying himself.

Smith-Ng looked at Lyle and then toward the ceiling as if seeking guidance. He placed his hand tentatively over Lyle's. His face approached the young man's as if moved by some external power, and he kissed him with the curiosity and then the intensity of an unsuspected passion he had just discovered. He drew back as if he could feel his world shattering in pieces around him and shook himself. "I understand that something interesting is happening on the roof," he said shakily. "Perhaps we should go find out what it is."

11:54 P.M. On the eve of the Twenty-First Century the United Nations Office of Population announced that the world's population has passed six billion. Of these six billion, it said, more than half were undernourished and one billion were actually starving. These figures, a spokesman said, raise serious questions for world peace as well as for the number of deaths by starvation and disease if world population doubles again, as predicted, in the next thirty-five years.

11:56 P.M. By the time the cameras arrived, the audience had swollen to fill all the chairs and the standing room that surrounded them. Krebs with Gentry behind her had reached the terrace just a few moments earlier, and Smith-Ng and his disciple were only a few steps behind.

The terrace had rippled minutes ago with the news of the President's hurried departure, but now it was quiet with the hushed expectancy of something momentous about to happen, as if by listening hard one could hear the last grains of sand trickling through the hourglass of the universe.

In the ballroom five floors below, the crowd was frantic in

its effort to greet the new millennium with life and laughter, like savages at the dawn of civilization trying to frighten away disaster with noise or appease it with celebration. Below Saturnalia was in progress. Here on the rooftop a congregation as solemn as that of any true believers awaiting the day of judgment on mountain top was contemplating the eternal.

People were here because of who they were, choosing this kind of celebration rather than other kinds below, because of the occasion and its star-reaching site, and because of Barbara Shepherd. She stood now like a sacrificial virgin, her hymen restored with her faith, her arms outstretched, her hands clenched into fists, her voice lifted in exultation.

"Now has the moment come," she said, "the time arrived, the stroke of the clock about to sound as we listen. Now we must demonstrate our faith or lose all faith forever and be forever damned. Faith can save us yet. Faith will save us. Have faith! Have faith!"

"I'm frightened!" Hays said to Landis.

"What are you frightened of?" he asked gently, tightening his arm around her as if to create a fortress for two.

"Everything," she said. "The world ending. The night exploding. Bombs. Change. Everything."

"Don't be afraid," he said. "Maybe we found each other too late, your sense of the drama of life and my search for its purpose. But if we make it through this night, I have a suggestion: let's create a new world, for ourselves and whoever wants to join us."

"I'd like that," she said. "If we make it through."

"I'm frightened, too," he said. "But it's not catastrophe I'm afraid of. What I fear is our love of catastrophe."

Barbara Shepherd turned and ran toward the back of the platform like the acrobat she once had been. As she reached the middle, she did a flip backward, landed on her feet, and flipped again. The second took her off the end of the platform. For an instant she seemed to disappear from view. Then her figure reappeared, propelled upward with surprising speed, head high and facing the audience with the composed features and confidence of a saint, rising, rising, clearing the railing that surrounded the roof top and floating free in the air beyond it. Her gown fluttered; her arms reached out and, like wings, seemed to support her body in the crystalline air, even to lift it toward the heaven she addressed.

The audience waited, shocked into immobility, shocked out of skepticism, expecting miracles and fearing them, fearing catastrophes and expecting them.

But as the stroke of midnight sounded and maddened noise broke out in the city below and in the ballroom behind like celebration or like explosions and machine guns and the screams and drying cries of victims, and the spinning world seemed to hesitate in anticipation of catastrophe, the figure of Barbara Shepherd faltered in the air before it fell, with growing velocity, glittering, through the night.

The Giftie

O wad some Pow'r the giftie gie us
To see oursels as others see us!
—Robert Burns

It all started at the little bookstore where Adrian liked to browse when he had the time. Browsing in the chain superstores wasn't the same. In the superstores you could find almost any kind of book you wanted, and anything you couldn't find could be located by computer and made available a day or so later. That assumed you knew what you wanted, or could find it in the current maze of instant literature. But there were so many books that you couldn't *browse* in an eclectic jumble of old and new. Anyway, the superstores didn't *smell* right. They smelled like, well, like department stores with air recirculated every thirty seconds. Bookstores should smell like old leather and good paper and printer's ink and maybe a little dust.

The book was on a table labeled "Remainders—Cults, New Age, UFOs." The books once had been stacked neatly—the proprietor of the Book Nook, a Mrs. Frances Farmstead of elderly years but a youthful devotion to books nourished by some sixty years of reading and handling, liked them arranged so that all the bindings could be read at a glance—but now they were jumbled in a heap as if someone else already had rummaged through them.

That honed Adrian's edge of irritation over his inability to get any closer to the goal he had been pursuing since childhood, ever since he had looked up at the stars and, like John Carter, had wished himself among them. The feeling of irritation had been growing in recent months. His ambition to be an astronaut had been grounded by the inarguable facts that he was physically unimposing and his hand-and-eye coordination had always made him last to be chosen at pick-up games. But he had a nimble and inquiring mind, and he had settled for the next best thing: aerospace engineering.

He had worked his way through the University, joined a major aerospace firm after graduation, and resigned after a dozen years of routine assignments that got him no closer to his goal of reaching the stars, through surrogates if not in person. He had set up his own one-man consulting business, and was able to pick and choose assignments that appealed to him and seemed to get humanity closer to freedom from Earth's gravity. But even second-hand space adventuring was hung up on chemical propulsion and obsolete vehicles. His own ambition, like the space program itself, was drifting. Humanity needed something totally new. The irritation had brought him into the Book Nook time and again; browsing had proved, over the years, a treatment if not a cure. But now someone else might have found the one text the book gods had intended for him, for which their mysterious hands had guided him into the store. These remainders were all one of a kind, and once one was removed it was gone forever.

Ordinarily he would not have chosen this particular table—he had a skeptic's fondness for books whose naive pretensions or whose paranoid conspiracies he could ridicule to his friends or even to himself—but he was not in the mood for such cynical amusements. The jumble attracted him, however, and he worked his way through the pile, re-stacking them neatly on the table, binding up, in the way Mrs. Farmstead would have done herself. *The UFO Conspiracy*, *UFOs: The Final Answer*, *UFO: The Complete Sightings*, and *Cosmic Voyage*, along with *The Secret Doctrine of the Rosicrucians*, *The Truth in the Light*, *Psychic Animals*, and other annals of magic and the occult. Adrian could feel Mrs. Farmstead's approving gaze from the antique wooden desk at the front of the store.

He held the book in his hand, turning it this way and that. The book had lost its dust jacket, if it ever had one, but it had a pleasant feel to it, and the title was catchy: *Gift from the Stars*. Perhaps it was a Von Daniken clone; he always enjoyed their innocent credulity.

He opened it. The book had a frontispiece, unusual in a cheap text like this. It showed the vast metal bowl of the radio telescope at Arecibo, with the focusing mechanism held aloft by cables strung from three pylons. The title page listed a publisher he had never heard of, but that wasn't unusual: fringe publishers were common in the cult field. The copyright page said that the book had been published half a dozen years earlier.

Adrian glanced at the first page. It was the usual stuff: Have we been visited? Are there aliens among us?

He leafed through the book, half decided to put it down, when he came across an appendix filled with diagrams. Not diagrams of cryptic incisions on arid plateaus in Peru or carved around the entrances to ancient tombs. These seemed to be designs for some kind of ship. Not "some kind of ship," he decided with the gathering excitement he recognized as the eureka feeling, but a spaceship, and not the sketchy drawings of some putative crashed UFO concealed in a hangar in New Mexico or Dayton, but engineering drawings such as Adrian worked with almost every day. He took it to the desk.

"Found something you like, Mr. Mast?" Mrs. Farmstead asked. She was old but cheerful about it, with a plump, grandmotherly face and gray hair braided and wound into a knot pinned on top of her head with an oversized barrette.

"Enough to pay good money for it," Adrian said. Mrs. Farmstead didn't accept charge cards, but she had been known to run an account for someone short on cash who had fallen in love with a book. "Any idea where it came from?"

"Of course I do," Mrs. Farmstead said. She maintained careful records that kept her in the shop, Adrian suspected, long after the time of its official closing. "But you don't expect me to look them up for a three-fifty remaindered title, do you, Mr. Mast?" Her sharp glance over plastic-rimmed glasses dared him to ask for special service.

"Not this time, Mrs. Farmstead," he said, paid his money, and took his hand-written receipt and his newfound treasure and walked out of the store, feeling no longer irritated but elated, almost trembling, as if what he had found there would change his life forever.

Nobody was dependent on him except those space travelers not yet liberated from the surly bonds of the solar system, perhaps not yet born; for a dream he had sacrificed hopes for wife and family. Who was he kidding? His problem was that the women he was interested in weren't interested in him, and the ones who were interested in him he found less exciting than his work. Ordinarily, then, there was nothing to draw him back to his one-bedroom apartment, but now a curious anticipation hastened his step.

He delayed gratification by changing to comfortable sweat pants, getting a cold can of beer from the refrigerator and a bottle of peanuts from the pantry, and settled into his easy chair in the living room opposite the television set he turned on only for the news, the science channels, and the sci-fi series. Only then did he open his *Gift from the Stars*.

The first chapter was titled "Where Are They?" Although it seemed to be a discussion of aliens and the possibility that they might have visited the earth in ages past and even might be keeping track of us now, Adrian recognized a subtext the ordinary reader would never have noticed. A conclusion seemed to say that evidence of alien visitation may have been deliberately concealed by nameless government agencies, but that other alien contacts had occurred or were yet to happen that anyone with an eye to the sky or a mind to understand could be aware of. Read with greater sophistication, however, the chapter suggested that the evidence for alien visitation was not only thin but probably nothing more than the connecting of random dots; that aliens were the modern equivalent of angels and demons; and that belief in alien visitation and abduction was a substitute for antiquated religions whose answers no longer seemed appropriate to contemporary questions.

Written between the lines, however, was an argument for the existence of aliens. Logic said that with all the stars in the Milky Way galaxy alone, a good number of them would nourish life and a good number of those would develop technological civilizations capable of interstellar travel. Good scientists had agreed on all that. Surely there must be aliens older, wiser, and more advanced then humanity. But, as Fermi asked, where are they? Why weren't they here by now?

The UFO believers, of course, thought they were here, observing us, maybe abducting people for their experiments, maybe having accidents that left their spaceship wreckage and alien bodies strewn across remote areas of the world to be hidden by government agencies concerned about popular panic or paranoid about alien takeovers, or committed to their own researches and fearful of the release of dangerous information. . . . But *Gift from the Stars* suggested, subtly, that aliens had their own reasons for not visiting Earth, reasons that we could never know, unless, perhaps, we should go visit *them*.

The question Adrian had to answer was more immediate: why should the book he held in his hands be titled and written in such a way that it was virtually indistinguishable from a hundred, maybe a thousand, other books on UFOs and aliens? The only reason he could think of was that the author wanted to hide a message that would be found only by someone capable of noticing and understanding it. Like concealing a diamond in a heap of glass imitations. What better hiding place for obscure revelations than among the books that the only people who would take them seriously were the people that nobody took seriously?

Unable to restrain his impatience any longer, he turned to the appendix. Here were the drawings he remembered. They could be for any kind of vehicle, a submarine, say, or an airplane without wings, but the design had non-aerodynamic extensions as if intended for use where fluid resistance was non-existent. The drawings were curiously uneven as if they had been prepared by some gross process different from the customary draftsman lines. Gaps in the drawings seemed to indicate details yet to be added or filled in according to individual preferences. But Adrian identified what was clearly a propulsion system based upon reaction mass being expelled through nozzles at the rear of the vessel. The storage space for fuel seemed too small, however, and the reaction chamber itself seemed oddly shaped and also curiously small.

Adrian turned more pages. The book had a second appendix in which he discovered the design for an engine in which two substances would be combined and the energy obtained used to accelerate another substance through oddly shaped nozzles and past some kind of magnetic fields until it was released. A final sketch made sense of the limited storage space and the engine. It was a design for a container in which the substance within would never touch the sides. The substance was some kind of plasma contained by magnetic fields maintained by some kind of permanent magnets built into the vessel or perhaps the vessel itself was magnetic. A companion design showed how solar energy could be transformed into—what else could it be?—anti-matter. Its combination with matter—perhaps hydrogen encountering anti-hydrogen—would convert the mass of both entirely into energy and provide the means by which humanity could reach the stars.

Would it work? Somehow he doubted it. It was all too pat, like a science-fiction gadget. But maybe that's what all advanced technology looked like—not magic but obvious. And, like a cultist's scenario, it all made sense, granted the premises, and was not that much different from imaginative concepts discussed in aerospace engineering circles. The difference was that these looked as if they were working designs, not concepts, and even, somehow, as if they were antiquated, like museum pieces or re-designs of historic airships such as the Wright brothers' first craft. It would work, all right, probably better than the original, but it hinted at the existence of methods far more effective. Were those beyond the understanding or the technological capabilities of less-advanced species?

Adrian shook his head. He was allowing his imagination to take him into theories as weird as those of any UFO true believer. But that was what the book had done to him: he had picked it up as a minor contribution to a neurotic belief system and it had evolved into a document addressing his deepest needs. And, although the text did not say so, the title suggested that somehow these designs had come from somewhere else, perhaps from aliens. Perhaps they were, indeed, a gift from the stars.

Adrian showed the book to Mrs. Farmstead. "You said you could tell me where this came from."

"Yes," she said, peering up at him. She looked up at him owlishly over her glasses, her plump face framed in coils of gray. "But surely one of these is enough." She looked at his face as if reading his need. "Oh, all right, since it's you, Mr. Mast." She ran a hand-held optical scanner across the ISBN number on the title page and then punched a couple of keys on her computer. "It arrived six months ago in a box of remainders from a jobber. Cheap."

"All cult books?"

"Most of them, I expect."

"Could we find out who wrote it?"

She pointed at the name on the title page: George Winterbotham.

"Could you find an address for him?" Adrian asked. He apologized. "I know this is a lot of trouble."

Mrs. Farmstead seemed about to say something but instead turned back to the computer and called up *Books in Print*. Nothing. She tried several library databases, including the Library of Congress. Nothing. She laughed. "This may be the only copy in existence."

Adrian grimaced. "That may be more accurate than you think."

She looked at him. "What are we doing here, Mr. Mast? Is it illegal?"

"It may be dangerous," he replied, only half in jest, "but it's not illegal unless it is illegal to publish a book revealing information that some people might want withheld."

"Trade secrets?" she asked. "In that?"

He had hoped to keep Mrs. Farmstead out of it. Something about this situation that had a wrongness to it—the information that should not be in a book like this, the accidental way it came into his hands, the curious anonymity of its author. He flipped the book open to its appendices. "There are these," he said. "They're spaceship designs."

"How do you know?"

"You know books. I know spaceships," he said. "I don't think I've ever introduced myself: I'm an aerospace engineer. I work in designs like these."

"How very odd," she said and leafed through the appendices. Her expression told him they meant nothing to her. "I'll take your word for it."

"I'd like to find the author and ask him where he got the designs."

"I see," Mrs. Farmstead said. "But why would he publish them in a book like this?"

"Exactly," Adrian said. "It suggests that he wanted someone to find them, someone who would understand what they were—"

"Like you, Mr. Mast."

He nodded. "And nobody else would know they were there, particularly nobody who might want to keep them from the public."

"And that nobody, or even a group of nobodies, might be dangerous to someone who found out what they didn't want found out."

"I'm afraid so, Mrs. Farmstead."

"Well," she said and turned back to her computer. "I don't like people who want to keep things from being published." She tapped several keys. "We can look up the publisher."

The publisher, at least, was listed on the Internet. He had two books under his name, both UFO texts. Neither one was *Gift from the Stars*. Before Adrian could stop Mrs. Farmstead, she had typed in a telephone number. Somewhere a phone started ringing.

"Hello?" she said into a speaker so that Adrian could hear. "Is this Joel Simpson? The publisher?"

"Yes," came the hesitant reply. "Who's calling?"

"I have a customer who is trying to find another copy of a book published by you half a dozen years ago."

"I've only published two books," Simpson said.

Mrs. Farmstead raised her eyebrows at Adrian as if to say, "He's lying."

"*Gift from the Stars.*"

"There must be some mistake. I never published a book by that title," the voice said on the other end. "Who is calling?"

"Sorry for the trouble," Mrs. Farmstead said. "It must have been another publisher with the same name." She pressed a button that closed the connection. "Well, Mr. Mast? You may be right."

"I wish you hadn't made that call," Adrian said. "I have the feeling that somebody got to Mr. Simpson and scared him into suppressing the book and reporting anybody who inquired about it. Maybe this *is* the only copy."

"I never told him my name."

"There's such a thing as caller ID and even tapped telephone lines."

"I never thought of that," she said. "The way you talk about it sounds like some kind of conspiracy."

"I hope I'm wrong," he said. "I hope I haven't been reading too many of those cult conspiracy books."

"No matter," she said, her plump face tightened into a

look of determination, "we're going to get to the bottom of this, no matter what."

"We seem to have run into a blank wall," Adrian said.

"There are ways around a wall," she said darkly. "As you said, Mr. Mast, books are my business. Just give me a few hours with this computer, and I'll find the author for you—or, at least, where we can locate the author."

"We, Mrs. Farmstead?"

"I told you that I don't like people who want to keep things from being published," she said. "I don't like people who threaten other people, either."

"I won't turn down your help," Adrian said. "But I never intended drawing you into this."

"I am in, Mr. Mast," she said, "and unless you forbid me from helping, we're in this together. But tell me: what is it we're trying to do?"

"We're trying to discover where these designs came from and whether there are more of them," Adrian said. "And then we're going to build a spaceship and go to the stars."

"That's worth taking a few risks for," she said. "I've always wanted to go to the stars." She turned back to her computer.

That night the Book Nook burned down.

Next morning they traveled stand-by to Phoenix. Adrian paid for the tickets with cash that he had withdrawn from an ATM, but he had to give their real names to the young woman who sold him the tickets and demanded photo ID. He had tried to persuade Mrs. Farmstead not to go along, but she was determined.

"Your book store has just been burned," Adrian said. "Somebody doesn't want us to follow this up."

They were sitting in the coach section, Mrs. Farmstead in

the window seat, Adrian in the seat next to her, leaving the aisle seat empty. They had their heads close together like conspirators.

"Nonsense!" Mrs. Farmstead said. "The building was nearly one hundred years old, and the wiring was almost as old. It was an accident waiting to happen."

"But right after your telephone call?"

"People have a dangerous tendency to connect events, Mr. Mast—"

"Call me Adrian," he said.

"All right," she said, "and you can call me Mrs. Farmstead." She looked at him over the tops of her glasses and smiled. "Misconnecting events is what's wrong with the UFO fanatics. They get cause and effect all mixed up. Just because two events happen, one following the other or next to the other, doesn't mean they're related. *Ad hoc propter hoc,* it's called."

"So you think—?"

"Coincidence," she said. "That means 'happening together.' I've spent a lot of time with dictionaries. I like words, Adrian, and I think they need respect." They were passing over southwest Kansas with its circular green patches below attesting to the existence of central-pivot irrigation. "Now that's cause and effect, Adrian," she said, pointing out the window beside her. "Like the book that has sent us off on this adventure. Either those drawings are intended to make otherwise unlikely comments seem more believable—"

"Not that, Mrs. Farmstead," Adrian said. "I know legitimate designs when I see them."

"Or, as you suspect, someone has tried to hide a golden acorn on the forest floor."

"That's a good image, Mrs. Farmstead. Only"—he hesitated—"this may be dangerous business." He held up a hand to stop her response. “I know: you think recent events are unrelated, and that there’s no danger from people who don’t want that acorn found. You may be right. But you may be wrong, and you shouldn’t have to take that chance.”

“At my age, you mean,” she said.

“At any age. You should be home taking care of cleaning up the site of your store, or collecting your insurance.”

“And sitting in my rocking chair.”

“Rebuilding. Restocking. Whatever.”

“I don’t choose to retire and, to tell the truth, I was getting a little bored with the book business. People don’t buy good books any more. Hardly any books at all to tell the full story. Maybe the fire was a blessing in disguise. It may have liberated me to do something important, like giving humanity the stars.”

“That’s eloquent, Mrs. Farmstead,” Adrian said.

“Besides, as you said, your area is spaceships. Mine is books. How far do you think you’d have got looking for spaceships?”

He thought about it. “You’re right about that. You found the publisher and his address.”

“But not the author,” Mrs. Farmstead said. “The book must never have been registered with the Copyright Office.”

“But it had a copyright notice.”

“That’s the law. You can copyright it by putting on the notice, but you don’t have to complete the registration. The author may not even have wanted it copyrighted. The publisher may have printed the notice automatically.”

“So,” Adrian said, “what do we do next?”

“We find the publisher and force him to reveal what he knows.”

“The name and location of the author.”

Mrs. Farmstead nodded. “And that’s what we’re going to

do. But I've got a question for you: if your suspicions are correct, what does it mean?"

"I don't even like to talk about it—it's too bizarre."

"Trust me. I've read a lot of bizarre scenarios while I was waiting for customers."

Adrian looked out the window past Mrs. Farmstead. Time had passed, and they were flying over the mountainous northern corner of New Mexico. "I've got a theory," he said, "that Winterbotham, or whoever he really is, was in a position to intercept a communication of extra-terrestrial origin."

"From aliens?"

Adrian nodded.

"What kind of communication?"

Adrian shrugged. "Radio. Gravity waves. DNA. Some kind of message, anyway. It may have had some general images or it may have consisted only of the designs. Or Winterbotham may have received or deciphered something that looked vaguely like a spaceship and the engines that powered it, and invented the rest. Only somebody—maybe the people he worked for—didn't want him to publish in some normal fashion, and he had to sneak it out in a way that wouldn't be suspected."

"That's bizarre, all right."

They were silent for a long time, thinking about the bizarreness of their mission.

"The only thing that makes it seem at all plausible," Adrian said finally, "is where we found it."

"And your belief in it," Mrs. Farmstead said.

"There's that," Adrian agreed. "That most of all. Trained people recognize authenticity. There's something about all this that speaks to me."

"Like books and art," Mrs. Farmstead said. "Only sometimes even the authorities fail to recognize fakes."

Adrian nodded. "I didn't say it was infallible. Sometimes wish-fulfillment gets in the way. But there's more: the fact that there may be only one copy. The anonymity of the author. The denial of the publisher."

"The burning of the Book Nook."

"Even if we call that an accident," Adrian said. "My theory is that if the designs are real, aliens have sent us the means to reach the stars."

"Why would they do that, Adrian?"

"That's the question," Adrian said. "And there's no way to get the answer unless we build the spaceship and go visit the aliens. There may be people who don't want us to go. Or don't want the world to have the technology implied by those designs. And they're the ones we need to watch out for."

By that time they were preparing to land in Phoenix, and there was no more time for speculation.

Joel Simpson lived in a small town in northern Arizona. Adrian had rented a car in Phoenix. He and Mrs. Farmstead had argued about that and the need for Adrian to produce a driver's license, until Adrian had pointed out that his name had never been associated with the book or Mrs. Farmstead's store or her telephone inquiries. They had driven north on Highway 17, through deserts and national forests, past Indian reservations, through Flagstaff and close by the Lowell Observatory where much of the world's apprehensions about aliens had started with Percival Lowell's observations of the "canals" on Mars and his speculations about intelligent Martians nourishing their dying planet. Adrian wanted to stop, but Mrs. Farmstead vetoed the idea.

"The fewer marks we leave along the trail, the more difficulty anyone will have trying to follow us," she said.

They came to a stop, toward evening, in a little town not

far from the Grand Canyon. Mrs. Farmstead wanted to make a side trip to see the gorge carved out by the Colorado River over the ages. "I've always wanted to see it," she said. "I never thought I'd be this close, and I may not have another chance."

Adrian vetoed that notion. "We don't have time. Maybe in the morning." But he knew, and she knew, that if their mission was successful they would be leaving in a hurry.

Mrs. Farmstead looked at the town with dismay. There was a business section two blocks long, with a grocery store, an official building of some kind, two filling stations, one with a cafe attached, and several vacant storefronts. This was a town that was being emptied of its citizens like water evaporating from a desert pond. "A town this size," she said, "strangers will stick out like weeds in a flower bed. And all we have for an address is a post-office box."

"We'll stop at one of the filling stations for gas and ask for a motel or a bed-and-breakfast," Adrian said. "Say we're going to head on over to the Grand Canyon in the morning."

Mrs. Farmstead looked at him with admiration. "Nothing like sticking close to the truth," she said.

They chose the nearest filling station. A talkative clerk told them about the best bed-and-breakfast this side of Flagstaff, run by his aunt Isabel and if they told her that Sylvester had sent them, she'd be sure to treat them right. "And give him a fee for touting the place," Mrs. Farmstead told Adrian later. Now she said to the clerk, "Isn't this the place where that fellow publishes those UFO books?"

The clerk looked blank.

"I've read some of them," Mrs. Farmstead said. "Simpson, I think his name is?"

"Never heard of him," the clerk said.

His aunt was more helpful. "Simpson? He must be the odd

duck who believes in flying saucers. I've heard he had something to do with books. He lives the other side of town."

"How would we find it?" Adrian asked.

Mrs. Farmstead added quickly, "If we wanted to look him up, maybe say 'hello.' "

"I'd have to draw you a map," Isabel said. "No house numbers in a town like this."

Adrian looked from the map to Mrs. Farmstead. "Thanks," she said. "Maybe we'll drive past there on our way to the Canyon in the morning." She gave Adrian a nudge.

"We're sort of night-owls," he said. "Do you suppose we could have a key to the outside door in case we come in late?"

"A key?" Isabel said. "Nobody locks their doors around here."

Adrian looked at her astonished.

"How wonderful!" Mrs. Farmstead said. "Come on, dear." They had introduced themselves as mother and son, and now, being maternal and filial respectively, they linked arms and walked out into the narrow street, redolent with the smell of desert wind and cactus. Adrian half-expected to see a tumbleweed rolling down the street.

Simpson's house, if that was what it was, was dark except for a single lighted window, perhaps a study or a bedroom or a living room. The night was black, but they could make out the outline of the building—it seemed square and low, perhaps adobe or imitation adobe. When the light went out, Mrs. Farmstead reached into her handbag and pulled out a flashlight.

"You are resourceful," Adrian said.

"A woman living alone has to be prepared for anything," Mrs. Farmstead said. She led the way to a detached garage.

"We're not looking for a car, Mrs. Farmstead," Adrian said.

"A small publisher can't afford to pay for storage," Mrs. Farmstead said, "and it makes sense to keep his records where he keeps his stock."

The side door to the garage was unlocked. Isabel had been right about doors. They entered quietly, and Mrs. Farmstead played her light around the inside. The only trace of an automobile was old oil stains on the concrete floor and a lingering odor of gasoline. But one wall was filled with books on rough shelves; sealed cardboard boxes were stacked against the back wall; on the near side was a gray metal desk, a telephone, a fax machine, and a gray metal filing cabinet.

Adrian inspected the books, and Mrs. Farmstead looked through the files in the cabinet, starting with the bottom drawer. "Simpson was right," Adrian whispered. "There's only two books: *The Aliens Are Here* and *UFOs and What They Mean*. No *Gift from the Stars*."

"Means nothing," she said. "No Winterbotham file either, but then there wouldn't be, would there." She riffled through the files in the other drawers. "It would take days to go through all these. I've always wondered about movies, how they can come up with the incriminating file in a few minutes."

"Wouldn't there have to be tax records?" Adrian asked.

"Ah!" she said and turned to look for files marked by the year. She chose the one for six years earlier. "Ahah!" she said. "Publishing costs for *Gift from the Stars*, and payment of one hundred dollars to someone named—"

"Peter Cavendish," a voice said from the door.

They jerked and turned. A small man in a red-and-black plaid robe over blue pajamas stood in the doorway with a large shotgun in his hand. It was pointed at Mrs. Farmstead.

The garage was redolent with the electric scent of tension,

but Mrs. Farmstead stared coolly. "You're very quick to reveal information you've been asked to forget!"

The barrel of the shotgun began to droop. "What do you mean?" the stranger asked.

"Maybe you'd also tell us where we can find Peter Cavendish," Mrs. Farmstead continued.

The shotgun barrel lifted again. "Why would you ask that?"

"The people we work for would like to know how much you'd reveal to strangers."

"You mean you work for—?"

"What do you think? You know what you were told: To turn over all copies of the book and wipe out all evidence of its existence. Well, we've discovered that at least one copy of the book has survived, and people are making inquiries. And now we find, Mr. Joel Simpson, that a record of the author survives in your file."

The shotgun pointed to the stained floor. "I didn't know," Simpson said. He was thin and nervous. "I wish you people would make up your minds—the IRS says I gotta keep the information, you say I gotta get rid of it. What's a guy to do?"

"Bull!" Adrian said, entering the conversation for the first time. "The IRS doesn't care any more. You just forgot."

"Just like you're going to forget Peter Cavendish," Mrs. Farmstead said. "And just to prove it you're going to tell us where he is."

Simpson's eyes got suspicious. "If you're one of them, you know where he is."

"Of course we know," Adrian said. "We just want to know if you know, so that when we tell you to forget it, you'll know what to forget."

Simpson turned that over in his mind without seeming to

unravel it. "He's in a mental hospital in Topeka, Kansas," he said.

"That wasn't so hard, was it," Mrs. Farmstead said. "Now forget it! Forget Peter Cavendish! And forget you ever saw us!"

"Yes, ma'am," Simpson said. "You bet. I never want to see any of you again. You're worse than aliens."

"What do you know about aliens?" Adrian asked sharply.

"Nothing!" Simpson said. "Nothing at all! I'm sorry I ever heard of them. I'll burn my books."

"Too much of a giveaway," Mrs. Farmstead said. "Keep everything as it was. Just forget the rest!"

"Yes, ma'am—and sir."

Outside, in the car, Adrian said, "Quick thinking back there."

"I read a scene like that in a spy novel," Mrs. Farmstead said. "Ian Fleming, maybe. I've read so many I get them mixed up. You were quick on the pick-up."

"Do you think he'll notify anyone?"

"Not for a while. Then maybe the shock will wear off and he'll begin to think about it, maybe wonder why we were sneaking around in the middle of the night, maybe analyze your nonsense about revealing Cavendish's whereabouts so that he would know what to forget."

"It was all I could think of at the time," Adrian said.

"Don't apologize for anything that works."

"Maybe he doesn't have a contact."

"Not likely," Mrs. Farmstead said. "They always leave a number to call in case people start making inquiries or start nosing around. Sooner or later he'll think to check."

"So sooner rather than later we'd better get out of here," Adrian said.

When they got back to the bed-and-breakfast, Isabel wasn't around. She was in her room asleep, they hoped. They messed up their beds to look slept-in, Adrian left money for the night's stay on the end table in the entry hall along with a note Mrs. Farmstead had written saying "Decided to make an early start for the Canyon. Here's money for the rooms. Thanks for everything," and they tiptoed out, easing the door shut behind them.

They headed back to Flagstaff, bypassing the Grand Canyon and the Lowell Observatory once more, before turning east on Highway 40. Mrs. Farmstead dozed in the passenger seat until the sun came up just before they reached Gallup.

"A mental hospital, Adrian?" she said. "I think I was dreaming about mental hospitals and a patient named Cavendish."

"I've been thinking about that, too. But it figures, doesn't it? Where's a better place to stash Cavendish? Where he can talk all he likes about aliens and messages from outer space and spaceships."

"We've got to figure out a plan of action," Mrs. Farmstead said, "and how we're going to protect ourselves."

By the time they arrived in Albuquerque their plans were complete, and all they had to do was to check in the car and catch the first flight to Kansas City. Adrian used their own names again, trying not to glance around the pueblo-style airport to see if someone was watching. "In movies," Mrs. Farmstead said, "people always give themselves away by acting as if someone was watching them. Almost as if they expect to be nabbed, and, of course, they are."

"By now, of course," Adrian said, "they may have traced the license plate on the rental car and have my name. They could be here in a few hours, maybe, but surely not before we've left. I wish we'd thought to make up fake IDs."

"In novels," Mrs. Farmstead said, "pursuers never get thrown off the scent. They'll be waiting for us in Topeka."

"Life isn't a novel," Adrian said. "In a book people get caught because the plot gets more complicated if they're caught, and if the pursuers were thrown off, that would be the end of a story, wouldn't it?"

Mrs. Farmstead nodded. "But it helps to anticipate the worst scenario. That way we won't be surprised."

"We'll have our insurance," Adrian said.

At that moment their flight was called and they passed through the metal detectors and onto the plane, not looking back.

Topeka had three major mental hospitals, the Veterans Administration, the state, and the Menninger Foundation. The first two had developed mostly because of the psychiatrists and reputation accumulating around Will Menninger's pioneering work. They weren't far apart, but Adrian thought random inquiries would only tip-off pursuers. Maybe he and Mrs. Farmstead could think of a way to narrow the search.

"He probably wouldn't be a veteran," Adrian said.

"But a government agency might be able to put him away there," Mrs. Farmstead said. "Maybe manufacture documents? Pull strings?"

"Possibly," Adrian conceded. They were sitting in another rented car in a large shopping center, having already spent some time in a computer service center. On this occasion Mrs. Farmstead had signed for the car in Kansas City, leaving a different trail to slow potential pursuers. "But government red tape might make it nearly impossible to contact a patient, at least in the time we have."

"Before they catch up with us."

"Or intercept us. As for the state hospital—I don't know the rules in this state, but wouldn't he have to be a resident before he could be admitted?"

"You'd think so," Mrs. Farmstead said. "That leaves—"

"The Menninger Clinic." He glanced at the rear-view mirror and then back at Mrs. Farmstead. "Do you ever feel like we may be fleeing from phantoms?"

Mrs. Farmstead nodded. "The guilty flee . . ." she said. "But the worst-case scenario—"

"I'm tired of subterfuge," Adrian said. "Let's play it straight."

Ten minutes found them on the campus of the Menninger Clinic. It was an attractive place, not like a hospital or institution at all, with trees and lawns and garden beds and buildings scattered here and there, with the breezes and green odors of a park. In the middle of everything was an office building. After five minutes of winding roads, and half an hour of questioning by security guards, they finally reached a reception desk.

"We're looking for a patient named Peter Cavendish," Adrian said. "We've been told he was hospitalized in Topeka, and we thought he might be here."

"Are you relatives?" the pleasant young woman asked.

Adrian shook his head. "We came across a fascinating book he wrote, and we thought we'd take the chance we might be able to meet him while we were passing through."

"A book?" She turned to her computer and clicked a few keys. "Yes, we have a Peter Cavendish, but you need a written request in advance that must be processed by the resident's treatment team."

Adrian and Mrs. Farmstead exchanged glances.

"Golly," Mrs. Farmstead said, "we're only going to be in Topeka a few hours."

"It might help Mr. Cavendish to talk to someone who has read his book," Adrian added.

"And admired it," Mrs. Farmstead said.

The receptionist hesitated. "Let me call his attending psychiatrist, Dr. Freeman." She turned to her telephone and soon began talking to someone. She swung back to Adrian and Mrs. Farmstead. "What's the name of the book?"

Adrian hesitated and said, "*Gift from the Stars.*"

The receptionist gave the title into the telephone and listened while Adrian's breath caught in his chest. "Okay," she said, "I'll get an orderly to take you to the unit."

The building looked like a two-story brick apartment building. Inside, it was like an attractively laid-out and furnished home. They waited in an off-white "day room" with a cream-colored sofa and brown, tapestry-covered easy chairs, framed landscapes on the wall, and a television set in one corner, while the orderly disappeared down a hallway. He returned in a minute or two with a medium-sized man in a dark shirt and slacks and a cheerful Scandinavian sweater; it was white with red reindeer. The newcomer had his hands in his pockets. He seemed to be middle-aged, perhaps in his fifties, with blond hair and blue eyes and a calm expression. Adrian wouldn't have given him a second glance on the street unless he had looked closer and noticed the stiff, almost apprehensive set of the man's shoulders and the way his eyes kept scanning the room but never looked directly at Adrian or Mrs. Farmstead.

"Peter Cavendish?" Adrian said.

The man nodded.

"I'll be in the next room if you need me," the orderly said.

Cavendish looked after the orderly until he was clearly out

of earshot and said, "Are you from *them?*"

"Them?"

Cavendish's glance flicked back and forth. "You know. *Them.*"

"No," Adrian said. "We just came to see you. We read your book, *Gift from the Stars.* We wanted to talk to you about it."

"*They* don't want me to talk about it."

"They're not here. You can talk to us."

"How do I know it's not a trick?"

"Do we look like tricky people?" Mrs. Farmstead said. She leaned forward, her hands spread open as if to show that she was concealing nothing. "I sell books. He designs airplanes."

"And spaceships," Adrian said.

Cavendish looked at them for the first time, and his face relaxed, as if he had been wearing a mask and the fasteners had broken. Adrian realized that Cavendish had been holding himself together. Tears appeared on the lower lids of his eyes. "You've come to rescue me," he said.

"The orderly said you could walk away any time," Adrian said.

"That's what they tell you," Cavendish said darkly. "The orderly's one of *them.*"

"But we have come to rescue your ideas," Mrs. Farmstead said. "Could you tell us about the book?"

"It's all true," Cavendish said.

Adrian nodded. "We believe it. But what part—"

"Everything. The aliens are here. You may be aliens for all I know." Cavendish's body tensed again.

"We're just people," Mrs. Farmstead said. "Like you."

"That's what they'd say, wouldn't they?"

"I'm interested in the spaceship designs," Adrian said.

"I'm an aerospace engineer, and I think I could build a spaceship from those designs."

"Yes," Cavendish said. "I got them out of there, you know."

"From the NASA project?" Adrian guessed.

Cavendish looked puzzled. "From SETI, of course. Cosmic rays. Energetic stuff. Too energetic to be natural, the physicists told me. Figure it out, it makes a picture. Right? You've got to decipher the code. But they make it easy. They want you to figure it out."

"Anti-cryptography," Adrian said.

"But then you don't know," Cavendish said. He looked bewildered. "Do they want you to come? Why don't they come here instead? Why don't the others want the information to get out? What will happen to the world if everyone knows?" He was getting agitated. "Why did they tell us? Why do they want us to come? Do they want to torture us? Dissect us? Make us slaves? Eat us?" Tears began trickling down his face.

"It's all right, Mr. Cavendish," Adrian said. He felt like backing away from the man standing in front of him, looking almost normal but acting strangely.

Mrs. Farmstead had better instincts. She moved forward and put her arm around Cavendish's shoulder and led him to the sofa. She sat down beside him and held his hand.

"Are there any other drawings?" Adrian asked.

"They destroyed them," Cavendish said more quietly. "The other aliens. The ones who are here. The ones who don't want us to go." He glanced around slyly. "But I hid the real ones." He looked apprehensive again. "Maybe they're right, though. Maybe it was all a mistake."

A change in the light and a puff of breeze alerted them more than the muffled sound of the door opening behind them. "I think you've talked long enough, Peter," a calm voice said.

Cavendish jumped up nervously as Adrian and Mrs. Farmstead turned toward the door. A tall, sandy-haired man in a tweed jacket and imitation horn-rimmed glasses stood framed in the doorway. He looked a bit like Cary Grant but sounded more like Clint Eastwood.

"Fred," he said, and they turned to see the orderly in the entrance to the hall, "I think Peter has had enough company for one day. Take Peter back to his room and give him a Xanax."

"Yes, Dr. Freeman," the orderly said. He took Cavendish's arm and they disappeared down the hallway. Cavendish gave a single anguished look back at them before he returned to his unnatural calm.

"So," Adrian said, turning to the psychiatrist, "you're Cavendish's physician?"

Freeman nodded. "And who are you?"

"My name is Adrian Mast. And this is Mrs. Farmstead."

"Frances Farmstead," she said.

"We were hoping to get some information from Cavendish about a book he published half a dozen years ago," Adrian said.

"The famous book," Freeman said.

"What's famous about it?" Adrian asked. "As far as I know there's only one copy, and we've got it."

"Peter talks about it a lot," Freeman said. "Maybe we'd better sit. We may have more than a little to talk about." He walked into the room and sat down in one of the easy chairs, and motioned Adrian and Mrs. Farmstead to the facing sofa. "You're not casual visitors as you suggested to the receptionist."

Adrian and Mrs. Farmstead looked at each other. Adrian said, "Not casual—in the sense that we weren't just passing through. We sought Cavendish out. But casual in the sense that we represent nobody but ourselves and our curiosity."

"Curiosity about *Gift from the Stars*?"

Adrian nodded. "Do you believe in the book, Dr. Freeman?"

"I've never seen a copy."

Adrian looked at Mrs. Farmstead. She unzipped her large purse, rummaged around in the central pocket, pulled out the book, and handed it to Adrian who passed it on to Freeman. The psychiatrist turned it over in his hands and then opened the cover to thc title page and to page one. "Now I believe in it," he said and held up a hand, "though not in the sense you mean. But, more to the point, you believe in it."

Adrian cleared his throat nervously. "At this point I have the urge to convince you that we're not crazy. We're not UFO believers. We don't think aliens are zooming around, abducting people, maybe even passing for humans. But could some of the book be derived from reality rather than imagination?"

"Anything is possible, Mr. Mast," Freeman said carefully. "You can find truth in some unlikely places and, as the French say, even a stopped clock is right twice a day. But this is the sort of book I'd expect a paranoid schizophrenic to write if one wrote a book. Not many of them do; they don't have the attention span. But Peter wrote this book before he came to us."

"And how did he come to you?" Mrs. Farmstead asked. "Was he more disturbed then? Did he have any explanation for his condition?"

"Those are not the kind of questions I feel free to answer. Speaking as his physician." Freeman put his hands together. "You're the ones who need to justify your presence here."

"Turn to the appendices," Adrian said. He waited while Freeman leafed to the back of the book. "Those are spaceship designs. I'm an aerospace engineer, and I would stake my reputation on the fact that those designs are genuine. I could build a spaceship from these if I could find something more detailed. And if I could develop the technology they imply."

Freeman nodded slowly. "I'll take your word for it. Not that I believe it. I have no proof, you see."

"Any more than you have proof of Cavendish's—condition," Adrian said. He almost said "insanity" before he realized that psychiatrists probably found that word offensive.

"Could it have been induced?" Mrs. Farmstead said. "Is Cavendish on drugs? Was he placed here?"

Freeman shook his head. "He is on drugs, of course. He needs to be calmed occasionally, as you saw just now, and we're trying to restore his sense of reality by restoring his chemical balances. But paranoid schizophrenia is a genetic predisposition sometimes triggered by an emotional crisis."

"Not by drugs," Adrian said.

Freeman chose his words carefully. "He came here talking about aliens and conspiracies, referred to us from a hospital in California. This is a place less conducive to theories of persecution. It was thought he had a better chance of recovery."

"And what if we told you that there may be evidence of a conspiracy to suppress the distribution of this book?" Adrian said. "Maybe Cavendish isn't crazy." There, he had used a word even more likely to offend.

Freeman didn't seem offended. "He suffers from schizophrenia. You can take my word for that. And for the fact that I'm not a member of any conspiracy. I am trying to cure his condition, not cause it." Freeman stood up. "I think you're reading far more into this than is there. Peter Cavendish was a member of a team searching for signs of extra-terrestrial intelligence. He had the background and ability to draw these designs, even make them plausible, perhaps even workable. But, like you, he surrendered to his desire that what he wanted to be true was really true. To oversimplify, the conflict created in him by this self-deception, and the necessary supporting details of a conspiracy to keep him from going public, triggered a psychotic reaction that brought him here. When he is able to recognize that, he will be on the road to recovery."

"You mean," Mrs. Farmstead said, "when he's willing to accept your version of reality."

"The world's version," Freeman said.

Adrian and Mrs. Farmstead stood up. Adrian shook his head as if trying to avoid the inevitable. "I hope," he said, "you won't find it necessary to report this incident."

"There is nobody to report it to," Freeman said, "except the team that supervises Peter's case. I have to note your visit, but if I can I won't elaborate on your beliefs. In return I'll need something from you: by your support for Peter's delusions, you have given his treatment a setback, and I would like your promise that you won't disturb him again."

Adrian and Mrs. Farmstead nodded.

"Goodbye, Mrs. Farmstead," Freeman said. "Mr. Mast. Give up this notion. You're only wasting your time."

"Goodbye, Dr. Freeman," Adrian said, "and thanks for your consideration." He reached out his hand. Freeman looked at it for a moment and then, with a start, returned the copy of *Gift from the Stars*.

Adrian sat disconsolately at the counter in the coffee shop, a cup of black coffee cooling unnoticed in front of him. "So Cavendish is crazy, and so are we for chasing after something as weird as this."

"You're taking Dr. Freeman's word for it?" Mrs. Farmstead asked.

"Aren't you?"

"Well, maybe. Freeman could be working for the people who stopped Cavendish's publication, who wanted him hospitalized. But he seems genuine." A wicked smile creased her face. "But just because a person is crazy doesn't mean he doesn't have a few sane thoughts. Like Dr. Freeman said about the stopped clock."

Hope flickered in Adrian's eyes. "That's right."

Mrs. Farmstead took a sip of her hot tea. "Dr. Freeman suggested that maybe the stress of writing the book, of inventing what he wanted to be true, set him off. But what if it wasn't that—what if it was the predicament of knowing he had stumbled over some fantastic truth and then it was suppressed?"

"And of not knowing the right thing to do," Adrian picked up excitedly. "Maybe, he thought, the people who wanted to destroy the information were right. Why were the aliens sending the plans? What did they want from us? Why did they want us to have a spaceship that could reach the stars? Why didn't they simply hop in their spaceships and come to visit us?"

"Exactly," Mrs. Farmstead said. "Those aren't easy questions. They might make anyone flip out. That's what Cavendish kept trying to say."

"I'll admit," Adrian said, "questions about the aliens and their motives have run through my mind, too, while I'm trying to go to sleep and sometimes when I wake up during the night."

"And like the bumper sticker when I was young," Mrs. Farmstead said, " 'just because you're paranoid doesn't mean people aren't after you.' "

"But if that were the case," Adrian said, depression edging back, "you'd think that somebody would be tapping us on the shoulder about now."

"Mr. Mast, Mrs. Farmstead," a voice said behind them. "That sounds like a cue."

They turned. Behind them was the orderly named Fred. He had been wearing white pants and a white jacket at the Clinic but now he had changed to a rumpled brown jacket over his white pants, and he looked like a bookish graduate student.

"You?" Adrian said.

Fred nodded. "You know how much orderlies make? They paid me pretty good just to keep my eyes open and let them know if anybody came around asking about Mr. Cavendish. Look, there's somebody wants to talk to you."

"Suppose we don't want to talk to him?" Mrs. Farmstead said.

Fred shrugged. "Up to you. But sooner or later you're going to talk to him, and the sooner it is the sooner you can stop looking over your shoulder."

"Are you threatening us?" Adrian asked.

Fred spread his hands. "You see any threats? You know, working around a mental institution you get some insights into behavior. I've learned this much: it's better to face the unknown than to run from it."

"And where do we do this?" Adrian asked.

"Is this where some goons throw us in a black limousine and whisk us off to Washington?" Mrs. Farmstead said.

"You been watching too many thrillers," Fred said. "You can go wherever you want, or you can follow me to Forbes Field, where a man has just arrived in an Air Force jet. He's waiting for you."

Adrian looked at Mrs. Farmstead, and Mrs. Farmstead

looked at Adrian. Adrian shrugged. "Let's get it over with," he said.

By the time they reached Forbes Field, the sun was setting. It had been a long day that had started far from this spot, and there had been little sleep and less food. They were tired and hungry.

Waiting at the back of a unused hangar at the airfield was a fat man sitting at a folding table. Mrs. Farmstead nudged Adrian and said, out of the corner of her mouth, "Sidney Greenstreet." The fat man didn't laugh like Greenstreet, however, from the gut, his whole body shaking. He didn't laugh at all. Sitting behind a portable table, he scowled at Adrian and Mrs. Farmstead as if assessing what kind of punishment he could mete out to the civilians who had made him travel all this distance and put up with such discomfort. It *was* discomfort. He overflowed the metal chair he sat on, gingerly, as if it were about to collapse beneath him.

"Well," Adrian said, "then it's all true."

"Truth depends on where you stand," the fat man said.

"Or sit," Adrian said, looking around for other chairs. There were none in that vast expanse of empty hangar. Greenstreet was going to make them stand in front of him like convicts awaiting judgment. "Let's have some truth, then. I'm Adrian Mast, and this is Frances Farmstead, and we've been looking for Peter Cavendish and the alien plans for building a spaceship. Now, who are you and why have you asked us here?"

The fat man was wearing a dark suit. It had a matching vest; nobody wore vests any more, but his had a purpose. He reached into a vest pocket, retrieved a calling card with two fingers, and flicked it onto the table in front of Adrian. Adrian picked it up and looked at it. It read: William Makepeace. And under that: Consultant.

"William Makepeace," Mrs. Farmstead said. "Wasn't that Thackeray's name?"

"My parents were great readers," Makepeace said.

"And what gives you the authority to summon us here?" Adrian asked.

"I'm in charge of the Cavendish affair," Makepeace said.

"It's an affair, then," Mrs. Farmstead said, "like an Agatha Christie mystery."

"An affair," Makepeace said, "is something less than a case and something more than a situation."

"Hah!" Adrian said.

"Let us be reasonable," Makepeace said. "You are idealists; I am a pragmatist. You deal in dreams; I deal in what is. One of us has to convince the other."

"You first," Adrian said. "Are the spaceship designs authentic?"

"As far as I know," Makepeace said. "But I'm no expert in alien communications, nor in deciphering codes, nor in spaceship design. I've been told by those who ought to know that they seem genuine."

"And will they work?"

Makepeace shrugged. It was like a tide of jello under his coat. "We haven't gone that far."

"Why not?"

"That part was unimportant."

"My god! What was important?"

"You want to go to the stars," Makepeace said. "I see that. Sensible people, of whom I am one, want to see that we don't destroy each other. We don't care if you go to the stars, Mr. Mast, as long as we can survive in some approximation of civilization."

"What in the name of everything holy does that have to do with building a spaceship?"

"Nothing," Makepeace said, "but our experts point out that the anti-matter collectors—" He stopped as Adrian jumped. "Yes, they are designs for anti-matter collectors, according to people who ought to know. If we built them, Mr. Mast, what do you think would happen?"

"Besides getting us to the stars," Mrs. Farmstead said.

"Quite right," Makepeace said. "Besides that."

"I suppose they would lead to the development of new energy systems, maybe generation in orbit," Adrian said.

"You are quick, Mr. Mast. No wonder you caught on to the designs in *Gift from the Stars*. But what comes after energy generation in orbit?"

Now it was Adrian's turn to shrug. "I give up. What?"

"Cheap energy for one thing," Makepeace said. "Our experts predict that we could beam down energy from orbit at a fraction of the cost of current sources."

"What's wrong with that?" Adrian asked.

"What do you think will happen when entire industries get displaced, virtually overnight?"

"It's happened before," Adrian said.

"But not so quickly, and not in a way that will transform the balance of power. Do you think that the energy-producing nations won't fight, maybe resort to financial strategies that would upset the world's economy, or terrorism, or even war?"

Adrian shook his head. "Buy them off. Buy them up. Cut them in. Give them free energy. Give them a share of the process. Anyway, oil and gas are far more valuable as biological raw materials than as fuel."

"Ah, Mr. Mast, that requires forethought and rational decision-making, and the nations of the world aren't good at those things."

"Maybe they could see that cheap, inexhaustible energy

makes everything possible," Mrs. Farmstead said, "from feeding the hungry and housing the homeless to raising their standards of living to the level of the western nations without destroying the world's resources, without pollution. We could clean up the environment. We could do anything."

"Cheap energy could make a heaven on Earth," Adrian said. "It could solve all our problems."

"Mr. Mast, Mrs. Farmstead," Makepeace said pityingly, "that will never happen. People aren't willing to give up their little disputes, their ancient hatreds, their petty jealousies. And, you see, anti-matter makes one other thing possible."

"What?"

"Bigger and better bombs. Big enough to shatter this planet, I'm told. Do you have an answer for that?"

Adrian looked down. "No," he said. "You just have to have faith that people are better than that, that they will see the promise and hold off on the destruction. That's your job, you and the people you work for, to convince them."

"I haven't convinced you."

"We're on the side of the angels," Mrs. Farmstead said. "Or the aliens."

Makepeace spread his arms out, palms up, as if helpless in the face of irresistible facts. "But we can't take the chance. Sure we could have a lot more of everything or we could end up with nothing at all. In that scheme of things, the status quo wins every time. So, you see, you have a choice. Either you give up this foolishness or—"

"Or what?" Adrian said fiercely.

"Or we will have to discredit you," Makepeace said. "We can do that, you know. The resources of the government are massive; they can be mobilized to make you part of the UFO fringe cultists. You will be destroyed, along with that book you have in your possession and whatever copies you may have made."

Adrian shook his head. "I don't think so."

"What do you mean, Mr. Mast?" Makepeace said. "I hope you haven't done something foolish."

"Depends on what you mean by 'foolish,' " Mrs. Farmstead said. "You know those old movies where the hero leaves the information in the hands of his lawyer, in case he gets killed, or in a safe-deposit box?"

"Ridiculous," Makepeace said.

"That's what we thought," Mrs. Farmstead said. "They're always killing the lawyer or looting the safe-deposit box, or the newspaper editor is part of the conspiracy. So we put everything on the internet this morning."

"Bah!" Makepeace's relief was clear. "The internet is filled with junk nobody believes."

"We know," Adrian said. "So we labeled the statement as a NASA news release—we didn't know then that it was SETI. But first we inserted the designs into NASA's database."

For the first time Makepeace looked uncertain. "You can't do that!" He shivered as he considered Adrian's confidence. "They can be found, erased."

"By this time they're all around the world. People must be accessing the database already."

"The designs can be discredited, ridiculed."

"Scientists and engineers will recognize their validity just as I did. Particularly scientists and engineers in other countries. You'll never know who might be taking the designs seriously. As in the race for the atom bomb, the U.S. can't afford to come in second."

"The genie is out of the bottle, Mr. Makepeace," Mrs. Farmstead said. "I think you'd better make your three wishes."

"You poor, stupid people!" Makepeace said. "You don't know what you've done!"

"We've just given humanity the stars," Adrian said. "It's your job to see that humanity doesn't destroy itself first."

"And how do you propose we do that?"

"I suggest you mobilize all those resources you were talking about, get them behind the release of the designs, take credit for it, swing public opinion into the realization that this is a legitimate gift from beneficent aliens, and we have been given the chance to make everybody rich and happy."

"And let some of us go to the stars," Mrs. Farmstead said.

"Oh my god!" Makepeace said and put his face down into his hands. Then, slowly, he pulled himself to his feet and plodded toward the hangar exit like a man who had just realized that he was old and fat and would never feel any better than he did now.

Adrian looked at Mrs. Farmstead. "Well, Frances," he said. He held out his arm and she took it. "I hope I may call you 'Frances.' "

"Any time, Adrian."

"What we opened may be the genie's bottle, or it may be Pandora's box," Adrian said. "Whichever it is, we're going to live in interesting times."

"If it's the genie's bottle, let's be sure we make the right wishes," Mrs. Farmstead said. "If it's Pandora's box, we must remind ourselves to be patient."

And they walked out of the hangar into a night in which the stars seemed close enough to touch.